SUN, SEA, and MURDER

A Locked Room Mystery

J S SAVAGE

Copyright © J S Savage 2024

All rights reserved.

No part of this book may be reproduced, or stored in a retrieval system, or transmitted in any form or by any means, electronic, mechanical, photocopying, recording, or otherwise, without express written permission of the publisher.

This is a work of fiction. Unless otherwise indicated, all the names, characters, businesses, places, events and incidents in this book are either the product of the author's imagination or used in a fictitious manner. Any resemblance to actual persons, living or dead, or actual events is purely coincidental.

ISBN: 9798876840257

Editor: Kathryn Hall www.cjhall.co.uk
Formatting: Elaine Denning

For Corinne, (again)

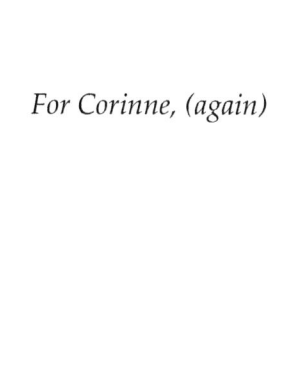

Also by the author:

THE MYSTERY of TREEFALL MANOR

An Inspector Graves locked room mystery.

[The Mystery of Treefall Manor: An Inspector Graves locked-room mystery eBook : SAVAGE, J.S.: Amazon.co.uk: Kindle Store](#)

The Narrators:

Marley - On holiday with her mum, Marley feels she is more of a carer than a companion. Eager to enjoy herself, she is looking forward to recharging her batteries and also planning her next steps in life. A keen artist, she decides to keep a journal to keep her creative juices flowing…

Terry - Holidaying with his wife, Marjorie, Terry can't wait to spend the days lazing by the pool, working on his tan to show off to the locals in The Rambler's Arms back home in Yorkshire. Two weeks of Spanish sun is just what the doctor ordered (literally). A few murders won't do his blood pressure any good, but will they spoil his holiday?

Sally - Being the niece of the hotel's owner has its perks; Sally is looking forward to enjoying a cut-price holiday with her best friend, Jasmine. Having just completed her English degree, Sally is dreaming of cocktails, Spanish waiters, and tapas. Unfortunately, murder is also on the menu…

Sanjay - Frustrated with his stagnant career, journalist Sanjay is looking forward to a break away from his overbearing editor, and for an opportunity to repair his damaged relationship with his boyfriend, Luke. Will two weeks together in a luxury hotel bring them closer together? Or will murder separate them forever?

1

Marley

I hate flying. I mean, I really hate it. I don't mean to sound negative, that's not me at all. I'm a chilled out, cheerful girl. However, the fear of flying can turn the whole airport experience into an anxiety-filled nightmare. Children laughing and playing would normally be a warming and wholesome sight, but in an airport lounge the vision is distorted into watching little demons snarl and cackle while their indolent parents sit and flick through *Hello* or *Top Gear* magazine, their minds not on the glossy pages but on the gallons of sangria they will no doubt consume over the next fortnight. And who can blame them?

The queues at the airport, worrying about your baggage weight, constantly checking the time in case the gate closes without you, what sane person could enjoy any of it? And then the worst part of all: the flight. Sitting on the tarmac, waiting to move, it's almost as if the pilot is toying with you, building the dread and anticipation as they power up the engines before releasing the brakes and hurtling you down the runway. I hate being flung backwards into my seat and feeling the weightlessness as the earth is left behind, as though the ground beneath has ceased to exist, perhaps a chasm has opened, a shortcut to hell. I'm shivering thinking about it. Okay, deep breaths, we'll be there soon.

I hope Mum is not exaggerating about how wonderful the hotel is. It needs to have topless Spanish waiters and daily soothing massages to justify the hideousness of this journey. Still, it will be good to get away, it has been so long since I've been on holiday. I can't wait to wake up in the morning and hear the waves lapping against the shoreline instead of the clanging poles and jolly shouts as Brixton market starts a new day.

Mum needs this holiday too, much more than I do. I wonder what it will be like for her going back to the same hotel. Part of me is surprised she asked me to go with her this year, I thought she would ask her sister. Another part of me is surprised she wanted to go back at all after what happened last year. I tried to coax her into branching out, try somewhere different, maybe even a different country. I even suggested she go back to Jamaica and stay in a nice resort, and to see where she spent her childhood – kill two birds with one stone, but no, she's a stubborn old lady who can't be talked around by anybody, least of all her daughter. "If you think you know better than your mother, Marley, then you don't know your mother at all." Those words will be engraved on her tombstone and will still be resounding in my ears until I'm under my own, I hear them so often. I remember once she said them when I suggested she try extra virgin olive oil instead of Crisp'n'Dry. Still, that's mothers, isn't it? They always know best.

She's snoozing next to me now; her pursed lips are vibrating as if she's trying to blow bubbles, and her glasses are balancing precariously on the tip of her nose.

I'm writing this on my phone, I can't concentrate on the book I'm reading. The drone of the engines is faint, and I worry in case I cease to hear them at all. I promised myself that I would keep a journal, a way to stay creative whilst I'm away. I can't draw, or paint as I love to, so this feels like the next best thing. I imagine it will be a dull, pleasant holiday, where each day is a repeat of the last: breakfast, sun, swim, dinner, repeat. Nothing exciting ever happens to me…

2

Terry

I love flying, absolutely love it! Everything about it! I love getting to the airport nice and early, chucking the bags in, and that's it, then; once that boarding pass is tucked into my passport, I'm in holiday mode. I take a wander through duty free, maybe get a bottle of something to enjoy when I'm sitting on the balcony in the evening watching the sun go down - perfect!

Always try to get a lunchtime flight, that's my motto, that way you can wake up at a reasonable time, not hurry yourself too much, have a nice brekkie in the departure lounge and still arrive while there's a few hours of sun left to enjoy.

Marjorie, on the other hand, well, she can take it or leave it, she says. She didn't say much in the airport, it's all the hustle and bustle I suppose, some women find it very tiring. The bigger airports are like mini cities, aren't they, and although we live in a small town, Marjorie has always felt more comfortable in the peace of the countryside. She grew up in an old mining village you see, clean air and dirty faces all around. She says she wants to move back to the countryside in a few years when we retire. Says she wants a nice little cottage with a wooden gate and a thatched roof. I'm not sold on the idea myself. What would someone like me do all day in somewhere like that? I've spent my whole life in the thick of it, fighting for the workers and the union, fighting for better pay and conditions, fighting my ex-wives. Someone like me doesn't belong in the sticks with church fetes and golf courses. Terence Smith is a man of action, a man who doesn't know how to stop.

Having said that, I am looking forward to a few weeks away, a chance to relax and enjoy myself. Doctor seems to think I need it too, the old blood pressure is through the roof apparently. Well, is it any wonder?

I don't put much store by what doctors say as a rule, but when they show you those graphs and charts with the red lines and bold letters, it can make a man sit up; even me. Stress can kill you, he said, you need to take it easy. Well, I've got no issue with going on holiday, but I draw the line at yoga and meditation. Does you the world of good, according to the doctor. Well, all I'll say is, the NHS must really be skint if that's what they're prescribing nowadays – stand on your head and hold your breath, Mr Smith, maybe all that cholesterol will fall out of your arteries – cheers, Doc.

So, here we are: the compromise. He said if I'm not willing to do the meditation or see a head doctor (which I'm not!) then I must keep a journal as a way of releasing the tension built up inside me, a way of expressing myself. Well, you can't say fairer than that, can you? Besides, it might be fun to set down my thoughts and record my adventures for a bit. My old mam used to keep a diary, I found it in her pillowcase after she passed, very interesting it was, too. Maybe when I'm finished, I'll bury mine in one of those time capsule thingies, you know the ones I mean, the ones that get dug up after a couple of hundred years? I suppose there'll be aliens by then. I quite like the idea of some spacemen gawking at my pages. How the other half live and all that. Maybe I'll put a bottle of ale in for them to enjoy while they read it.

We're on the plane now, did I mention? Marjorie is reading a book about a girl on a train, she bought it in the airport at WH Smith (no relation) when I was buying this notebook. You'd think someone would write a book about a girl on a *plane*, that would sell loads more copies in an airport. Anyway, that's enough for now, my wrist is getting sore. I haven't done this much writing since my O levels.

3

Sally

I don't know how I feel really. Jasmine and I have been friends our whole lives, our mums are best friends and I guess our relationship is quite like theirs, but I can't help feel that we've drifted apart over the past few years. I suppose it's since I went to university, naturally I saw less of her then. I'd always look forward to coming home and seeing her during the holidays but it's not the same seeing someone every few months when you're used to spending time with them every day.

In my first year we would both plan our adventures and what we were going to do when I got back. Jasmine would be the first person I'd go to see after Mum, of course. We'd go on day trips or spend hours walking through town, shopping, or drinking in the pub, catching up properly, giving meaning to all the short, snatched WhatsApp messages sent whilst drying hair or running for a bus. But as the years passed, we'd see less of each other and for a shorter length of time; a quick drink at the Christmas market, coffee instead of dinner. Yes, Jasmine got a boyfriend while I was away, but she went out with someone else during secondary school and we were still inseparable then.

I worry that we are changing, that we have already changed; that we are two petals in the same flower and as we grew, we stayed close, but now, we are opening up to the world and splitting, each going in different directions.

And, of course, there's the other thing, but I'll try not to think about that. The past is the past.

Anyway, I'm back now, degree in hand, mission accomplished. I hope this holiday will bring us closer together. We've never been on a girly holiday, just the two of us. A fortnight of sun, relaxing and cocktails, then I can think about the next steps in life, like job applications and finding somewhere to live. The first is nerve racking and I hope I can put it out of my mind. I've researched the publishers I would want to work for but even a first-class English Literature degree doesn't give me much of an edge in such a competitive industry. Of course, my passion is writing, and I am loathe to continue describing myself as an aspiring writer. If you write, you are a writer, so here goes. I shall keep a journal to practise my craft while on holiday, and then use my honed skills to write a Man Booker winner when I get home. Easy, right?

Perhaps starting my journal now isn't one of my best ideas. I'm a little bit tipsy from all the prosecco we sank in the airport. Jasmine was adamant it was the proper, and indeed only way to start the holiday. The first mouthful flushed away butterflies I felt in my stomach. I couldn't put my finger on why I was feeling nervous, I guess it was the combination of excitement about the holiday and apprehension that maybe there would be an awkwardness between Jasmine and me. The conversations between us up to that point were mostly confined to the usual airport related worries. "Did you remember to pack suncream?" "I just need to nip into Boots to grab a few miniatures." "Where's my passport? Oh, here it is, phew!" The type of conversations that all passengers are having half the time.

By the time Jasmine ordered the second glasses (about ten seconds after the drowning of the butterflies), I had let known my excitement about the holiday.

"I can't wait to get away. My final exams were really stressful, and I just need a break," I said.

"Yeah, work has been crazy busy at the minute, we've had so many appointments I'm struggling to find the time to increase my following."

Jasmine's new, or second career, as an 'influencer' is somewhat alien to me I must admit. I understand a select few can make a lot of money from it, but the complexities of navigating your way through the social media world to become someone who makes an income from flicking their hair whilst holding a bottle of Evian is bizarre to me. She is, of course, a stunningly beautiful girl, but does she have something that sets her apart from all the other wannabes? I don't know. I don't even know what that 'something' is and I doubt it is tangible.

"How's uni going?" she asked before taking a long sip from her slender glass.

"I've finished, remember?" The blank expression which faced me made me doubt my sanity. Surely, I'd told her I was coming back home for good? And I had literally just mentioned my *final* exams. Maybe I'm being too harsh on Jasmine, everyone is self-centred to varying degrees and although she can be forgetful at times, while at others I'm not sure she really listens, she can be the sweetest girl.

"Anyway," I said, changing the subject back to the holiday, "all I want to do is sit by the pool and read for two weeks."

"Have you been to the hotel before?" Jasmine asked.

"Yes, but not for years. I went with my mum when I was a kid."

"I thought it was an adult only hotel?"

"It is, but Uncle Russell made an exception for me. You can do that when you own the place. The other guests didn't seem to mind. Our mums went together before we were born, I think."

"They did? My mum never mentioned it," she said, frowning in surprise. "How long has your uncle owned the hotel?"

"He built it about forty years ago. He rarely comes back to England; running the resort is his whole life. It's a shame I don't see more of him, he was always my favourite uncle growing up."

"He's my favourite now, too. Giving us a half-price holiday has endeared him to me before I've even met him. Cheers!"

We clinked our glasses and drained them of their last drops.

4

Sanjay

It's not often that being in a relationship with a solicitor has perks, although I suppose Luke would say the same about being with a journalist. There are no fancy dinners to attend, no yearly bonus, and no John Lewis vouchers at Christmastime. In fact, being with a solicitor is about as boring and predictable as you might imagine. So, it is fair to say that my surprise and delight were in equal measure when Luke said his company wanted him to go to Spain to see a client. The fact that this client is also a hotel owner seemed fateful as we've been saying for ages that we deserve a good holiday and combining business and pleasure seemed like a no-brainer. Luke can spend a few days going over accounts or books or whatever it is he's there to do while I sit by the pool drinking cocktails and listening to podcasts. Then, once Luke has finished his work, we can spend some quality time together. We need it.

The past year has been hard. I don't know why my editor hates me, but she sets impossible deadlines and berates me when I miss them. Working for a small newspaper shouldn't be this stressful. It's only you, my dear diary, that has kept me sane. I love and hate you at the same time. You are always there when I need you, when I feel my head is about to explode unless I unleash my thoughts, which you selflessly collect. But you are also a bit too much like work, which is what my brain needs space from, and although that's my fault for being unable to stop thinking and recording all I see, I feel that I can never get away, can never escape from who I am. How pathetic to have a friendship with a diary. I feel like Tom Hanks in that film with the volleyball.

Luke has been so busy with work this past year; it seems like I haven't seen him at all. I worry we're growing apart and are suffering the seven-year itch. I've seen it happen too often to too many friends, but I've always thought Luke and I are stronger, as though our relationship is held together by a thicker glue.

I hope these two weeks give us a chance to reconnect, and that our hectic work lives are the problem and not a symptom of a problem. I want Luke to enjoy this break for his *own* good as much as for *ours*.

I turn my head and look at him now, asleep beside me. I don't understand how people can sleep on airplanes, especially in the middle of the day, but Luke can sleep anywhere. I remember once at Glastonbury he was asleep on his feet, held up by the tightly knit swaying crowd. In his defence, we had drunk a skinful of spiced rum, and it was Coldplay on stage.

That's all for now, my friend, the flight attendant has just told us to turn off all electrical devices as we are about to begin our descent to our destination.

Welcome words.

5

Marley

Obviously, no one would wish to have a mother who's in a wheelchair, but you have to take the rough with the smooth, right? Mum's arthritis is severe. Crippling, in fact. But the pain is not constant and there are times where she can walk with the aid of her sticks (safely out of sight in the luggage hold). So, I wasn't complaining when the flight attendant made a fuss about getting her off the plane first, or when the other attendant insisted on getting our bags from the overhead compartment. We were escorted all the way to Passport Control where even the stony-faced officer in the glass cubicle was given a theatrical and completely unnecessary show of pain induced grimaces, as though this would speed up his stamping hand.

Mum is always in a hurry, or at least, she is always hurrying others, which is almost the same thing. I was just happy to be off the plane and free to walk more than two feet in any direction, but as I explained to Mother, we would be waiting for the other passengers who were getting the same coach transfer, so racing to the arrivals lounge was a waste of energy. Of course, I realised the futility of my words as soon as they left my mouth. After all, whose energy would be wasted? Certainly not Cleopatra's as she was carried along in her litter. Regardless, we proceeded at a fair pace only for Mother to express a wish to stop at the toilet. By the time it took us to complete that logistical operation we were the last people to arrive at baggage reclaim. "I told you to go fast, Marley," said Mum, when she saw the throngs of people jostling around the carousel. "When are you ever going to listen to your mother? And don't roll your eyes." How did she know?

I watched as people fidgeted and shifted their weight from one leg to the other. They were either impatient for their bags and to begin their holiday proper, or they should've stopped off at the facilities like we did. Holidays are like that I suppose. There is a refrained tension in the air until you step out of the airport building, then there's a collective sigh and relaxing of shoulders. I was just thinking about this tense atmosphere when a girl stormed past me and drowned out the low, rumbling voices with an angry challenge. "Dylan, why didn't you wait for me?" she shouted, drawing a few interested stares, not least from Mum. She stood a few metres from me, hands on hips and feet square apart, waiting for a reply. The subject of her anger was a tall, dark-haired man in his mid-twenties who reddened as he noticed the interest his girl garnered.

"Elle," he replied, making his voice low as if by doing so she would reply in kind, "I told you to meet me here."

"No, you didn't! I only stopped at the toilet for a minute, why wouldn't you wait for me?"

"I told you to meet me at baggage claim. Don't you remember?" he asked.

"I'm not deaf, Dylan. Why on earth would you leave me to go through Passport Control on my own instead of waiting all of thirty seconds? Eurgh, you're so frustrating at times."

Dylan pulled her closer and spoke into her ear so that the rest of us couldn't hear what he said. The girl looked up, her hands still on her slender hips. She seemed unmoved but also done with the argument as she shook her head and shrugged. Dylan put his arm around her waist placating her more and our spectator fun was over, much to Mum's annoyance. "Is that it?" she said in shrill disbelief. "She gave in too easy that girl. Far too easy. Getting abandoned in a foreign country, anything could have happened to her. She should've given him a clip round the ear for doing that. Poor girl."

"Never fear, Mother, the bandits didn't get her this time," I said, laughing at how she would think nothing of making disparaging comments about a country she loved if she felt robbed of entertainment.

With the excitement (if you could call it that) over, our few fellow spectators turned back to the empty carousel and their own business. All except one. She stood about ten yards away from us, but through the tangle of people I was struck by the look on her face. She was gawking, mouth open at the scene she had just witnessed. The look on her face was so exaggerated in its surprise that I almost wondered if I'd missed some shocking part of the drama. She had jet black hair which fell in a bob to her shoulders and a rather plain face, if that's not too unkind a thing to say. I took her to be alone, but almost as soon as I noticed her, another girl, who was by no means plain with intense blue eyes, floated towards her from behind the mass of people and spoke. The first girl flushed, and in an instant turned her gaze away from the direction of the couple. She cupped the second girl's elbow in her hand and twisted her away, leading her further down the carousel. I watched them go and wondered what they were talking about until they were lost to me in the crowd, girl number two's golden hair swishing out of sight.

"What are you staring at, Marley? What have you seen?" asked Mum.

"I don't know," I replied, honestly.

6

Sally

I can't believe he's here. It was all going so well.

As soon as I finished typing on the plane, Jasmine woke up. The combination of sleep and alcohol had made her drowsy and needy. She snuggled into my shoulder, and we talked in whispers until we landed; the kind of sleepy talk that means so much and yet so little. We spoke about when we were little girls and the fun we used to have at sleepovers. We talked about how close our mums are and reassured one another that we were just as close, that we would always be friends and nothing could get in our way; how great it was that I was moving back and how much we would see each other. I rested my cheek on her head, happy in that moment.

She didn't see him in the airport. That airhead he's with shouted, turning a few bored heads. I looked up and there he was. Dylan. I watched him and then heard Jasmine's excited voice; a deranged combination. Luckily, I managed to distract her before she saw him, and moved her out of his line of sight. For a moment I thought it would all be okay, I thought we could still have a great holiday without Jasmine ever being aware he was here. We got our bags and headed for the exit; the coach driver ground out a cigarette beneath his heel as we approached. "What hotel are you ladies going to?" he purred in his Spanish accent, his eyes fixed on Jasmine.

"The Orange Tree Hotel," I said, shaking.

"Excellent, this is the correct coach, please allow me," he said, taking Jasmine's suitcase. "That is a very nice hotel, a marvellous hotel."

I couldn't get aboard quick enough and we made our way swiftly to the back where I got the window seat, my eyes fixed on the terminal exit. The coach was three quarters' full when the hope that had risen in my heart plunged and smashed into a thousand jagged pieces. *They* were walking straight towards our driver. A thought flashed through my mind that maybe they were going to a different hotel, maybe it would still be alright. Then, through the open door, I heard the driver speak and the girl reply, "The Orange Tree Hotel."

"What's wrong?" asked Jasmine.

Apprehension must've shown on my face. I wondered if I could disguise it as excitement, but my better judgement told me that two conflicting emotions would form two conflicting expressions and I replied with some feeble lie about travel sickness. For a moment I considered telling her that this might not be the fun holiday we were hoping for, that an outside element had upset the balance of things, that her ex-boyfriend was on the coach with his new girlfriend, and they were staying at the same hotel as us.

7

Terry

I tell you what, Mr Spaceman (if you're reading this), get in your UFO and fly it to Spain. And when you get there and land, prepare yourself for one of life's greatest joys: stepping off the plane (or in your case spaceship) and feeling that Spanish heat hit you in the face. There's nothing else like it. I remember the first time I felt it. It was the summer of '82 and me and a few lads from work flew over to watch the World Cup. Unforgettable days. Bryan Robson scored twice in the first game when we beat the frogs 3-1. We went unbeaten the whole tournament, though we didn't win it mind, can't remember who did, but great days all the same. When I stepped off that plane this afternoon and closed my eyes, I was taken back; I could almost feel the perm blowing against my neck in the warm breeze.

There was a bit of a kerfuffle at the baggage claim. Some young lass accusing her fella of ditching her and going through on his own. I thought we might see round two when they got on our coach and sat right in front of us, but no luck, he put his headpods in and she just stared out the window. Not sure what she was looking at mind, all I could see was blinding tarmac and plain-looking houses with metal shutters over the windows.

Though, I must say, the hotel is nice. Marjorie did a cracking job choosing it. It's small, very small in fact, but that suits me. No screaming kids, no drunken louts, just a pool, restaurant, and bar. What more could you ask for? Oh, and there's a gym. I might even go one day. It's harder to keep the weight off at my age, though I'm not as fat as I might be. You've got to have a bit of pride in yourself even if you are nearing sixty.

I'm sitting on the balcony writing this. The room is overlooking the pool, which is just bigger than a penalty box. Marjorie is doing the unpacking. I wouldn't bother personally, what's the point in taking everything out of the suitcase and hanging it up? We're only here for two weeks, doesn't seem worth the effort to me, but she insists. Ah well, if it keeps her happy, who am I to complain.

The room has one of those fancy coffee machines where you put in a little capsule and press a button and it makes a popping sound and then the steam appears, but all the TV channels are in Spanish. What's the point in even having it?

There was a note left on the bed from the owner, addressed to us by name. It said that we're invited to a special welcome dinner tonight along with all the other new arrivals. Well, I suppose there's no harm in being social, you never know, there might even be a free drink or two going.

8

Sanjay

The hotel is perfect! As soon as the taxi dropped us off outside, I smiled and felt a wave of relief rush over me. The building is only two-storeys and looks more like a colonial villa that you'd find in India during the Raj rather than a boutique hotel in Spain. It's quaint and airy. The walls are white and huge potted plants are dotted along them between tall French doors. The reception is surprisingly large and is littered with teal-coloured sofas and velvet foot stools. Despite it being small, I was desperate to explore, so as soon as we checked in, I had the first shower while Luke unpacked.

"There's a note here from Russell," he said, as I emerged from the bathroom drying my hair. "It says we are invited to dinner with the other new guests."

"Oh, well that's nice."

"Is it? My idea of 'nice' isn't sitting listening to strangers talk about their boring lives. Besides, I thought he would've wanted to have dinner with us on our own. After all, we're here because he has some delicate business matters to discuss."

"Yes, but he can't very well discuss them in front of me, can he? He probably throws a little soiree for new guests all the time. I know you think you're special, Luke, but you're not that special."

"Bloody am." He smiled, and I laughed, but we both knew there was a glimmer of truth in his arrogant joke. "You're probably right. We're here for a fortnight, and it won't take me too long to sort his affairs I imagine. He's probably in no great hurry."

I left the room to the sound of water sloshing from the shower, eager to begin exploring.

The layout and design of the hotel is simple. The guest rooms are divided between the East Wing and the West Wing. All the guest rooms are on the first floor and beneath the East Wing is a bar and lounge area. The restaurant, where breakfast and dinner are served, is on the ground floor in the West Wing. I glanced in as I got out of the lift, the tables are plainly set and close to each other. On the walls are paintings of flamenco dancers and matadors, deep reds and dark yellows of swishing capes and dancing skirts complimenting the walnut panelled walls.

At check-in, the receptionist told us that all new arrivals that day were allocated to rooms in the West Wing. Apparently, all bookings are taken on a week-by-week basis. The hotel prides itself on its easy-going culture but also likes a group atmosphere, so this morning all the residents in the West Wing left and we then came and took their rooms. The East Wing will empty and refill in seven days' time. I had to suppress a smile as we were being told this; I could feel Luke tense beside me and sense his jaw clenching at the words 'group atmosphere'.

In a group of his choosing or with people he likes, Luke is always the centre of attention; he's loud, funny and his personality is magnetic. Forced fun or conversation is anathema to him; he says being made to speak to those you don't wish to is akin to being strapped to a chair and tortured by the Gestapo. He really sees few differences between the two. I'll admit it's one of the less attractive sides to his personality, that he doesn't consider the other person and how they feel, that his time is worth more than theirs. I remember challenging him about this once with a drunken outburst after an admittedly boring Christmas party at my office. "You complain about having to speak to my editor, do you ever stop to consider that she might find *you* dull?" He actually thought I was joking. He looked at me, laughed, and poured himself another glass of wine, spilling it everywhere as the bottle shook in his convulsing grip.

The two wings are divided by the lobby, behind this is the lift and a door leading to the pool area which has a pop-up style bar and a dozen or so tables in front of it.

I walked past the pool to the bar and got an Aperol spritz. I was in two minds whether to lounge by the pool or sit at a table when my decision was made for me by a girl sitting a few feet away. She had a wide afro and an even wider smile which she was flashing towards me. Her arm waved, and for a second I did that thing you do when you're not sure if you are the object of someone's attention. I half-looked behind me but there was no one near and when I turned to her again, she was nodding as though she'd perceived my doubts. "Hi, I'm Marley," she said. "I saw you on the plane."

Of course, I am much more friendly and approachable than Luke, but I'm still an introvert (unlike Luke, ironically) and would usually brush off the half-invitation with a polite *Oh, hi!* and my most convincing smile before disappearing to the remotest corner of the lounge. Now, however, I found myself unable or unwilling to do so; the girl's smile was so warm and genuine that to walk away would have felt like abandoning a bouncy puppy who just wanted to play.

"Hi, I'm Sanjay," I said, as she pulled out a chair for me. "I must have missed you on the plane."

"We were first on, so I watched everyone as they filed past. You never notice the people sitting at the front, everyone always looks down the aisle to find where they're going to be sitting."

"Who are you with?" I asked, before sipping my drink.

"I'm with my mum, super cool me! You're with your boyfriend, right?" She said it without hesitation. She could've asked who I was with, but she didn't, she took the reins. Being gay is the same as being straight except for one thing: everyone else. Because we hide this side of ourselves growing up like it's some dirty secret, we are left with the hangover of it into our adult lives, long after we accept ourselves and celebrate who we are.

"His name is Luke," I told her. "I've no doubt you'll meet the handsome devil at dinner. I won't tell you too much about him, I'm sure he'll do that later. If you want to get off on the right foot, compliment his hair, or his clothes, or anything about him, really."

"Is he vain?" she asked, and laughed.

"Yes. Unfortunately, the better looking someone is, the vainer they are. I've even programmed our Amazon Echo to respond to 'how do I look?' so I don't have to. What about you, do you have a boyfriend?"

"No, I'd struggle to find the time at the minute. Since my dad died, I've spent a lot of time helping my mum."

"Is there no one else who could chip in?"

"No, just me. My three brothers are always out. They're not bad but they are a bit wild."

"You all live together?"

"Yeah, in South London. I'm the youngest but we're all pretty close in age. The boys come and go at all hours, day and night. The only time you're guaranteed to see them is for church on Sunday morning. Mum would kill them if they missed that."

Marley spoke about her family and London, about how much she loves the City. She hopped from one topic to another, often with no discernible correlation between them. She smiled constantly and laughed at everything. The warmth from the sun, and from her, relaxed me. In fact, I think it was the first time I've felt truly relaxed in weeks. It was with reluctance that I told her I must leave her, that Luke would be wondering where I'd gotten to and that I looked forward to seeing her this evening at the welcome dinner. She beamed and said she couldn't wait. I believed her.

9

Marley

The receptionist checking us in was efficient and polite. She got a colleague to take Mum to her room while I filled in the necessary forms. That guy Dylan was checking in next to me. He sent his girlfriend off to the bar to get some drinks and no doubt hope to improve her mood. The receptionist dealing with him was as polite to him as mine was to me, but the courtesy wasn't returned. When she said, "Enjoy your stay, Mr Freeman," she received a grunt as a reply. He then strode off towards the bar leaving his bags at the desk, presumably expecting them to be taken to his room. I made sure Mum was settling in okay before I dashed off to explore the hotel.

I met a man named Sanjay at the bar, who is lovely, and later, I met a lady called Penny Haylestone, who is a mystery. After chatting with Sanjay, I sat with my face in the sun and thought that if Mum hadn't emigrated from Jamaica, I could be enjoying this feeling every day. I think I read in a magazine that there's something in the sun's rays that makes you happy, which explains a lot when you think about it.

I was nearly dozing off when a chair scraped the tiles at the table next to me. I opened my eyes and saw an older lady sitting down beneath an orange tree. "Oh, sorry, dear, I didn't mean to disturb you," she said. "These damned chairs sound like fingernails on a blackboard. You probably don't remember blackboards, do you, everything's digital now I imagine."

She wore pearl earrings and a pearl necklace. Her pale blonde hair was coiffured in a chignon, the kind that in a few years will turn to grey and lose none of its elegance. "I love your dress," I said, looking at a thin, flowing red day dress with long sleeves.

"Thank you, dear. M&S. Can't go wrong." Her voice sounded a bit posh but there was a knowing twinkle in her eyes. "Have you just arrived?" she asked.

"Yes, about an hour ago."

"In that case you need a drink. Paulo, my dear," she said to a passing waiter, "will you bring us two gin and tonics, please? You're a darling."

"Si, Senora Haylestone," he replied and bowed.

"I'm Penny. You must be Marley," she said, giving a slight bow.

"Oh, how did you - "

"I was chatting with Russell earlier; he said your mother is a regular guest and was arriving today along with her daughter. I saw you signed your names in the guest book when you arrived, no magic or conspiracy, dear, don't worry."

"Do you know Russell well? My mother speaks very highly of him, which is unusual. She can be quite fierce." I laughed, making light of the truth.

"Yes, I've known Russell for years, since before he bought this place in fact. Actually, it was my husband who gave him the idea. We used to work together but Russell wanted to try something new, so Anthony suggested buying a hotel in the sun. A daft idea, really. What does Russell know about hotels? I said. He can learn, said Anthony. And so, he did." Penny lifted an arm and swung it, her reach taking in the whole hotel. "Thank you, Paulo, dear," she said, as our drinks were set before us. "Cheers, Marley, I hope you have a marvellous holiday."

"Cheers. Is your husband with you?" I asked.

"No, he's dead."

"Oh! I'm so sorry!" I spluttered, fearing I'd put my big foot in it. Penny, however, just raised her eyebrows and looked surprised.

"Why are you sorry, dear? Everyone dies, it's a fact of life. And don't feel sympathy for me, either, I won't have it. People always scrunch their faces up and assume helplessness. Do I look helpless to you?"

"Absolutely not," I said earnestly, before taking a large gulp of fizzy gin.

"Quite right, dear. It's a funny old business bereavement. People refer to my 'late' husband. Late. What a funny word. Anthony was never late for anything. He was the apotheosis of precision and reliability. Well, until he was dead, of course."

"My father's dead," I said, though I don't know why.

"Is he? Well then, cheers to the dead-men-club." Penny reached over and we touched glasses.

"To the dead-men-club!"

10

Sally

Uncle Russell knocked on the door and caught us at a terrible time. We were finishing getting dressed for dinner; Jasmine was straightening her hair and wearing a cream silk dress which clung to her slim frame. I'd just told her that Dylan and his girlfriend were staying at the hotel. She'd glared at me when the words fumbled out of my mouth, her beautiful face frozen in either shock, disbelief, or fury: it was hard to tell which. The knock came before she could process my words and she stood in stunned silence when Uncle Russell introduced himself and held out his hand. She took it in her own after what seemed an age but still she stood, not speaking, just staring at my uncle. "How great to see you," I said, turning his attention away from the statuesque beauty beside me. "It's been so long! Thank you for squeezing us in."

"It's no bother at all, really. The hotel is always busy, but how could I not make room for my favourite niece?"

The years living in the sun have treated Uncle Russell well. He's a few years older than my mum so he must be closer to sixty than fifty but there are only a few flecks of grey among his thick blond hair. He obviously takes pride in his appearance; he's toned and tanned. The latter easily achieved in this place, of course, but the former must be gotten through hours of effort in the gym just down the corridor. As I looked at him, I couldn't help but wish I'd inherited his bright blue eyes.

"Are you girls nearly ready for dinner?" he asked.

Jasmine, seeming to have regained some composure, smiled her sweetest smile and said, "I promised I would phone my mum to let her know we got here safely. You two go on ahead and have a drink and a catchup, I'll be right along."

There were a few guests already seated near the pool, I recognised one or two from the plane and the coach. I saw the large man with the mousy wife talking to the gay couple. The big man seemed to be doing all the talking (and drinking, for that matter); the words poured from his mouth even as he poured his beer into it, and his wife handed him a constant stream of napkins to wipe his chin with. The gay couple didn't look a bit interested in what he was saying, the good-looking one didn't even look at his torturer and instead his eyes wandered, examining everyone else. The other one nodded politely and tried to draw the loud man's wife into the conversation but didn't appear to enjoy much success. She sat and smiled at him in return, tilting her head in what looked like unconscious sympathy.

Uncle Russell asked me what I would like to drink and went behind the bar to fix it himself. I looked to my right as I waited and saw a woman sitting on her own beneath an orange tree. She was watching me, assessing me even, and made no attempt to hide the fact. She smiled when we made eye contact but continued appraising me without a hint of embarrassment. I would put her at sixty, though she looked very elegant in her pearl earrings and necklace, the type of woman whose confidence could reduce men to quivering wrecks. How I wish to have an ounce of that.

"Here you are, Sally," said Uncle Russell, handing me a daiquiri. "Ah, there's Penny, you should meet her, she's an old friend, and an exceptional woman."

"How did you meet?" I asked, thinking 'old friend' was code for new girlfriend. I was wrong.

"Oh, it was long ago. Before I came out here. We used to work together in a way: a different life."

"What did you do before you bought the hotel? Mum has never mentioned."

"That's because your mum never knew. Penny!" he said, as we moved within hearing distance, "this is my niece, Sally."

"Hello, my dear," she said, regally taking me by the hand and guiding me into the chair next to her. "How nice to meet you. I know Russell has been looking forward to your visit. He said you have just finished university, have you got a job lined up?"

"Good heavens, Penny!" interrupted my uncle. "The poor girl has barely had a sip of her drink and you are trying to recruit her. And might I remind you that you are now retired!"

"I don't need reminding, Russell; the mirror tells me every day." She turned to me and lowered her voice. "Forced retirement, can you believe it? Ridiculous. I don't look sixty-five and I sure as hell don't feel it. I'm as sharp as I ever was."

"*That* I won't argue with," said Russell.

"If you argue with any of it, you'll wake up tomorrow morning cradling your tongue in your hands."

"I thought forced retirement had been outlawed," I said. "You can work until you drop these days, no?"

"My profession has always adhered to different rules, dear. Now then, where's your friend? Russell said her name is Jasmine?"

I instinctively looked up in the direction of the hotel lobby, but instead of Jasmine, I saw Dylan and his beau exiting and walking towards the bar. He saw me and stopped; his face contorted in horror. His mouth moved to form the word *no* and all I could do was raise my eyebrows in recognition and give a half-smile. Yep.

"Who's that?" asked Penny, following my gaze.

"That's Dylan. I don't know the girl's name. He's Jasmine's ex-boyfriend, he left her for that one."

"Cancel the fireworks, Russell, I don't think we'll need them."

My uncle groaned, no doubt thinking that the peaceful holiday atmosphere which he had created was going to be destroyed by jealousy and drama. "The girl is checked in under the name Elle," he said, after a pause.

Elle, sensed something was wrong. Dylan, stopping in shock, had not failed to notice and he was now speaking rapid words in her ear as they passed our table on the way to the bar.

The three of us spoke in more hushed tones than before, the fraught ambience of the evening broken by the large man who was oblivious to any tension in the group and who was still regaling his companions with what I could only assume was boring and possibly inappropriate stories, judging by the looks on the gay couple's faces.

"That's Terry Smith," my uncle said, looking at the loud man. There was an edge to his voice, a mixture of regret and apprehension.

"He was on our plane, too. Do you know him?" I asked.

"We're old schoolmates, though school acquaintances would be a more accurate description."

"You don't like him?" I asked, glancing at Penny to see if she was familiar with this information, but her eyes were still fixed on Dylan as he took his drinks from the bar and made his way to a table near Terry. They sat by the nearside of the pool, the table which was to be used for dinner being on the far side.

"We didn't get on too well, though I'm not the kind of man to bear a grudge. I can't say the same for Terry, mind."

"What would he begrudge you for?" I asked, intrigued by the hardness in my uncle's voice and eyes.

"Oh, it was all such a long time ago, he probably doesn't even remember me. He hasn't shown any recognition when he's looked over this way."

"Maybe you should introduce yourself to see if he does remember you."

Before Uncle Russell could consider my suggestion, our group became larger. Penny had spied two women exiting the lobby, one pushing the other in a wheelchair, and she hailed to them.

"Marley, my dear. Over here, let me meet your mother." Penny rose and fanned out the chairs to make room. "Marley, that dress is beautiful, the colours are so vibrant, so exotic. Here, let me get you something to drink. Paulo!" A very handsome waiter appeared at her elbow in a flash and was given firm instructions. He flashed me a wide smile before disappearing behind the bar to create a maelstrom of shaking and clinking.

Uncle Russell rose to greet the lady in the wheelchair, stooping over and taking her by the hand. "My dear Agathe. It is so good to see you again here at The Orange Tree Hotel."

"As it is to see you, Russell, you look the same as always. The good Lord seems to have blessed you with eternal youth. This is my daughter Marley," continued the woman, taking hold of the girl's arm. "She's here to look after her old mother, isn't that right, Marley?"

"And to have some fun I hope?" said Penny, smiling at the girl.

"Mum, this is Penny, the lady I met earlier. Remember I mentioned her?"

"Oh yes," said Agathe, looking at Penny over the top of her bifocals. "You are Russell's friend, no?"

"Yes, we go back a long way, we used to work together, I taught him everything he knows."

"Oh, I see. In the hotel business as well, are you?"

"No, I -"

"Ah, here is Paulo with your drinks," interrupted Russell. "Allow me to raise a toast: To friends, family, and having a good time. Cheers!"

11

Terry

The smug bastard sat there like king of the hill, surrounded by his harem of worshippers, laughing and joking and raising toasts, pretending he hadn't seen me. Aye! Like hell he hadn't. I saw his face fall flat when he walked out from the lobby and clocked me sitting there. He looked like someone had shoved a cattle prod up where the sun don't shine and give it a good buzz. Shaking he were when he saw me, shaking with fear, as well he might.

Sickening it were the way he stood up and bowed over the woman in the wheelchair, like he were some gracious lord deigning to greet a commoner. Of course, they all loved it. They all smiled and thought to themselves how wonderful he is, how kind, how well-meaning. Well, I know the truth. I know what kind of horrible, vindictive man Russell Aspell is. It may have been near four decades, but Terence Smith wouldn't forget a feud like that if it'd been four centuries.

Still, I'm on my holidays and I won't let the likes of him spoil it, though I do resent putting money in his pocket.

Before dinner we sat and had a drink with two fellas that are here together. The Indian one seems a nice enough bloke, but the other one, well he's a bit mardy. He didn't seem interested in what I had to say, even when I told some of my best jokes.

Marjorie seems to have perked up a bit now that we're here, though. She was talking to Sanjay about his job and about living in London and that. She said how she's always wanted to go to the Chelsea Flower Show then had the cheek to say she's never been because I won't take her. "Well," I said, "what were you doing for the fifty years before we met? And if I'm dragging my arse all the way down to London, I'll be watching football or rugby, not sniffing a bunch of pansies." Luke said something I didn't quite catch and the three of them laughed, but at least I'd made my position on the matter clear: if I'm going to London to be surrounded by all those Southern fairies, I want to see some balls being played with.

"I do envy you, though," said Marjorie. "Living in a small town can feel a bit, oh, I don't know, limited at times. I suppose you're never bored in London with all the theatre shows and fancy restaurants and shops to go to. It must be wonderful."

"It is. We love it," said Sanjay. "Although it *is* easy to take for granted. Sometimes you just don't bother with those things because they're on your doorstep and you know you can enjoy them at any time, then inevitably you never do. I've never even visited the Tower of London to my shame."

"Well, there you have it," I said. "If something's not worth doing right now then it's not worth doing at all, that's my motto. Therefore, London can't be all it's cracked up to be. Sure, there's nothing down there we don't have up our way anyway."

"Except the Tower of London," said Luke, like an arse.

"We have plenty of towers and castles of our own, thank you very much," I replied, determined not to be riled. I took a long sip of my beer and admitted to myself that as cold and refreshing as it tasted, it was nowhere near as good as a pint of bitter in the Rambler's Arms but still better than anything they'd scoop from the Thames and charge you a tenner for.

"London also has beautiful parks, stunning architecture and world-renowned tourist attractions."

"Aye, and smog, unaffordable house prices, and bloody tourists, too!" I replied, unable to help myself.

Marjorie laid a hand on my arm and said, "Well, each to their own I suppose. I would love to see more shows and the like, but I'd miss the country walks I enjoy so much, so I guess you can't have everything no matter where you're from."

"We saw a great show the other week, didn't we, Luke?" said Sanjay.

"What was it?" asked Marjorie, leaning forward all eager and conciliatory, wrongly thinking I was annoyed.

"*Magic Mike*," said Luke, smiling. "Brilliant it was, like nothing else we've seen."

"Paul Daniels came from up my way! And Dynamo!" I said, unable to take any more of their cockney nonsense.

"Actually, I meant *Les Misérables*…" replied Sanjay, before being interrupted by a loud voice over at the other table.

"Ladies and gentlemen, dinner shall be served in a few minutes, we are just waiting for one more of our party to arrive," said that tosser Russell. "Ah, here she is now!"

He was looking at a tall, slim girl in a white dress who was coming towards him from the hotel lobby. As she strode across the tiles, she turned her pretty little head in our direction and glared at me, or at least I thought she did, until I realised it were that young fella she were looking at, the one sitting nearby who had the bust-up in the airport.

You don't get three ex-wives without getting a few hard stares along the way but none of my romantic mistakes ever looked at me like that; there were pure venom in that glare.

"There's history there," whispered Marjorie, following my gaze. "She looks like a woman scorned if you ask me."

She's not often wrong is Marge, but I'll not often tell her. She's got that woman's institution where their first guess is usually the right one. My old mam was the same; they *know* things, there's just no rhyme nor reason as to how they know them. Institution or intuition?

Anyway, as we got up to go over to the table where the food was being laid out Marjorie said, "Aren't Luke and Sanjay a lovely couple?" It never occurred to me that they might be gay. But if there's one thing that Terence Smith is not, it's a bigot! A bigamist, yes. Wife number three came before wife number two was fully out the door, but a bigot? No! Each to their own is my motto, they can do what they like and that's fine by me as long as they keep their eyes to themselves! God sculpted Terence Smith for the eyes and pleasure of the deadlier species.

Anyway, that's enough from me for tonight, I don't want to think about what happened after. I want to go to sleep now and dream about strangling Russell bloody Aspell!

12

Sanjay

Marjorie is lovely, and Terry is…well, he's vibrant, shall we say. He's loud with zero filter and is probably the type of man that thinks all gay men are attracted to them, you know, because they're gay. They never stop to consider that all straight men aren't attracted to all women so why would we be different, but hey-ho.

Luke didn't take to him but that's only to be expected. Terry's boisterousness isn't entirely compatible with Luke's preening snobbishness.

I think Terry had pushed our tables closer together as there didn't seem much space between us, and he started talking as soon as we sat down. I hope he's taken Luke's rude hints and doesn't try to engage with us too much on this holiday, otherwise I can envisage my role. I'll be like the circus performer who walks on the tightrope with the balance pole, only sitting at opposite ends of the pole will be a loud Terry and a grumpy Luke.

Maybe the incident after dinner will have inflicted an embarrassed shyness into Terry. Dinner! How delicious it was. It was served informally with the food laid out on a large table.

Marley came over and introduced herself to Luke, and I could see his icy mask begin to thaw under her relentless, exuberant charm. She wore a fabulous green and yellow dress with matching heels, but I was sad to see her shoulders slump when she spoke, and her entire body rigid when she walked, as if she didn't possess the confidence the outfit required, or perhaps she was unused to wearing such an elegant number.

Confidence is one thing the other girl is not in short supply of. She was introduced to me as Jasmine. She has gorgeous blue eyes, and she wore a cream silk piece with a slit that ran the length of her endless leg. She tossed her flowing hair, and her thick red lipstick creased as she smiled at everyone. Everyone except the young couple that is.

Curious as to the cause of the animosity, I shamefully commented on the girl, Elle's, dress hoping Jasmine would in turn respond with at least a nugget of information to satisfy my journalistic thirst for truth. I was not disappointed.

"It's a disgusting rag! I mean, just because you're a whore doesn't mean you have to dress like one."

"You know the girl?" I asked, sipping my prosecco to hide my shamed face.

"I know all I need to. You see the guy she's with? That's Dylan. We were a couple until that little slut came along. I should be thanking her really; she did me a favour. Dylan is not who he pretends to be. Beneath the pretty boy looks he's rotten to the core."

She spoke these words loud enough for all to hear. The chatter hushed and most eyes fell on Dylan, who reddened and scuttled off to the bar followed by Elle. In that moment I became aware of the warm breeze, the sweet scent of oranges, and the starry sky. The dramas of the others made me forget the strife in my own life and I was grateful to them for it. Music started playing, perhaps to remedy the awkward silence that lingered as a result of this scene, which I had a hand in creating.

The group inflated and deflated like bellows blowing air on hot coals as people drifted in and out, fetching food, or going to the bar. Terry had dragged his chair over with him and was talking to Agathe. I wondered if the poor woman was suffering or if the crucifix around her neck gave her more patience than the average mortal.

Russell was talking to Marjorie, who appeared to be complimenting him on the food as they were both peering at the loaded plate in her hand and pointing at various items. She looked like she was stocking up for the fortnight. There were glazed sausages, prawns, stuffed vine leaves, chicken thighs, and a mountain of chips on the plate. Jasmine left me to join them. Marley, excited, broke off her conversation with Luke and called everyone together for a group photo. Terry wheeled Agathe into the centre and after Marley had taken a photo, insisted on taking one of his own. It became contagious as Sally was next to command everyone to bunch together to fit in the shot. Dylan and Elle stayed by the bar. After picture time, I was accosted by Penny, who I must say is a lively character.

"My good man, that shirt does absolutely nothing for you. Just because you are in a sunny place does not mean you need to wear ridiculous tropical shirts; you're not in Hawaii, you know. No, dear, stick to plainer designs. A nice salmon pink would suit your skin tone quite well I should think. That shirt your boyfriend is wearing is much more appropriate."

Luke was wearing a spotless, white cotton shirt from Hugo Boss, and although it suited him well, I know he doesn't like us dressing similarly and he doesn't mind me showing off the more colourful side of my personality.

Before I could reply or defend my fashion tastes, Marjorie appeared at my side.

"What lovely food that was! I've just had a whole plate of things, delicious, all of it. Have you tried any, Sanjay?"

"No, not yet."

"The minced beef wrapped in vine leaves was to die for. I've never had ought like it before. I should cook more really, you know, from scratch I mean, but sometimes it's easier just throwing something in the oven. Terry can't cook and neither can my daughter, bless her."

"How old is your daughter?" asked Penny.

"She'll be twenty-six in a fortnight's time. That's one of the reasons we're here now, Terry wanted to fly out next week, but I couldn't miss Sarah's birthday. Have you any children, Penny?"

"No, my husband and I were never blessed, not that we ever really tried, to be honest. Work always came first for both of us."

"I know what you mean, people are very career driven these days. Nick, my ex-husband, was the same. I wanted a bigger family, but he was always trying to grow his business. A car salesman he is. We only had Sarah, but I'll never complain about that. Such a sweet girl."

"Terry's not her father, then?"

"No, Terry's my second husband. We married four years ago. This is our first holiday together. Do you want kids, Sanjay? You can do that these days, can't you?"

I could swear I saw Penny raise her glass to her lips to suppress a smile. The old minx is a mind reader I believe, or certainly a face reader and, in that moment, had divined the whirlwind of thoughts Marjorie's innocent question had created. I mean, is asking someone their desire for progeny socially acceptable? And is it less acceptable to ask a gay man or should I be glad of the assumed equality? And that's before you even start to consider the physical practicalities of surrogacy, adoption, whose sperm would we choose, and all this to be summed up and presented in a simple yes or no.

"No," I replied, more due to a desire for simplicity rather than to confer honesty.

"Oh! What time is it?" asked Marjorie, startled. "I told my Sarah, I'd ring her at nine o'clock and I've left my phone in my room." She peered into her handbag.

With Marjorie gone, Penny and I joined Russell, who'd waved us over to his group. He was standing by the food table with Luke and had brought Dylan and Elle into the fold, also. Luke gave me a cold look as I approached, no doubt angry at me for abandoning him. We chatted for ten minutes or so when Russell, noticing I wasn't holding a plate, said, "Sanjay, you haven't eaten! Here, try a crab claw." I took one, our host offering the dish around. Everyone took a claw except for Dylan, who stepped back from the plate as if it were a hissing snake.

"No, not for me," he said, eyeing the food with disgust. "I have a severe allergy to shellfish, one bite of that and I'd be a goner."

"Quick, shove it down his throat!" shouted Jasmine, who was standing in the other group a short distance away. A few of us gave a nervous laugh as though to make light of the comment but it was plain to see the young beauty had not intended to sound funny. The gorgeous gorgon stared at her ex-lover, her face set with contempt. Dylan shook, whether through anger or embarrassment I couldn't tell, but I wondered if his face would still be so pale after two weeks of Spanish sun.

"My Marge don't like shellfish neither, Dylan, so you're in good company," said Terry, I think to ease the tension.

"I didn't say I didn't like it, I said it will kill me, you idiot."

"Alright, steady on, lad."

Dylan is undoubtedly attractive. He is tall and dark, though slim to the point of lanky. He has a certain charisma, a danger to him almost, but his rudeness is not an attractive quality.

Conversation resumed, Luke asked Russell when he would like to begin the work he was there to carry out.

"Now's not the time to discuss that, my good man, now is the time to enjoy yourself. You don't talk shop with a beer in your hand, isn't that right, Sanjay?"

"Absolutely," I replied, clinking glasses with our host. "I must say, Russell, this really is a wonderful hotel."

"Thank you. Have you seen the beach yet?"

"No, but I'm looking forward to it."

"We have our own private beach here. There are steps leading down to it just over there past the end of the pool, beneath the gym. Directly opposite the beach is an island about three hundred metres out. It's called Stork Island, because many of the breed nest on an old, ruined lighthouse. The island is small and uninhabited but a great place to go snorkelling and kayaking. In a few days we'll all go on my boat and have a barbeque there. If it was just a little lighter, you'd be able to see it."

Russell pointed in the direction of the island, and as he flung out his arm, he caught Terry who was walking past him, presumably to the bar. The sudden impact knocked Terry, who was already unsteady on his feet, and he stumbled headfirst into the pool, sending a plume of water high into the air. Gasps could be heard over the soft music, mine amongst them, until frantic splashing and churning water drowned out all else. Terry, choking on water and words, grabbed hold of the side of the pool and clung on. Luke and Marley were the first to react, reaching down to help the man out, but he waved them away in his anger and shouted at Russell.

"You bastard!"

"It was an accident, Terry, I didn't see you," replied Russell, his hands held out in front of himself, a futile conciliatory gesture.

"Accident my eye!" Terry screamed. "An accident like all those years ago? I haven't forgotten that, and I won't forget this!"

13

Marley

Oh, what a beautiful morning! Oh, what a beautiful day! I love singing in the morning, even when I'm writing. The sky is so blue without a hint of cloud, and the sun feels glorious on my skin. Russell told me last night that the hotel runs day trips to Seville, and that the East Wing lot are going in a few days' time, with us due to go next week, but if the weather stays like this I'll want to stay here. I want to enjoy the sun, not sit on a stuffy coach.

I hope Terry is okay after last night, at least he won't catch a cold out here, but still, the shock of the water can't be good for him, not at his age and in his condition. I hope he makes use of the gym while he's here. I went this morning and I'm still buzzing from the feeling. All those endorphins zapping around my brain like lottery balls during the big draw. At least that's how I imagine them.

The gym is pretty basic but perfectly adequate for my needs. There are three treadmills, a ski machine thing and a weights section with metal frames and that sort of thing. Only one of the walls has windows, though, so I didn't stay too long because I missed the sunshine.

The receptionist said Russell has exclusive use of the gym between seven and eight, so I decided to have a workout as soon as I was able then have breakfast after. Mum was tired after the travelling yesterday and said she didn't mind eating a bit later.

When I got to the gym, Russell was still there but he had finished his workout. He was measuring a length of the wall with a tape measure but as he extended it, the tape folded under its own weight. "Need a hand?" I asked.

"Marley, I didn't hear you come in. I'm just seeing if we have space for a rowing machine, sure you don't mind?" I took the tape measure and Russell walked backwards stretching it out, talking about the gym as he did so. He's a nice man. He's warm and friendly; I can see why my dad liked him. Dad always said he looked forward to sitting by the pool in the evening, drinking rum, chatting with Russell. Now that I think about it, it must be strange for Russell to see Mum here without my dad, and to see me instead. "I think we can just about squeeze one in, don't you think?"

I didn't answer, I yelped. The tape slipped out of Russell's grasp and retracted towards the plastic housing I was holding, slicing the edge of my finger as it travelled. Russell was so mortified I had to laugh. Anyone would think he'd run me over in his car he was so apologetic and sweet. I assured him a dozen times that I was fine but he insisted on examining the cut, which had barely a trickle of blood seeping from it. Only after my thirteenth assurance that there was no harm done and no bad feelings did Russell nod his head and rein in his concerns. "I'll leave you to your workout before I cause any more harm," he said over his shoulder as he walked to the door.

The gym empty, I grabbed a yoga mat and played *Yoga with Adrienne* on my phone, happy that I wasn't disturbing anyone else. Then, I worked up a sweat on the treadmill, but stayed clear of the dumbbells and metal bars and all that. I wouldn't know where to start and would definitely do myself an injury. I'm not sure our travel insurance covers diabolical use of gym equipment.

As I was rolling up the mat getting ready to leave, I heard the electronic beep of the door access-reader and saw Elle come in. I hadn't spoken to her up to this point and now felt a little ashamed that I hadn't tried to last night. She has long blonde hair like Jasmine, and is beautiful (Dylan obviously has a type!), but she smiles less than Jasmine and there is little warmth about her. She seems stand-offish whereas Jasmine has a more 'take me or leave me as I am' way about her. Maybe I'm being judgemental, the poor girl probably feels ostracised for being with Dylan. If I were in her heels, I'd be paranoid, thinking everyone is talking about me behind my back. Of course, in her case, we are.

"Hi, you're Elle, aren't you?" I asked, in my friendliest tone.

"Yeah. Marley, right?"

"Yeah. Here for a workout?" Groan. What a dunderhead I am, what else would she be in the gym for. She pursed her lips and gave a curt nod in answer to the stupid question. "I wanted to come and say hi last night," I said quickly. "But you know what it's like, *so* many people and so many drinks and - "

"And your mother to run around after . . ."

"Yeah, that too," I replied, feeling my face burn a little.

"Why is she in that wheelchair? Did she have a careless accident or something?"

"No. She suffers with pain in her joints, actually."

"Can't be much fun for you though, can it? Being at her beck and call whenever she rings her little bell."

"She doesn't have a - "

"Good chat. Bye."

She slung a towel she was holding over her shoulder and walked to a treadmill.

This encounter dampened my mood, but it was soon recovered by the delicious breakfast we had. The restaurant was bright and airy, and the only sound heard over the clattering of crockery and the din of cutlery was the faint whirring of the ceiling fans as they wafted warm air around the room.

I helped myself to a bowl of melon cubes, orange slices, diced strawberries, and natural yoghurt before enjoying some Parma ham, Emmenthal cheese and a croissant. I got Mum the same, although she declined the ham as I knew she would.

The coffee was delicious. I peered over the top of my cup and glanced around the room like Audrey Hepburn in Tiffany's. Jasmine and Sally were sat by the window which faced onto the pool. They weren't speaking, Jasmine was playing with the food on her plate as Sally scrolled on her phone. Sanjay and Luke were talking to a waitress who was clearing their table. There was no sign of any of the other guests until a few minutes later when Penny swooshed in wearing a light, flowery, long-sleeved dress. I waved her to the table beside us.

"Penny, over here, come and join us."

"Marley, my dear, what a treasure you are. Good morning, Agathe, did you sleep well?"

"Oh yes, I always sleep well at The Orange Tree Hotel, Lord knows I do. My late husband Reggie, he'd say if you want a good night's sleep, fly yourself here and ask Russell if he has a spare room, but don't be surprised when he says no, because tis the finest hotel in all of Spain. Lord knows it is."

"What are you planning to do today?" Penny asked me as I put a forkful of Mum's ham into my mouth.

"I don't know really; it depends on how Mum is feeling. What do you fancy today, Mum?"

"I'll be alright by the pool watching films on my tablet or doing my wordsearch. I don't mind you leaving me there for a few hours if you want to go down to the beach."

"Actually, I was thinking of taking a walk into the town. I need to buy a plug adapter, I forgot to bring one."

"You'd forget your head if it wasn't screwed on, girl."

"I've got to pop into town to go to the bank," said Penny. "Maybe we can go together?"

"Perfect."

14

Terry

Get up nice and early when on holiday, that's my motto. You must make the most of it, after all, you've paid for the pleasure of being here, so why waste it asleep. Well, strictly speaking, Marjorie paid for this holiday, she holds the purse strings; says I can't be trusted with money; says I'd spend it all down the Poacher's Arms given half the chance. And what's wrong with that might I ask? A man needs his little reward at the end of a hard day's graft. And when you're between jobs like I am now, you need a pint to lift your spirits in the afternoon. Where's the harm?

Of course, things have been a bit tight lately, what with the economy and the job market and all that, and I admit Marjorie is more frugal than I am, and she's more determined when it comes to saving. Still, she must've got a cracking deal on this place, it's much nicer than I was expecting, but then I've heard those last-minute deals can be very reasonable, some right bargains to be had.

Plus, you know what women are like, they can make money stretch farther than men. Food, too. I remember my old mam could feed the lot of us for a week with just a few potatoes, carrots, and onions.

At breakfast, Marge badgered me to tell her the whole story about how I ended up soaking wet. Anyone would think it were my fault the way she went on. "I left you for ten minutes to call Sarah and you go and fall in the pool drunk!"

"I didn't fall, he hit me. And I wasn't drunk!" And she says I don't listen to her half the time!

After brekkie we went to the pool. Luke and Sanjay were on the loungers next to us. I thought I heard Luke say something about the incident last night, but I couldn't be sure, so I didn't pursue it. He's got a smart mouth on him that one, he'd better watch it, or my fist will make it dumb.

The heat is glorious by the way, by mid-morning the mercury was over thirty and I could almost hear the oil sizzle on my back. Marjorie spent the morning reading on her kindle thingy. She had her umbrella up from the get-go, her not being a fan of the sun. Umbrellas are for rain, that's what I said. I didn't fly all the way to Europe to sit in the shade; I could go to Grimsby if I wanted to do that.

When it got to lunchtime, we packed up our things and dropped them back in the room. Marjorie wanted to eat in the town, but I put my foot down. We didn't know how far it were, what if I fainted on the way there, walking in this heat on an empty stomach, it's a recipe for disaster. No, I said, we'll eat here in the hotel before we go anywhere, and that's what we did. I had a juicy steak baguette with a lovely dollop of mustard on the side. French mind, not English, but I shan't complain. Now that I think about it, the Spanish mustn't have learnt to make mustard, you never see it in shops, do you?

Anyway, in the end the walk to town wasn't too bad, about ten minutes all told. Porta del Costa or something the place is called. We walked past a few houses that looked deserted with shutters pulled down over the windows, and dusty wasteland containing broken bottles and rocks and the odd abandoned tyre; nothing to put in a brochure.

The town itself is a nice seaside haven, although a bit hilly for my liking. There's restaurants and bars, ice-cream shops and tattoo parlours, everything you could wish for. Marjorie said she wanted a new hat, but after the third shop I'd had enough and told her I was going for a pint in an Irish pub I'd spotted and for her to meet me there when she were done.

The Irish Rover, now this is more like it. I know I'm not out of place in the fancy hotel with miniature shampoos and towels provided, but a good boozer is where I fit right in. There's old black and white photographs on the walls showing men in bowler hats, posing beside a mountain of barrels. There's Guinness prints with tortoises and toucans, and a sealion doing a balancing trick with a pint of the black stuff on the tip of its nose. It's like being in Dublin, only hotter.

After my first pint I headed for a seat outside; the sun was still shining after all. I was sitting on a patio that faced onto the main pedestrianised road so it would be easy for Marjorie to see me. I was just thinking how easy it would be to nod off, what with the sun on my face and the beer in my belly, when a voice woke me back to the present.

"Hello, Terry. Enjoying the local amenities, I see. You're looking a bit pink; would you not be better in the shade?" Penny, standing there with Marley, obviously went to the same school of thought as Marjorie, although she's not as pale as the missus. Has a bit more colour about her, does Penny.

"Not a bit of it, Penelope! A bit of sun never done no one no harm, ain't that right, Marley?" She'd be on my side. "Come and sit down, ladies, I'll buy you a drink!"

Women have always found it hard to say no to Terence Smith and these two were no different. I fetched two gin and tonics and returned to beaming smiles.

"I do hope you're alright after that horrid incident last night?" asked Penny.

"Takes more than a bit of water to dampen my spirits, Penny!"

"I daresay! I thought you handled the situation very well I must say, Terry. Truly marvellously."

"Well, that's kind of you to say so," I replied, taking a swallow of my beer.

"And I know Russell feels terrible about it . . ."

"Does he now?"

"Indeed, he does, he told me so this morning. Very remorseful he is."

Ah, the fairer sex. So predictable and gullible. I saw what the game was. Russell had obviously roped Penny into trying to make amends on his behalf, the coward, and the poor old gal had obviously fallen for the Aspell charm, hook, line, and sinker, the poor mare. You read about these things don't you: wealthy widow falls for hotel manager on holiday only to be taken to the cleaners. Well, if there's one thing everybody who knows me agrees upon, it's that Terence Smith is as gracious as they come, so I decided to take it easy on her and not break her heart by telling her the truth about Russell bloody Aspell. If he has no scruples and is willing to involve a lady into our feud that's up to him, but I won't be drawn into using the same dirty tricks. No sir!

"Penny, I've known Russell for many years, I know his capacity for remorse," I said, quite pleased at my cryptic response.

"You've known him longer perhaps, but I know him better," she smiled.

"You what?"

"I've been friends with Russell for forty years, he was the best man at my wedding."

"I had no idea. I thought you just met him a few days ago."

"Good heavens no. I know Russell better than anyone, and I know there's bad blood between you, though I don't know why, but what I do know is that until yesterday you hadn't set eyes on one another since you wore school ties, so whatever the cause of this resentment, it happened when you were practically children, so it's about time you both grew up!"

These last words were so sudden and so much louder than the rest that even Marley raised her eyebrows before exclaiming, "You should've been a teacher, Penny. You would've terrified the children."

"Children don't need terrifying, dear; they need convincing that they should behave how you tell them they ought to. But they're not stupid, they need to see adults live by the rules they themselves set and lead by example. A bit like us and politicians."

"Except we're smarter than politicians, eh?" I said.

"So are most children. Anyway, my point is, Terry, do not ruin your lovely wife's holiday over some childish, petty feud. Ah! Speaking of your wife, here comes Marjorie now."

I looked down the road and saw Marge strolling along, a shopping bag swinging from each hand. Honestly, you'd think there were no shops in England. Do women think that men are magicians who can just conjure up more space in suitcases for taking all this clutter home? Give me strength. And she'll be eyeing up the hotel towels! I told her to pay for extra baggage allowance!

Marley waved. "Hello, Marjorie!"

I got another round of drinks. By the time I got back to the table, Marjorie had pulled over a large umbrella and half the table was covered in darkness.

"It really is a gorgeous hat," said Marley. "Where did you get it from?"

"There's a little boutique down a cobbled side street -"

Why is it when given half a chance women will immediately begin talking about clothes? I was only gone to the bar for two minutes and I'd come back to Madrid Fashion Week.

"Such a nice shop it was," she continued. "I saw a pair of boots just like ones my Sarah would wear when I'd take her horse riding when she was a little girl. Such a shame we can't do that anymore."

"What else did you buy? Did you get anything for me?" I asked, though I received a glare from my lady wife who doubtless would say my interruption was rude. I'll tell her later, that rude is talking about clothes and fashion when I'm not interested in any of it.

"I bought a bracelet for Sarah, and some more suncream, if you must know!"

"I need to get a plug adapter," said Marley. "I forgot I'd need one and can't charge my phone."

"They sell them where I got the suncream," said Marjorie. "They sell everything in there. It's just down that street." She pointed.

"I don't know why these foreigners have to be so awkward," I said.

"How do you mean?" asked Marley.

"Well, why have different plugs? Why drive on the wrong side of the road? Why use different money? It's like they've got nothing better to do than annoy us Brits. And they all sleep in the afternoon!"

"So do you!" said Marjorie, looking at me with her disbelief face.

"I've earnt the right! Besides, I'm not a shopkeeper, my sleeping habits don't stop other people from buying a pint of milk or getting their prescription! Speaking of which, I don't suppose you ladies saw a chemist shop on your explorations?"

"What do you want a chemist for?" asked Marjorie.

Imagine asking me a private question like that in polite company. Marjorie really doesn't think at times, she has no decorum.

15

Marley

Poor Marjorie. I wish we could've taken her with us to go shopping. We did ask but she said she ought to spend some time with Terry, not that he seemed bothered. "You crack on, love," he said. "Enjoy yourself. This is your holiday too. I don't mind having a couple more pints if you want to go off with the girls."

"No, we ought to get back to the hotel," she said. "Otherwise, we'll be in a rush to get ready for dinner."

"Suit yourself."

I'll try to prise her away for a drink later, though. I think she needs to let her hair down a bit. She's very tense, on edge, even. She seems to walk on eggshells around Terry, though I would say his bark is worse than his bite. In fact, he doesn't really bark, he's more of a yappy mongrel. Still, I'm sure he means well.

Penny, on the other hand, is quite the opposite. She's like an elegant dragon. She walks with confidence and grace and yet in her company you're left in no doubt that you are in the presence of a formidable woman. It's the intelligence behind her bottomless eyes and the knowing smile that plays on her lips. I wish I could be more like her.

We left the Irish Rover and followed Marjorie's directions.

"What did you do for a living? I know you weren't a teacher," I ventured to ask as we entered the shop.

She looked me up and down and took a good minute before responding. "Very well. I used to work in the Security Services."

"You were a spy?" I asked, stunned.

"No, dear. I was most definitely *not* a spy, although I did work with them. In fact, I recruited them. Recruitment and interrogation were my specialities. Reading people is what I'm good at. Knowing when someone is lying and getting the truth out of them."

"And Russell?"

"No questions about Russell please, that's for him to tell, not me," she said, lifting a warning finger. "I've told you more than I should already, certainly more than I'm allowed to. But as you know, I'm retired now. Forced retirement, so screw them."

The shop was like an indoor market selling toys, buckets and spades, cosmetics, drinks, and all kinds of bric-a-brac. The shelves and aisles were overflowing with goods which made walking through the place no easy task. Beginning to feel claustrophobic by the overhanging clutter I asked a passing shop worker in my worst Spanish where we would find what we were looking for. He answered with a torrent of words in his native language, and I was saved by Penny who answered him fluently.

"He said past the electric toothbrushes and left at the home security section."

"Penny, you speak Spanish!"

"I can get by, dear."

We found the adaptors on a shelf next to those doorbell security cameras. "We've got one of them at home," I said. "Mum got one after she ordered the *Downton Abbey* boxset from Amazon and the delivery driver said he left it behind the recycling bin. She kicked up a fuss when it wasn't there, threatening to sue Jeff Bezos, only to find out Lizzie next door had taken it in because she was worried it might rain. Still, clever inventions."

"Oh, they're nothing new. Back in the eighties we had tiny cameras in tie pins for interviewing suspects. The live feed would be watched in the Control Room by behavioural experts who would analyse body language. I had one in a necklace: ties don't suit me."

"No, I can't imagine you in a suit, Penny."

"Of course, what you'd wear would depend on the suspect."

"How so?"

"Well, dear, if I were interrogating a young man, I might wear something quite low-cut, let the cleavage do half the work. You'd have to be careful though, there was always the chance they'd see the camera in the necklace, but ninety times out of one hundred they didn't, and besides, they were already in custody anyway, so it didn't really matter if they discovered our tricks, they were never going to get the chance to tell their mates. Should we stop for a cocktail on the way back to the hotel?"

The cocktail bar was much nicer than the dank, dark Irish Rover. Chandeliers hung from a high ceiling and the chairs were upholstered with red velvet. We were seated by the rear window which looked out over the beach. It was the first time I'd seen a beach in years, since my cousin's hen do in fact, and that was in Brighton, so it doesn't really count. Apologies to any Brightonians but if it's a stony beach, it ain't a beach!

The sea sparkled blue and stretched to the horizon. I thought it daunting yet awe-inspiring that it stretched all the way to Jamaica and that if you floated away, you could eventually find yourself in Kingston.

"Have you ever been to Jamaica?" asked Penny,

"How did you know what I was thinking?"

"Because you were trying to see something. Something far away, but all you can see out there is a blue desert. You're in a sunny place now, I doubt you would be longing for England, so your ancestral homeland seems the natural place that your mind would wander to. Can I say that by the way? Ancestral homeland? Or is it racist? It's hard to keep up these days."

"No, it's fine to say, and no, I've never been," I replied between laughs. "I would love to go but we could never afford it when I was a kid. Mum raised us and Dad worked, there was never anything left at the end of the month to pay for a holiday for us all. They started coming here about six years ago when I was old enough to look after myself."

"I know what you mean. The first time I left Blighty I was twenty-two and had to interrogate a Stasi officer in East Berlin, who claimed he wanted to come over to our side. My job was to find out whether he was genuine. I'd never known anything other than fish, chips, and bread and butter pudding, and all of a sudden I found myself being ferreted through security checks with barbed wire and machine gun posts everywhere you looked. Still, I'm sure you'll get to Jamaica one day, dear."

"I tried to persuade Mum to go this year instead of coming here. I thought coming here would be too painful for her."

"Because she used to visit here with your father? Too many memories?"

"Yes, but also because this is where Dad died. At The Orange Tree Hotel, I mean. He had a heart attack one morning."

"Oh, Marley, how terrible, I had no idea." Penny took my hand in hers and gave it a squeeze. I turned again to the window and gazed out to sea.

"Thanks. Mum never talks about it. Everything I know is from the coroner's report which I found in a cupboard at home. Dad had just been exercising in the gym and was walking back to his room when he collapsed. Russell tried to use the hotel defibrillator on him, but the battery in it was flat. It was supposed to have a yearly servicing, but it was missed somehow. Russell paid to have the body flown to London and helped Mum sort out the legal paperwork. Still . . ."

"It is such a shock when one loses a parent. My father died when I was eleven, it was very hard."

"And your mother?" I asked.

"She's still fighting against the inevitable. She's ninety-nine and lives in a leafy care home where she's fussed over from dawn til dusk. Not that she wishes to be, of course. She's still fiercely independent for her age, raising a child on your own during the post-war years will make you like that. We need hardships in our lives, dear, they mould our character. It's just a shame when those hardships include the permanency of losing a loved one like your father. Breaking up with a boyfriend, well, that's much more like it. It makes you tougher and better prepared for the next one. Do you have a boyfriend you can break up with?"

"No. I don't have time, what with Mum and - "

"Oh, nonsense, dear. What you have are excuses. You're a beautiful girl, Marley, I refuse to believe that young men are not making fools of themselves everyday trying to win your affection. Back in my mother's day it was called 'walking out' when you'd meet your sweetheart at the kitchen door and steal away for an hour to get to know them, then in my day it was called 'stepping out' and now you youngsters call it 'going out', but nine times out of ten it all ends up in falling out. It's that one time, when you know he's the one, that's when you grab him and hold on for the ride of your life."

"You make it all sound so easy and romantic, Penny."

"Well, the last bit was a dirty joke, but the rest of it *is* easy, that's how you know he's the one: it's easy being with that person. Love isn't expensive gifts and grand gestures that can be recorded on Instagram, it's the little things."

"Has anyone ever told you how very wise you are, Penny?"

"Dear, most of the conversations I've had in my life have been with terrorists, murderers and psychopaths. I've been called all sorts of vile names more times than I can remember, but never wise." Penny then gave several examples of what she considered to be the worst things she's been called, and which she considered to be accurate.

It's always shocking hearing older ladies saying the foulest words imaginable, but Penny does so with characteristic grace and a shrug of her shoulders. Even so, the other patrons of the bar hushed at the words and cast their glances in our direction, not that Penny seems bothered in any way. "Oh look," she said, "here comes Sanjay and Luke."

The two men were entering the bar and gave us a wave before being seated by a waitress at the far end of the room, away from us.

"Should we have another drink, my dear?"

I looked at my phone, it was still mid-afternoon, and I had received no text messages from Mum, so although I couldn't be sure, I imagined her napping in the shade or watching a film as she sipped a pineapple juice. I knew I should go back to check on her, but I was having so much fun with Penny, I couldn't say no.

"Okay, but just the one! I should really check on Mum."

"Your mother's fine, dear, she's asleep under a palm tree. I have Paulo giving me regular updates," she said, waving her phone at me.

One drink turned into three as I relaxed, knowing Mum was okay and being looked after. After a particularly punchy rum cocktail I nipped to the toilet, only to find there was one unisex toilet, and the lock said ENGAGED in bold red lettering. I hopped around outside the door holding it in, when I became aware that I could hear the person in the cubicle talking on their phone.

"You bastard!... How am I supposed to do that?... It's too much money... I'm warning you; I'll kill you!"

After a moment, I heard the lock snap open. I jumped behind a nearby plant pot, not wishing for the toilet's occupant to see me and think I was eavesdropping. I needn't have worried, as when the door slammed open the person flew past me blind with rage; I might as well have been invisible.

It was Luke.

16

Sally

We've been here for three days now, and so far, the holiday is living up to my (reduced) expectations, despite a few bumps in the road.

Jasmine has spat venom about Dylan every time he is in sight, but only in conversation with me. There has been no repeat of her outburst on the first night and I'm hoping she'll mellow more as the holiday progresses and she gets used to him being here.

Uncle Russell has plied us with free drinks and last night took us to the best restaurant in the area. Jasmine didn't say much during the meal and when she did it came across as rude and ungrateful, but again, I'm sure it was all because of Dylan. Dylan, Dylan, Dylan! Part of me wants to talk openly and honestly with her but I still have my secret to keep, and besides, the more we talk about Dylan the more of a problem his presence here will be. We are supposed to be enjoying a relaxing holiday!

Uncle Russell told us about the trip to Stork Island he has planned in a few days' time. We spoke about the other guests, but I noticed he was tight-lipped about Terry and every time I mentioned him, he would move the subject on to someone else, usually Penny, who he holds in high regard. What the 'work' was that they did together is anyone's guess as Russell is as evasive on that topic as he is on Terry. I texted my mum asking her what Russell did for a living before he bought the hotel, but she was clueless, replying, "I don't know, love, why don't you ask him? P.S. Did you take my hair straighteners?"

I'm sitting on the balcony, the only sounds I can hear are Jasmine's faint, melodious singing and the gushing water which slaps the tiles after hitting her body.

Today we went to the beach, and an annoying amount of my time was spent taking pictures of Jasmine in an attempt to kill the proverbial duo of birds. She would upload the photos to her Instagram feed, where she said a talent spotter was sure to see them, and at the same time Dylan would pore over her teeny-weeny bikini shots and cry over what he was missing.

Of course, *I* was behind the lens taking the action shots whilst she thrashed in the surf. She flung her hair back so many times I'm surprised she doesn't require a neck brace. Jasmine's been in the shower for forty-five minutes now after spending an almost equal amount of time complaining: "Eurgh, sand gets, like, everywhere, and why does my hair smell of salt? Gross!"

Still, it will all be worth it when she's getting paid a million dollars to post a video of herself 'accidentally' spilling a Starbucks mochachocalattechino on a pair of Jimmy Choo's with her arse in the air.

What made the photoshoot worse was the fact that the beach itself is, in fact, glorious. Deserted golden sands stretch between the cliffs and the sparkling blue waves. I just wanted to lie there and read about the crawdads singing as I listened to the squawking gulls and the swelling sea.

The beach is private, accessed from the hotel by a zig-zagging wooden staircase that's secured to the rock of the cliff-face. There's a road which can get you there, but the journey takes three times as long because you have to drive away from the hotel and loop back around. Russell brought Agathe this way. Jasmine had finally decided she'd taken enough snaps for the day (apparently, the sun was beginning to fall as it was past noon and she didn't like the shape of her shadow), and we lay down to relax when Marley and her mum appeared with Penny. Uncle Russell helped the old lady walk from the car to the middle of the beach and set up a deckchair and umbrella for her. Penny came over to say hello.

"Sally, that swimming costume looks gorgeous on you. You look like Cindy Crawford."

I was wearing a simple black one-piece but appreciated the kind words. "Thanks, Penny. You're not going for a swim?" She was wearing a light, long-sleeved dress and dark shades.

"No, dear, I'm just going to enjoy the sun and have a bit of a read. But first I think I'll take a walk along the beach. Would you girls care to join me?"

Jasmine declined, but I was happy to agree. Over the past few days, I have gotten to know Penny better than any of the other guests. Of course, her being a friend of Uncle Russell is partly the reason, but I do like the lady, and I am ashamed to say I have enjoyed her company more than Jasmine's. She has a mystery to her, yet a kindness, too. She's the type of person who makes you feel comfortable in their presence immediately, and who you feel you can open up to.

"How is the book you're reading?" she asked, as we began our barefoot walk.

"Good and bad," I replied. "Good because it's so well-written and has a captivating plot. Bad because it's so well-written and has such a captivating plot that it makes an aspiring writer feel like a talentless fraud."

"Oh, Sally, dear, you must turn those feelings inside out. If there are no works better than your own there would be nothing to aspire to, and the quality of your own literature would suffer as a result. Use the book you are reading as a guide, break it down to the bare components to see what works and why. It will help you. When my career was in full swing, I became better at, ahem, problem-solving by watching those I worked with who had more experience. I watched them get to the root of a problem by breaking it down and asking the right questions."

"Was that when you worked with Uncle Russell?"

"I recruited your uncle, dear, we worked in different departments; it was a big company. Anyway, on to more important matters, did I detect a little tension between you and Jasmine when I arrived?"

I told Penny how Jasmine obsessed over Dylan, how she obsessed over herself and how she was distant with me, like at dinner the previous night. As I spoke, I realised that Jasmine was only interested in me when I could be of some use to her. Taking photos, the free holiday, etc. She wasn't actually interested in me, her friend.

Maybe I'm being harsh, maybe tonight Jasmine will be full of fun and laughter, and it'll be how it used to be, we'll see.

I can no longer hear the shower running so she must be drying herself. Mum's hair straighteners are hot enough to use now, so it's time for me to get ready.

17

Sanjay

It seems there's been a murder! I saw the police and ambulance crew show up as we were leaving the breakfast restaurant a few hours ago. The paramedics had a folded-up body bag and sombre sort-of-expressions on their faces, which is to be expected of them. The kind of look that says, "Yes, this is grim, but don't worry, we will work quickly and quietly, we've done this before."

As we left the restaurant Luke tried asking the receptionist what was going on, but only received a tearful, babbling response which couldn't be deciphered. We then went to the pool under the pretence of sunbathing and assumed the place would be abuzz with activity, but only old Agathe was there, sitting in the shade, holding her crucifix in one hand and her Bible in the other. As I approached her, she gripped the cross tighter as she does when I speak to her.

"Good morning, Agathe."

"Morning, young man."

"It's very quiet around here, you don't know where everyone is, do you?" I asked, fishing.

"How should I know? Marley sent me a text message saying there had been an accident and that her and Penny Haylestone were trying to get to the bottom of it, but I don't know any more than that. She's forgetting her old mother, that girl, forgetting her place!"

At that moment, a young, tall, and rather handsome police officer approached us and spoke in broken English. "Excuse me, senors and senora. I have been ordered to escort you to your rooms until the inspector de policia is ready to talk to you. What is your rooms?"

"My room? Now listen here, young man, I've just dragged myself all the way down here, and now you want to drag me all the way back up to there? You better have a good and honest reason to make such a demand on an old and frail woman, Lord knows, or there'll be trouble, and don't think old Agathe ain't capable of stirring no trouble! Now tell me, *what* has happened?"

"Senora, the inspector will explain everything in good time. Now, what is your room?"

"Excuse me," I cut in, seeing Agathe ready to explode. "When you say escort us to our rooms, do you mean we are to stay in our rooms until your inspector sees us?"

"Si, that is what I mean."

"That does seem quite unusual, perhaps if you were to tell us what has occurred, we might be inclined to follow your instructions more, erm, enthusiastically. . ." I nodded my head in the direction of Agathe, hoping the young officer would see sense and relinquish some information, thereby giving himself an easier time with the old woman and giving us something to discuss whilst locked in our room.

"All I can say, senor, is that a person was found dead in the gym this morning and that one of the hotel guests is insisting that it is a case of murder." The police officer rolled his eyes as he said the last words, no doubt imagining some busybody kicking up a fuss to spice up their holiday and give themselves a good story to tell their friends in the hair salon when they got home.

"I see, and you don't believe this is murder you are dealing with?" I asked, taking a step closer to Luke, though I'm not sure why. The officer gave a disinterested shrug, as though he didn't really care, and said, "Maybe, but the gym was empty other than the body when it was found, and the hotel computer shows that only the victim used their access card to enter the gym before the body was discovered, so I don't see how it can be murder. But that is enough, I tell you. What is your rooms?"

"105," said Agathe.

The policeman then turned to Luke who had seated himself on the edge of a sun lounger. "103," he said.

"And you?"

"Also 103," I said. Agathe snorted, then squeezed her crucifix.

"Am I under arrest?" asked Agathe, as the officer began pushing her chair around an umbrella and past the empty bar.

"No, senora, you are not under arrest."

"I should think not, if you know what is good for you, young man. Being in this chair doesn't make me weak, you know; I'll wring your neck like a chicken if you try to lock me up in one of your filthy jails, don't you know."

"Yes, senora." The officer pressed the button for the lift in the lobby. "Wait here senors, I come back for you."

"And bring some water, it's inhumane. And find my daughter! And - " Agathe's voice hollowed as the doors closed and the lift stuttered up to the floor above.

"Goodness, Luke, who do you think is dead?" I asked, as we waited alone.

"Could be anyone," he replied. "Well, except Marley and Penny, who we know are alive from what Agathe told us. And Terry, of course."

"Terry? How do we know Terry is alive?"

"The body was found in the gym. . ."

"Cruel, but fair point," I conceded. "I hope we aren't waiting too long for this police inspector to come along."

The lift doors opened in front of us, but instead of the youthful policeman, we found ourselves confronted by Penny and Marley.

"Marley," I said, "your mum is looking for you, the police have just taken her to her room, they say there's been a terrible accident-"

"There has been no accident," cut in Penny, sharply. "Russell has been murdered."

18

Sally

Uncle Russell murdered! I can't get my head around it. I know I must be in shock, but I don't know how to describe it. It's like my mind is a dull void and my senses have fallen into a coma. Words spoken have little meaning until my brain captures them and interrogates them for value. I missed much of what was said, my sentinelled hearing shields my overwhelmed mind from useless words or blunts their thrusts as best it can. It allows only the light in, that which is needed, and banishes the worthless, the platitudes which will bring me no closer to understanding. But the shock was not sudden, it has seeped in since I was told the news a few hours ago.

Jasmine and I didn't get in from our night out until close to two o'clock in the morning. We had dinner in a seafood restaurant on the beachfront. Jasmine's spirits and attitude were lifted somewhat by the lively atmosphere and chilled vibe of the place. The waiters, all of whom gave Jasmine dedicated service, glided around the tables as though they were ballroom dancers. In any other restaurant they would've seemed rushed and overrun, but there they looked in complete control. One waiter in particular caught Jasmine's eye, the miraculous result being that the name Dylan wasn't mentioned for our entire two-hour stay.

We then went to a few bars where we shot too many shooters and gulped too much prosecco, the outcome being a terrible and confused hangover, which was reverberating around my head when there was a loud rap on our door this morning. Jasmine didn't stir in her bed across the room, so at the third knock I wrapped a gown around myself and blearily opened the door only to squint at the invading light and a policeman.

"There has been an accident, stay please, in your room until I say so. Good morning." I was already back under the covers, hand stretching for a bottle of water before the words had any effect on my cognitive curiosity. What sort of accident? Why were the police here? Why did we have to stay in our rooms?

I was drifting off again when there came another tap on the door. This time I checked the peephole and saw Penny and Marley standing outside looking up and down the corridor. I flung open the curtains and shook Jasmine awake before opening the door.

"Sally, my dear, can we come in? I think we better had."

Jasmine rubbed her eyes awake and put on the matching gown to mine.

"Marley, fire up the coffee machine, dear, I think it's going to be needed. Now, girls, have the police been to see you yet?" Penny asked, leading me to the desk chair and ushering me down on to it.

"Yes, I'm not sure how long ago," I replied, time being lost in my foggy brain. "They said there had been an accident and we were to stay here." I looked at Jasmine who seemed bewildered, her beauty sleep having not been broken by the policeman's thunderous raps.

"That's all? They didn't say anything else?" asked Penny. I shook my head. "Well, dear, I'm afraid to tell you, your uncle is dead. He was murdered this morning in the gym during his morning workout."

The words were quietly spoken, their gravitas being at odds with the soft tone in which they were shared, being at odds with the bright sunlight that poured into the room and lightened the faces of those who heard them.

I sorted the confused thoughts in my mind, the jumble of questions vying for prominence. "But the police said it was an accident..."

"This was no accident, my dear. I've seen the body myself. Marley found him and called me straight away. Russell suffered a fractured skull, there were three separate impacts: no, this was no accident. The police are not yet aware that you are Russell's niece, I omitted to mention that, otherwise they would've come to see you before I could have, and I thought it best you heard this news from me."

My thoughts were disrupted by a hiccup coming from Jasmine. She was sitting on the edge of her bed, her hand covering her mouth. She returned my gaze for a moment then bolted into the bathroom where we heard her vomit into the toilet, heavy splashes echoing as the bile plunged into the water.

"Thank you, Penny. Who… I mean, what… there must be some mistake… Uncle Russell? I mean, why?" I said, powerless to reply with anything more meaningful.

Marley stood. "I'll check on Jasmine," she said, and walked into the bathroom.

"Oh, Penny," I whispered, as she put an arm around my shoulder. "What can we do?"

"You can tell your mum the news. The police will be here to interview you soon; phone her before they do. As for me, I'm going to find whoever killed your uncle, you mark my words, dear, I'll uncover the person who killed Russell Aspell, I swear it."

19

Marley

I guess the beginning is a good place to start.

This morning, I met Marjorie in the lobby at quarter-to-eight. I'd got talking to her yesterday by the pool and she'd said how she's always fancied trying yoga but had never given it a go. She said she didn't have the balance for it and was worried she'd look a fool. I encouraged her to join me for a session today, after all, it would likely just be me and her in the gym, and after a lot of arm twisting, she finally relented and agreed.

Marjorie was in the lobby before me, her eyes were glued to her phone; she was bidding on eBay for a necklace to match the bracelet she'd got for her daughter's birthday and the auction was nearly closed. She showed me the potential gift. It was an emerald on a golden chain and was advertised as being 'Art Deco Design'. I smiled at her, seeing the excitement and nervousness of the bidding in her eyes as the clock counted down, but my heart panged at the sight of the necklace. My mother had bought me something similar for my fourteenth birthday and I had treasured it. . . until I lost it on a school trip to Stratford-Upon-Avon. Mum was furious. She swore she'd never buy me jewellery again, and she never has.

"I'll just increase the offer to be on the safe side," Marjorie said, tapping her phone. "No one will bid over the top of one hundred, will they?"

"I doubt it. I think that will be a safe offer," I reassured her.

"I'll phone Terry to get him to keep an eye on the auction while we're doing our yoga." She looked pleased as she put the phone to her ear, and again I felt a pang of guilt, or was it jealousy? This woman next to me clearly loved her daughter, that much was obvious, but would someone say the same if they saw my mum with me? Do they say that? Elle's snide remarks in the gym had burnt a hole in my pride and been at the front of my mind since.

"No answer," she said. "Typical. I bet he's fallen asleep on the beach, that would be just like Terry to do."

As we walked up the stairs and along the corridor, we were blissfully ignorant of the scene which was about to confront us. I tapped my keycard on the reader and watched the LED turn from red to green. The door made a *clunk* sound (Penny later told me this was the sound of the electromagnet de-energising allowing the door to be opened) and we entered. At first, I didn't notice anything unusual, the gym seemed deserted. It was only as I flung out my yoga mat, unrolling it, did I see a pair of feet in the middle of the room. I yelped in shock and dashed closer, manoeuvring around a shoulder press machine to give assistance to what I hoped would be a fainted guest. As I got to within a few feet of the figure, I noticed dark red blood oozing from the man's head. A thin streak of crimson trickled across the victim's cheek; I could see without doubt that I was looking down at Russell's lifeless corpse. For perhaps a minute I stood frozen, unable to move or think. He was so still it seemed his body hushed the room. Marjorie drew by my side and took my hand in hers. Together we looked down at the vacant, unseeing eyes which stared lifelessly across the room. Russell was wearing a grey t-shirt specked with blood, and a pair of black running shorts.

"Is he. . .?" Marjorie's question hung in the air as I bent down and took Russell's wrist in my hand. It was still warm, but I could find no pulse. Without thinking, I pulled my phone from my pocket and called Penny, relieved we'd exchanged numbers the night before.

When she arrived, she swept into the room, her long kaftan skirt trailing behind her. She took us both by the hand and asked if we were okay before giving me a long and much needed hug. Only when reassured and satisfied that I was as fine as could be did she turn her attention to the situation in hand and the body of her friend.

"Listen, both of you, it's important that we preserve the crime scene. You haven't touched anything, have you? Good. Marjorie, go to your room and phone the police, then stay there. Tell them your room number and they will come to you. Where is Terry?"

"He went for a walk along the beach, I said I would meet him for breakfast at nine o`clock."

"I see," replied Penny, glancing at her wristwatch. "No doubt he'll come back to your room when you don't show for breakfast. Marley, dear, I'm going to need your help. . ."

Marjorie staggered from the gym to her peaceful and corpse-less room. I doubt she will ever agree to do yoga again.

"Now what do we do?" I asked when it was just me and Penny.

"We have to inspect the scene before the police get here."

"Have you done this type of thing before?"

"What type of thing?"

"Inspect a bloody crime scene."

"No. I've made a few though."

"Pardon?"

"*Interrogation* is a very loose term, dear. So is recruitment, in fact."

"How can recruitment be a loose term?" I asked, bewildered.

"Recruitment, seduction, and manipulation are three sides of the same triangle, dear. Now, be a doll and check to see if those windows are locked."

I went to the three windows. All three were snapped shut.

"Open them," said Penny once I'd conveyed the information. "But use your sleeve, we don't want the police finding your fingerprints where they shouldn't be."

I pressed the key button and turned the handles on each of the windows and pushed. They were horizontally hinged at the top and opened outwards at the bottom, but each window only opened to a maximum of six inches. Their purpose being just to let some air in, I assumed. "No way anyone could get in here, Penny," I called. "They only open a smidge."

Penny joined me at the windows. I suspected she was trying to keep me away from the body and the trauma associated with it because despite me explaining that the windows snapped shut, she proceeded to examine them herself. She pushed a window open, watching the two extending restrictors on either side of them straighten until the hooks locked in position. She then pushed the joint with her finger so that it folded like an elbow and watched as it fell shut under its own weight.

"Hmm, you're right, a cat couldn't get in through that gap, never mind a person." She then pressed her nose to the window and peered down. Below the gym was the swimming pool area to the right, windows looking out onto the sea, and Stork Island to the left as you looked out to sea.

"Surely you don't think the killer got in any way other than the door?" I asked.

"I agree that is most likely but don't forget, the door is on card access. Anyone entering will be registered on the system. If this murder was committed in the heat of the moment, our killer will be in custody before lunchtime. If, however, this killing was premeditated, then I would imagine the killer considered the access card reader and planned accordingly..."

"Did you find anything interesting on the - ?" I couldn't quite bring myself to say the word body, so I nodded my head in Russell's direction.

"Only that there is more than one impact wound on his head, in fact, there are three. Two of the impacts have made quite a dent, the third one is more of a glancing blow which has made a cut and a bump, but wouldn't have been lethal on its own. There is also a bar propped against the stanchion next to where he lies. Come, I'll show you. If you're up to it that is?"

"Yes. I think I am," I said, taking a deep breath.

The blood around Russell's head was beginning to pool and congeal. I tried not to look at it and instead I inspected the bar Penny had mentioned. It was a type of weightlifting bar about five feet long where you slide different weights onto each end, commonly used for bench-pressing. The bench I assumed it belonged to was a few feet away. The bar had no weights attached and rested upright in the rectangular nook of an I-beam stanchion which supported the ceiling. The stanchion was joined to another I-beam at the top, which ran the length of the ceiling.

"Do you think that's the murder weapon?" I asked.

"It's certainly heavy enough, and the dents in the skull would correspond with the curvature of the bar, I would say. Forensics should let us know for sure. If it is the weapon, then it has been wiped clean; I can't see any bloodstains on it."

"It's so horrible the way it's resting there, impotent and shiny, as if the murderer has wiped it clean in thanks for a job well done." I shivered, despite the warmth of the room.

Penny made a quick search of Russell's body. The only things in his possession were a water bottle lying next to his right leg, a metal key, and his access card, which was in the left-hand pocket of his shorts. Penny pocketed the card and the key. We then checked out the rest of the room. Penny rummaged in the bin while I scoured the floor for anything the killer might have dropped. The gym looked just as it had every other day that I'd used it. Mats were heaped along the wall, weights and dumbbells were stacked in racks or lying on the floor next to them. Spray bottles of disinfectant and blue roll were placed strategically around the equipment for users' convenience. It was unimaginable that a room intended to promote health and prolong life should be the setting for a brutal slaying.

"The police should be here soon," said Penny. "Let's inspect the door before they arrive and tie our hands."

With the door shut, the electromagnet was engaged. Penny instructed me to grab the handle with her, and we pulled as hard as we could, but our strength could not overcome the magnetic power and the door didn't budge. Penny then used her access card and pulled the door open. We then stepped into the corridor and tried to push the door open from the other side but again we had no joy. It was clear that anyone entering the gym would have to use an access card.

It was then that we saw a Spaniard with a clipped moustache and wispy bird's nest hair approaching. He walked past the hotel rooms, seemingly in no hurry. He was wearing a light blue shirt which bulged around his belly, and a pair of desert beige chinos. He was chewing gum with his mouth open and waited until he was within a few feet of us to exclaim, "I am Policia Inspector Moreno, please step away from the door!" From his back pocket he took a notepad and flicked it open. "Names, senoras?"

"Marley Williams and Penny Haylestone," I replied, seeing that Penny wasn't likely to. She was looking at the policeman as an Arsenal fan would look at a Spurs supporter, or a Millwall fan would look at, well, anyone.

Inspector Moreno chewed and spoke at the same time, something I found to be repugnant yet impressive. "What are you women doing here? You know there's a body in there, si?"

"Yes, we know. We are waiting for you," said Penny. "I didn't expect to wait this long."

"Oh. I see. Your New Scottish Yard police, they would have arrived and caught the murderer and sentenced him in the Old Bailey already, si? Well, this is my town, senora, I'm your Sherlock Holmes here. I work how I want to, understand?"

Moreno picked the gum from his mouth and flicked it into a nearby plant pot, revealing dark sweat patches under his arms as he did so. "Now, get out of my way," he continued. "I must inspect the body, unless there is anything else you think I should know?"

"You don't want to know what I think," said Penny.

Moreno smirked. "Go to your rooms, I will interview you fully when I am finished here. No one is allowed out of their rooms before they have been interrogated by me or one of my colleagues!" He gave us one last sneer and pressed an access card against the reader to open the gym's door. Penny took me by the wrist and led me down the hall past the hotel rooms. I thought I saw her wipe her eye, but whether the cause was a tear or something else I couldn't be sure.

"I can't believe they've sent that man to find Russell's killer. That odious man! You saw how slowly he walked down the hall, like there was no need to hurry, as though there wasn't a dead man behind that door, a *good* dead man!"

"Oh, Penny," I cried. "Don't worry. If that detective can't find Russell's killer, I have no doubt you will."

"Thank you, dear, I've no doubt I will, too, and I won't be waiting for Inspector Moron to fail before I attempt to succeed."

"Where are we going to now?" I asked.

"We're going to find Paulo. He can get us access to the hotel's computer before the police. We need to find out who went into the gym this morning."

Paulo was more than willing to help. He waved away Penny's warnings that by assisting us he risked the wrath of the police with careless determination. "I want to help find who killed Russell," he said. "He was a great man."

"Very well," said Penny. "Let's crack on then." We went behind the reception desk, conspicuous by our lack of uniform. As we crouched behind the monitor, we watched a police forensics team and other officers passing through the lobby to the lift and stairs. None bothered us, presumably because we were with Paulo who looked stern and fearsome in his grief. With a few clicks of the mouse, he brought up a log with all entry and exit times recorded on the gym's door. I took a photo of the screen on my phone.

Date	*Time*	*User*	*In/Out*
15/07	18:56	Room 107	In
15/07	19:42	Room 107	Out
15/07	22:10	Master	In
15/07	22:30	Master	Out
16/07	07:11	Master	In
16/07	08:01	Room 104	In
16/07	08:07	Room 101	In
16/07	08:12	Room 106	Out
16/07	08:35	Room 101	Out
16/07	08:39	Master	In

"Who is in room 107?" asked Penny.

"Dylan and Elle, they have a keycard each, it's not possible to know which of them used the gym last night," Paulo explained.

"Is there no CCTV in the area?" I asked, proud that I'd asked such a practical detective-like question.

"No, miss, only at the front entrance and car park."

"I'm room 101," said Penny. "So you must be 104, right, Marley? Marley?" My mind had drifted off to wondering how you go about auditioning for *Death in Paradise* and what I'd look like in a police hat. Do they have special afro accommodating ones?

"Sorry, Penny, say again?"

"Are you in room 104?"

"Yes, how did you figure that out?"

"Because Marjorie left the gym at 08:12, so presumably you arrived there together this morning and used your card to enter at 08:01?"

"Yes, that's right."

"Okay, so Russell obviously used the master-card. Is there only one Paulo or more than one?"

"The cards are programmable, we can take any card and turn it into a master, but we keep a record of how many are in circulation at any one time."

"How many were there between noon yesterday and eight o'clock this morning?" asked Penny.

"Just one."

"Which must have been Russell's. Why would he go to the gym last night? He went religiously between seven and eight every morning."

"Sometimes he liked to check that the place was tidy and to make sure none of the equipment was broken, that sort of thing."

"Well thank you, Paulo, you're a darling."

We then left the reception desk and I turned to Penny and asked the question which was tormenting my mind. "How did someone enter a locked room, commit a murder, and then vanish?"

20

Terry

Bloody hell! Marjorie told me there's been a murder! I didn't believe her at first, thought she must've been dizzy after the zoomba, or whatever it's called, and told her to lie down, but not half an hour later the Spanish fuzz are knocking at the door telling us to stay in our room, and would you believe it? There's been a murder! And you'll never guess who . . . Russell bloody Aspell. Well, I'm sorry it weren't me who got to batter him, that's all I can say.

I suppose the other way of looking at it is someone's robbed me of my rival, and what's a man without a nemesis? Terry Smith and Russell Aspell, Hector and Achilles, Tyson and Holyfield, Ken Barlow and Mike Baldwin. It's good for a man to have someone to butt heads with, reminds him he's still got the old primeval instinct kicking about inside him somewhere. We've become too civilised if you ask me, well I certainly have, anyway.

Of course, the Policia dos Stasi wanted to know where I'd been this morning between the hours of seven o`clock and dead o`clock. Well, I told them, I couldn't sleep (not that it were any of their business) so I went for a walk along the beach where I had a little snooze on a sun lounger. Then I came back here to the room to wait for Jane Fonda so we could go for breakfast. Of course, what, with what happened, it weren't all that long before Marjorie returned, quivering and shaking and playing up.

"Have some sympathy," she said, when she told me Russell had been beaten to death in the gym.

"Sympathy?" I said. "Sympathy? The man made me look a fool a few days ago and that were forty years after he'd already ruined my life!"

"Not sympathy for him, Terry, for me! How do you think it made me feel finding him there like that?"

Typical bloody woman, eh? Me, me, me. Speaking of which, it never rains, it pours, because before you know it, there was another knock on the door (I might as well have a red light hanging outside it), and lo and behold there's Inspector Penny Haylestone and Constable Marley Whatsername come to interview the prime suspect. (Speaking of Prime Suspect, Penny ain't half like that what's her face off the telly, Helen Mirren, that's it, especially when she raises an eyebrow.)

"Here we go," I said. "Come to interview the suspect numero uno, have you? Well come on in, I've got nothing to hide. Marjorie, put the fancy coffee machine on." I sat down with my back to the desk and folded my arms, it just seemed like the done thing.

"Terry, I don't have a lot of time, and I'll have less of the wise cracks, thank you. But yes, I suppose to many you would be assumed the most likely candidate for the murder. I, however, make no such claim and I make no assumptions. I ask questions and I get answers. I will ask *you* questions, and you will provide *me* with answers, understand?"

"And what authority do you have to do that then?" I asked. Honestly, the sheer bloody cheek of the woman!

"None. I don't deal in authority; I deal in leverage. If you don't give me full, frank answers I will dig into your past, present and future, and I will find something, some succulent secret, a glinting little nugget of information, anything, anything at all. Tax evasion, benefits fraud, you name it. If you're squeaky clean I'll invent a crime, plant evidence, bribe a false witness, I'll do whatever it takes to get the information I need to find out who killed my friend. Do you understand?"

"Blimey, love, steady on!"

"And don't call me love, or I'll get a pair of bolt croppers. Now, shall we begin?"

I nodded, anything to get rid of the psycho. I glanced around; was Marjorie smirking?

Marley handed Penny a cup of coffee, I hadn't even noticed she'd been making one. "Sugar?" she asked Marjorie, who shook her head and held out her hand. Where the hell was mine?

All of them were watching me, Penny had pulled up the comfy corner chair and was sitting right in front of me, elbows on knees. "Now," she said, "let's begin. What time did you wake up this morning?"

"I tossed and turned most of the night," I said. "But I eventually called it quits around six-ish."

"What did you do at six-ish?"

"I got up, thought I might catch the sunrise. Marjorie woke, too, as I got out of bed, you remember, Marge? I told you I was off for a walk down the beach and would see you back here."

"Did you see anyone on your walk?"

"Not that I can think of. Although I did nod off while I was there, so someone may have seen me."

"How did you get to the beach? Did you go through the lobby and around the hotel, or did you go past the swimming pool and down the cliff-steps?"

"Past the pool."

"So you won't have been picked up on the lobby security cameras, then. What time did you get back at?"

"I checked my watch when I woke up, it was seven-forty-five, so I would've got back here around eight o'clock."

Penny took a sip of coffee, but her eyes never left mine. "Russell Aspell was killed between 07:11 and 08:01. Did you murder him?" she asked after what seemed a long time.

"No, I did not!"

21

Sanjay

The good-looking policeman didn't seem surprised or even curious as to how we'd learned Russell had been murdered. He didn't answer any of our questions and instead led us to our room like a pair of naughty schoolboys being escorted to the headmaster's office.

"Stay here, do not move," he said. "Inspector Moreno will come to see you and you answer his questions, si?"

Luke, either through boredom or perceived injury of his self-importance, launched a fruitless, if elegant monologue about 'his rights' claiming that he was being detained against his will and that if he was 'imprisoned' here for one minute longer, he would see that the young policeman (name and rank? - Agente de Policia Garcia) Agente Garcia would be dragged to the Hague to answer for his crimes. Was that what he wanted?

Luke then demanded to speak with Inspector Moreno immediately and claimed that he possessed information in relation to the murder. Agente Garcia, unfazed by Luke's wagging finger and by the European Court of Human Rights, retorted simply, "Two minutes ago you didn't even know who was murdered, now you have information about it?"

"Yes. Yes, I do!"

Agente Garcia shrugged and moved towards the door. Luke, thinking his threats had taken effect asked, "So you will fetch the inspector?" to which Agente Garcia replied, "No, he will see you when he's ready." Agente Garcia then opened the door and exited before Luke could scream dramatically that he couldn't handle the truth.

"Coffee?" I asked, picking up a Nespresso capsule.

"Tea," Luke replied, so I flicked on the kettle.

"Don't worry, I'm sure the inspector will be along in no time."

"Yeah, you're probably right," Luke said. "Still, that was quite fun. Agente Garcia didn't bite as much as I expected, he barely blinked when I threatened to sue him."

"Probably didn't understand half of what you said," I reassured him as I handed over his tea.

"Bleurgh. The tea here truly is awful," Luke said. "Is it the tea or the milk? I can never tell. I'm beginning to understand why people bring their own. I bet Marjorie has a suitcase full of Tetley in her room."

"Don't be ridiculous," I said. "It would be Yorkshire Tea if anything."

Luke took a bottle of sparkling water from the mini-bar and poured himself a glass to wash the taste away. "Who do you think killed Russell?" he asked.

"I haven't had time to think about it," I replied. "It's such a shock. Of course, we didn't know him well, but regardless, you don't expect something like this to happen, do you?"

A thought occurred to me. "Luke, you *were* joking, weren't you?"

"About what?"

"When you said that you had information relative to the murder. You said that so we could be interviewed quicker and get out of this room, didn't you?"

"Hmm, kind of."

"What? What do you mean?" I asked, shocked by his response.

"Oh, nothing much. Only, as you know I've spent a few hours each day looking over Russell's accounts and things. There are one or two irregularities in them. Nothing I saw would quantify murder, but. . . well, you never know, do you? What some people might do."

"What sort of irregularities?"

"I won't confuse you with technical terms or details, but the long and short of it is The Orange Tree Hotel is going under, or at least it was until Russell received a cash injection to the tune of one hundred and fifty thousand euros."

"What? Where from?"

"That's the dodgy bit. I don't know. But I do know he paid no tax on the sum, it's an off-the-books transaction."

"If it's off-the-books, as you say, then how did you find it?"

"Pfft. Please. Remember who you're talking to, Sanj, I'm *very* good at what I do."

Our discussion was disturbed by a loud rap on the door. I opened it to find a moustachioed man wiping his brow with a handkerchief. "I am Inspector Alberto Luis Alejandro Juan Flores Moreno. You can call me sir or Inspector, whichever you prefer." He barged past me into the room, stopping in the centre to look around. He looked at me, then Luke, then at the bed, then at me again, then Luke, then the bed again. "Hmmph," he said, before pausing for a moment. He took a stick of gum from his pocket and began chewing loudly. "Which of you two has information for me about the murder of Russell Aspell?"

"That would be me," Luke said. He was standing by the window and his eyes were boring into the policeman; he made no attempt to hide the distain he felt.

"Go on. I don't have all day; I'm having lunch with the mayor in an hour."

"I'm sorry Russell being murdered has inconvenienced you," I said, unable to contain my surprise at the man's demeanour.

"It's not your fault," he replied, ignorantly waving away my sarcastic words. "These things happen, you can't plan Englishmen getting themselves murdered into your diary, but neither can you dismiss the possibility, either. So, what can you tell me?" he finished, turning to Luke.

"You know, I've completely forgotten," said Luke, forcing a smile at Moreno.

"Typical," replied the inspector. "You English, too much litres of your Carling in the Irish Rover last night no doubt. . ."

"Not likely."

"Too many shots of your sour whisky," continued the policeman, ignoring the interruption. "No doubt you covered the street in vomit or fell asleep on the beach. Too often times I've complained to the mayor about you tourists filling up our hospitals with your alcohol poisoning and sunburnt skin. Alright, if you remember, you tell me, okay? Now, on to other matters. Names, occupations, all the usual stuff you see on TV, come on, hurry," he said, opening a notepad. "I don't have all day."

Luke told the inspector his name, but when he mentioned he was a solicitor he didn't admit the fact that he was here in a professional capacity and Moreno showed little interest anyway. I, on the other hand, generated much more interest.

"Ah, a journalist. No doubt you have already telephoned your bosses with lies about the case. Your British tabloids will be besides themselves with joy. I should remove your mobile device from your possession, but I won't, no, I won't! Don't let it be said by the Daily Sun and Stars that Inspector Alberto Luis Alejandro Juan Flores Moreno is an unreasonable man."

I tried to interrupt to explain that I worked for a small local newspaper with a depressingly modest circulation, but the man was in full flow.

"I have solved many cases, many baffling cases and I shall solve this one also if the killer has not already fled the country, which, I admit, is likely." The man droned on, chewing gum all the while. He recounted his apparent successes and expounded on the various methods he had used to catch the most dangerous and hardened criminals. "Catching the man responsible for this killing will be easy, even if he has left the country."

"Really? How can you be so sure?" asked Luke.

"Because smart men don't kill people with metal bars, they use a gun that is untraceable, or a poison that makes death look natural. No, no, no, this shall be as you English say, the piece of the cake!"

"Why didn't you tell him about the accounts," I asked, five minutes later when the door had closed, and the sound of chewing ceased.

"Because I dislike the man and don't want to help him."

"Even if it could bring Russell's killer to justice?"

"We don't know for sure the money has anything to do with it, besides, if Inspector Moreno is as clever as he says he is, he'll find the monetary discrepancies himself."

22

Marley

After leaving Paulo at reception, I suggested to Penny that I go to my room to change out of my gym wear. Really, I wanted to check on Mum and also write down the morning events in this journal so that I didn't forget anything. You never know, maybe by writing down the clues and conversations, I might be able to help solve the case.

Mum was sitting in the chair in the corner of her room when I entered. When we arrived here a few days ago, the receptionist had kindly given me a key to Mum's room so that I could check on her without her having to get up to let me in.

"Where have you been, Marley?" she asked. "Your mother has been sitting here worrying and fretting, not knowing what's going on. What's this I hear about an accident?"

I told her about Russell, and that his death was deliberate. I said the police would be along soon to interview her as they wanted to speak to everyone in the hotel. She sat still and silent, then after a few minutes asked me to leave her alone so she could pray. I took the opportunity to change and write, then I left my room to find Penny and continue our investigation.

The sun had burnt off the morning haze, leaving a glorious blue sky. The temperature was sizzling towards thirty degrees when I passed a good-looking police officer in the lobby and made my way towards the pool. The policeman nodded at me as I passed, but didn't challenge me, presumably assuming that I'd already been questioned by Inspector Moreno and had been authorised to leave my room.

Penny was sitting at a table in the bar area with Dylan and Elle. She didn't sit like she had done every other day, languishing and relaxed. She was leant forward, her elbows on the table, alert and focused. Her blue eyes gleamed, two freezing flames giving a cold, resolute stare. She beckoned me to join them but didn't break from the conversation she was having.

"What did the police ask you? Was it Inspector Moreno who questioned you?"

Elle answered, "Yes, he said we were the first to be interviewed as our room was closest to the gym. He asked us if we had seen or heard anything suspicious this morning, anyone creeping past our door."

"What did you tell him?"

"We woke early and were the first down to breakfast, so if someone did sneak past our door, we wouldn't have heard them then, although, the whole thing is ridiculous."

"How so?"

"If someone were going to the gym to murder Russell they wouldn't be sneaking, would they? They would carry themselves normally and hope not to be seen, not draw attention to themselves by darting from plant pot to plant pot like in some bad movie."

"How long were you at breakfast for?"

"Half an hour or so, until seven-forty-five, then we went back to our room."

I looked at Dylan, who hadn't said a word. He sat upright, like he was at a job interview, a stony expression on his thin face. He's not exactly handsome, not in my opinion anyway, but there is something about him. He has swagger. He's tall and slim, like a long-distance runner, but he has cold, cruel eyes that are strangely magnetic. He must have felt my assessing gaze, because without moving his head his eyes darted to meet mine, and the power in those eyes was too much for me to bear and I broke the trance, feeling an unpleasant tingle at the base of my spine.

"When was the last time you saw Russell?"

"Why are you asking us that?" asked Dylan, angry. "Like we had something to do with his death."

"I don't think you had anything to do with his death," replied Penny. "I want to know if Russell seemed himself before he died, or if there was anything worrying him. Anything that might indicate he was expecting some sort of attack or knew he was in danger."

"You were his friend, weren't you? Surely, you'd know if anyone would?"

"A lot can happen in the blink of an eye, in a split second a bullet can be fired, or a button can be pressed; everything can change in an instant. If, for example, I saw Russell at nine o'clock and he was his happy, usual self, at five-past-nine someone whispers something in his ear that turns his world upside down, at ten-past-nine you stumble into him, then his demeanour will be much changed than from when I saw him. That's why it's important to know who the last person was to see him alive, barring the killer, of course."

"What would I gain from telling you anything?"

"You mean as opposed to telling the police?"

"No, that's not what I mean. Why would I tell you *or* the police anything? What's in it for me?"

"To help catch the killer of an innocent man," answered Penny.

"Again, I ask, how would that benefit me?"

Penny looked at Dylan, her thoughts hidden behind a smiling mask.

"Young man," she said, her gaze not faltering as she stared at the cruel eyes, "do you know what psychopathy is? You exhibit all the traits as far as I can tell, and I struggle to believe that you have made it this far through life without someone other than myself recognising the signs."

Elle shifted in her chair, her uneasiness pronounced by increased fidgeting. "If Dylan doesn't want to talk about Russell, I don't see why he should. It's a free country, isn't it? But I can tell you we saw Russell last night. Right here in fact. You were here too, if you remember? Just about everyone was. That was the last time we saw him."

"And you didn't see him this morning? Not on the way to breakfast, or on the way back?"

"No. I told you. Last night was the last time."

"Actually. . . I did see him this morning," said Dylan with a grin. "Before breakfast, around seven o'clock I went to the petrol station at the end of the road to get cigarettes. I saw him talking to someone in the stairwell on my way down. They were having a very heated discussion."

"Who?" demanded Penny.

"Now that's a question you'd love to know the answer to, isn't it?"

23

Sally

The police came to see us. The main one, Inspector Moreno I think his name is, was still ignorant of the fact that Russell was my uncle. He offered no condolences when I told him, and tutted instead. At least the other one that was with him, Agente Garcia said a few kind words. He is tall and *very* good-looking. To my shock I don't think Jasmine even noticed him, she was still suffering with the shock of the news and the after effects of last night's drinking. She sat on the edge of her bed looking pale despite the impressive tan she's managed to acquire in the space of just a few days. She hugged a bottle of water to her chest like it was a flotation aid and to be without would mean certain death.

"This uncle of yours, tell me about him," commanded Moreno. What could I say? He was Uncle Russell.

Was. That horrible, definite tense.

"He bought this hotel a long time ago," I said, "so I didn't know him as intimately as I might had he lived in England. He was my mother's brother. He was a nice man; I don't understand why someone would want to do this to him."

"He had no enemies that you know of?"

"No, but I wouldn't know, would I?" For a moment, Terry's face flashed through my mind. He had, of course, been humiliated by Russell when he was accidentally knocked into the swimming pool, and had threatened Russell at the same time, but he wouldn't kill him, would he? I was in two minds whether to relay this to the police when the decision was taken out of my hands.

"There is another guest here who threatened Russell," said Jasmine in a weak voice.

"Who? What is the name of this other guest?"

"Terry. I don't know his surname."

"Smith. Terry Smith," I said. "He and Uncle Russell were old schoolmates but there was bad blood between them, although I don't know what the cause of it was. I can't see Terry resorting to murder because of a silly little feud, can you?"

"Senorita, I have seen many things over my time in the Cuerpo Nacional de Policia, things that would shock, terrify even, little girls like yourself. Things that would give even Agente Garcia here the sleepless nightmares. But I tell you this, the most shocking thing of all is that people will commit the most terrible crimes for the smallest reasons, because what seems small and insignificant to you does not necessarily seem so to a murderer. A minor car collision, a stolen watch, even a book lent and not returned, si, all of these I have investigated and found in each case to be the motive for a murder. (I can sympathise with the last one.) Si, there is a terrible, how do you say, darkness, in the soul of man."

Inspector Moreno gave this impassioned speech with his chest puffed out and his eyes on the ceiling as though he were conversing with a higher power, who alone could appreciate his wisdom and experience. It was the only time during his stay in our room that he ceased to chew his gum, such was the importance of his soliloquy.

"Who is this Terry Smith here with?" asked Agente Garcia, notepad at the ready.

"His wife Marjorie. Their room is a few doors down, I don't know the number," I said.

"I will find, have no fear."

Inspector Moreno then asked us questions which I suppose would be considered 'routine'. He asked our whereabouts 'at the time of the murder' yet couldn't tell us with any certainty when the murder occurred. He asked us if we had ever used the gym, when we last saw Russell, and could anyone corroborate our alibis despite us not actually giving any.

"Look," said Jasmine, "we were out all night and then asleep until Penny woke us this morning to tell us Russell had been murdered."

"Penny? Penny Haylestone?"

"Yes. Penny Haylestone."

"When? When was this? I told her to go straight to her room! She is interfering in my investigation and disobeying my orders!"

Moreno's face glowed red, like a Halloween pumpkin when you light a candle inside it. He harumphed and grumped, spitting Spanish at Agente Garcia before turning angrily to us.

"You are not permitted to speak to anyone about this investigation except for me, do you understand?"

We both nodded, eager to be rid of the man. He confiscated our passports and informed us they would be kept in the safe in reception along with all the other guests' until he consented to release them. He then turned on his heels and fled the room without giving us so much as an adios. Agente Garcia nodded to us and followed his superior in silence.

"What a horrible little man," said Jasmine, once the door was closed.

"I know," I agreed. "And that chewing. . . gross, he sounded like a steam train churning through a swamp. At least he's gone now."

"Hopefully we won't be seeing too much of him."

"Fingers crossed. Besides, it shouldn't be too hard to catch the killer."

"What makes you say that?" asked Jasmine.

"The police can check our room cards on the hotel system, so they'll know who was in their rooms and who was in the gym at the time of the murder, if they can figure out when that was of course. The pathologist should be able to narrow it down, though."

"I don't understand."

"Well, say for example Russell was killed at seven o'clock, they'll know it couldn't have been us because we didn't use our cards to leave the room all morning. Are you feeling okay? You look very green."

Jasmine didn't answer but ran into the bathroom to throw up again. Poor girl, she won't be doing any more shots for a few days I don't think.

24

Terry

As if being interrogated by Penny bloody Haylestone wasn't enough, the Spanish plod then came knocking not five minutes after she'd left. I might as well get a revolving door put in. Two of them there were, a big one and a little one. I made some remark about being questioned twice and the smaller one, PC Morenzo or whatever he's called started shouting about Penny bloody Haylestone, too. Looks like she's proper rubbed him up the wrong way. Well, I can understand it, can't I? Coming in here, throwing her weight around, who does she think she is? Miss Marple?

Anyway, this policeman fellow weren't messing about, there were no niceties with him! Straight out with it he was: "Did you kill Russell Aspell?"

"Did I kill Russell Aspell?" I said. "No way, Jose!"

"My name is not Jose," he said. "It is Alberto Luis Alejandro Juan Flores Moreno, Inspector of the Cuerpo Nacional de Policia, you can call me sir or Inspector, whichever you prefer."

"Alright! Keep your moustache on! I'll stick with inspector, thank you very much, sir reminds me too much of school."

"As you wish. Tell me, Mr Smith, what were your whereabouts this morning?"

I told Inspector Lorenzo the same story I told Penny; couldn't sleep, beach, snooze blah, blah, blah. Marjorie, always needing to do something with her hands, made us a cup of tea, even though we men declined her offer. And she says *I* never listen to *her*!

"Mr Smith, it has come to my attention that you and the deceased had unfriendly relations, is this so?"

"Yeah, he was an arsehole, what of it?"

"You had motive to murder Mr Aspell, no?"

"No, I wouldn't say that. If I wanted to kill Russell, I would've done it back then, not wait forty bloody years."

"I see. What was the cause of this dislike?"

"If you must know he broke my leg in a football match. Broke it bad."

"That's it? A broken leg?"

"It wasn't just the physical pain I suffered that made me hate his guts, he didn't just break my leg; he ruined my future! It were a warm-up game for the school's cup final, first eleven versus the reserve team. I played centre forward for the firsts. The day after that match I was meant to sign a contract with Leeds United! It were all arranged, they'd sent a scout to watch me a few times, he were there that day too, only instead of seeing me being carried off on my teammates' shoulders, he watched me being carried off on a stretcher."

"Perhaps it was an accident?"

"Accident my eye! Russell claimed it were a fifty-fifty challenge, I'd like to know how when he came through the back of me with both sets of studs at knee height! He didn't even get sent off! I could've made it to the top. European Cup, England, Wembley, you name it. And don't think I'm exaggerating either because I'm not! I could've been like George Best only better looking. Instead, here I am. Always between jobs, twenty different pensions worth ten pence each, no savings and no Miss Worlds (no offence Marge). I'm even a little tiny bit overweight because I can't exercise properly because of the lasting damage done by that man. It wasn't just a football injury, Inspector, I had more reason to kill Russell Aspell than anyone alive, but I didn't do it."

I took a sip of tea, but it tasted funny, whether it were the foreign milk or a bitter taste in my mouth from the memories just recounted I don't know. One thing's for sure though, it weren't the teabag at fault; Yorkshire never lets you down, you can even get ones nowadays specially made for hard water. Maybe I ought to get some and put them in the time capsule. I'll set a reminder on my phone.

Anyway, Inspector Flamenco wrote all this down without saying a word, and just chewed on a piece of gum. The tall fella whispered something to Marjorie, and she handed him our passports which were in the desk drawer.

"Oi, oi, oi," I said, "what do you think you're doing with them?"

"We are taking them so that you cannot flee the country," answered Inspector Maracas. "You will receive them if and when I am satisfied that you did not kill Russell Aspell."

"Flee the country? We paid good money to come here, I'm not leaving before I've had my two weeks of sun. Besides, I told you I didn't kill him, does the word of Terence Smith count for nought these days?"

"In Spain, most definitely it does not. Now, you, senora," he said, turning to Marjorie, "what were your movements this morning while your husband was sleeping on the beach like a vagrant?"

"Like a wha -"

"Silence! I am talking to your wife, not you."

"Well, Inspector sir, I went with Marley you see."

"Marley," he consulted his notepad, "Williams?"

"That's right, Inspector sir, Marley Williams. A lovely girl she is, so happy and friendly. Yesterday I had a drink with her out in the bar and she invited me to do yoga with her this morning. Well, I've always fancied trying it but it's not the type of thing I'd do on my own you see, wouldn't know where to start. Exercise videos in front of the telly is my comfort zone, but I thought, well I'm on my holidays aren't I, live a little Marjorie I said, so I agreed."

"Si, and what time did you meet Marley Williams?"

"A quarter-to-eight or thereabouts. Mr Aspell had the gym to himself between seven and eight you see."

"How did you come to know this?" he asked, chomping away on his gum.

"They told us at reception when we checked in, the girl working, Maria I think her name was, a lovely girl, she said Mr Aspell was very strict with his routine and the gym opened to guests at eight o'clock sharp." Marge then glanced at their empty cups. "Would you like another cup of tea? Agente Garcia, would you like one? No? Well, if you change your mind just you let me know."

"Then what did you do?" asked Inspector Mourinho, as he replaced the gum in his mouth for a fresh piece.

"We went in, and we found him. Such a shock! Marley, she was wonderful, handled everything perfectly. Me? Forget about it, I was a shaking wreck, wasn't I, Terry?"

"She was."

"Don't know what I would've done if I'd been on my own. Marley phoned Penny, 'Penny will know what to do,' she says. And she did, bless her. Was there in a flash, issuing orders, but not bossy like, more, I don't know... controlled, that's the word. She told me to come here and phone you, and that's what I did, isn't that right, Terry?"

"That's right."

"And there you have it, Inspector sir."

"The body, did you touch it?"

"Heavens no! Marley tried to find a pulse, but I wouldn't touch it for all the tea in China. Not good with blood and gore and all that type of thing, am I, Terry?"

"Can't even watch *Casualty* or *Holby City*," I confirmed.

"Then Penny came and asked us if we'd touched anything, and I said no."

"Thank you, Mrs Smith, I think I need to go and find Marley Williams and Penny Haylestone before they do further damage to my investigation!"

"Another cup of tea, Terry?" asked Marjorie, as the door closed, leaving just the two of us.

25

Sanjay

I got into journalism to make a difference, or so I tell myself. When you do something for ten years, your original incentives get distorted by time and paying the mortgage quickly becomes your main motivation. Of course, you expect to climb the ladder, to move diagonally from publication to publication always in a more prestigious and higher paying role than the last one. In my naivety I always imagined being the editor of *The Times* or *The Spectator* by the time I reached thirty, not still doing features for the Streatham Gazette for a horrible boss who demands the impossible. So maybe (as horrible and terrible as this business is) this killing could be the ignition my career needs. I mean, I am on the spot to report on it, right in the hot zone, I am intimately involved with the case and, I can write it from the inside. Perhaps I could turn this tragedy into a true crime book. Something to think about…

Anyway, after being cooped up in the hotel room for most of the morning, it was with great relish that we descended to the pool to enjoy the sun, sangria and gossip. I was disappointed to find the pool area practically empty. I figured that most of the guests had probably been confined to their rooms before they had had a chance to eat breakfast and were out making up for it.

We settled on a pair of sun loungers, and I was halfway through a podcast about a serial killer in Massachusetts when I heard Agathe giving orders.

"Over there, wheel me over there to the shade, no, not that way, there! Lord, where is Marley when I need her?"

She was being pushed by the tall, handsome police officer who received the instructions without answering back, his face showing no sign of annoyance or impatience.

"Yes here, that'll do." The final command. Agente Garcia gave Agathe a slight bow and strode away, his long legs taking only a few strides before he disappeared out of sight past the lifts and into the lobby.

I waited for Agathe to take her knitting equipment and Bible from her bag before I got up and walked past her on the way to the bar. Luke stayed by the pool, the evenness of his tan being his number one priority.

"Oh, hi, Agathe, I see the police must be finished with you?"

No bite.

"I'm just going to get a drink, would you like one?" A suspicious look as her hand gripped the crucifix.

"I don't drink."

An opening.

"Well, you must drink something, I'll get you a pineapple juice." I dashed to the bar before she could decline my generous offer. After all, she had just said Marley was nowhere to be seen and being in her advanced years, I felt it my Christian duty (or in my case Hindu) to ensure she was looked after, especially in this heat.

"There we are," I said, setting down her juice and a large gin glass brimming with sangria before taking a seat next to her. "I hope those policemen didn't upset you too much. They can be nasty brutes you know."

"I think it was I who upset them," she said, stirring her ice with a straw.

"Really? Well, I'm sure you were fully justified. Did I mention I'm a journalist?"

"No."

"Indeed. Last year I ran an article about a church group who were having trouble with vandals, you know the sort, young louts breaking windows in the church hall and spraying graffiti, that type of thing. Well, the head of the church committee complained to the police, but the cries fell on deaf ears, 'nothing we can do about it' they said. 'Underfunded, overstretched, no CCTV,' the usual claptrap. Well, Agathe, I tell you, if there's one thing that really gets my goat it's good people being let down, and the fact that it was a church, that cornerstone of all that is good and righteous, well, that was the last straw for me. I wrote an article shaming the police, calling them out on their excuses, and do you know what? They installed the CCTV cameras the day after the article was printed, paid for by the constabulary no less. Still, I suppose no two police forces are the same. I'm sure Inspector Moreno will catch Russell's killer in no time..."

"I wouldn't count on it! I've watched enough *Quincy* and *Silent Witness* to know the clues needed to solve the crime are on the body. That's why they get them pathologists to inspect them in the mortuary. What time was Russell killed, I asked him. Don't know he says. Pfft. How did the killer get in the gym, I asked? We're looking into it he says. Pfft. Looking into it? I know what that means, it means he hasn't the foggiest."

"I'm sorry Agathe, I don't understand, how do you mean 'get in', surely the killer used the door?"

"They may well have done, young man, but those doors are card activated both in and out. I remember my Reggie's card stopped working one day a few years ago when he was having his morning workout. He had to holler at me through that little gap in the window up there, then I got Russell to let him out." Agathe pointed across the pool to the first floor of the building. There were three windows, all slightly open.

"I'm afraid I still don't follow," I said. "So, the door is opened and closed using a room keycard, how does that help catch the killer?"

"Lord, give me strength. Because, whoever's card is used it's logged on the hotel computer, and according to Marley no one entered while Russell was in the gym. In the books they call it a locked-room mystery," she added, knowingly.

I let Agathe's words take hold. If she was correct about the gym door, then maybe Russell's death wasn't murder after all, maybe it was an accident. But if it was murder, who committed the crime and why? And more intriguingly, how? The whole thing was impossible.

26

Marley

The hotel's wings are symmetrical in shape and size, but where the West Wing has a gym, the East Wing holds Russell's office and living quarters. Penny, waving the metal key she retrieved from Russell's body, said we had better inspect the office before the police did, otherwise they may remove evidence which we would need to solve the murder.

My hand trembled as she said 'we'. This woman of unfathomable experience was relying on me to help her solve the murder of her friend, placing her trust in my abilities. Why? Why was she putting her faith in me?

We walked along the East Wing corridor without seeing anyone except one of the housekeepers who was pushing a laundry trolley. The poor woman had tears in her eyes, the news of her employer's demise obviously having reached all the corners of the hotel. Seeing her so upset made me want to give her a hug, but also made me wonder about the man whose murder we were investigating. What was he like? I only knew him through a few casual drinks we shared, and from what my mum had told me of him, but now I was with someone who had known him for two-thirds of his life and surely if I were to assist in the capture of his killer I ought to know more about the victim?

"Penny," I said, as she unlocked the door to Russell's office. "What was he like? Why would someone want him dead?"

"That, my dear, is a very good and timely question. Take a seat." She pointed me to a winged armchair as she strode to a mahogany bureau on top of which sat a whisky decanter and two crystal cut tumblers. As she poured two generous measures, I looked around the room. It was large but cool, the faint hum of the air-conditioning unit keeping all thirty of the degrees outside at bay. The office area took up most of the space. Behind a thin curtain I could make out a small room containing a bed and a wardrobe. By the windows facing out onto Stork Island is a large wooden desk. The walls are filled with bright abstract paintings, vibrant blues clashing with dancing yellows, each picture a tropical maelstrom of colour and disorder, as though Picasso was in a hurry. In the far corner of the room there sat a safe with a keypad on it like you see in the movies. The centre of the room has a long, low, walnut coffee table and is flanked by two chairs. I sat in one and Penny joined me in the other, handing me a glass.

"What if the police come?" I asked. I'd hoped she would answer my question about what Russell was like whilst we searched the room, rather than taking a break with a glass of whisky each.

"Don't worry about that dear, I've got Paulo keeping an eye on them, he'll ring me if there's any danger. Now, you were asking about Russell?"

"Yes, I just want to know what he was like as a person, to see if there are clues as to why someone might want to kill him."

"He was a wonderful man, to me, anyway. Terry would disagree. He was friends with my husband, they went to university together. Of course, I wasn't on the scene then, I met Anthony, that's my husband, through work. I recruited him. I recruited them both as a matter of fact. You see, in those days the best universities were the breeding grounds for spies, they were littered with lecturers and professors who were friendly to the service, usually through wartime involvement themselves. They would give us the heads-up on students who they thought were either exceptional or who would fit into the service. It's not like in James Bond, you know, there are no flash cars or beautiful women, me being the exception, of course. The work is often dull, there's a lot of paperwork and bureaucracy, and the pay is terrible."

"So why do people do it?"

"Because recruits don't know any of this before they join, and once you're in it's hard to get out."

"Because they make it hard? Because you know too many secrets?"

"No, not like that, it's a kind of magnetism, it's difficult to leave because the job is never finished, and people don't like committing time and effort to something and not see the end result, so they keep stumbling on. When one terrorist is caught, they are quickly replaced by another, so the job never has an end."

"But Russell left?"

"Yes. He only served a couple of years. In a way he was one of my failures because as a recruiter I was judged on how long my apprentices stayed in the service for."

"And your husband?"

"He never left. We actually saw very little of each other in work, us being in different departments. When I was sent to the university, I was only supposed to assess Anthony, but once I was satisfied that he was suitable he said he had a friend I should look into: Russell. I could see straight away he was the right sort, too. Clever, handsome, but lacking charisma, you don't want to stand out you see, dear. He was just the right cut, so I took him on as well, plus, he spoke fluent Spanish which is just what I was looking for."

"Why?" I asked, recovering from a sip of whisky.

"You're too young to remember, dear, but in the 1980s the IRA was importing weapons and explosives from North Africa. We needed a man here keeping an eye on shipments going through the strait of Gibraltar. A Spanish speaker came in handy."

"And Russell stayed here after he left the service?"

"Yes, he bought this place."

"How did he afford it?" I asked, mystified.

Penny didn't answer the question, instead she raised her eyebrows and stood up. "Come on," she said, "we had better search this office before Inspector Moron does."

"What are we looking for?" I asked, opening a desk drawer.

"Anything out of the ordinary. Any ledgers, any letters, some death threats would be useful."

"But if Russell was a kind and honest man like you and Mum say he was, then why would someone want him dead?"

"He wasn't honest, dear; he was a spy. It's possible he had an enemy from his days working in the service. Or he may have owed someone something and couldn't keep up his end of the bargain. Russell wasn't what an accountant would call 'fiscally responsible'. He had a certain nobility to his character, and I was indebted to him, but don't be under any illusions: the best men can be the most dangerous ones, and dangerous men attract enemies."

The first two drawers I inspected contained a few pens, and some blank stationery. From the desk's third drawer I took out an unsealed envelope and shook out two pieces of paper. I scanned the text and felt excitement rise within me. "Here! I think I've found something," I squealed, unable to keep the excitement from my voice.

"What is it?"

"It looks like a warning!"

I held out the first sheet of paper and Penny abandoned her search of the bureau to take it from me.

THE WAGES OF SIN IS DEATH

The paper was thin and stained yellow with time. It was soft and creased. The second sheet, however, was white and crisp, as if it had been produced just yesterday.

REMEMBER THIS: WHOEVER SOWS SPARINGLY WILL ALSO REAP SPARINGLY, AND WHOEVER SOWS GENEROUSLY WILL ALSO REAP GENEROUSLY

"They're quotes from the Bible," I said, looking at the Google hits on my phone. "The first text is from the Book of Romans, Chapter 6, Verse 23, the second is the Book of Corinthians, Chapter 9, Verse 6."

"Is there anything else in the desk?" Penny asked.

"Not that I can see." Although my mind was still thinking over the notes and not wholly focused on the drawers. "It's a threat, isn't it? In other words, you reap what you sow."

I opened the camera on my phone and clicked and snapped at everything and anything while Penny carried out a quick search of the bedroom area. She then walked to the safe, and to my surprise began punching in numbers with confident rapidity.

"Penny!" I said. "You know the code?"

"Yes, dear, three-zero-zero-four, although I'm surprised the thing is locked. Usually, Russell would just leave the door open. For a spy he wasn't very security conscious." The safe made a dull clunking sound and the door swung ajar. I peeked over Penny's shoulder to see some loose sheets of paper, a passport, and a wad of cash. Penny examined the papers though she exhibited no sign that there was anything interesting about them.

"How much cash is that?" I asked.

"Twenty thousand euros. It says so on the sheath of paper wrapped around it."

As she said this, her phone beeped. "It's from Paulo," she said, looking down at the screen. "He says Inspector Moreno is on his way here. Come, quick!" Instead of going down the corridor where we ran the risk of colliding with the police, we crossed the hall and Penny used the master-card which gave us access into a cleaning cupboard. After only a few seconds the voice of Inspector Moreno could be heard grinding towards us. His words were indistinct until he was right outside the door. When he spoke, Penny whispered the translation into my ear.

"Es esta habitacion?" "*It is this room?*"

"Si," came the reply. "*Yes.*"

"Gracias, puedos volver al vestibulo" "*Thank you, you can return to the lobby.*"

"Y si ves a Penny Haylestone y Marley Williams me avisas inmediatamente!" "*And if you see Penny Haylestone and Marley Williams, you let me know immediately!*"

"He must've asked Paulo to show him the way," Penny whispered. We heard the beep of the card reader and the click of the door closing but Penny put a hand on my shoulder and gave a gentle squeeze.

"Okay, let's go," she said, still in a low voice when she was satisfied the coast was clear. We scurried down the hall and made for the pool. Out of the corner of my eye I saw Penny give Paulo a wink as we passed him standing behind the reception desk, a lingering policeman preventing a vocal thanks.

Mum saw me as soon as my feet touched the tiles. She was sitting at a table with Sanjay next to her, three empty glasses in front of her. "Marley, where have you been?" she demanded. "Your mother's been left here all on her own with some crazed murderer running loose."

"Not quite on your own, Mum, it looks like Sanjay has been keeping an eye on you," I said, acknowledging him with a smile.

"How do you know he isn't the murderer? Only the Lord knows who that is."

"Sorry, Sanjay," I said. "She doesn't mean any offence."

"Marley, what have I told you about thinking for me and speaking on my behalf? Your mother has been thinking and speaking long before you were born, you hear?"

"Yes, Mum."

The wind taken out of my sails, I offered Sanjay a drink by way of thanks and apology, but he politely declined and instead went back to Luke who was on a sun lounger typing on his laptop. I got myself and Penny two large gins and Mum a pineapple juice.

When I returned to the table, Mum and Penny were talking about Dad and Anthony.

"My husband was the same," said Penny. "He'd notice things about people, the good and the bad. He could see through them and know what they were feeling, but he never noticed anything else around him. I remember buying a plant for the living room, it was nearly as tall as him. Three months it sat there next to the television before one day he said, out of the blue, 'where the hell did that thing come from?'"

"That's men, isn't it. Although my Marley's the same, very like my Reggie in that way, she is -"

"I'm sitting right here, Mum," I pointed out, only to be ignored.

"Her head's in the clouds, always has been. I remember when she was at school- "

I groaned and rolled my eyes. Mum has a habit of talking about me like I'm invisible when I've annoyed her. I know she wasn't angry at me because I wasn't there to look after her like she said, it was because I wasn't there to find out the gossip for her. She'll have seen couples with heads touching, talking in hushed tones and whispers and she'll have needed my legs to eavesdrop on her behalf.

I decided that instead of sitting there listening to her elaborate on my many shortcomings, I would go and apologise to Sanjay on *her* behalf.

"Hi, Sanjay, hey, Luke." I sat on the edge of the sun lounger next to them. "I just wanted to say sorry about Mum. I'm sure she doesn't really think you're a murderer."

"There's no need to apologise, really. I know better than anyone that a parent is not a reflection on their offspring."

Luke laughed. "Too true," he said. "Sanjay's parents aren't exactly comfortable with his sexuality and definitely not with mine. They come from a time and place where a child's duty first and foremost is to bring honour to the family. Funnily enough, that doesn't include coming out as gay at your parents' thirtieth wedding anniversary party."

"Not one of my most inspired ideas," Sanjay admitted. "But I was eighteen at the time, I was full of rage at the world and my parents and I wanted to hurt them."

"They still haven't accepted that their beautiful boy is gay," Luke continued. "They refuse to meet me as that would be all too real for them. They've even threatened to cut Sanj out of their will - as if he's going to leave the best-looking bugger in blighty and turn straight for a few quid!" Luke laughed again, but Sanjay gave a feeble smile and cast his gaze downwards. I felt sorry for him, torn between the people he loved. I was trying to think of something comforting to say when an echo sounded in my brain. What had Luke just said? A will! Of course! Russell's killer had to benefit from his death in some way, maybe they stood to gain inheritance.

"What are you looking so confused about?" asked Luke, his hands resting on his laptop.

"Nothing," I said, "I was just wondering who inherits Russell's estate now that he's dead."

"Sally does," Luke said, matter-of-factly.

"I'm sorry?" I asked, surprised, and confused by the immediate answer.

"Sally is sole beneficiary. I checked an hour ago."

"How? How would you know?"

"Didn't I mention? I'm Russell's solicitor."

27

Sally

I needed fresh air and to get away from Jasmine. The room smelt stale and sweaty, a horrid, sweet scent permeated throughout: sickly tears and vomit. The room was becoming more and more oppressive with each passing minute, not only the overbearing odours of alcohol and regurgitation, but also the weight of grief and emotion that filled the place. In the passing hours the four walls had become synonymous with the death of Uncle Russell. This was where I had learned of the fact, where I had chewed on the news and digested it and tried to make sense of it all.

I couldn't bear the thought of seeing the other guests who would undoubtedly offer condolences and hollow words, nor could I face the sun lest the heat stoked my hangover back into life, so I decided to go to the indoor bar knowing it would be quiet, and tuck myself into some corner, preferably by an open window.

I needed to escape Jasmine's zombie-like presence, her dead-eyed stares, and pathetic sniffles.

Paulo served me an orange juice but wasted no words on me. Instead, he gave my shoulder a gentle pat and left me to my own dark thoughts. Who could have killed Russell? And why? Was it someone here at the hotel, someone I'd shared a drink and a joke with?

I sat feeling the limp breeze touch my cheek, listening to the distant rumble of traffic through the open window. I don't know how long I sat there with my knees pulled up to my chin, it could have been minutes or hours, but when Penny and Marley came and stirred me from my reverie, the ice in my orange juice had completely melted and the glass was warm to touch.

"How are you coping, dear?" I looked up at Penny's face but produced no words. "I know you probably want to be left alone but I have a few more questions for you I'm afraid."

"I'm fine, just a bit tired, that's all." I wondered if my face portrayed the bravery I tried to muster. Penny smiled; there's no fooling her.

"Would you like a drink, dear?" She raised her own glass as if to entice me.

"I don't think I could stomach it, Penny, we had quite enough last night."

"Hair of the dog. Marley, see if you can find Paulo, he should be around somewhere, and get him to bring a bottle of champagne and three glasses, we need to toast Russell's life. It's only fitting." Marley did as she was instructed, returning a few moments later. Penny poured the golden liquid into the flutes, and we raised them in unison. "To Russell!" she toasted.

Marley and I echoed her cry before taking a sip. The cold bubbly gave me a rush instead of inducing the hammer blow headache that I anticipated.

"I've never had proper champagne before," said Marley. "It must be expensive; it tastes so clean and crisp."

"One hundred euros a bottle, dear, but don't worry, I'll have Paulo add it to Russell's tab. Don't worry, Sally, I'm sure you only inherit the money and not the debts." For a second, I sat stock-still, my brain not possessing the energy to decipher the meaning of Penny's words *and* send signals to the rest of my body, commanding it to move. "What do you mean?" I managed to ask.

"Don't you know? You are in line to inherit Russell's estate, whatever that consists of." The words were spoken delicately and were tinged with curiosity.

"I had no idea," I spluttered. Penny's hard eyes ravaged me, seeking a lie or deception. I felt as though I sat before a Roman emperor, waiting to see which way the thumb would point.

"I believe you, dear," she said after an eternity. "I had to be sure, inheritance can complicate matters."

"I've never even thought about money, or any of it. Did you really think I would kill my uncle for a few measly quid?"

"I think it unlikely but not impossible. Many people would, you know."

"Wait a minute, how do you know I stand to inherit? There's no way you could know that already. Did you lie about it to see how I'd react? To see if I'd give myself away as a murderer?"

"No, dear, although that would've been a good trick. No, I'm afraid we do know because Russell's solicitor told us. I've seen the proof myself, thanks to Marley here." I gawked at the girl who looked abashed. She smiled at me and shrugged. "Soz."

"Do you know who your uncle's solicitor is?" asked Penny.

"Of course I don't, why would I?" I asked, incredulous.

"That's what I thought. It's a large firm, London based, they deal with all manner of affairs - conveyancing, probate, even commercial law. One of their solicitors is here at the hotel, he showed us the will."

"Surely that's breaking some sort of code, ethical or otherwise."

Penny shrugged. "Probably, but you won't hear me complain. He also told us something else, something quite unusual."

"What?" I asked, wondering what could be thought of as 'unusual' on the day my uncle had been murdered in a locked room and I found out I would inherit his hotel.

Penny took a gulp of champagne and topped up our glasses before continuing. "Russell instructed this solicitor to have some paperwork ready for next week. He wanted the forms ready to be signed on the day the solicitor leaves this hotel and flies back to London..."

"Okay... what forms?" I felt a knot in my stomach and my hands shake, though I don't know why.

"A blank will."

"Why?"

"I don't know, dear, presumably so he could make a new one... and change the beneficiary."

28

Terry

This was supposed to be a relaxing holiday, and now Russell bloody Aspell is ruining it by being dead. If he hadn't gotten himself killed, I wouldn't have the police banging on my door, and Penny Haylestone barging in all guns blazing with her little sidekick in tow!

I needed to get away, I needed to think.

I weren't too happy with Marjorie, neither. She enjoyed me being questioned like I'm some sort of criminal, I saw her smiling. "I'm just a nervous smiler," she said when I challenged her. A nervous smiler? What's one of them when they're at home, I said.

After a few cross words, I left her in the room feeling sorry for herself, still grumbling about finding a dead body. I don't know what she's so upset about, she didn't even know him. I remember finding my old mam lying at the bottom of the stairs, now that's something to be upset about, the woman who raised you, lying lifeless, knowing she died on her own, knowing that you couldn't help her, that you couldn't save her. But did I get upset about it? No, I got on with it. It never did me any harm. Don't bottle it up Marjorie says, bottle what up? Everyone dies, don't they, it's just something you have to face in life. Still, if I was to be upset, I'd have every right to be, wouldn't I? The woman who raised you…

Time for a drink! That's what I thought. Who wants to be depressed on their holidays, eh? I left Marjorie to do as she pleased. She said something about phoning Sarah, no point in sending a postcard I suppose. I told her I'd be back in a couple of hours.

I walked into town, I knew that if I were to have a drink in the hotel terrace bar, Marjorie would be plonked next to me in half an hour and I wanted to get away.

It were proper hot by the time I got to the Irish Rover, the sweat was dripping off me, but I was determined to sit outside, I'd already missed enough sun for one day being locked up in the hotel room waiting to be investigated, I weren't going to miss anymore!

There weren't too many people there, most were probably at the beach or by their hotel pools. I sat at a table next to a family who were just having their plates taken away by a ginger-haired waitress. Two of the little kiddies were pestering their mum to take them back to the beach, pulling at her arms. I smiled and looked at my pint, rather you than me, love. The little'uns soon got their way and away they all went, that's when I saw Dylan sitting behind where the family had been. "Ey'up," I said, getting up to join him. "Did the police interview you as well?" I asked.

"Yeah," he said. "I suppose you were the first person they came to see."

"How do you mean?" I asked.

"Well, you had the strongest motive, didn't you? He pushed you in the pool and we all saw it." He lit a cigarette, and the smoke wafting up my nose gave me a pang. I had to resist the temptation to ask for one. Two years with no ciggies is something to be proud of, but by heck, you don't half miss them sometimes.

"Listen. If I killed Russell Aspell, I'd say it. Terence Smith is an honest man if nothing else. Sure, I didn't like him, who did? But I didn't kill him."

"Penny Haylestone liked him."

"Aye, don't I know it. She were round interrogating me before the police! Did she give you the fourth degree too?" I asked, taking a swallow of my beer.

"She tried to get some information out of me. She left disappointed."

"So you know nothing too, then."

"That's not what I said, is it? Penny asked me when I last saw Russell, I told her the truth. But what I didn't tell her was that I know who killed Russell Aspell."

"Why the hell not? Those idiot policemen will finger me for this, you could clear my name."

"I could, but you'd have to make it worth my while." The scheming little sod rubbed his thumb and forefinger together.

"How much?" I asked. He leant over and whispered in my ear, the smoke on his breath tickling my nostrils.

"I don't have that much you little rat! What kind of man are you, anyway? Trying to extort an innocent person, you could be lying for all I know, maybe you know bugger all about who killed Russell."

"Maybe," he said with an arrogant shrug, "or maybe I could tell the police it was you I saw talking to Russell this morning before he died."

I slammed my empty glass on the table and staggered down the street. How did Dylan know I'd spoken to Russell that very morning? And where would I get the money to pay him off?

29

Sanjay

The podcast I was listening to was no longer gripping me. A serial killer running rampage through Massachusetts is all very exciting and thrilling, but when there's a real-life flesh and blood murderer in your midst, the ghoulish romanticism of true crime evaporates. Knowing that a violent killer could be sitting a few feet away is terrifying and not as exciting as one might expect. There is safety in headphones and narration, in knowing that the crimes you are listening to were committed long ago and that there is a vast ocean separating yourself from the country where the bloodletting took place, an ocean which I can see sparkling on the horizon.

After Luke's nonchalant revelation, a detail which might alter how the story now progresses, I took myself to the terrace bar to mull things over. Luke hadn't seemed surprised or interested that Sally was in line to inherit Russell's fortune, or that the murdered man had intended to change his will. Whether he realised the gravity of the implication I'm not sure, perhaps he couldn't envisage sweet, plain Sally as a cold-blooded killer. One thing I do know is that Luke enjoys knowing things that other people don't, so if he freely told Penny about the will, I'd bet there's something else he knows that he hasn't shared. He enjoys watching people struggle, knowing that the smallest effort from himself could save them a heap of trouble. I remember one Christmastime I had forgotten to get a 'Secret Santa' present for a lady in work and needed to dash to the shops before they closed. I couldn't find my car keys anywhere. I searched the whole house top to bottom while

Luke sat watching me run around like a headless chicken. Earlier in the day his little nephew had been to visit and had hung them on the Christmas tree like a decoration, the last place I'd think to look. When I eventually found them, Luke shrugged and said, "Did you not see Sebastian hang them there? You were supposed to be watching him." I'm getting angry just thinking about it. Deep breaths, Sanjay!

I ordered another sangria and felt my eyelids droop, an alcohol and heat-induced weariness starting to take a gentle hold of me. My alertness sprang back to life when I saw Jasmine exit the lobby with a towel draped over her shoulder, clearly intending to enjoy an afternoon of sunbathing. I had other ideas. I called her name and waved her over, the girl hesitated, no doubt wanting peace, but as Sally was my main suspect, I wanted to find out more about her, and who better to ask than her best friend.

"Jasmine, come have a quick drink, you look gorgeous by the way," I said, knowing she would find it harder to refuse if she was flattered.

"Hi, Sanjay," she replied, sitting next to me at the table. "I don't think I can face a drink, I had far too much last night." She wore a red sarong over her bikini and dark sunglasses. Her nose was slightly red, and I suspected that if she were to remove her shades I'd see red tear-burnt eyes.

"How's Sally? She must be in a terrible state."

"She seemed okay-ish, but I haven't seen her in a while, she went to get some fresh air. I thought maybe she would be here." Jasmine's head turned towards the pool, but only Agathe, Luke and Marjorie were there, each minding their own business.

"Still, it must be a terrible shock for her, a death in the family is always so hard to cope with. I'm sure not even the money will be any consolation right now."

"What money?"

"Oh. Didn't she say? I feel like a right idiot now. I've royally put my foot in it…"

"What money?" Jasmine repeated.

"You didn't hear it from me, okay?" The apprehensive nod I received didn't reassure me, but I had committed myself. "I happen to know, though don't ask me how, that Sally will inherit all of Russell's money, hotel, everything."

"I see. Well, she is his niece after all."

"That's not all. Russell had intended to change the will…"

"Why?"

"I would imagine to favour someone else, but who?"

"Maybe Sally's mum? Or Penny. You could see they were very close." Sally's mum was a potential beneficiary that I had already considered, but the suggestion of Penny Haylestone was an intriguing angle. Was that why she seemed so hellbent on finding out who killed Russell? Because the murderer had robbed her of one day gaining great wealth? Jasmine had gotten my mind whirling. What was the relationship between Penny and Russell? They were certainly close, but how close? Had they had an affair when Penny's husband was still alive? Did they kill him together to be rid of him so that they could be a couple? No, that didn't make sense because they weren't a couple, were they?

"Does Sally know Penny well?" I asked.

"No, she hadn't met her before we came out here. Sally hadn't seen Russell in years though, so it's not surprising she didn't know Penny."

"So this is your first time here? You and Sally don't visit together every year?"

"No, this is the first time."

"If I had an uncle who owned a beautiful hotel on the Spanish coast, I'd be here every chance I got!"

"Me too! It was me who suggested it. Well… I suggested we go on holiday together; it was Sally's idea to come here."

"So, you'd never met Russell until a few days ago?"

"Yeah, that's right. Why?" The beauty hadn't removed her sunglasses, but I was positive that behind those dark lenses her eyes were wide and staring.

"Just curious," I said. "For some reason I assumed you knew each other."

The 'some reason' being that last night when I sneaked away to enjoy an elicit cigarette, I saw them have a violent argument in the car park which resulted in Russell grabbing Jasmine's arm before she wrenched it free and slapped him in the face.

30

Marley

Sally had offered little information and nothing revelatory. We had left her alone to process her grief and confusion and made our way to the pool terrace. As Penny and I crossed the lobby, we were ambushed by Inspector Moreno whose face was scarlet with rage. "There you are," he growled. "I told you two to stay in your rooms. You have disobeyed a direct order of a Policia Inspector of the Cuerpo Nacional de Policia, a most grievous offence!"

"But not a criminal one," interrupted Penny. "Tell me, Policia Inspector, have you made much progress in your investigation?"

"The investigation is in its infancy, not that it's any of your business, and not that I would expect you to understand, Senora Haylestone. A murder investigation is like the cooking of the paella. You require all the correct ingredients; in an investigation this is the suspect statements. The suspects are like the tomatoes, you must squeeze them, check their firmness, you cannot ask a bad question, or you will get a rotten answer. You peel back the layers of the onion, see the true flesh that lies beneath, that is what goes in the pot, not the dirty skin, the lies, and deceptions but the truth beneath! You shell the prawns, remove the armour, make the suspect naked before you with nowhere to hide their shame and then… then!" A finger was thrust into the air in fevered gesticulation. "You throw all the suspects in the pot together and watch them simmer and stew until finally it is ready, and the truth will be served."

"You're making me hungry, Inspector," I said, remembering I hadn't eaten all day.

"Come! We go somewhere quiet where we will not be disturbed." The Inspector spun on his heels, and we followed him to the restaurant which was deserted. The breakfast plates had long been cleared away and the tables were set ready for dinner, which was still a few hours away. The policeman took his notepad from his pocket and led us to a table by the window. I seized the opportunity to grab a banana from a fruit bowl which we passed and had shoved half of it in my mouth by the time I sat on the chair Penny had pulled out for me.

"Okay, since you did not wait for me in your hotel rooms, I shall question you here." Penny smoothed out an invisible crease in the skirt of her kaftan with one hand and gripped the stem of an empty wine glass with the other.

"Be quick about it," she said. "We didn't kill Russell and we have more productive things that we could be doing than sitting here watching you try to imitate competency."

"We will start with you, Miss Haylestone."

"It's *Mrs* Haylestone. Just because my husband is dead does not mean he's not still my husband."

"*Mrs* Haylestone. Where were you this morning between seven a.m. and eight a.m.?"

"Enjoying my morning bath."

"Can anyone confirm this?"

"Unfortunately, not."

He then turned to me. "And you, Miss Williams, where were you?"

"I woke at seven-fifteen, had a cup of coffee, checked out some photographers and artists I follow on Instagram and then met Marjorie in the lobby at seven-forty-five."

"You didn't see your mother before you went to the gym?"

"No. Mother usually sleeps until eight, by the time I finish yoga, she is ready to go to breakfast."

"Your mother is in a wheelchair, are you telling me she can dress herself? She doesn't need your help?"

"The wheelchair speeds up getting from A to B. Sitting down also eases the pain in her joints, but she can walk and do things for herself, she just needs help sometimes."

"So, your mother would be capable of walking the short distance from her room to the gym?"

"You think my mum killed Russell? That's hilarious." I laughed at the ridiculousness of the suggestion, but a cold fear clenched my heart. If this man could suggest something so ludicrous, was he capable of following through with a wrongful arrest?

"You just told me she is more physically able than she appears," he continued.

"I said she can dress herself, but even that takes ten minutes. I didn't say she could run to the gym, somehow break in, and pick up a ten-kilogram metal bar and bash someone over the head with it. She might not be completely disabled, but I did have to drop out of uni to look after her, for goodness' sake! If you're looking for suspects, there's a few more standout ones than my mum."

"Such as yourself, for instance…"

"Me? Why would I kill Russell?"

"For the same reason as your mum, perhaps. You blamed him for the death of your father. Don't look so surprised, your mother told me about it. Your father died because Russell had not maintained the heart equipment correctly, si? That sounds to me like a motive for murder. You are more physically able than your mother, perhaps you are in on it together. Tell me, Miss Williams, could you lift a ten-kilogram bar? I think so. You also have no alibi."

"This is ridiculous, I just told you where I was. And if my mother and I did plot to kill Russell together, do you not think we would have provided each other with an alibi?"

"She's got you there," declared Penny, patting my shaking hand. "Besides, does Marley really seem the vengeful type to you? She's a sweet girl, and you are a buffoon."

"A buffoon with handcuffs and prison cells at his disposal, who counts the local magistrate and mayor as among his closest acquaintances. Speaking of which, I had to postpone my lunch because of you two, I ordered you to stay in your rooms and instead you decide it would be fun to play the hide and the seek with me. Well, count this as your last warning, do not interfere with my investigation again."

"We're not interfering with your investigation," replied Penny. "We are conducting our own, and so far, I'd say we are making more progress."

"Is that so? It may surprise you to learn that I have found a very important clue already in this case, not just a clue, but a threat upon Russell Aspell's life!"

"I see, so you've found the letters in the third drawer down on the right-hand side of his desk."

"How do you know about them?" he shouted. The man's eyebrows rose so far up his forehead in rage and surprise they nearly covered his balding crown. "I should arrest you for trespassing on a crime scene!"

"Russell wasn't killed in his office, it's not a crime scene," replied Penny, twirling the empty glass in her hand.

"Then I should arrest you for perjury."

"I haven't lied…yet."

"Then I will arrest you for obstruction! Interfering with evidence before a Policia Inspector of the Cuerpo Nacional de Policia has examined it!"

"And I'll say Russell showed me the two letters yesterday afternoon."

Out of retorts, and steaming at the ears, Inspector Moreno gripped the edge of the table until his knuckles turned milky white. He let out a grunt like a wearied bull and stormed from the restaurant.

"What now?" I asked.

"It's four o'clock," said Penny, looking at her sleek wristwatch. "Shall we see if your mother is okay?"

"You don't really think he would arrest Mum, do you?" I asked Penny, as we walked out of the restaurant towards the pool terrace.

"I wouldn't put it past him. But don't worry, we'll catch the killer and then he'll have no reason to. Tell me, dear, did you really leave university to care for your mum?"

"Yeah. Dad did so much, but then when he…"

"I understand."

"But it hasn't hindered me in any way. Not really. I mean, what do you go to university for anyway? To learn or to get a qualification? If you're like me and want to create art, you can do that in your bedroom as well as a classroom, right?"

"My dear, I went to university in the seventies, you went to have sex. Moreso than the sixties because you were angry that you missed that decade and felt you had to make up for lost time. But I take your point, you can pursue your art and look after your mum at home, you can't do both at university."

We found Mum sitting with Marjorie, who insisted that we join them.

31

Sally

Penny dropped the bombshell about the will, and then sped off to continue her investigations elsewhere once she was satisfied that I wasn't lying to her. She didn't stick around long enough to see my reaction to the news, which was confusion. Confusion as to why Russell would choose me, and confusion as to why he would then apparently change his mind. He did always describe me as his favourite niece, but the truth is he only has one other, my mum's sister's daughter, and we haven't seen either of them since they moved to New Zealand twenty years ago. I barely remember my Aunt Mary, only that she taught in my Sunday school and was forever quoting the Bible. *'And do not fear those who kill the body but cannot kill the soul.'* That one is the book of Matthew something or other, I think. It's amazing how words spoken so long ago can linger deep within the mind. We get a Christmas card from them every year and that's it. Always a nativity scene, always a short, formal greeting written within. I wonder if Mum even has Aunt Mary's phone number to let her know the news.

It's true that I have never thought of inheritance, after all, Russell was in great shape and death always seems a far-off thing when you've never known it intimately before.

If what Penny said was correct, then this hotel will soon be mine. What do I know about running a hotel? I yearn to be a writer, not Basil Fawlty.

Although, this would be a gorgeous place in which to write. Russell's office looks out over the sea and towards Stork Island.

When I went to see him there yesterday, I stood at the window and watched a stork glide through the air; it was the only movement to be seen, other than the rippling, sparkling waves. Such beautiful scenery would surely inspire my pen as much as it would distract my mind.

The hotel was quiet, half of the guests being on the overnight trip to Seville. I suppose that will make the task of finding the killer easier for the police, their suspect range being narrowed down.

Soft Spanish music was playing in the bar, but the plucking of guitars was beginning to sound repetitive, each song seeming to be a slight variation on the last. I estimated that I'd been sitting there unmoved for two hours, and was starting to feel my legs stiffen. I decided to see if Jasmine was feeling better. I found her lying on a sun lounger with her earphones in. She may have been asleep; she didn't stir when I walked onto the terrace. Marjorie was sitting at one of the tables and waved me over. Agathe was sitting next to her, the wheelchair vacant beside her.

"Hello, Sally," said Marjorie, before offering the expected condolences which were solemnly endorsed by Agathe's nodding head.

"I don't know why anyone would want to harm that lovely man," said Agathe. "He was a real comfort when my Reggie died. Sorted everything he did, all the Spanish paperwork and flights and all that. A real gentleman he was, and there isn't many of those left now, is there?"

"That's right," agreed Marjorie. "I don't envy you young girls these days, Sally, bless you. Men have no manners, no upbringing. They don't want a nice girl, they want flash cars and expensive champagne with sparks flying out of the bottle to show off on the Instagram."

"Not like in our day. I was lucky with my Reggie. God never made a harder working man. He was on the London Underground you know, for forty years, man and boy. Fixing them tracks and making sure it was safe for the trains to run, carrying all those passengers. Forty years of night shifts and then only two years of retirement he enjoyed before the Lord called him home. And it was those two years when I started needing this thing." Agathe gave the wheelchair next to her a resentful kick. "And I need a new one, this wheel here keeps jamming, I go round in circles if I'm not careful."

"Let's have a look," said Marjorie, who got down on her knees beside the demonised chair. She lifted one side off the ground and spun the wheel, generating a squeaking sound. "Sounds like you have a bearing on the way out. It should last you until you get back home."

"*If* we get back home. Don't forget there's a lunatic running about the place."

"Agathe…" Marjorie gestured towards me as though my sensibilities were so vulnerable they were susceptible to being overwhelmed by hearing true words spoken.

"It's okay, Marjorie, Agathe is quite right. There is a madman here, it's the only explanation for why someone would want to kill Uncle Russell. I don't believe for a second Terry would harm him because of some old squabble, and I certainly didn't kill him to inherit this hotel. No, I'm afraid some deranged killer is the logical explanation, which means we had better be on our guard."

"Heavens," said Marjorie. "I hadn't considered that the murderer might kill again. It sends a chill down my spine just thinking about it. And that policeman took our passports from us so we can't even fly home to safety. What a thing to do."

"I expect that's a formality," I said.

"Even so. It's irresponsible. Oh, look, here comes Elle," said Marjorie, distracted from the prospect of being murdered in her sleep. "I got chatting to her yesterday. Poor girl, going out with *him*." These last words were whispered as the pretty blonde drew closer.

"Hi, Marjorie," the girl said, though she gave a small wave at all three of us.

"Sit down, Elle, here, there's plenty of room, the more the merrier," said Marjorie. The girl hesitated for a few seconds, giving me an apprehensive glance, then obeyed.

"I only came down to give you back the magazine I borrowed." She handed Marjorie this month's *Grazia* edition.

"Would you like to read it, Sally?" Marjorie offered. "I enjoy reading it with my Sarah." I took the magazine and slipped it into my bag. I won't read it but didn't want to appear rude; fashion magazines aren't my thing but I'm sure Jasmine will flick through it.

"No Dylan this afternoon?" asked Marjorie.

"He went into town to buy cigarettes after the police interviewed us," replied Elle. "He should be back soon; he's been gone a while. Did they give you a tough time too?"

"They were fine with me, the tall one's a nice big fella, very polite. They had Terry squirming a bit, though. It's no secret him and Russell didn't see eye to eye. How about you?"

"They asked us what time we went for breakfast, that type of thing. I think they were trying to determine where we were when the murder was committed, except I got the impression they didn't know themselves when it happened. And, well, Dylan can be quite cagey, he doesn't like people prying into his personal life. I told him not to worry, he didn't kill Russell, so all he can do is answer the routine questions and there's nothing to worry about, but sometimes it's like talking to a brick wall. Then we came down here after the police spoke to us and Penny started asking us the same questions as they did. That really got Dylan's back up. He said she had no right to ask him anything and who did she think she was, although he did tell her he saw Russell arguing with someone this morning before he died."

"Who was he arguing with?" I asked, shocked by the revelation.

"He wouldn't say, not even to me. He told me not to ask him again because I would be wasting my time. Then he went into town in a mood, and I haven't seen him since."

"I wonder who it was…" I said.

"He might not have seen anyone, maybe he's lying," offered Elle as way of explanation.

"Why would he lie?" I asked, shocked that Dylan's girlfriend could speak so openly and uncaringly about the fact her boyfriend could be an unconscionable liar.

"Dylan likes playing games, it would amuse him to think Penny was wasting her time chasing a false lead. I know what you're all thinking, how can I be with him when he can be so…cold. Well, he's not perfect, but who is? Besides, he hasn't had an easy life…"

32

Terry

Don't get angry, get even. That's my motto. I don't know how, yet, but I'll take that little rat Dylan down a peg or two, maybe when we take the trip to the Stork Island, when he's out of his comfort zone and least expecting it. Who does he think he is, threatening Terence Smith?

It's hard not to get angry, though, despite my motto. I left Dylan smirking in the sun, and walked through the town, but I wasn't going in any particular direction and had nothing in mind other than to think. I sat on a bench and watched the seagulls for a bit, they're all huge out here, like eagles they are. I saw two of them fighting over last night's kebab scraps. No wonder they're so big if they're eating that every day, eating like kings. The hornets are bloody big, too, one buzzed past my head and I thought it were a 747 coming into land. I scarpered away from it and carried on strolling down the cobbled streets in the old part of town. The buildings are whitewashed, and the windows aren't level with one another, they're different sizes and offset. Wonky-eyed builders must charge a lower hourly rate over here, either that or they haven't invented spirit levels yet.

It's authentic here though, if you know what I mean. The streets are so narrow you know the houses were built before cars were invented. The locals hang their washing out on retractable lines which stretch between the buildings, and cats roam or lie in the shade without a care in the world, probably owned by no one yet looked after by everyone.

The streets and alleys are never quiet, distant shouts and squeals of playing kids are forever echoing off the walls. It's a happy place. There's bright colours everywhere you turn, and around every corner is a different smell, whether it be the aroma of dinner being prepared in some hidden kitchen, or the plants and flowers which guard the narrow doorways and climb the walls. I was quite happy being lost in the warren of sunburnt houses, where I couldn't understand anything of what was being shouted and had no wish to, neither. But in the end, I knew I had to face the music and go back to The Orange Tree Hotel; Marjorie would be waiting for me, and besides, maybe some evidence had come to light which would clear my name. That would wipe the smirk of Dylan's face.

The sun was beginning to sink as I walked the desolate road back. The broken glass on the wastelands shone orange, illuminated by the falling light. I were panting by the time I saw the palm trees standing either side of the hotel entrance and looked forward to taking the weight off my feet.

As I approached, the coach from Seville pulled up behind me, and a heap of exhausted-looking tourists staggered off, each one looking like they were ready to fall into bed. I wondered if they had been told of Russell's death, so much had happened it had seemed like two days squeezed into one, and I were surprised to find my watch telling me it were still early evening.

Marjorie was sitting by the pool when I found her. She were sitting with Agathe, Sally and Elle. I nearly swerved them unseen; I didn't want to sit with all of them, but Agathe spied me and flagged me down. "Terry, how was your afternoon?" she asked, in her thick accent.

"Fine. How was yours?" I looked at Elle who didn't so much as glance at me. I can't tell whether she's in cahoots with her boyfriend over his blackmail scheme or not. If she is, she hides it well.

"We've had a nice chat, haven't we, ladies," replied Agathe.

"Sure have," said Marjorie, patting my arm. "Agathe was just telling us of her childhood in Jamaica. It sounds so beautiful there, Terry, we must go some day."

"Aye," I said. "The day we win the lottery. Those cross Atlantic flights are a rip-off. Virgin? You'd be verging on bankruptcy using them. I'm sure this place cost an arm and a leg and all, and this is only Spain."

"You mean you've come on holiday, and you don't know how much it cost?" asked Agathe looking at me over the top of her glasses.

"Marge takes care of all the financial matters in our house, and I wouldn't have it any other way. What do I need with PIN numbers and sort codes and the like? Marge does the weekly shop and sorts out the council tax and whatever else, and I get a few notes to spend in the Rambler's Arms, ain't that right, Marge. Works for us. I daresay your Reggie never paid a bill or pushed a trolley around Tesco?"

"Of course not, he'd have done it wrong. Never had a head for money my Reggie, I took care of all that. It's a good thing he went first; he'd be lost without me."

"See, there you have it. I can tell by looking around this place that it costs a bob or two, but if Marge says we can afford it, then that's good enough for me."

"We did get a good deal," said Marjorie. "I think it all depends on when you book it. The earlier the cheaper, I think. If we'd have waited a few more weeks, I doubt this place would've been in our price range, it's ever so nice."

"I don't know how much it costs either," said Elle, who was twirling her blonde hair with her forefingers.

"I see," said Agathe. "A kept woman. That explains a lot. Dylan flush with cash is he?"

"Not at all, I don't know how much the hotel costs because I won this holiday in a competition. The most I've ever won before is a toaster."

"I didn't think you'd be entering competitions with all that fancy jewellery on…"

"My mum treats me sometimes. Dad's loaded but he's as tight as anything."

"Well, that's a stroke of luck, isn't it," said Marjorie, smiling at the girl. "Oh, it is lovely when young people catch a break, it's so hard these days, and there's so many traps and pitfalls out there. Take credit cards for example, these poor young people getting themselves laden with debt because they don't understand the interest repayments. We never had any such issues, did we? If your wages didn't cover it, you weren't getting it, it was as simple as that."

"What sort of competition was it?" I asked, thinking I were missing a trick. "One of them phone-in ones you see on the TV ad breaks?"

"No. I don't know if they still do them, I don't watch TV, I stream mostly."

"You what?"

"I hate adverts. No, I enter competitions on Instagram, that type of thing. There's loads to be won. When I won this, I was given the choice between here and Turkey, but I went to Turkey last year and got food poisoning, and swore I'd never go back, so here we are."

"Well, that's bad luck ending up in the middle of all this murder business," I said. "You'd be better off in Turkey with a dicky tummy."

"I'm not so sure, it's not like anyone's going to murder me, is it? And I won't be arrested because I've done nothing wrong. As long as I get my passport back, I'll be happy. Anyway, we don't know that it was murder, do we?"

"Penny Haylestone said it was," protested Marjorie.

"I know what she said, but Russell was found dead inside a locked room. How could anyone have murdered him?"

It was Agathe who provided a theory. "They're saying someone got in and killed Russell in the gym, between 07:11 and 08:01, right? Well, is it not possible he was killed last night, and his body put in the gym this morning to make it look like he was murdered in there?"

"But, why?" I asked.

"Maybe someone wanted to make it look like he died this morning to give themselves an alibi for then?"

"How?" I asked, confused.

"Okay, let's say, for example, Russell was murdered in the early hours of the morning and his body hidden in a cleaning cupboard near to the gym. The murderer could leave his room this morning, take Russell's card from his body, carry him to the gym and dump the body making sure the door was wedged open. That way, it would look like Russell had entered the gym using his card and not left it. Meanwhile, the murderer could run down to reception and pass a few meaningless words with some other guests to create an alibi. All of it could be performed in just a few minutes. I remember a similar thing happening once."

"You've been involved in a murder before?" shrieked Marjorie.

"No. I saw it on an episode of *Columbo*."

"An accident is much more likely in my opinion," Elle said, adjusting the sunglasses on the bridge of her nose.

"What sort of accident?" I asked, feeling a mysterious excitement in my belly.

"I have a cousin who's a builder. One of the lads on his building site got hit on the head by metal poles that were being swung by a crane. It gave him a nasty bang, but he said he was alright. A few hours later he collapsed and died at home. The impact had caused a bleed on the brain or something. Maybe the same thing happened to Russell, maybe he got a bump on the head somewhere else and then died later when he was in the gym?"

The ladies around the table looked at each other, the explanation offering hope that a murderer was not on the loose after all. Only I remained glum, because if Elle's theory was right, then surely I killed Russell Aspell after all.

33

Sanjay

I spoke to my editor and informed her that I was at the centre of a murder investigation. I may have embellished the truth a little, and added a flourish here and there of artistic creativity with regards the danger we are all in, and hinted that I myself am a suspect in a baffling and mysterious case of international intrigue, but let's face it, if it helps her support me in my endeavours to chronicle the story with the aim of publishing a true crime book, or even a podcast, then what's the harm? I recently read Truman Capote's *In Cold Blood*, about the writer's relationship with two murderers who slaughtered an entire family in chilly Kansas one November night. Capote was close to the investigation when the police were searching for the killers and his book became an astonishing success, but even he was not involved at the beginning like I am now. If the murderer of Russell Aspell is unmasked, then I will be in a unique position to document the case from beginning to end, *and* from the inside. The story of an impossible murder at a sunny resort, where tensions are high and hatred simmers beneath the surface. Perhaps I'll call my book *In Warm Blood*.

By the time I got off the phone with my editor (after ensuring I told her that my passport had been confiscated as I was a 'flight risk'), it was early evening. The sun had fallen behind Stork Island, leaving an orange glow shrouding the ruins of the lighthouse, giving away its existence. From our balcony I could see the glow of the fairy lights around the pool bar and could hear the faint murmur of voices and laughter. I told Luke I would go down for a drink while he got dressed for dinner.

As I got to the pool terrace a large group walked past me heading for the lift I'd just vacated. They had been on the day trip to Seville and each of them looked exhausted. Despite Russell's death we were informed that our own trip to Stork Island would be going ahead. It will only be a short hop over in a boat and the plan is to have a barbeque, swim, and wander around the island, so I don't think we'll be as tired as those poor zombies.

The bar terrace was quieter now that the large group had left. I saw Terry sitting and staring at a beer in front of him. He looked morose, as though he had received some bad and unexpected news. My first instinct was to pretend I hadn't seen him and to sit behind him, but there was something so pathetic in the unguarded gloominess, the lack of self-awareness brought on by whatever worry the man had, that I felt obliged to check on him. "Hey Terry, you alright for a drink?" He looked up at me, his eyebrows raised, but it took a full five seconds before he recognised either myself or his surroundings.

"Alright, Sanjay, how's it going, son? No, I'm fine for a drink lad, still supping this one." He pointed at a flat pint in front of him and pulled out a chair for me. I sat down and a waiter took my order of sangria.

"How was your day, Terry? I didn't see much of you, what with everything that's happened."

"Oh, you know, as to be expected I suppose. The police were pestering me, and Penny Haylestone, too, so I took a walk into town. I got back an hour ago and had a drink with the women. They've all gone to get dressed for dinner now. Did the police take your passport away too, or was it just me?"

"Yes, they did. I think they confiscated everyone's who was here when the murder was committed."

"Hmm. I thought it were just me. Suspect numero uno, don't you know."

"Really? Did the police actually say that?" I asked.

"They don't have to, do they? I was seen threatening Russell when he knocked me in that pool, and everyone knows there was bad blood between us."

"Do you not have an alibi? Where were you this morning when Russell was killed?"

"Down the beach. Alone. Where were you?"

"I was out jogging, Luke was working. The police didn't seem too interested in our whereabouts to be honest, that Inspector Moreno seemed more interested in talking about himself. He didn't even ask me where I went on my jog or anything about Luke's work."

"It doesn't seem like anyone has much of a watertight alibi, does it?"

"No. Nor does it seem like the police have much of an idea how to run an investigation."

"Look, here comes Dylan." Terry announced the new arrival in a tone of unexplained resentment. Dylan made a beeline straight for us and Terry scraped his chair back on the tiles. "I'll leave you to it," he said.

"Is everything alright?" I asked him, wondering at the man's eagerness to flee, or at least not be in Dylan's company.

"Er, yes, I, er, just have somewhere to be, that's all. I'll catch you later, Sanjay."

"Ah, Terry! Not leaving on my account I hope?" said Dylan, his thin face widening into a horrible smile.

"Of course not, I just have somewhere else to be, that's all."

"I see, well, have you thought any more about our little chat earlier?" Terry threw me a quick frightened glance, and his face grew even redder that usual.

"Er no," he replied, rather sheepishly I thought. "I still have to work a few things out. I'll see you both later." He disappeared into the lobby faster than I would've thought possible for a man his size.

"Care for a drink?" I asked Dylan, when the two of us were alone.

"Sure, why not." I got myself another sangria and Dylan ordered a gin and tonic. He lit a cigarette while he waited for the waiter to bring our drinks and I must've been staring at the glowing end with hungry eyes, for he held the packet out towards me without saying a word. I took one and looked at my watch before lighting it. Luke takes ages to get ready, and I calculated he wouldn't be down for at least a quarter of an hour. I was safe.

"Luke doesn't like you smoking. Same here."

"At least you don't hide it from Elle like I do from Luke. I should just come out and admit my addiction, but no one likes acknowledging they're not their own master, do they? When Luke and I met, I promised him I'd quit, and I did, for a year or so, but you know how it is, when that moment of weakness happens…"

"I'm sure Luke has his moments of weakness, too."

"Chocolate is Luke's weakness. He eats it in secret and hates himself for days afterwards. He's so obsessed with his waistline he'll have one square of chocolate then stand and stare in the mirror for an hour as if it's going to grow in front of his eyes. What's your weakness?" I asked the question playfully, and expected a jocular answer in reply, but Dylan stared at me through the rising wreaths of smoke as though considering how honest to be before simply replying, "Money."

"Is that a weakness? It's something we all need."

"It's what you're willing to do in order to get it which tells you whether it's a weakness or not. Me, there's not much I wouldn't do for money."

Despite the warm breeze, a chill ran through me as he said these words because I could hear, without doubt, he was speaking the earnest truth. I wondered for a moment whether Dylan would in fact kill for money, and if he could in any way benefit financially from Russell's death. He must've been reading my thoughts, for he added quite nonchalantly, "I didn't kill Russell, by the way, I had no reason to. But I do intend to profit from his death."

"Really, how?" I asked, taking the bait.

"Because I know who did kill him, and I will keep my mouth shut for a price."

My mind was so enraptured by these words I failed to hear the faint ping of the lobby lift, nor did I see Luke as he approached our table. I only became aware of him when I heard his angry voice demand, "What are you two talking about? And why are *you* smoking?"

34

Marley

Mum had a great afternoon, swapping between the sun and shade, and gossiping with Marjorie and Elle. Of course, she is upset about Russell, but the loss is made easier to bear by the fact that his death was so mysterious and dare I say, juicy. I, on the other hand, had a frustrating and typical afternoon. Typical, because it's just like me to lose my phone when I need it most. I'm such an empty head at times.

After spending a little time with Mum and seeing that I wasn't really needed, Penny took me to one side and set me a task to find out when was the last time people saw Russell. I reached into my pocket for my phone only to find that it wasn't there. I then went back to Mum's table where I assumed I must've left it, but no one had seen it. I'm sure it will turn up, but it was annoying having to rush into town to buy another and then hurry back to set about the task Penny had entrusted to me.

We already knew what Elle had told us, that she had last seen him by the pool bar last night, and Dylan, well, there seemed no point asking him again, I'd only receive a shrug and a smirk.

As it was, my task turned out to be easier to accomplish than I anticipated, because tonight before dinner, when I entered the bar area, the tables were occupied with the people I wanted to see.

Luke and Sanjay seemed to be sitting in frosty silence, and I think Sanjay was glad of the intrusion when I walked up to them and asked how their afternoon had been. He quickly pulled out a chair and began making small talk. "Are you looking forward to going to Stork Island tomorrow afternoon?" he asked.

In truth I hadn't given it any thought, and I used this fact to steer the conversation where I wanted it to go. "It's completely slipped my mind, what with everything that's happened. I haven't thought about it since last night when Russell was talking about it. Now that I think about it, that must have been the last time I saw him. He was sitting where you are now, Luke, and was telling me about the barbeque he had planned. He seemed very excited. Then he left, I think he said he was going to talk to you?"

"Did he?" asked Luke. "Oh yes, I remember now, he wanted to talk about work, but he could see I was enjoying myself and said it could wait until morning. I guess now I'll never know what he wanted to say."

"How did he seem?"

"A bit drunk, to be honest. He was very happy, giddy almost. He would start conversations then change topic halfway through. He was in the middle of telling me about the trip he runs to Seville when Jasmine caught his eye, and he went over to talk to her. I found it a bit rude, leaving us like that."

"Us?"

"Yeah, Sanjay was there, too. I doubt he would've left if it was just me."

I looked at Sanjay, who gave me a half-smile. "Yeah," he said. "That was the last time I saw him too… with Jasmine. Anyway, what time are we leaving for the island tomorrow?"

We chatted for a few more minutes, then I excused myself. I'd spotted Jasmine at a table on her own and told the guys that I needed to talk to her about some vague topic. I could hear the frosty silence between them return as I walked away.

"Hi, Jasmine," I said, taking the presumptuous step of pulling out a chair and plonking myself down on it. "I haven't seen much of you today…"

"Eurgh, I had, like, the *worst* hangover! Then I fell asleep by the pool for an hour only to wake up and find Sally laughing and joking with that bitch!"

"Who?"

"Elle, of course. Or whatever her name is. Sitting right there they were, chatting away like old chums."

"Maybe Elle was just offering her condolences about Russell."

"Not likely, the ice in my lemonade isn't as cold as her. They're made for each other."

"Who? Elle and Sally?"

"No! Elle and Dylan. Keep up. I wonder how long they were at it before I found out."

"You mean you didn't ask him?"

"No, I was too furious. When I got that message, he was sitting in my mum's kitchen. Luckily for him, the plates were the closest things to hand and not the knives. Mum was furious when she came home and found the broken pieces lying on the floor."

"Sorry, I'm confused. What message?"

"The text message. It was from an unknown number, it simply said, *'I think you should know; Dylan has been seeing someone else. Ask him about Elle.'* So, I did. Right there and then."

"And what happened?" I asked, trying to piece together the snippets of information in my head into something like a big picture.

"His head ducked out of the doorway just as the first plate smashed into the wall. I never saw him again, not until a few days ago, here, with *her*."

"Maybe she didn't know about you. After all, you didn't know he was seeing her until you were told, maybe she didn't know he was seeing you."

"Yeah, right. I'd find that hard to believe."

"Sorry to bring it up, let's talk about something else. So, you went out into town last night?"

"Yeah, me and Sally went to a restaurant and then a few bars. It was such a good night; I got some really super pics, too."

"Did Russell not go with you? I thought Sally said he went to a seafood restaurant with you."

"No, that was a few nights ago. Last night it was just me and Sally."

"You're right, I must be getting confused. Actually, now that I think about it, I think I saw you saying goodbye to him last night as you were leaving to go into town." I was fishing quite unashamedly, and expected a casual denial or agreement from Jasmine, but I watched her body go rigid, and she seemed to glare at me as though I was accusing her of something.

"No. I didn't speak to Russell at all last night."

"Are you sure? I could've sworn you chatted to him right over there." I pointed to where Luke had indicated they had been standing.

"Not that I remember, but like I said I had a lot to drink, my memory is a bit hazy. If I did speak to Russell, it must've only been for a few seconds. In fact, maybe I was just saying goodbye like you said, nothing more." Jasmine clammed up then, and I looked around the terrace for other fish to fry.

Terry and Marjorie were getting drinks served to them by Paulo when I joined them. "And whatever young Marley will have," added Terry as I sat down. "What'll it be? Rum? Malibu and coke? A nice pina colada?"

"Just an orange juice, please. I don't often drink, but I've really been putting it away this holiday, I think I need to ease off."

"You do what your body tells you, love," said Marjorie, patting my hand.

"Besides, if I have too much to drink, I won't have the balance for yoga in the morning. I don't suppose you want to join me again, Marjorie, after what happened this morning?"

"No, I don't think so, dear. I don't think I could go into that gym again. I just know I'd see him lying there, the image scorched in my mind."

"I doubt the police will allow the gym to be open just yet," I said. "I'll probably go to the beach for my morning yoga, might even get up for the sunrise."

"Like Terry did this morning, ain't that right, Terry?"

"What? Oh aye, this morning. Beautiful, that sunrise…"

"I know what you mean, Marjorie," I said, preparing the bait. "I keep seeing Russell lying there too. Awful image. But what I've found that helps is instead of thinking of him lying there dead, I remember the last time I saw him alive, you know, happy and laughing. It was here actually, last night. He told Mum and me stories about the times he took my dad fishing."

"Aww, that is nice, Marley. Although I don't remember the last time I saw Russell, at least I don't think I do. When was it, Terry?" Marjorie's face was contorted in thought.

"How should I know when the last time you saw him was? I'm not your biographer."

"Well, it was probably the same time as you saw him, wasn't it?"

"What? Aye, oh, right enough. Good thinking, Marge. Yeah, it would've been last night then I suppose, we probably saw him talking to you, Marley. We had a drink here, didn't we, Marge, near enough everyone was here, I think. I remember seeing you and your mam. How is your mam?" continued Terry. "I suppose she must be terribly upset over all this business."

"Will she be coming to the Stork Island tomorrow?" interrupted Marjorie.

"Of course she won't be coming, she's in a bloody wheelchair!" said Terry.

"Well, actually," I began to contradict, before being cut off.

"Terence Smith! Just because the lady is in a wheelchair, doesn't mean she can't be taken places to enjoy things, as you should know well! She's not like…like…"

"Disabled?"

"Yes, disabled. And even if she was, I'm sure there's ramps and things to assist. I do apologise, Marley. He forgets who he's talking to sometimes."

"That's alright," I reassured her.

"I don't need anyone apologising on my behalf, thank you very much! Honestly, you'd think I were a child the way you get on sometimes."

I left Terry in a grump and Marjorie smiling after me sweetly. I got a vague impression that she didn't want me to leave them, but

I'd seen Penny exit the lobby and wanted to catch up with her to let her know my findings.

"Inside bar," I whispered to her, and she spun around in the direction she had come from without so much as raising an eyebrow.

"I take it you've found out when the last time everyone saw Russell was, then?" she said, as we walked through the deserted lobby, the only sounds being the soft Spanish music playing and the clacking of our heels on the polished floor tiles.

"Yes, although I don't think I've found out much that will be of interest."

"I'll be the judge of that. Let's hear it."

I recounted my conversations verbatim as much as I could. I regret not recording the chats on my phone, like they would in one of the movies my mum likes to watch, but I'll remember to do that next time. As I spoke, a waitress brought us two glasses of cold, crisp, white wine. Penny sipped from her glass, her eyes never leaving mine as I told my tale.

"Hmm," she mused when I'd finished speaking. "Okay, forget the words for a minute, banish the conversations from your mind. I want you to imagine you are watching the people you spoke to but can't hear their voices. Like you are watching TV on mute. What were your impressions of them?"

"You mean like their body language?"

"Yes, exactly like that. Who was nervous, who was lying, who was uncomfortable?"

"Well, Terry was acting very odd. He kind of switched between being overly defensive and highly agreeable. Like when Marjorie asked him when they both last saw Russell, he jumped down her throat, but then when she explained to him that they were most likely together he went the opposite way; *clever you, Marge*, type of thing."

"Interesting. What else?"

"Jasmine was on edge, too. She was angry when talking about Sally, Dylan and Elle, but she was defensive when I asked her about Russell. She flat out denied speaking to him then changed her tune when I said I saw them together, which was only a little white lie. Then she was as tight-lipped as could be, as though she didn't want to say the wrong thing or let something slip. I think we should keep an eye on her."

"I think we should keep an eye on all of them. It seems that everyone has something to hide around here. What about Luke and Sanjay?"

At the sound of Luke's name, I froze. How could I be so forgetful!

"Marley, are you alright?" asked Penny. "You look like you're having some sort of episode that you're far too young to be having."

"Oh, Penny, there's something I forgot to tell you."

"Well, there's no time like the present, dear."

"You remember a few days ago we went to the shop to get me a plug adapter, then stopped off at the wine bar for drinks?"

"Yes, what of it?"

"Well, I went to use the loo in the bar but there was only one cubicle. I heard someone in there speaking on their phone, threatening someone."

"What did they say?" she asked, swirling her wine.

"They said, *'You bastard! How am I supposed to do that? It's too much money. I'm warning you. I'll kill you!'* Then the door opened, and Luke came out."

"Did he see you?"

"No, he flew past me in a rage."

"I see. I wonder what that was about…"

35

Sally

I don't know where to begin! So much has happened today, there's no way I can write it all down in one sitting, or even process it all in my head while it's all still so raw. Today's turbulence eclipsed even yesterday's when Uncle Russell was murdered. I suppose if I wish to attempt to straighten out all the events in my mind, I had better start at the beginning.

Jasmine spent most of last night in a mood with me. Apparently, I'm a *'traitor'* and *'why don't you go off and have a good time with your new bezzie, Elle?'*

She can be so childish at times, like she still has a high school mentality. My uncle had just been murdered and she was angry at me for having a drink with her stupid ex's new girlfriend. Does she not realise how lucky she is that she's no longer in a relationship with that horrible creep? If anyone should be having a drink with Elle it should be Jasmine herself, and she should be paying, thanking Elle for taking Dylan off her hands. Maybe I should come clean to Jasmine, especially after today's events. I've been carrying around my secret for too long and need to get it off my chest.

This morning, I enjoyed breakfast on my own. Croissants, ham, cheese, and then Greek yoghurt topped with strawberries and chia seeds. I was coming to terms with Russell's death and was determined to enjoy his hotel and all it offered as I thought he would wish me to, and that meant not letting my spat with Jasmine further dampen my already soggy spirits.

We were due to meet in the lobby at midday for the trip to Stork Island, and so, I wanted to spend the morning by myself. I wanted to see if I could enjoy my own company, to see if it *was* actually enjoyable. As I was leaving the restaurant, I stopped to fill up my water bottle at the jug next to the fruit juices. It was only as I got to the hotel lobby that I realised I'd left my phone on the breakfast table. I hurried back but found the table had been cleared by Paulo. Oddly, Paulo was adamant that there was no phone on the table when he cleaned it, and I suppose the shock of recent events must've affected the reliability of my memory, though I'm sure I took my phone to breakfast with me. I looked around for a few minutes before giving up. I guess it must've fallen out of my pocket.

The early morning sun filtered through wispy clouds, which burnt off as I trod the dusty road into town. Hibiscus and lavender defied the arid odds and brought colour and life to the otherwise bare and thirsty landscape. The only sounds, other than the chirps and twitter of small sparrows, were the dry slaps of my sliders on the cracked pavement and the occasional barks of distant dogs.

The main street of the town was deserted, though the detritus of the previous night's revelry still littered the cobbled stones. Cigarette butts peppered the ground, plastic pint glasses lay, crushed flat under the heels of thousands of unsteady feet. Fast food boxes and wrappers cascaded from the overflowing bins, spilling onto the pavements like scree from a rubbish-spewing volcano. I turned off into a side street, the smell of vomit and urine being gradually replaced with the spicy scent of red carnations and geraniums. As I inched closer to the domestic normality of cramped family homes in hidden alleyways, and away from the hedonistic wreckage wrought by sweet little Tony's and Tina's, cut loose from their mothers' apron strings for the first time, I breathed more freely, unburdened by the warmth of my new surroundings. The houses were rustic, sun-baked and colourful. Flowers and plants filled every crevice and decorated every ledge. Bougainvillea crawled along the walls and roofs, snaking along with the winding streets. My eyes were dazzled by every colour imaginable, my nose teased by the baking bread of the morning as well as the flowers of the summer. I could hear children's muffled laughter behind the thick walls and wooden-shuttered windows. Despite the life surrounding me, I saw no one for five minutes until an old woman, bent forward and muttering to herself, passed me clutching a cross. We were in the narrowest part of a steep alley, and I had to flatten myself against a house to give her a respectful enough berth. She carried on down the slope, paying me no attention or thanks, completely absorbed in her incantations or prayers, whatever they were.

I carried on my aimless wandering through the maze of streets until I came to the harbour. It's not a big harbour, but the jetty runs out into the deep blue, so I walked to the farthest bench and watched the fishermen at the end cast their lines while the greedy gulls overhead swooped and circled, crying out for food. I watched, entranced as one of the fishermen cast his line, then retracted it with his electric reel, repeating the process over and over, the swaying, waving rod swinging like a pendulum, the fisherman mystic with hypnotic powers. The glittering calm soothed my soul, the unfathomable depths elating my spirits as happens when you are faced with something so enormous that the realisation of your own insignificance can seem a joyous thing, as your worries and woes shrink, and you laugh at it all.

I don't know how long I sat there for, staring from one blue abyss to the other. I didn't care whether I was late back to the hotel, or if the group went to the island without me, I was indifferent to it all. I stopped at a coffee shop before I even looked at my watch and was surprised to find it was not yet eleven o'clock. I ordered a macchiato and watched the streets fill, describing the scene to myself in my head as though I were writing it in a novel.

The child stopped and stood wide-eyed as the inflatable dolphin undulated down the street, taking the man along with him. The little girl did not notice the melting ice cream drip over her knuckles and plop into a growing white puddle at her feet. Her mother soon did.

I then took a slow walk back to the hotel, stopping at a shop to buy a second-hand phone. It was eleven-thirty when I rounded the bend in the road and saw the hotel. As I approached, I could see Sanjay in the carpark smoking a cigarette, he was pacing back and forth as though he was agitated. He didn't see me as I entered the lobby.

I walked to the lift, but as I reached out my hand to press the button, the doors opened. Jasmine stood in front of me.

"Sally! Where have you been?"

"For a walk. Why?" I asked, seeing a buzzing excitement in her eyes.

"Haven't you heard what's happened?"

"No. What? Tell me."

"There's been an arrest. Terry has confessed to murdering Russell."

36

Terry

In the films you get a phone call, don't you. Well, it turns out it's the same in real life, too. Do you want to make a phone call? Inspector Morpurgo says. Who the hell am I going to call? I asked him. Call your lawyer, he says. Call my lawyer? I says, I don't have a lawyer, I told him, I'm not Al Capone you know, and if I did, he'd be in England, wouldn't he? Honestly, if I hadn't have handed myself in, that plonker never would've caught me. They should pay me half his wages for this week.

That Agente Garcia's a nice enough bloke, though. Can I get you anything? he asked me when they put me in the cell. Don't suppose you could find a pen and paper, I said. And sure enough, five minutes later, the letterbox thingy on the door opens and in pops what I'd asked for.

I have to say, I'm quite fond of this diary-keeping lark now that I've started. I'm not quite sure my blood pressure is any lower, but I like it all the same. Well, what else am I going to do to pass the time? I don't think they're going to let me have a pint, or a key to the cell, so I might as well keep up to date with the old diary, mightn't I?

I couldn't sleep a wink last night. I kept tossing and turning, Elle's words going round and round in my head. I mean, that's it, isn't it? It must've been me who killed Russell, I just didn't know it at the time. When Elle told us that story about her cousin or whoever that got a bash on the head on the building site, I knew that Russell must've died from a delayed reaction after I threw that rock at him. I lay there, Marjorie snoring next to me, staring at the ceiling. Well, I won't have anyone say Terence Smith doesn't take responsibility for his actions, so at around three this morning I decided to come clean. Straight after breakfast, I decided, I'd march down to the police station and hand myself in.

I told Marjorie first, of course, as a husband should. "Marge," I said, as she tried to open one of those rectangle blocks of butter without getting any on her fingers, "I've something I need to tell you." She stopped what she was doing to look at me. "Marjorie, my love, it were me who killed Russell, and I'm going to the police station after I've finished my bacon and eggs."

"What?" she asked, setting down the butter.

"You heard me. I did him in."

"How?"

I then told her all. I explained how Russell had come upon me on the beach that morning, had woke me up to apologise for knocking me in the pool, and how like a bear with a sore head I'd argued with him. I explained how I lost my temper and as he was walking away, I picked up the nearest thing to hand which happened to be a rock and I lobbed it at him, hitting him on the head.

"How hard did you throw the thing?" she asked.

"I don't know, really; how do you measure these things? I know I'm a big old lump though, so I must've given it some welly."

"Don't be so ridiculous, Terry, he would've died there and then, surely."

"Maybe not. You heard what Elle said."

"And how do you know she didn't make it up? How do you know she didn't see you throw the stone and told you a load of cobblers to make you confess?"

"Why the blazes would she do that?"

"Maybe she's the killer, and she wants you to take the fall for it. Or maybe Dylan killed Russell and she's trying to protect him."

"Don't talk rubbish, Marge, I threw the rock, I killed him. It's the only explanation."

"What was Russell's reaction when the rock hit him?"

"He just, sort of, rubbed the back of his head, then muttered something and stormed off." I began to wish I'd waited until I'd finished my breakfast to tell Marge. With all these questions, my eggs were getting cold.

"Well, there you go. He wouldn't have decided to go for a workout in the gym if you'd done any damage, he'd be feeling dizzy. Besides, what about the blood? I didn't look too closely because it was all so horrible, but there was blood on Russell's face, you couldn't have done that."

"I'm not sure, Marge. I looked it up on the Google last night, what Elle said can happen, there's reports of it. Concussion, swelling on the brain, all sorts of medical things. The blood on the face may have come out of his ears if there was bleeding in the brain." She seemed unsure. The thing with Marjorie is, she always does the right thing. I can read her like a book. On the one hand she knows that me handing myself in is the right thing to do if I did kill Russell, on the other, she can't bear the thought of being without me, the poor mare.

"You're really going to go to the police?" she asked, her breakfast now cold and forgotten.

"I have to, Marge. I hated Russell bloody Aspell, but I didn't mean to kill him, I'd never have wilfully murdered him, but I'm responsible for his death all the same."

"You have your principles, Terry; I'll give you that."

I walked slowly to the copshop; I was doing the right thing, but I was in no hurry about it. I wanted to savour the last rays of sun that I was going to enjoy for a while. When I did eventually get here, the inspector and Agente Garcia were just coming out of the building. They stopped when they saw me approach.

"I was just on my way to The Orange Tree Hotel," said the inspector.

"No need. I've come to confess."

"Aha! I knew it. Didn't I say, Agente Garcia, that I, Inspector Alberto Luis Alejandro Juan Flores Moreno of the Cuerpo Nacional de Policia would solve this impossible mystery?"

"You what?" I said. "I bloody solved it if anyone did, I've delivered the killer right into your hands. Me!" He waved my words away.

"Come," he said. "We talk."

At the reception desk, the two policemen stood either side of me as another behind the desk filled in some forms. They took my belt, my wallet, everything. Inspector Moreno then looked down at my feet, probably for shoelaces in case I wanted to do myself in inside the cell. "What have you got on your feet?" he asked.

"What do you mean, are you blind? I'm wearing flip-flops." He opened his arms and looked around himself as though he were addressing an invisible audience.

"Who comes to be arrested wearing flip-flops?"

"And why the hell not? I am in Spain you know; it's thirty bleedin' degrees outside."

Anyone would think I nip down the local bobbies all the time and should be an expert in how to be arrested.

"Come. Follow me, we go to the torture room."

"You what?"

"Ha! A little joke, see, I thought you British like to laugh. Agente Garcia, fetch our murderer here some agua." We went into a small dark room containing only a table and three chairs.

"Sit. Good. Now, Mr Smith, please tell me everything. Do not hold anything back for I shall know if you do." The little fella puffed out his chest and put a stick of gum in his mouth. Instead of agua, Agente Garcia handed me a bottle of water and a paper cup, then I told them both exactly what I had told Marjorie earlier. Beach, rock, et cetera, et cetera, blah, blah, blah. The two men listened in silence then looked at one another. Then they looked back at me.

"Mr Smith, are you saying you killed Mr Aspell, but you did not hit him in the gym?" asked the inspector.

"For the umpteenth time, I bumped into him on the beach, we had an argument, and I threw a bloody rock at him on the beach. Are you deaf?"

"Me? Perhaps you are the one who is deaf. Perhaps you weren't listening yesterday when I came to your hotel room and told you Russell Aspell was bludgeoned to death in the gym. Idiot!"

"What did you call me?"

"An idiot!"

"Now hold on a -"

"I will hold on to nothing. Tell me, how many rocks did you throw?"

"One. I told you a hundred times."

"Well, Russell Aspell was struck three times. Uno. Dos. Tres. One. Two. Three. Do you know what that means? It means you didn't kill him! Agente Garcia, take Mr Smith to a cell, he will spend the rest of the day there as punishment for his stupidity."

"Ey'up! We're meant to be going to the stork's island, I don't want to miss that!"

And there we have it. Turns out I didn't kill Russell after all. And if Marjorie wasn't so bleeding squeamish and had looked at the body proper, I wouldn't be missing the barbeque and the storks right now.

37

Sanjay

When I heard Terry had confessed, I thought my idea for a book or podcast might be a non-starter. After all, a confession isn't as gripping or intriguing as a case being solved by a detective using flair and genius, is it? I needn't have feared, however. Terry may or may not have killed Russell, but he couldn't have been responsible for the second murder which occurred this afternoon. Terry was locked away in a police cell in the middle of town: nowhere near the island.

I'm getting ahead of myself…I had no idea of the tragic events that were to unfold when I woke this morning to the sound of splashing water and Luke's melodic shower singing.

The hotel was abuzz with murmurs and excitement over Terry's arrest when we went down for breakfast. I could see from the rapid nodding of peoples' heads and animated conversations that something of note had occurred, but it wasn't until we were seated at the breakfast table that we found out exactly what. Marjorie was sitting at the table next to us, only a foot or two away. She was crying into a tissue and was being comforted by Marley. Agathe and Penny were also at the table, each drinking coffee.

"Marjorie, are you alright?" I asked, seeing the sodden tissue in her hand.

"No. That oaf of a husband of mine has gone and confessed to killing Russell, but he didn't do it." Penny then filled in the blanks and explained that Terry had thrown a rock at Russell on the morning of the murder, thinking that was what killed him.

"Which is of course ridiculous," Penny stated. "As I've just told Marjorie, when I examined the body, I could see quite clearly that Russell had suffered more than one heavy blow. It's simply not possible that Terry killed him. At least, not in the way he says he did. Don't worry, Marjorie, I've no doubt Terry will be released before you know it. Even Inspector Moron will see that Terry is talking nonsense."

"I do hope you're right," Marjorie replied between sniffles. "You've made me feel much better, Penny, thank you. And you, Marley, such a comfort. She's a credit to you, Agathe."

"Yes, I raised all my children good and proper, Lord knows I did."

"Are you coming on the trip to the island, Agathe?" I asked.

"Why wouldn't I?" she shot back, clutching her crucifix.

"Oh, I only meant…" my words trailed off. What did I mean? Marley, being the doll she is, intervened.

"Sanjay was just being polite, Mum. I told him yesterday that you hadn't decided on the trip yet, that's all." This was a fib, but I was grateful for it.

"So, we're back to square one," said Luke, changing the subject.

"How do you mean?" I asked.

"Well, if Terry didn't kill Russell, the killer is still roaming about the place."

"Ask Dylan, he knows," Agathe said matter-of-factly.

"Mum, what are you talking about?" asked Marley, her voice rinsed with shock.

"He told me. He's been telling everyone as far as I can make out."

"Told you what, exactly?"

"That he knows who murdered Russell. He spoke to me yesterday when you were off galivanting like Nancy Drew. Sat himself down next to me, uninvited I might add, and just started chatting away. I was suspicious immediately. He's never shown much interest in me before and why would he? I'm an old woman, and a God fearing one, too. I daresay we've little in common, but down he sits himself nonetheless and starts talking about the weather of all things. Well, I smelt a rat, and sure enough it wasn't long before he's telling me that he knows who the killer is and that he'll go to the police with the information soon. Obviously, he's trying to get money out of someone. A dangerous game to play in my opinion."

"Indeed, it is," murmured Penny.

"Why didn't you tell me this?" asked Marley.

"Why would I? I've been waiting for that policeman to turn up to tell him. Besides, Marley, when would I tell you? I've barely seen you since Russell was killed."

"It sounds to me like Dylan is telling a few porkies," I said.

"How so?" Agathe said reproachfully, as though I doubted her testament.

"If Dylan did know who the killer was, he would approach them directly. Instead, he's using you to spread the word in the hope that the killer comes to him and offers him money or whatever to keep his mouth shut. He's best ignored." I noticed Penny looking at me keenly, though it was impossible to determine whether she agreed with my assessment. Those intelligent eyes give little away; it would be a foolish fellow who would bet much on what she's thinking.

The breakfast ended with Marjorie smiling, reassured that Terry would soon be back with us and out of chains. Marley even convinced her to come on the trip to the island, although it took much persuasion.

The rest of the morning was spent sunbathing, there was hardly a spare lounger, everyone waiting for midday to come so we could board the boat.

Dylan lay nearby to us, Elle next to him. I watched him and wondered if I was right; was he just a greedy opportunist? He has a scar that runs the length of his leg, it shone white in the sun, more distinctive than when I first noticed it a few days ago, as it was now surrounded by bronzed skin.

Close to midday, Paulo came onto the terrace and clapped his hands for attention. He then waited a few minutes while we all gathered our belongings, then he led us around the pool, through the gap under the gym, and down on to the beach where the boat was waiting. Jasmine stayed by the pool, telling Sally quite loudly even though she was standing right next to her that there was no way she was getting in a boat with *him*. Sally shrugged, picked up her bag, and walked away without saying goodbye to her friend, leaving Jasmine open-mouthed and attention starved.

Paulo made an honourable fuss over Agathe as he helped her aboard, the old woman recounting her many afflictions and hardships. Once she was settled, Paulo reversed the boat out and swung it around before opening the throttle. It was a pleasant ride; the sea was calm, the only disturbance being the white frothy surf made by our propellers. It was good to feel the tiny droplets of sea spray hit my face as we skimmed along. I wished the journey could've been longer, but the island is no great distance from the shore, and in a few minutes, we once again had sand sinking beneath our feet.

"I'll set up the barbecues. In the meantime, please explore the island," said Paulo, taking a knotted bundle of twigs in one hand, and a bag of coals in the other, laying them next to two flame-blackened barbecues.

"Surely one barbeque would be enough?" I asked, as Luke took some sunscreen from his rucksack, and the rest of the group dispersed off the beach. "There's only a handful of us."

"Si," replied Paulo. "But the one with the nasty face says he has allergies and so I must cook separately for him."

"He must mean Dylan," I said to Luke as we headed off, following the mingled footprints left in the sand by the others.

"Yeah, he's allergic to shellfish."

"It must be quite severe to merit having an extra barbeque."

"Not worth taking the risk I suppose. I know I wouldn't fancy spending time in hospital when I'm meant to be enjoying my holiday."

The rugged island is named after its avian inhabitants. The storks are not so great in number that they are always visible, but their clacking is frequently heard and every now and again the great birds would swoop overhead and glide to their rocky nests, their crooked wings cutting silently through the air.

We climbed to the summit (if you could call it that, more of a rocky outcrop with a small, ruined lighthouse on it than a peak) and admired the changing blues of the sea, from the gentle teal shallows to the terrifying cobalt depths. I imagined the array of creatures hidden beneath the waves, each participating in the endless struggle for survival, each doomed but unaware of the fact. Looking across the island, we could see the other members of the group scattered about the place. I could just about make out Agathe sitting in her wheelchair talking to Marjorie while Paulo tended the smoking barbeques next to him. Paulo had told us the food would be ready at two o'clock, which meant we had just enough time to go for a quick dip.

The climb down the slope was more fraught than the clamber up; the risk of slipping on the uneven tracks and loose stones made more dangerous by my terrible balance which has plagued me throughout life. Luke, being athletic, pranced down like a mountain goat and stood waiting for me at the base of the slope with his arms folded and head tilted to one side. I waited for a snide remark about my slowness or inelegance but was surprised to receive none. Instead, he dictated a brisk pace on our way to the beach, one which had me puffing and panting and caused me to renew my vow to quit my smoking habit once more.

The cool water was very welcome when we reached it, and for half an hour we floated and frolicked, leaving ourselves fifteen minutes to dry out in the blazing sun.

We were the last to return. Paulo had equipped everyone with a drink from cool boxes on the boat and seeing us walk along the shore he fixed us a gin each, handing them to us with a smile. The smell of roasted pork and chicken hit my nose, my mouth watering after the hunger brought on by our exertions. We all stood chatting and drinking, eating with our hands from paper plates. Every time a piece of meat was served up, it's place on the grill was taken by something else. Sausages, prawn kebabs, even thin peppered steaks. It was all very civilised and relaxed until Elle, her eyebrows knit close together and her voice strained, said to Dylan, "That's my plate, stop eating!" Dylan, who was holding a chicken leg in one hand and a glass of gin in the other, began spitting mushed up white bits onto the sand.

"What is it? What's the matter?" asked Agathe, leaning forward in her chair.

"I'm sure it's fine," answered Elle. "Dylan just took some chicken from my plate instead of his, that's all. Are you okay?" she asked him, her voice lower but still strained with concern.

"I didn't take anything, you handed me the plate! You were eating prawns from that! You can be so stupid sometimes, Elle!" He took a mouthful of gin and swirled it around like mouthwash, then spat it towards the sea. Elle didn't reply, she just reddened with embarrassment and bowed her head. Dylan began berating her further but stopped after a few words, his eyes slowly widening in horror. He threw down the glass from his hand and clutched his throat, then began clawing at it as we all stood silent, staring, but unable to do anything. Elle rushed to the boat and reached into her handbag, pulling out what looked like a pen. She sprinted back to Dylan whose face was going lobster red, and lifted his shorts, revealing more of the shining scar which ran the length of his leg. She pressed the pen against his thigh, holding it for a few seconds before withdrawing it, a long, thin needle now visible.

"What's that? What's happening? Marley, move out of the way so your mother can see."

"Mum, be quiet," came the reply. "Will he be alright?"

"Yes, he should be fine now," replied Elle. "The epinephrine decreases the reaction to the shellfish and reduces the swelling."

But Dylan began waving his right arm while his left still clutched his throat. He looked around at each of us wild-eyed, the red blood vessels in his eyeballs getting brighter and larger with each passing second.

"I...I don't think it's working!" gasped Luke next to me. Sally, beside him, was covering her mouth with her hand, holding in a cry. Elle looked from the EpiPen in her hand to the convulsing face of her boyfriend and back again.

"I don't understand! It should be working but it seems to be making it worse." Tears were now streaming down her face as she watched Dylan drop to the sand and begin to writhe in agony. He could form no words; his whole body shook like he was having a spasm. It was a horrid sight, but worse was the sound… the screech. The man's gasps for air turned into a shrieking wail of absolute pain, as though he was being tortured on a medieval rack. This event, which will forever haunt my dreams, lasted for a few more minutes, minutes filled with useless words and futile actions, a hand held, a makeshift pillow placed beneath his head, until finally, the man's torment was over, and his convulsing body stilled, his face a reminder of his anguish as it set in death, a deformed mask of misery.

38

Marley

Today has been a frenzy; first Terry confessed to killing Russell, although was soon exonerated, and then Dylan was murdered. The manner of Dylan's death was so horrific I can barely remember anything that preceded it. He took a bite of chicken, and the next thing we knew, he was lying on the sand shaking like he was being electrocuted, until finally he stopped: dead. The rest of us stood there, frozen with shock, unable to think of anything which might save the man, or at least alleviate his suffering. It's the eyes which will haunt me. Dylan looked at each of us...it's hard to convey how. If I said a pair of eyes could accuse you of impending murder, yet also be blinded by fear and panic, all the while leaving you in no doubt of the agony being felt, how could I communicate that in a few words. Some emotions are so intense they are nearly indescribable, usually those of grief and pain.

When we were left in no doubt that we were standing around a corpse, it was Penny who took control of the situation. She whispered to Marjorie to take Elle away from the body. The poor girl was sobbing, still staring at her lifeless boyfriend. She allowed Marjorie to twist her away, and together they stumbled along the sand towards some large rocks that would shield us from them.

"Paulo, do you have a sheet or a tarpaulin in the boat which we could use to cover the body?" asked Penny. He nodded, and Luke and Sanjay went to fetch it while Penny walked closer to Dylan. She crouched on her haunches and sniffed at the dead man's open mouth, a hideous and ridiculous sight. Then she patted his pockets.

"What are you doing?" I asked. Penny ignored my question and asked one of her own.

"Tell me, Marley, how did he die?"

"He had an allergic reaction to the food. The chicken must have had some shellfish on it."

"I'm afraid not, my dear."

"How then?" demanded Mum, who still sat in her wheelchair, absorbed in everything.

"I'm not sure. An allergic reaction would cause his throat to close up, which is what happened to begin with. But…" Penny picked up the gin glass Dylan had been holding. The curvature of the glass still held a tiny amount of liquid, and Penny held it to her nose. "Hmm." She stood the glass upright and buried the base in the sand to prevent it toppling over. Then, from her handbag, she took a piece of paper and scooped up the EpiPen as you would a dead wasp.

"You think he was poisoned with the pen, that's why you don't want to get your fingerprints on it?" I ventured to say.

Luke and Sanjay came back with a folded sheet of tarpaulin. They stood, awaiting further instructions from Penny. With a nod of the head, she indicated that they could cover the body, then they went to find stones to place on the edges of the sheet to ensure the slight breeze did not unveil the indignity of Dylan's death. Sally went with them, eager to be of some use.

Penny turned to me. "Yes, dear, I think it very probable. When the police take away the EpiPen for testing, I think they'll find some traces of poison contained within. Paulo, you had better call Inspector Moreno. He needs to get out here."

"But he ate the chicken," said Mum. "We saw him eat it!"

"Yes, but there may not have been any shellfish traces on the chicken. Elle may have been wrong in thinking she gave him the wrong plate. If Dylan was murdered, as I have no doubt he was, then the killer had to guarantee he would have an allergic reaction. It's more likely that whatever substance caused the allergic reaction was in the gin."

"I see," I said. "So the killer puts traces of shellfish in the gin and then guarantees death by putting poison in the EpiPen, which is then injected into Dylan."

"Precisely."

"But how did they spike Dylan's gin and no one else's? We all had gin."

"Then I suspect we've all drank traces of shellfish, but only Dylan was allergic to it. It would be much easier for our killer to contaminate the bottle of gin therefore covering all bases, rather than just Dylan's glass. Besides, the risk of being caught is much higher if trying to drop something into his glass while we were all standing around here. The killer could've squeezed a prawn into the gin bottle at any time and no one would've noticed. They probably brought the contaminated bottle with them and switched it with the one Paulo brought when no one was looking."

"And it's not like any of us would be able to taste a few drops of shellfish juice in the gin, is it?" I asked.

"No, gin would mask the taste quite well I should think."

As we waited for the police to arrive, we chatted in low voices around the sheeted body. It didn't seem right to move away from Dylan, to leave him alone. Luke seemed in shock, he had done what Penny had commanded meekly without question or complaint and had shown none of his usual bravado or ego. Mum was talking to Sanjay, clutching her cross. I hate it when she does that, but she is completely unaware that she is doing it and would never wish to deliberately offend anyone. Sally sat cross-legged in the sand and gazed out to sea.

Penny whispered in my ear, "Let's go and speak with Elle. See how she is." We slipped quietly away, Mum still engaged with Sanjay while Luke stared at the moulded tarpaulin. As we walked, Penny told me that Dylan's phone was not in any of his pockets. I couldn't tell if she was frustrated or curious by this, but I remembered my own missing phone, and Sally's, and a foreboding took hold of my mind.

Elle was sitting on a rock, her head resting on Marjorie's shoulder.

"Hello, dear, how are you holding up?"

"It's all my fault!" she wailed.

"Nonsense…" Penny then told her the theory of the gin bottle. "I'm sure I'm right, dear," she concluded. "The police will be here any minute, they'll take samples to confirm."

"But who would want to harm Dylan? Why? I don't understand, Penny."

"Well… Dylan did let it be known far and wide that he knew the identity of the killer. Perhaps his murder was an act of self-preservation."

"But why like that? It was so – horrible. So – evil. Seeing him in that much pain…"

"That is a very good question."

"So, you think Dylan's killer and Russell's killer are one and the same?" asked Marjorie.

"Yes, I do. We have a very clever foe on our hands. By the way, dear, Dylan's phone isn't about his person. I don't suppose you have it?"

"Yeah, he put it in my bag when we were by the pool waiting for the boat to take us here. Why?"

"Nothing, dear, don't worry about it now."

"Well, at least my Terry can't be suspected of this one, he's still locked up in the police cell."

Penny made no reply, but I was convinced she was thinking along the same lines as myself. If the EpiPen did contain poison, and the gin bottle contaminated, this meant that the murder was premeditated, and the killer wasn't necessarily with us on the island. Terry wasn't out of the woods yet.

My thoughts were interrupted by the sound of a boat's engine, loud with urgency. I looked up to see Inspector Moreno standing at the bow like a saviour coming to rescue marooned shipwreck survivors.

39

Sally

Terry's confession was false, but Dylan's murder was all too real. I felt a jolt of panic when his eyes widened and he grabbed his throat, but my fear melted as Elle sprang into action. In fact, I felt relief when I saw her produce the EpiPen and administer its contents. That relief, though, was short-lived and quickly morphed into pure horror as I watched Dylan die an agonising, torturous death.

Everything else became a blur after that, the sun's rays lost their potency, the small waves lapped the shore in silence, even the storks ceased their clacking; everything united in confused shock. My mind only focused on the present again when the police arrived. Inspector Moreno hailed to us from a little motorboat, then almost fell overboard when he was subjected to the shudder caused by the bow running aground on the shore. Agente Garcia hung a ladder over the boat's side and the Inspector clambered down it in a comically unwieldy fashion. In the time it took him to do this, Penny had led Elle back, the girl shivering despite the afternoon heat.

Judging politeness and tact to be luxuries ill-afforded in times of murder, Moreno rushed up the beach and demanded to see the body. He flung back the tarpaulin without giving warning to Elle or any of us who might find the sight upsetting.

"Were you all here when this happened?" he asked, looking around the group. We nodded and murmured. "Well! What happened?"

"Dylan had an allergy to shellfish," said Penny. "He had a reaction and his EpiPen was administered. He then died. Those are the facts."

"Ah! Those are the facts, are they? You, Mrs Haylestone, think a great deal more, don't you? The facts, pah! Tell me what you really think."

"I think the bottle of gin we were all drinking from is laced with traces of shellfish, and that the EpiPen that was used contained some sort of poison which is what really killed him."

All eyes looked at Inspector Moreno, intrigued by how he would react. He hesitated a moment, keenly aware of the situation Penny had put him in. She had spoken her words so confidently, that the man must fight his natural inclination to automatically disagree or challenge her statement. On the other hand, he was loathe to publicly give weight to her words and so had to choose his retort carefully.

"I would not wish to make such assumptions, Mrs Haylestone, that is exactly why I have a forensics team, and laboratory technicians, and the scientists. It is they who will tell me how the victim died, and they will tell me precisely, not with the generic term 'poison'. They will evaluate the chemical compounds of the substances that they find, *if* there are any to be found."

"They'll find them, I'm sure of that."

"Excuse me, sorry to interrupt, Inspector Moreno sir, but I was just wondering when you were going to release my Terry."

Moreno looked at Marjorie with disdain. "I released your husband before I set off to come here. I have another body to deal with and a murderer still to catch, I can't have my cells filled up with idiots who waste my time. Now, Agente Garcia will take each of you over there and take your statements."

Elle was the first to go. Marjorie tried to accompany her to provide comfort and support, but Inspector Moreno was adamant that having one suspect hear the testimony of another could jeopardise his investigation. I thought him unnecessarily cruel.

When it was my turn, I followed Agente Garcia the short distance along the beach until we were out of earshot of the others.

His stern jaw and dark brown eyes gave rise to butterflies in my stomach, and I was shocked and ashamed at myself to feel that kind of excitement when we were in such tragic circumstances.

"I'm sorry for the loss of your uncle," he said before we began the formal part. "I hope you are alright."

"Thank you. Still a bit of a shock, but now all I can think about is what's happened to Dylan. It was so awful."

"You knew the dead man?"

"Yes. He was my friend Jasmine's ex-boyfriend."

"Jasmine is not here?" he asked, looking over my shoulder.

"No, she didn't want to spend any time in Dylan's company. I'm sure the walk around the island and the barbeque would've been fine where she could distance herself from him, but the trip over in the tiny boat seemed too much, I think."

"I see. There was bad blood between them?"

I hesitated, not wanting to throw suspicion onto Jasmine, but I quickly reasoned that the other guests will no doubt mention their attitude to one another, and it would be better for me not to lie. "Yes."

"And you? What were your feelings for the deceased?"

"I disliked him. He betrayed my friend with someone else." I nearly spilled my secret but caught myself before the words came out.

"Tell me, just before Dylan was killed did you notice anyone acting suspiciously?"

"You mean like preparing the murder or doing something out of character?" I thought back, it had been a relaxed atmosphere, everyone happy and enjoying themselves. No one had been behaving strangely.

"And after he was dead? Did you notice anything then?"

"No, I think everyone was in shock. Penny took control of the situation; she told Paulo to phone you and ordered the guys to cover up the body. No, no one acted oddly considering the circumstances." I hadn't really paid much attention to the others, and I didn't want to give Agente Garcia feelings or impressions when he wanted facts, so I didn't mention Luke's demeanour. It's not that he had behaved strangely as Agente Garcia had asked, his behaviour and reaction to the murder was the same as the rest of us, but that is what I found odd. Luke is full of bravado, always conscious that he is being seen and as a result never lets his guard down. He's one of those people who project themselves how they want to be seen, as though everything is an act, but when Dylan died, the mask slipped; I saw Luke's vulnerability. He stared at the body, unaware of himself. Maybe he was frightened that he himself will become a victim of whoever is killing us, I don't know, but I'm sure Dylan's death affected him more than he would care to admit. I even wondered if maybe the face I was seeing was of someone who was watching the result of their actions…

40

Terry

Well, that were a stroke of luck, weren't it? Dylan getting himself bumped off while I was locked up in a police cell; if you're wanting an alibi, you'd have to try hard to find a better one than that. Even these idiot police can't suspect me of this one.

Marjorie was very excited when she got back. Not in a good way excited you understand, more twittering and buzzing about, unable to sit still. "Oh Terry, t'was horrible," she said, describing Dylan's last moments. Poor bugger. I know the rat was trying to blackmail me, but even so, the way Marge tells it, no one deserves to die the way he did. "It was like there was a demon stomping around inside his head, giving him torment," that's what she said.

I knew something was up because that Inspector Moreno was in a right hurry getting me out of the police station. He just threw a couple of forms in front of me to sign and then shoved my bag of belongings into my arms and practically pushed me out the door. Then, he and the big fella hurried into the police car and away they went, sirens blaring. I took a slow walk back to the hotel, taking my time to enjoy breathing the free air. I was relaxing by the pool when they all got back. They trudged up the wooden steps into the pool area from the beach, a more depressed, sorrier looking bunch you never did see. "Ey'up," I said. "What's up with you lot? Did Paulo burn the sausages?" That Luke threw me a venomous glare and stormed past me towards the lobby. Jasmine, who had been asleep on a sun lounger since I got back to the hotel, woke up and propped herself on her elbows. Young Sally scurried over to her and sat down next to her, quickly whispering something in her ear. The girl's eyes were hidden behind dark shades, but I could see her mouth flatten from a smile into a thin line. That's when Marjorie caught sight of me. She bustled over, setting down her bag next to me before telling me all about it in her serious voice, which is a bit like her phone voice, only faster and quieter. She stumbled over her words, eager to tell all but getting ahead of herself now and then. "Marjorie!" I told her, "slow down, woman. It's like hearing the story backwards listening to you. Tell me from the beginning and tell me slow!" And to be fair to her she were much more coherent after that. Sometimes she just needs telling what's what, that's all. It's a good thing they let me out of jail otherwise there'd be no one to keep her right.

Once I was fully up to date with the latest occurrences, I looked around me. One of my fellow guests must have killed Dylan, but who? Jasmine was here all afternoon, I could vouch for that, but she had the strongest motive, didn't she? Then again, Dylan and Elle had a pretty fiery relationship from what I had seen. She had a right go at him in the airport, then didn't even speak to him on the coach ride here, and they were forever having cross words over a drink or by the pool. Maybe she'd had enough of him and decided to end their relationship forever, although murder seems a bit over the top.

I were turning these thoughts over in my head when Penny bloody Haylestone came over to us, her lapdog in tow. "Evening, Penny, Marley," I greeted them. "I hear you've had quite a day. Here, let's go to a table and have a drink, my back can't be doing with this lounger for too long."

I wanted to hear what they had to say about the murder business just in case Marge had forgotten a detail or two. "What'll you be having?" I asked.

"I'll have a gin, thank you, Terry," said Penny.

"Me too, thanks."

"A gin?" said Marjorie. "I don't think I could ever have a gin again for the rest of my life after today. How do you know it won't be poisoned like what happened to poor Dylan?"

"Poor Dylan," I said, unable to help myself. "You called him a horrible toad the other day, and now he's 'poor Dylan'?"

"Well, I mightn't have thought much of him, Terry, but that's no reason to speak ill of the dead, is it?"

Typical woman, they'll call you all the names under the sun but as soon as you're dead you turn into a bleeding saint. I bet I'm the bloody exception when my time comes.

"I don't think we need to worry about poison now, Marjorie," said Penny. "I think Dylan was deliberately targeted."

"Maybe, but I'll stick to lager all the same."

Paulo fetched us the drinks and Marley suggested we toast Dylan as a mark of respect, the foolish, sentimental girl that she is. I agreed. "To Dylan," I proclaimed out loud, raising my glass. "May he never blackmail me again," I said inwardly, allowing myself a little chuckle. Penny looked at me as our glasses touched, her eyes boring into me. Ha! Even *she* couldn't suspect me of killing Dylan, I thought to myself, I was miles away when it happened.

"Did you kill Dylan?" she asked, causing me to splutter my beer all over my belly.

"How the bloody hell could I have killed him? You're obsessed with me killing people. I was nowhere near him all day."

"Terry was in the police station, remember?" said Marge. "He couldn't possibly have killed Dylan."

"The killer didn't have to be there for their plan to work..."

"Well, it weren't bleeding me!"

"Alright, I meant no offence. Killing can be a terrible crime but it can also require guts to carry out. It takes nerve and, in this case, intelligence."

"Ha! You won't trick me that easy. You think you can butter up my ego and get me to confess. Nice try."

"I won't need the killer to confess: when I find whoever they are, I'll prove their guilt. Already a few interesting points have presented themselves, clues, if you will." I tried to coax these so-called clues out of Penny, but she were too wily, only hinting vaguely while batting away my questions. I even tried pretending that I didn't believe she knew anything, that she were full of hot air

- reverse psychology I think they call it, or is it sociology? Anyway, it didn't work, she sipped her gin and looked straight through me.

Marjorie were performing her own mental gymnastics, tugging on her fingers as though she were trying to count or work something out. "What I don't understand, is why kill Dylan like that. I mean, if it were someone he was blackmailing who did him in, why not arrange to meet him and pretend to pay him, then bosh him on the head like Russell with no one around to see?"

It were Marley who offered an explanation. "The problem with that theory is that the killer couldn't guarantee they wouldn't be seen, or that Dylan wouldn't give himself some kind of insurance."

"Insurance? How do you mean?"

"If Dylan was chancing his arm and claiming he knew who the murderer was but really didn't have a clue, then the murderer would be revealing their identity by offering to meet to pay the blackmail money. Dylan could then take precautions, like leave a written note saying who he was going to meet to stop the killer from harming him. By poisoning Dylan the way the murderer did, it helped conceal their identity."

"But if the killer agreed to meet Dylan to pay the money, they could do so without giving their name. They could slip a note under his door with a time and place to meet written on it."

"You're right, Marjorie, they could, but what if they turned up to meet Dylan and he took a photo of them and emailed it to himself as insurance before they could do anything. There are loads of ways Dylan could cover himself; the killer knew this and took no chances."

41

Sanjay

The police arrived on the island quicker than most of us expected. I suppose having one murder to contend with is a bit of a challenge for the local law enforcement, but two applies real pressure to the detective in charge. I can imagine the local governmental representative wanting a more experienced investigator from Madrid to take charge of the case, I know I would.

Inspector Moreno came ashore full of his own importance. He chewed his gum and waved his arms around, gesticulating in Spanish to his handsome subordinate. When he pulled the tarpaulin sheet from Dylan's body, I could feel a collective shudder from the group at the wanton inconsideration. He then spoke to each of us, though his interrogation techniques have not improved since Russell's murder. He asked us to recall the events leading up to Dylan's death, from arriving on the island to the final choking gasp. He sought no motive, nor did he ask for our impressions of others, only the chronological facts as we saw them. He spoke to Luke and me simultaneously, though I did most of the talking.

Luke seemed deeply affected by the horrific events, more than I know he would admit to. He stared at the sand or out to sea. On the few occasions he did mutter the odd word he made no eye contact, his gaze shifting to the dead body then snapping away, his body turning with it.

The boat ride back was undertaken in silence, only the hum of the engine and skimming water could be heard. We came back with Paulo, one less than when we set off. As we climbed the cliff steps leading to the hotel, Luke mumbled something about a shower and made a beeline for the lift. Elle, shaking, was helped along by Sally who asked if she could do anything. The bereft girl shook her head and said she wanted to lie down, leaving Sally by the pool before following in Luke's footsteps. Sally then made her way to Jasmine who was watching the solemn scene from a sun lounger, propped on her elbows, the fading sunlight glistening on her toned, oil-lathered body.

At a loss for what to do I sat on a lounger near the girls and put my earphones in. I didn't turn my podcast on, as if I had done, I wouldn't have been able to hear what they were saying.

"Are you okay? You haven't said anything."

"I'm in shock! You've just told me my ex-boyfriend was murdered!"

"Oh, Jasmine, I'm sorry!"

"What are you sorry for? I'm ecstatic. Shocked, but ecstatic."

"You're what?"

"I hated him. I'm glad he's dead, I can't believe it. This is fantastic."

"Fantastic? Have you lost your mind? A man has been murdered and you're happy about it. That's really sick, Jasmine."

"Sick? He was the one who was sick."

"How do you mean?"

Jasmine hesitated. I was wearing my shades and had been extremely careful not to move to avoid drawing attention to myself, but I got the feeling she was looking at me and was worried that I might be listening. I felt myself getting annoyed that she could think so little of me. When she did continue to speak, her voice was lower and I had to strain to hear what she said.

"Nothing…I don't mean anything. But if you knew what he put me through you'd be glad he was dead, too, at least you would if you were truly my friend."

"I am your friend, so why don't you tell me what you mean? I know your break up hurt you, but -"

"What? You think I'm angry because of a stupid break up?"

"Well…I mean -"

"You don't understand anything, do you? The break up was a good thing, it was what came after…" Jasmine's voice faded, lost in her memories.

"Oh Jas, I don't know why you hate him so much and if you don't want to tell me, that's fine, but you can't let it be known that you're happy he's dead."

"Why not?"

"Because that bumbling little policeman will think you killed him and then he'll arrest you!"

"But I couldn't have killed him, I've been here all afternoon."

"I haven't told you how he died…" Sally leaned her head closer to her friend's and whispered so low I couldn't hear. I was glad. I didn't want her words forming that image in my head again, the red face looking like it was about to explode; it was all too much.

Sally's description must have been vivid though, for Jasmine, who a few minutes ago had been exuberant at Dylan's death, clutched her own throat and spoke the words, "That's horrible."

"It was," agreed Sally. "It was awful."

"And Penny thinks the gin was poisoned?"

"Yes, which means your innocence can't be presumed. Fortunately, it seems whoever killed Dylan also killed Russell and you have no motive for that, otherwise you'd be top of the list of suspects.

"Yeah…"

42

Marley

I was quite pleased with the theories I presented to Marjorie. Penny listened to them but gave no opinion, which I hoped meant that she agreed with my hypotheses. Of course, Dylan's murder has complicated things. Up to now, we have been trying to catch Russell's killer by trying to determine which of the guests had a motive for his murder. Now, we must continue our investigation into Russell's death, but also try to work out when the murderer poisoned the gin bottle, and if they switched bottles or poisoned the one Paulo brought. When did the killer decide to kill Dylan? Did something occur which forced the killer's hand? Was Dylan really on to them or had his bluff gone terribly wrong? Then there was the other possibility, which, if true, would confuse matters even further; what if there were two killers and the two crimes were separate? I sat mulling these things over in my mind as Terry and Marjorie spoke to Penny about life back in England.

"My husband and I used to go to Devon for a few weeks every summer," said Penny, as I zoned back in.

"I'd love to go to Devon," cooed Marjorie. "And I hear Cornwall is nice. They're beside each other, aren't they?"

"You should go, take a few weeks to explore England a bit, it really is beautiful."

"It's a long way though, isn't it. I couldn't leave my Sarah for that long."

Terry shook his head. "Too bloody right, it would take us ten or eleven hours to drive all the way down there, you could fly to Australia in that time."

"Well, not quite."

"You ever been down that way, Marley?" asked Terry.

"I went to an art exhibition in Exeter once, but it was only a flying visit. One night in the Travelodge then back the following day. The cathedral was worth a visit, though," I said.

"I forgot you said you liked art. Have you been to the gallery here? I noticed there's a small one in the town," Marjorie informed me.

I made a mental note to check it out, this writing thing is great and I'm enjoying it more than I thought I would, (the excitement of the murder probably helps), but I regret not bringing a few pencils and paper to sketch with; my fingers are yearning to stroke and not tap. Maybe a visit to the gallery will gratify my artistic cravings for a while. I'll go when I get a chance, or when I need a break from murder-solving (it can get a bit tiring on the brain).

The couple left us to get changed and ready for dinner. I could hear Terry's voice chatter, until the lift doors closed on the garrulous man.

"Penny, I've been thinking," I said, when we were alone. "What if there are two killers and the murders aren't connected?"

"That crossed my mind too, dear, but at the minute I don't think it's likely."

"Why?"

"Because both crimes were clever. Russell was murdered in a locked room and we still don't know how. Dylan was murdered and although we know the EpiPen contained poison and the gin bottle contained something to trigger his allergy, or at least we will know soon when the lab results come back, we have no clue who swapped the bottles or poisoned the pen. Although..." Penny raised her head as though in thought. Her fingers caressed the stem of her glass, but her drink was forgotten now.

"What? Have have you thought of something?"

"Only that the EpiPen itself might be a clue."

"You mean we might get fingerprints from it? Maybe there are fingerprints on the gin bottle, too."

"No, I'd be surprised to find the killer's prints on anything. No, what I mean is, whoever replaced the adrenaline in the EpiPen must have known how to do it."

"So, we're looking for a doctor, or a nurse?"

"No, dear, anyone could use a web browser to work out how to do it, therefore the answer we're looking for may be on someone's internet search history."

"But how will we find that out? We can't just ask people to show us their internet history."

"We won't need to, dear; I may be retired but I still have friends who owe me favours. All I'll need is a list of names to give to one of my contacts and they'll do the rest."

"Okay, so what now?"

"We see Paulo at reception. I know everyone's surname except for Jasmine, Elle and Dylan."

"Why Dylan? Surely, he's the last person we need to check up on."

"Because Elle had access to Dylan's phone. If she's our killer, and if she's smart, she'll have used his phone to do the search. Oh, and another thing, Elle told us Dylan's phone was in her handbag, but I looked in it when we got back on the boat and there was no phone there."

"Meaning what?"

"Probably nothing, she might have been mistaken, the shock of seeing her boyfriend die will have befuddled her memory. The phone must be in their hotel room."

We found Paulo in the lounge bar serving Luke what looked like a large whisky. With one wink from Penny, Paulo politely excused himself and strode over to us. "Senora Haylestone, you need me?"

The lobby was deserted, most of the guests I assumed getting their glad rags on for dinner. I looked at a blue velvet armchair with envy; despite, or perhaps because of the day's excitement, I felt tired, and wished I could sit and put my feet up for an hour. No such luck.

"Paulo, I need a list of the guests' full names," commanded Penny.

"Si, Senora Haylestone."

Paulo did not question the order or show any curiosity and instead tapped at his keyboard, causing the printer to stutter into life within a few seconds. He handed Penny the list which I peered at over her shoulder.

West Wing

Habitación de hotel 101 – Penelope Haylestone
Habitación de hotel 102 – Sally Oldfield
Habitación de hotel 102 – Jasmine Colwell
Habitación de hotel 103 – Luke Rowlands
Habitación de hotel 103 – Sanjay Pandit
Habitación de hotel 104 – Marley Williams
Habitación de hotel 105 – Agathe Williams
Habitación de hotel 106 – Terence Smith
Habitación de hotel 106 – Marjorie Smith
Habitación de hotel 107 – Dylan Forester
Habitación de hotel 107 – Elle Caplan

Penny thanked him, took her phone from her purse and scanned the document. "Right, I'll email this off to my confederate and give him a ring."

"That's strange," I said.

"What is?" asked Penny, catching the confusion in my voice.

"Dylan's surname. If you'd have asked me what it was I couldn't have told you, yet now that I see it, it doesn't look right."

"Maybe your mind doesn't think his surname suits him, like a large man called Little."

"No, it's more than that, I'm sure I've heard Dylan's surname mentioned, and it wasn't Forester."

43

Sally

When we returned to the hotel, Jasmine was lying by the pool. Most of the guests headed to their rooms or to the bar to get a drink so we were quite alone. I began telling her about Dylan's death and was shocked by her reaction, her glee. I was so shocked, in fact, that I didn't notice that Sanjay had taken up residence on a sun lounger behind me until Jasmine and I had already spoken of murder, alibis, and something even more sinister, the details of which were still a mystery to me. Jasmine had hinted at a side of Dylan's character that was somehow darker than that which I already knew, yet she would elaborate no further.

Sanjay, I noticed, when I half turned around to look, had his earphones in and sunglasses on, but there was something about the unnatural rigidity of his body which gave me the impression that he was perhaps not listening to music but was instead listening to our conversation; being a journalist, I wouldn't have put it past him. It was just a feeling, like when you're lying in bed next to someone and you know they are awake. I may be overthinking it, and I feel bad for judging him, but at the same time I trust my instincts, so I lowered my voice once aware of his presence. I think Jasmine, recovering from the shock of the news, became uncomfortable by Sanjay being so close too, because when we were talking about her motive (or lack of in Russell's case), she clammed up and changed the subject. She looked ashen pale, and I wondered if the brief euphoria she felt at the demise of her hated ex-lover had now evaporated, leaving a residue of shame and worry.

I, too, felt burdened by emotion. I had carried my secret around for so long, but now Dylan's death meant the end of something, and when something ends, something new takes its place. I wondered that if I came clean to Jasmine maybe our friendship could heal, and we could become as close to one another as we once were. I made up my mind.

"Let's go to our room," I said.

"Good idea, I need to get changed for tonight."

We saw no one on the way and we didn't speak until I gently closed the door behind us. The room was grey, the setting sun's rays reaching the window onto the balcony and no further. I turned on my bedside lamp, which cast a cold, white light into the air. "Jasmine, please sit, there's something I want to tell you."

"Is it about Dylan?" she asked, sitting on the edge of her bed, her hands resting on her knees.

"Yes."

"Something you didn't want to tell me by the pool. What could be more horrible than that?"

"It's not about Dylan's death, it's…" My words stuck in my throat. "Jasmine, it was me who told you about Dylan. About Dylan and Elle, I mean."

"What? I don't understand. Someone texted me…"

"Yes. Me. I texted you."

"Why? Why didn't you tell me in person?"

I had imagined this moment many times, and on each occasion, I had envisaged Jasmine's face contorting with anger, reddening with rage, but as I looked down upon her, I could see that all my words had wrought was confusion.

"I didn't tell you because I was afraid."

"Afraid of what?"

"Of how you would react. I thought you would blame me, or that you wouldn't believe me, I thought…I…" Sobs stymied my words. Jasmine rose and put her arms around me.

"Are you mad? You thought that I would blame you? Oh Sal."

Two years' worth of worry melted and rolled down my cheeks onto the shoulder of my friend. "You're not mad?" I whimpered.

"No, of course not. Why would I be mad? If it wasn't for you, I might still be with that horrible creep. But wait a minute, how did you find out about Dylan and Elle?"

"I overheard him on the phone one day when the three of us went out for a drink. Dylan went outside for a cigarette, and I walked past the door on the way to the toilet. I could hear him talking to someone, he called her Elle and said some other stuff that I won't repeat. I couldn't believe my ears; in fact, I did actually doubt if I'd heard correctly. I didn't want to tell you in case you thought I was jealous of your relationship or something, and all I could think about was if I *had* misheard, you'd never speak to me again, so I decided to tell you anonymously. I bought a cheap phone in the market and texted you from that. I figured if I had got the wrong end of the stick, you'd be angry but at no one in particular, and if I was right, then you'd dump him and be better off for it."

"Oh Sal, of course I would've believed you. All this time I've been wondering who could've sent me that text and it was you all along. You should've told me this sooner."

"I wanted to, but you hated Dylan so much I didn't want you to associate me with that hatred. I didn't want to be a reminder of what he'd done."

"That could never happen. I don't hate Dylan for his affair, I hate him for something else."

"The thing you hinted at by the pool? What is it?"

Jasmine looked at me, deciding what to say. We were still embracing, and I could feel her body tense.

"Okay, I'll tell you," she said, finally making a decision. "Dylan was blackmailing me."

44

Terry

My head was hurting by the time we left Penny and Marley at the bar. The two of them had filled it with theories to the point of bursting, and Marjorie weren't much better. "What if this is what happened, what if so-and-so did that, what if, blah, blah, blah." I want a sore head from too much beer, not too much nattering.

Anyways, the more I think about it, the more I think Marjorie could be the killer. I mean, let's stop and think about it for a second. Who had the best reason to kill Russell? That's right, me. And who had the best reason to kill that blackmailing little toad, Dylan? Me again (although young Jasmine might argue that one). And who worships the ground I walk on and would do anything for me, and took a vow on our wedding day to cherish and look after me or something like that? See, Marge! Now, I know what you're thinking, Marjorie doesn't know Dylan were blackmailing me and you're right, but are you? Didn't I say women have intuition and that sort of thing? And don't they say that the female species is more deadly than the male? I think I remember David Attenborough saying on one of his programmes that the women black widow spiders eat the men ones after the old rumpy pumpy. That's proof enough in itself, is it not? Plus, she's always saying she wants a bit more excitement in her life, maybe she's decided to take matters into her own hands.

Then again, I hope it ain't Marge, I've got used to having her around. I met my first wife in the eighties on a picket line. I can't remember why we were on strike, but she got a real taste for it; as soon as we were married, she refused to do the cooking, the cleaning, the washing up, the lot. And the cheeky mare said she refused to do it because I never did anything around the house. How does that work? Two wrongs don't make a right, I said.

Wife number two weren't much better, I was glad to see the back of her, and that was before we split up; she wasn't much of a looker - she was a great cook, though.

Yeah, I could do worse than Marge. She's enjoying herself a nice lie down now; she deserves it, doesn't she. I mean, if she isn't on a killing spree, she's been through the ringer a bit, hasn't she?

After having a drink with the dynamic duo downstairs, we had a quick one here on the balcony, and Marjorie told me all about it properly. She started off talking about the weather, how sunny it was and how lovely to feel the sea breeze on her face as the boat made its way to the stork's island. "Alright Marge," I told her. "Don't rub it in, I was languishing in a dirty, dank prison cell while you were having such a wonderful time in case you've forgotten." Honestly, some people, eh?

Anyways, the way Marge tells it they all got there, and the fellas and younger ones were keen to explore, but she decided to stay with Agathe, keep her company you see. So as Paulo started with the barbeque, Marge helped him with firewood and the like, and chatted to Agathe. You know how women of a certain age can talk, well, it were like that by the sounds of it. "What did you talk about?" I asked.

"Well, I was curious about young Marley's love life," Marjorie said.

"Why would you be wondering about that?" I asked, dumbfounded by the way my wife's brain works sometimes. "If you want to know about Marley's love life, why don't you ask bloody Marley?"

"Because, Terence, I wouldn't want to embarrass the poor girl, would I? She's a lovely lass, and I just wanted to know if there was someone who cares for her, that's all."

"And is there?"

"Not that Agathe knows of. Flaky is how she described her, gets bored easily apparently, never sees anyone for too long before she drops him like a stone. She's young though, isn't she, you have no patience when you're that age. Painting and photographs and the like are the only thing she sticks at according to Agathe. At least there's something she's passionate about, I said. I remember wanting to dance when I was a young girl, younger than Marley mind, and I gave it up on a whim just because I had a friend called Judy who said -"

"Bloody hell, Marge, are we going to get to this murder or what?"

"There's no need to be rude, Terry! Where was I? Oh yes, I was chatting with Agathe. Did you know she came here with her husband every summer for the past six years. I said no wonder she just wanted to stay by the barbeque with Paulo, she must know the island like the back of her hand. Oh no, she said, this was her first time on the stork's island. How lovely for her, and to come all that way in the boat and with those sticks and that chair too, oh I do admire her."

"Why did she want to go now and never before?" I asked, taking a sip of the brandy that I'd bought in the airport.

"I don't know. Maybe her husband never liked boats. Or maybe she wanted to go because Marley was going. I never asked why, I was too busy having a nice time and the others started coming back then."

"And then the murder happened?"

"Yes, that's right. Terrible it was, Terry."

Marjorie told me the gory details, the contorted face, the popping veins, the panic in Dylan's eyes. She said it all happened so fast and was so awful that the aftermath was a bit of a blur. She took young Elle away from the body and tried to comfort her but can't recall what she said. Then the police came and took statements and all that rigmarole and still everyone stood around in shock, unsure what to do.

She did say one interesting thing though, she said Luke was acting a bit queer.

45

Sanjay

Sally and Jasmine began whispering to each other like a pair of schoolgirls at their lockers when a cute boy walks past. In this case (and for the first time ever) I was the heartthrob. I had been lying on the lounger when out of the corner of my eye I saw Sally twist her body and glance at me over her shoulder. Rumbled.

They quickly gathered their belongings and scuttled off in the direction of the lobby. From the little that I had heard, I formed the opinion that Jasmine had been delighted that her ex-lover was dead but not so thrilled when it was pointed out to her that she would still be a suspect despite having never stepped foot anywhere near where Dylan had died.

My prey now having ran free of my grasp, I decided to go to the hotel room. Luke would no doubt be wondering where I was, although he hadn't bothered to wait for me when we got back. When we got out of the boat, I'd helped Paulo lift some rubbish bags ashore and when I looked up, I could see Luke already climbing the wooden steps on the cliff face.

To my surprise I found the hotel room deserted, the only sign of anyone having been in since we'd left was the freshly made bed and clean towels, courtesy of housekeeping. I decided to quickly wash and get changed, as keeping those clothes on me any longer felt repulsive. It wasn't only that it had been a hot day and that I had worked up a sweat climbing to the lighthouse, it was the proximity to death. I felt as though death clung to me, sticking to my shirt. I knew that when I ripped it off, I was trying to tear myself away from the horror of the day and I knew how idiotic and absurd this might be, but it felt all too real. I set the shower to the coldest setting, but even then, the water felt warm against my skin. I dried myself and tied the towel around my waist, then opened the wardrobe and slid the hangers across the rail looking for my favourite silk shirt, but closed the doors empty-handed. Next, I rummaged through my suitcase but again found no shirt. I wondered if it had been packed in Luke's suitcase by accident. I unzipped the large wheely case which was tucked behind the chair in the corner of the room and took out a beach towel that was neatly folded on top, then I stopped, staring at something else that was also inside. I took a step back, my eyes still wide at what I was looking at. Recovering, I dressed in the first thing to hand and called Luke's mobile, but it rang out. Confused as to where he could be, I decided to check the rest of the hotel.

I hate it when Luke disappears or doesn't answer his phone, it sets my insecurities on edge, and makes my nerves bristle. If I call him and he doesn't answer, he'll call back an hour or two later and say he was in a meeting or ask me why I'm calling him when he's at work, even if it's way past the normal five-p.m. finish time. He makes me feel unreasonable when he reminds me that solicitors don't leave work when the bell rings like journalists working for the Streatham Gazette do. I know he's not intentionally trivialising my job, but he can be quite cutting, and his tone is defensive when he calls, as if I am accusing him of something, which, I don't know, maybe I am.

The gym was still closed, the police seeming to be in no hurry to reopen it following Russell's murder. As I wandered alone, I regretfully acknowledged that this would be the perfect time for a crafty cigarette, but I was focused on finding Luke. My nervous imaginings had evolved into wilder, more frightening notions when I remembered that there was a lunatic close by who had already killed two people.

My fears were unfounded however, and I shook my head at my colourful imagination when I found him sitting alone in the lounge bar, a large whisky in front of him.

"Hey, I tried phoning you," I said.

Luke raised his gaze from the amber liquid. "Did you? My phone must've died."

"Really?" I said, wondering if my tone carried the doubt that I intended it to. I pulled a chair out from the table and sat down opposite him.

"Why are you looking at me like that?" he asked, his voice thick with alcohol.

"Like what?"

"Like you're angry."

"I'm not angry," I lied. "I'm confused."

"Oh, really? Tell me, Sanjay, what are you confused about? What is it that you're worried about? Why were you trying to phone me? What is it you need from me now, because that's it, isn't it? That's what it all boils down to in this relationship, your neediness, and how much you need me?"

"What I *need*, Luke, is for you to explain what I just found hidden in your suitcase."

46

Marley

Penny had gone to the car park to call her contact at the security services, giving me ten minutes alone to update this journal When we parted in the lobby, I had gone to the lounge bar, but I'd only taken a few steps when my attention was drawn to a table by the window where Sanjay and Luke appeared to be arguing. Sanjay looked the angrier of the two, but Luke was the louder, and definitely more drunk. I backtracked before they saw me; I had no wish to interrupt their domestic, and wanted quiet to concentrate on my journal and ensure the details I recorded were faithfully accurate and in line with my memory. I skipped back through the lobby, past Paulo and out to the poolside bar, which entertained a few of the East Wing guests whom I barely recognised.

"Where to now?" I asked Penny when she reappeared.

"You know, I think we should see Elle, check how she is, and look at Dylan's phone."

We left the pool bar and made our way upstairs. I gave a sympathetic tap to the door of room 107 and we waited a few moments. Elle opened the door and stood to one side to allow us entry. I could tell she'd been crying by the pink, puffy skin around her eyes, but when she spoke, she did so with perfect composure. "Take a seat, please."

"Thank you," replied Penny. "How are you, my dear, you must feel exhausted?"

"Yes, I suppose I am." She slumped onto the edge of the bed, Penny and I having taken the two chairs.

"Tell me, dear, now that you're over the initial shock, did Dylan say anything to you that could hint at the identity of his killer?"

"What do you mean?"

"Well, the other day when we spoke, Dylan was keeping his cards close to his chest, he told us that he saw Russell arguing with someone on the morning he was killed, but he wouldn't tell us who. I thought perhaps he may have told you?"

"No, he didn't, honestly. For all I know he may have been lying about the whole thing."

"Did he lie often?"

"No, not needlessly, but if he didn't like someone, he would like to toy with them, to make their life difficult, and I don't think he liked anyone here at the hotel."

"Really? Why?"

"He thought everyone hated him. On the first night here, his ex, Jasmine, had told everyone how horrible he was, she was poisoning everyone against him. Dylan wasn't perfect, but you shouldn't judge someone without getting to know them first, right?"

"Absolutely, dear, I couldn't agree more. And you're right, maybe he didn't witness an argument that morning. Then again, he did tell people he knew who killed Russell, it seems like he wanted to benefit in some way, almost like he wanted to blackmail someone…" Elle's fingertips brushed a strand of hair behind her ear, and she coughed as though something was lodged in her throat.

"I don't know anything about blackmail," she eventually managed to blurt out.

"Well, if you did, I don't think you could get into any trouble now that he's dead."

"I said I didn't. Really, I don't know any more than you." Penny tilted her head, considering the girl, seemingly feeling no compulsion to speak.

"I don't believe you," I said, though I was thinking out loud.

"I'm sorry?"

My big mouth putting me in this position, I had to follow through with my thoughts. "I said I don't believe you, but I'm not talking about whether you know anything about Russell's killer, I'm talking about blackmail. I'm wondering whether you know about Dylan blackmailing someone else, at some other time."

"You know, Marley," interjected Penny, her eyes still assessing Elle, "I was just thinking the same thing. You see, dear, what I don't understand is why would a bright, beautiful girl like you stay with a man who, quite frankly, was a nasty, narcissistic psychopath? Let me tell you what I think. I think that Dylan had some sort of hold on you, something which was never explicitly spoken about but which you were both aware of. It was a ghost haunting your relationship and you were afraid of it. You knew that if you broke up with him, he could wreak a terrible revenge, but he was clever enough not to make a direct or obvious threat so you could go on pretending to yourself that you were in a relationship with him because you loved him. You might even have kidded yourself that he was a good person. You are a very beautiful girl, and Jasmine is also stunning, but you could give Dylan something she couldn't: money."

"I'm not rich, Penny!"

"You're not poor. Those are real diamonds in that bracelet you're wearing, and those designer handbags you own weren't bought here in the local market."

"Okay, so my dad runs a successful business, so what?"

"So, I think Dylan's ambition grew, as did his thirst for money. He saw you as a golden ticket, your beauty was an added bonus. Tell me, what was the hold he had over you?"

"I'm not talking about this anymore. You're insane." I thought the poor girl was going to demand that we leave but Penny continued to speak, cutting her off, though her voice was more conciliatory. Perhaps Penny also felt near the edge.

"I'm sorry, dear, me and my mad ideas. Tell me, satisfy my curiosity, how did you and Dylan meet?"

"At a music festival, last summer. My phone fell out of my pocket and Dylan saw. He picked it up and ran after me, we got talking…"

"I see. How did he get that scar on his leg?"

"He was in Afghanistan with the army. A vehicle he was travelling in hit a mine, Dylan was wounded in the leg. He was medically discharged."

"I see. I bet his medals were hung on his wall, taking pride of place."

"No, he said his time out there was traumatic. He didn't like talking about it."

"Still, I bet his parents were proud?"

"They died when he was a teenager, that's why he joined the army, he needed somewhere to go. A new beginning."

"Hmm, not an easy life."

"No, it wasn't, and now this. Murdered."

"Exactly, which is why we need your help to catch his killer. Think hard, did Dylan say anything that might be a clue?"

"I told you; I don't know anything!"

"I believe you." Penny stood and took Elle's hands in her own. "My dear, do you mind if we search this room?"

"Why? What for?"

"Because if Dylan did know who killed Russell, and he wanted to blackmail them, he may have written it down in case he was harmed so that his killer could be brought to justice. He was playing a very dangerous game. He would most likely make a note on his phone. You said it was in your handbag, dear, but I couldn't find it there so it must be here." Elle consented, but our search threw up no hidden note, and no phone.

"It was worth a shot," said Penny when we'd finished. "Sorry for the inconvenience."

Elle looked at Dylan's belongings that we'd searched and threw up her hands. "What am I going to do with all this? Take it back with me? It would feel wrong to throw it all away."

"Leave that to me, dear, I'll get Paulo to sort it out, you won't have to worry about a thing. I'll just need Dylan's surname in case there are any forms to fill out, you know how it is."

"His surname? Freeman. Dylan Freeman."

47

Sally

After Jasmine told me about how Dylan was blackmailing her, we held our embrace for so long I began to wonder if she had fallen asleep on my shoulder. I didn't care if she had, I felt close to my friend again. Then she whispered in my ear, asking me if I was hungry. I hadn't eaten since the ill-fated barbeque and was now faintly aware of a slight pang in my stomach.

We decided to go into town; we wanted to enjoy ourselves, to let our hair down and not have to worry about other guests seeing us and perhaps thinking we were celebrating a successfully executed murder.

Jasmine wore an emerald-green knee-length dress. She looked absolutely gorgeous. I played it safe with a little black dress, but she applied my makeup and I looked and felt like a different person when we left our room. I noticed Paulo do a double take as we passed reception, and to my surprise (and delight) it wasn't Jasmine he was looking at.

We took a taxi to town, the ten-minute walk along the dark road being incompatible with my three-inch high heels. The cab dropped us off at an Italian restaurant that Penny had recommended a few days ago, although now, after everything that had happened, it seemed like months ago.

The waiter seated us at the window and brought us menus and a carafe of water. The restaurant was softly lit with candles in old wine bottles on every table. Despite the intimate setting, the atmosphere was verging on boisterous. Nearly every table was occupied, and chatter and good-natured shouts drowned out the music. I looked around to see grinning faces, red either through too much sun or too much laughter, I didn't care which; it was good to get away from the hotel, away from death, drama, and everything in between.

As Jasmine pored over her menu, I watched the throngs of people walk along the street, two streams intertwining as groups glided in opposite directions, families and friends looking for somewhere to eat, drink, or rest their weary legs after a day of playing with their inexhaustible children on the beach. A man carried his little boy on his shoulders, the boy had a plastic bucket in one hand and a spade in the other. He saw me looking at him and smiled, waving the spade excitedly. I smiled back.

"I'm in the mood for champagne," I said to Jasmine.

"Champagne? Sure, why not, what are we celebrating though?"

"Us."

"Cool. For a second, I thought you were going to say Dylan being dead."

"That, too. After what he did to you, I have no qualms about raising a toast to that scumbag no longer being around."

"Sally, that's so unlike you," Jasmine replied. I could see genuine surprise on her face but also the hint of a smile.

I shrugged. "It's how I feel," I said with candour.

The waiter took our order and brought the champagne with gratifying promptitude.

"Cheers!" I said, raising my glass high.

"Do you think whoever killed Dylan also killed Russell?" Jasmine asked after taking a sip.

"I haven't really thought about. If it is one person, they've taken my uncle from me but have given you your life back, what a bittersweet, double-edged sword that is."

"To be honest, I thought Terry had killed Russell, but I can't see why he would kill Dylan."

"Hmm, I'm not convinced Terry would be smart enough to pull off these murders, no offence to him. I also don't think Inspector Moreno is smart enough to catch the killer."

"Penny seems pretty determined. She's got a real bee in her bonnet."

"Yes, I think she's quite extraordinary. Uncle Russell certainly seemed to think so. He told me being friends with her is like having a guardian angel by your side."

"Didn't work out that way for him. Oh, sorry, I didn't mean…"

"No, you're right. But she couldn't have known someone was going to kill him."

"Maybe that's why she's so hellbent on finding his murderer, because she feels she let him down, that she should've prevented his death."

"Maybe…"

The waiter brought our starter. We shared a plate of bruschetta, covered in juicy tomatoes and thick mozzarella drizzled in olive oil and lemon juice. The table next to us erupted into a chorus of *'Happy Birthday'* as a waitress brought out a large tiramisu with a few candles sticking out of it. Most of the other patrons joined in the singing but I had a mouthful of bruschetta that was so delicious I wasn't going to rush eating it, so as recompense I joined in the applause when the birthday girl blew out the flames.

"Have you thought about what you want to do with the hotel?" Jasmine asked when our empty plates were taken away.

"I haven't made any firm decisions. I want to keep it, it would feel wrong to sell it, as if to do so would be a betrayal to Russell. But I also want to pursue my career. I can only live here and write simultaneously if the hotel is making enough money to support me, and I would need someone to run it who knows what they're doing. Russell was very hands on, he built the place and made it how he wanted, but I don't have a clue about running a hotel."

"You have Paulo, he knows what he's doing."

"That's true, he's very capable."

"And I bet you'd like him to be more hands on…" Jasmine's eyes sparkled, and I could feel the heat in my cheeks as I blushed.

"Meaning what, exactly?" I asked, feigning ignorance.

"I think you know. It's obvious he likes you, why don't you ask him out on a date?"

"Call me old-fashioned, but if he wants to go on a date, he can ask me."

"Fine, but sometimes you have to grab life by the horns. You're both shy, so one of you must make the first move."

"I'm not shy, I'm introverted."

"What's the difference?" she asked, trying to hide a smile behind her champagne flute.

"Nothing! Introverted just makes me sound smarter." She set her glass on the table and laughed. "Anyway," I continued. "I can't make any major decisions about the hotel until I see the books, the financial reports, and all that sort of thing."

The main course was even more delicious than the starter. We both had squid-ink linguine with razor clams and shrimp, washed down with another bottle of bubbly. Jasmine suggested we go to a bar and have a few cocktails. I agreed but made a solemn vow to myself that when we got home, I wouldn't touch alcohol for a month.

The night was warm, the air lazy. No breeze stirred as we left the restaurant for the short walk to the bar Jasmine had in mind. We took a few short steps when I saw Penny, sitting on a bench licking an ice cream, staring into the abyss.

"Hi, Penny," I said, recalling her to the present.

"Oh, hello girls, sorry, I was miles away. You both look stunning, breathtaking in fact."

"Thank you. Are you just out for a nighttime stroll?"

"Yes, I thought I would get some fresh air and hopefully some fresh ideas. I had a drink with Marley and Agathe but declined their offer to join them for dinner. I'm afraid I've been hogging Marley a bit; she should spend some time alone with her mother."

"Fresh ideas? About the murders?" Jasmine asked.

"Yes. It's a complicated business, the pieces aren't quite falling into place. But don't worry, I'll unravel the mystery, have no fear. Where are you two off to? Somewhere nice?"

"Just a bar for some cocktails. Would you like to join us?"

"No, I couldn't possibly with you two looking like that, I look like the ugly aunt in comparison. Besides, I've still got my thinking to do…" This was of course, rubbish. Penny was dressed in a figure-hugging, long-sleeved flowery dress, her beautiful pearls being displayed around her neck and on her ears.

"Very well, we shall see you tomorrow."

"Yes, but not at breakfast I shouldn't think." She took a box of paracetamol from her handbag and handed them to me. "Take one now and the hangover won't be so bad. Goodnight, girls."

"Goodnight," we replied in unison.

"Oh, Jasmine, just one more thing…" We stopped and turned around having taken a few steps.

"What was Dylan's surname?"

"His surname? It was Findlay. Dylan Findlay. Why?"

"No reason, dear. Enjoy your night."

48

Terry

I was out like a light last night. I suppose all the excitement must've taken it out of me, what with going to prison, then being released, then the other murder and that. I slept like a log, only waking when Marjorie threw open the curtains this morning, letting the light pour in. Near gave me a heart attack she did, going from pitch black to blazing sunshine, it's like lying on a sunbed then being tipped into a freezing pool. It ain't right.

Tell you what though, those blackout curtains are just the ticket, I said to Marjorie, I said, "Marge, when we get home, get yourself down to Dunelm and get us some of those special curtains, I haven't slept so well since Thatcher resigned."

Marge, on the other hand, she wasn't so lucky. Says Sally and Jasmine woke her up around two a.m. singing and laughing as they came down the corridor, not that she minded she says, she was happy they were enjoying themselves, especially young Sally, what with losing her uncle in such an awful way.

The deep sleep had made me ravenous, so as soon as I was ready, we went down to the restaurant.

Sausage, bacon, eggs, (fried, of course) grilled tomato, mushrooms (sauteed, whatever that is), potato rosti (Spanish hash brown by the looks of it), beans, and toast, (proper bread, too, none of that sourdough rubbish you see everywhere these days), all washed down with a big mug of coffee. Can't beat it. Although, the sausages were smaller than my pinkie, which is fine so long as you load up on them; can't just be having three like you normally would. And the bacon is the streaky type, not back bacon, but it's tasty all the same, so I can't complain. Oh yes, always have a good breakfast to fuel you through the day, that's my motto.

Marjorie had fruit and yoghurt and granola all mixed together.

Granola?

Melon?

Papaya?

I've never seen her eat anything like that at home, ain't it funny what going on holiday can do to some people? Not me though, a leopard can't change its spots, as they say, Terence Smith knows what he likes and what he don't, and that's that!

Despite the good sleep last night, I felt a bit drowsy and tired after breakfast, though I'm not sure why, I guess your body just relaxes more on holiday. That, and the fact that I no longer had to worry about giving that blackmailing toad Dylan the twenty grand he was demanding.

We decided a bit of sunbathing was the order of the day, so we went out to the pool. On the way, we passed Inspector Moreno and his tall sidekick talking to Paulo and Elle at reception. I had to slow down; Marjorie's not as tall as me, she can't walk as fast.

"Do you have your boyfriend's phone? It was not on his body."

"No, it's gone missing. He put it in my handbag along with his EpiPen when we were waiting by the pool yesterday morning. I haven't seen it since, I've no idea where it is."

"You have no objection to us searching your room, senora?"

"I have no objection, but I doubt you'll find it or anything else for that matter."

"Why are you so sure?"

"Because Penny searched the room for clues last night, and she left empty-handed." I could see a vein in the police inspector's neck bulge as I walked past, and his ears redden. We'd just got past the lift when I heard the explosion coming from the little man. He were still screaming when I lay down and closed my eyes.

I must've dozed off, because when I opened my eyes again there were more people at the pool than when I closed them. Agathe was on the other side of Marjorie, the pair of them sharing an umbrella and chatting away. The opposite side of the pool was taken up by East Wingers, a strange bunch. I saw one of them, a big fella in his late fifties, shovelling food into his gob at breakfast like he hadn't eaten for a week. He had a bit of everything on his fork, and he sat there after with a bit of dried yoke stuck to his chin. Disgusting. Some people have no self-awareness, do they. No pride.

The only available sun lounger was on my left and this was soon taken by Elle. "Ey'up," I said. "I thought you were with the old bill?"

"That was an hour ago."

"Is that so." I were sleeping for longer than I thought. "Did they, erm, find anything?"

"No, nothing. Just like I told them. The inspector spent most of the time shouting about Penny. The other one had to keep steering him back on track, you know, ask questions about Dylan and stuff."

"Oh aye, like what?"

"Just about where he lived, next of kin, the sort of stuff you might expect."

"So, they left disappointed, then?"

"Not quite. Just as they were finishing the inspector's phone rang. He gibbered in Spanish, but I could see he was getting very excited. When he hung up, he spoke to the other policeman very quickly, I couldn't understand what he was saying but I did catch one bit. He kept saying 'Marley Williams' over and over, then he went into the corridor and began banging on her door, but there was no answer."

I was about to ask more questions, but as Elle finished speaking, her phone vibrated on the table next to her. She caught it before it rattled itself off the edge, looked at it and said, "Oh, I have to go, there's somewhere I've got to be," before scurrying off towards reception.

49

Sanjay

I woke to the sound of someone banging on a door somewhere down the corridor for what seemed like a century. Luke didn't stir. We had argued into the early hours, our anger and irritability being fuelled by the minibar which was now bare. Empty miniatures of whisky and brandy were scattered about the floor, a plastic minefield of misery. I doubted Luke would rise anytime soon, him being responsible for most of the empty bottles. Still, I dressed quietly, not wishing to wake him in case we picked up where we left off last night.

I slipped out of the room just in time to see Inspector Moreno walk away from Marley's door shaking his head. Agente Garcia was with him, they both walked to the lift and waited, I chose to take the stairs. Agente Garcia saw me as I was about to descend onto the first step, he nodded and smiled at me, a kind smile; it was exactly what I needed.

I ate breakfast alone, though I picked at my food like a petulant child, my appetite suppressed by tears throughout the night. I toyed with the idea of walking into town, but the truth was I couldn't be bothered. I was exhausted, not due to lack of sleep, but through emotional turmoil. I refilled my coffee mug and walked to the lounge bar opposite which I knew would be deserted at that time in the morning. I sat on a sofa and felt my hands shake and panic rise to my throat as I realised how truly alone I was.

Luke had said that I needed him, and he was right. I've always known it, ever since we met. He was confident, funny, and had a devil-may-care attitude, which I not only envied but desired. From the moment we got together I used to sometimes wonder if it was all a cruel joke that I wasn't in on, if perhaps he would laugh with his friends about me following him around like a puppy. After all, I couldn't figure out what he saw in me.

Most relationships have an equilibrium, a balance of qualities, but not ours. Luke tips the scale in looks, income, popularity, every metric imaginable, except, perhaps, kindness. How much solace can I take in that? Besides, being kinder than cruel doesn't make you kind.

Our argument last night was different than ever before, it had an edge to it: a finality. It was as if years of tension and unease had built up until the pressure was too much and the explosion happened. Of course, I know why this fight was different than all the others: I started this one. Usually, when we argue, I back down, the fear of losing Luke always superseding the will to come out on top, but this time it was I who was angry, and Luke didn't know how to handle that. The fact he'd been drinking heavily only exacerbated the problem. When I demanded the truth about what he'd been hiding, he got angry, accused me of snooping, and said it was none of my business. The argument got more heated as it reached a tired stalemate and then descended into petty point-scoring. We veered wildly from the source of my anger, Luke tried to hide the truth about my discovery, and used my apparent shortcomings to deflect my attention. I, on the other hand, shamed myself with hysterics, as the weight of the deceit became more and more apparent to me.

As I sat, my coffee mug between my hands in the lounge bar, I became aware of a disconnect with my surroundings. It was like there was a force field in front of my eyes protecting my grief-riddled self from the present reality. The faint clatter of crockery in the restaurant across the way, mingled with the subdued chatter of bleary-eyed guests seemed ethereal and distant, as though from another realm, a happier place, lost to me.

The chairs surrounding me were empty, there was a stillness in the lounge which I was unwilling to disturb. I sat tight, looking at the paintings adorning the walls, the granular remnants of brush strokes, the legacy of effort long dead, yet the effect immortalised in the vivid hues of the flaming skirts of the flamenco dancers and capes of the matadors.

The sad serenity was broken by the sound of dull thumping. I looked towards the lobby to see Agathe come unsteadily towards the lounge bar on her two walking sticks. She came all the way in, her head rotating, taking in the whole bar. She was only a few feet from me when she saw me through her thick lenses.

"Oh, it's you. Have you seen my Marley? I hear the police are looking for her." I shook my head, worried that if I spoke, my voice might crack under the weight of sadness. She tilted her head to one side, surveying me. "What's the matter?" she asked, her voice softer than I expected. Again, I could form no words. Agathe continued to assess me for a few more moments, then hobbled closer and sat in the chair next to me. She balanced her sticks against the table and raised her hands and I expected them to clutch her crucifix, but to my surprise she took my hands and clutched them instead. I could feel the warmth of her touch and her gesture, and the tears started flowing from me. She asked no questions, asked nothing in return for her kindness, she merely sat and squeezed my hand, the goodness given gratefully received.

"You must think me a fool," I spluttered, eventually.

"Now, why would I think that?"

"Sitting here, crying for no apparent reason."

"I wouldn't say there's no apparent reason. Only two things can overcome a person in this way: estranged siblings, grief, and love. So, tell me, has anyone you cared for died?"

I shook my head.

"Well, then," she continued. "It must be Luke." She took a tissue from her bag and handed it to me, then resumed squeezing my hand.

"I thought you didn't approve of us?"

"It's not my place to approve or disapprove. '*Judge not lest ye be judged*', as our Lord said."

"We had an argument last night, I found out he was keeping a secret from me, but that was just the beginning, it got worse the more we talked. It started when I found something he'd been hiding, he wouldn't explain it, he point-blank refused. I went on and on at him…"

"Good for you. You stood your ground."

"I almost wish I hadn't. In the end he told me he'd been seeing someone else, he said they ended it six months ago. I don't know what to do. I always knew this would happen one day, I could never hope to hold on to him."

"Rubbish. He's the one in the wrong, you could find someone better. He's a smarmy, arrogant one if you ask me. You're much more polite."

"Thank you, but I don't think politeness is a sought-after quality in a relationship."

"You'd be surprised. My Reggie was a gentleman, always nice to people, even when I knew he was annoyed or irritated, he would still be polite to folk. It shows character. It's one of the things I admired most about him. I'm not going to offer advice, you know yourself best, and Luke, for that matter. You know if you have a good relationship or if you don't. But if you need to talk to someone while we're here you can always come see old Agathe, you hear?"

I thanked her.

"And if you're ever alone and in need of comfort, you could always pick up a Bible. Psalm 120:1 would be a good place to start. *'I took my troubles to the Lord; I cried out to him, and he answered my prayer.'*"

50

Marley

I left the hotel early this morning. I wanted space and solitude to go over the facts of the case in my mind. I was thinking about Russell and how he could've been killed in the locked room. I tried to fit the Bible quotes we found in his office into the puzzle, but the pieces were too big. Then the facts surrounding Dylan's murder had convoluted my thinking; the two murders had happened so close together they were mingling in my brain, two fogs colliding. It seemed Russell had only just been killed when Dylan was then murdered to throw us off the scent. And we still couldn't be sure the two deaths were connected.

The revelation that Elle knew Dylan under a false name came as a shock but looking back, it was explained by some rather odd behaviour. I remembered being in the airport when Elle flew into a fury because Dylan went through passport control without her, was this so that she didn't see his passport which contained his real name? Maybe Dylan feared that the border control officer would say, "Thank you, Mr Forester, welcome to Spain." Although I imagine his fears would've been unfounded, those guards never so much as smile never mind speak, you're lucky to get a grunt out of them.

I then remembered when we arrived at the hotel, Dylan carried out the check-in process alone. They were queueing in front of us, and Dylan ushered Elle off to the bar to get some cocktails to toast the start of the holiday.

"Welcome to The Orange Tree Hotel, Mr Freeman," the receptionist had said. So when booking the room, Elle used Freeman as Dylan's surname and Dylan had got rid of Elle on every occasion that he might have been compromised. I could just imagine him explaining to the receptionist that Elle must've made a mistake on the booking, casting blame onto her.

Still, if Dylan was killed because he knew who killed Russell, then he must've seen that person going into the gym that morning, and we checked the usage of all the access cards, and none had been used except Russell's. Unless…someone saw Russell and the murderer enter the gym together. No, that made no sense, because how then did the murderer get out?

I stumbled over these thoughts as I walked the dusty road into town. Mum and I had been the first seated for breakfast, though neither of us ate much, I wasn't overly hungry having had a feast of paella for dinner last night, and Mum doesn't eat much as a rule. Being restricted by her arthritis she is careful with the amount she eats, as she can't burn it off through exercise. I'd left her by the pool and told her I was going to check out the art gallery in town, but I don't think she was listening as she made no response, her eyes fixed on the sudoku in her lap.

Today is another glorious day. As I walked, the sun climbed, rising slowly, like mercury in a thermometer, getting hotter with each step I took. Marjorie's directions had been vague, but I found the gallery without much difficulty. It's in a whitewashed building that stands alone and looks like it could belong in an old western movie, maybe as a bank or sheriff's office in some wild frontier town. The windows were covered with blue painted shutters shaped like saloon bar doors. I walked in and shivered, it felt like the aircon was spitting out ice. The girl behind the ticket desk smiled politely as she served me. She looked like a student with her pink hair and nose piercing, and I wondered what Mum would say if I dyed my hair afro pink. Hmm, maybe I'll find out.

The two-euros' entrance fee satisfied my thrifty alter-ego while also tempering my expectations. I thanked the girl and went through to the first exhibition, Spanish abstract art from the 1970s.

The pieces displayed varied in quality as well as in state of preservation, but it felt good to be among silent canvasses again, to be disturbed only by the occasional muffled cough, and to become absorbed in the colours and patterns in front of me.

I checked my phone and was pleased to see that I had no service. The old building blocked out the signal, almost as if it wanted you to enjoy its display undisturbed.

The next room contained a mixture of paintings and sculptures, the theme throughout seemingly a celebration of Spanish art. I saw no other nation represented, though the plaques beside each piece detailing the works were all written in Spanish, so my assumption may have been wrong. I spent two hours looking at the works and most of the time I was alone, the gallery appeared to me not to be to most tourists' tastes. It was as I was leaving that I saw something which both shocked and intrigued me. I was passing the third exhibition containing Impressionist works from northern Spain when I heard hushed voices. I turned my head as I passed the doorway and saw Jasmine and Elle huddled together in a corner. They hadn't seen or heard me pass, so I crept back along the wall and peeked around the doorframe, exposing as little of myself to them as possible. They were in the far side of the room and seemed to be deliberately keeping their voices low, so I couldn't make out what they were saying, but I saw Jasmine take something from the canvas bag that was slung over her shoulder and give it to Elle who quickly buried it in her Gucci Ophelia handbag. The exchange happened so quickly I couldn't see what the item was. Jasmine then started moving away from Elle towards the door, and me! I made a run for it, not wishing to be seen by either of the girls. I needed time to think, to digest what I had just witnessed. I whispered a hurried thanks to the pink-haired student and tumbled out into the street, momentarily blinded by the vicious sun. I suspected Jasmine wouldn't be far behind me, so I dashed as fast as I could until I came to a café where I sat inside next to the window, my eyes trained on the street outside. After a few minutes, Jasmine walked at a leisurely pace past the café but didn't look in my direction. I then watched her turn in the direction of the hotel, and she was soon lost to me among bustling tourists and blazing tarmac.

A waitress came and took my order. I opted for a green smoothie, though my mind was on other matters. As she left my table, I looked out of the window again and this time I saw Elle following in Jasmine's footsteps, also looking like she was in no hurry.

What could they have been talking about? These two girls were supposed to be sworn enemies, or so I thought, but their conversation had looked almost friendly. The fact they'd arranged to meet in the art gallery where I assume they imagined no one would see them is odd on its own, but the fact they exchanged something in such a furtive manner is downright suspicious.

I'm sitting in the café as I write this, trying to remove a small piece of kale from between my teeth. I have to stop thinking about Jasmine and Elle now, because a few moments ago my phone regained signal and I saw I had four missed calls from Mum as well as a text message from Penny:

Where are you, dear? The police are at the hotel. Apparently, they want to arrest you for murder.

So now I have to decide what to do: go back, or make a run for it?

51

Sally

I woke this morning to find Jasmine's bed empty. I had slept for much longer than I thought I would, it being mid-morning by the time I opened my eyes and stretched out my arms. I guess going through the range of emotions that I've had these last few days took it out of me more than I realised. That, and a considerable number of cocktails.

With a dull aching in my head, I threw on a pair of shorts and a t-shirt and made my way down to the restaurant. Breakfast is served until eleven, meaning I had ten minutes to get myself seated. Paulo was at reception when I passed. He smiled at me and wished me a good morning and I felt myself blush a little as I returned the greeting. I must've looked awful having just rolled out of bed and gone out the door without applying any makeup at all. I should've known he'd be standing at reception, or at least about somewhere; he always is, it's like the guy never has a day off.

The fruit on the platters in the restaurant was looking a little drier than I would've liked, but the coffee was hot and strong, so I didn't regret getting out of bed.

I was stirring a lump of sugar into the black abyss when Penny sat down opposite me. "Good morning, dear. How was your night out? Not feeling too rough I hope."

"Morning, Penny. I've felt worse, though I think I slept through the worst of the hangover."

"And Jasmine? Is she still sleeping through hers?"

"No, I'm not sure where she is, she was gone when I woke up. She may be sunbathing already. How was your night? Did you make any progress on the case?"

"Hmm. I managed to straighten a few things in my head I think, but I still don't know who killed your uncle…yet."

"I wonder if *he* is any closer to finding out." I pointed to Inspector Moreno who I saw charging towards us. When he reached our table, he wasted no time on pleasantries, instead coming straight to the point.

"Mrs Haylestone. Where is Miss Williams?"

"Good morning to you too, Inspector…"

"I do not have time for your English chit-chat. Tell me, where is your Miss Williams?"

"I don't know, I haven't yet seen Marley this morning."

"Lies! You two are the thick thieves, I have seen the way you carry on as if you are investigating this crime, *my* crime! You think you are so clever, don't you, Mrs Haylestone, well you are not, you can't be, because the murderer has been under your nose this whole time!"

"What are you talking about, you stupid little buffoon?"

"I am talking about Marley Williams murdering Russell Aspell! I have the proof! Now, tell me, where is she?"

"You think Marley is responsible for these crimes? You're even more incompetent than I thought."

"I did not say crimes, I will charge her with *one* murder for now, though there is no doubt that when I get her into my interrogation chair, she will also confess to the murder of Dylan Forester."

"Dylan who?" I said, confused. I looked at Penny, who gave me an almost imperceptible shake of the head, her eyes ordering me to be quiet.

"Tell me, Inspector," said Penny quickly, "what evidence do you have to suggest Marley killed Russell?"

"I have the DNA evidence, the most conclusive evidence in the world. Many a case, many a baffling case, have I solved with the DNA. Now, no more lies, where is she?"

"Paulo, dear," called Penny. He was clearing a nearby table and as he approached, I rested my elbow on the table and put my cheek into my palm, covering my face as best I could. "Paulo, have you seen Marley this morning?"

"Si, Senora Haylestone. Senora Williams left the hotel quite early, maybe eight-thirty, she has not yet come back."

"Did she go to the beach, or to town?" asked Moreno.

"To town, I believe."

"Gracias," said the policeman to his countryman before dismissing him with a flick of the hand. "Aha! You see, she shall not evade my capture." He took his phone from his pocket. "I shall get Agente Garcia to search high and low until she is found. And the search will be more successful than your efforts in Elle Caplan's room last night, Mrs Haylestone. Yes, don't think I don't know about that, Inspector Moreno of the Cuerpo Nacional de Policia, he knows everything!"

He barked his orders into the phone and put it back into his pocket before Agente Garcia on the other end of the line could ask any questions. "Now, where were we?"

"You were demonstrating your lack of cognitive reasoning."

"Ah yes, Marley Williams is the killer. We have the lab results back; Miss Williams' blood was found on the victim. That puts her at the scene of the crime."

"Of course she was at the scene of the crime, she found the body."

"Tell me, Mrs Haylestone, every time you find a body do you leave blood on it? No, of course not! It is obvious that Mr Aspell must have inflicted some sort of wound on Miss Williams when defending himself from her frenzied attack."

"I see," said Penny, rolling her eyes, "and how did Marley then get out of the gym?"

I took a sip of sweet coffee and watched Inspector Moreno redden as he realised he couldn't provide an answer to Penny's question.

"I will not discuss details of a murder inquiry with you, a civilian! Anyway, whilst we wait for Agente Garcia to find Miss

Williams, there are one or two questions I have for you, Miss Oldfield."

"Me?" I asked, surprised.

"Si, in my role as investigating officer, I have left no scone upturned as you English say. I have been looking into your uncle's affairs and I have found one or two financial irregularities which require clarification. If you would be so kind as to accompany me to your uncle's office, we can discuss the matter there."

"Can Penny join us?" I asked, wishing for a friend to be nearby.

"Absolutely not! Mrs Haylestone is a suspect in this murder, and as such is not allowed to listen to a witness being questioned."

"How can I be a suspect? I thought you said Marley is the deranged killer. Besides, I don't know what you think Sally will be able to help you with, she knew nothing of Russell's affairs."

"And you did?"

"More than Sally, certainly."

"Very well, Mrs Haylestone can join us, I look forward to hearing what light she can throw on Mr Aspell's accounts."

As we waited for the lift, I cast my glance out to the pool, half expecting to see Jasmine's glistening body, but there was no sign of her. I wondered where she could've got to.

Inspector Moreno took a shiny metal key from his pocket and opened the door to Uncle Russell's office. He then sat at the desk as though it was his own, leaned forward and clasped his hands in front of himself. He appeared to be contemplating us as we stared back at him, bemused and expectant.

"Miss Oldfield," he began, "it has come to my attention that you are the heir to Russell Aspell's estate, including this hotel in which we sit. Are you aware of this fact?"

"Yes."

"How do you know this?" he asked, his brows furrowed.

"Penny told me," I replied, tilting my head at the lady beside me.

"What? How did you know? Every step I take in this case you are there to stumble me, to deceive me!"

"I spoke to Russell's solicitor, there's no magic involved."

"Tell me then, Mrs Haylestone, since you are the knower of all things, why was Mr Aspell's financial position so precarious?"

"He made a bad investment, he put too much of his money into a Russian mining company; it went south when Russia invaded Ukraine."

"I see, and yet, from his financial records, it is apparent that Mr Aspell received a large cash injection which saved the hotel from liquidation only a few weeks ago. What can you tell me of that?"

"Nothing. I know he kept a small amount of cash in his safe like most hotels do. What do you mean by a large sum?"

"Over one hundred and fifty thousand euros with no tax paid on it and no record of where it came from."

"I'm afraid I can't help you, Inspector."

"Can't…or won't?" he snarled.

"Toss a coin."

Moreno glared at Penny who caressed her pearl necklace and appeared disinterested in what the little man had to say.

"Perhaps the answer I am looking for will be found in Mr Aspell's safe. Miss Oldfield, do you know the code? No? Okay, maybe you could make a list of likely ones, you know, birthdays, anniversaries, the usual unimaginative numbers."

"I don't think that will be necessary, Inspector," I said.

"Oh? And why not?"

"Because the safe appears to be open," answered Penny before I could. She was looking behind me, and for the first time since I had met her, I saw what appeared to be confusion etched on her face.

The three of us rose in unison and dashed the short distance to the safe. The door was only slightly ajar but had clearly not been forced; there was no sign of tampering, and it looked to me to be an expensive and secure unit. Even my ignorant eye could tell that the safe had been opened using the code.

Inspector Moreno swung the door fully open and took out a few sheets of paper which appeared to be deeds or some other legal documents. "Aha! Excellent. You see, good police work yields results. Leave this type of case to the professionals!"

At that moment Moreno's phone rang, he answered it with smug glee and spoke into it in English for our benefit. "Agente Garcia, you have good news I trust? Very good, take her to the station, I shall meet you there. Goodbye. Excuse me, ladies, you must forgive me leaving you, but I have a murderer to question. Adios." The odious man then tossed a piece of chewing gum into his mouth and swept out of the room.

"Penny," I said, when he was gone, "what are you confused about?"

"The safe was locked when I checked it, after Russell was murdered."

"Maybe it wasn't, maybe the door was ajar like how we just found it."

"No dear, I know it was locked, because I locked it. I knew the code, I opened it, checked inside, and closed it. And there was twenty thousand euros in there when I did, which is now missing."

"But...who else knew the code?"

"Only Russell and me. And Marley..."

52

Sanjay

I was grateful to Agathe for her comforting words, I wasn't about to join in a prayer meeting, or her local congregation, but I was thankful for the extended hand of friendship, nonetheless. We were still sitting in the deserted bar, her warm hand resting on mine.

"You said you were looking for Marley when you came in here, I'm afraid I haven't seen her," I said, remembering how I had been disturbed from my trance by Agathe's hobbled search.

"Well, I'm sorry, young man, but now that you've reminded me, I need to go and find her. The police are here, they want to talk to her, it sounds serious."

"Serious? What makes you say that?"

"That big oaf Terry heard from the young, pretty girl."

"Jasmine?"

"No, the other one, the girl that was going with the one that died."

"You mean Elle."

"If you say so. Well, according to her, the police were banging on my Marley's door, saying something about an arrest warrant. I need to find her to straighten this out. She's always been the same, too much energy, always getting herself into trouble. Nothing bad you understand, more curiosity that gets the better of her."

"But why would the police want to arrest Marley?" I asked, more to myself than to Agathe.

"I'm sure it's all a big misunderstanding. Still, I need to find her to get it all straightened out." The old woman's sticks trembled as she pushed herself up from the chair. Marjorie hurried into the bar and made straight for us.

"Have you found her?" she asked, breathless.

"No, I was just taking a little rest and talking to this young man. I'm going to carry on looking now."

"I've checked the whole hotel, and the beach, but I can't find her anywhere. Have you tried phoning her?"

"Yes, but it went to voicemail."

"Agathe, allow me to look," I said. "If she's not in the hotel as Marjorie said, then she must've gone into town. I'm sure you don't mind me saying I can cover more ground and quicker. You should stay here and rest." The truth was I wanted to return the kindness shown to me, and thought this opportunity was divinely presented.

"I'll go with you, Sanjay; four eyes are better than two."

Agathe agreed to the suggestion and Marjorie helped her back to her chair by the pool, ensuring she had all she required before we set off.

"I don't know what that policeman is playing at," said Marjorie as we passed through the lobby doors and were met with a wall of heat. "I mean, how anyone could think that lovely young girl would be capable of harming anyone, I don't know."

"I understand what you mean, but the police must have some sort of evidence to justify an arrest warrant. Inspector Moreno must answer to a higher power, a judge or someone who grants the warrant, he must provide proof of something. Anyway, we don't know which murder the warrant is for, or if it's for both. Maybe they found Marley's fingerprints on the EpiPen or the gin bottle and there's an innocent explanation. What exactly did Elle say?"

"I'm not sure, it was Terry who was speaking to her. I was next to them talking to Agathe. Elle spoke to Terry for a few minutes then ran off as if she were in a hurry to be somewhere." I pictured the scene in my head, the beautiful blonde girl being bored out of her wits by the loudmouth who was undoubtedly asking stupid questions while admiring her toned body. She had probably feigned illness or 'forgot' to do something in her room to get away from him.

"What did Terry say?" I asked, as we rounded a bend in the road, the town's variety of buildings becoming visible through the quivering air.

"Well, according to my Terry, the police were battering on Marley's door this morning, demanding that she come out with her hands up. According to Elle, he says, the police searched her and Dylan's room, but Penny Haylestone had beat them to it last night. Terry reckons Penny was looking for evidence of Marley's guilt, and that Penny was going to hide it from the police because her and Marley are so close, but I said that's nonsense and that he has an overactive imagination. 'What do you mean nonsense?' Terry said to me. Then I reminded him that Penny was the best of friends with Russell and that if Marley was the murderer, Penny wouldn't be hiding it from the police, she'd be giving it to them."

"And what did Terry say to that?" I asked, trying to keep up.

"He said, 'Give over, Marge, at least I'm trying to think who the murderer could be, unlike you, who just thinks the best of everyone.' Which, by the way, is a load of old tosh. I *don't* think the best of everyone, I look for the best in people, there's a difference."

A few clapped-out cars passed us as we made our way past the apartment blocks on the edge of the town. Small restaurants with umbrellas advertising local beers outside and white plastic chairs, gave us a guard of honour along the way until we reached the main strip.

"Which way do you think we should go?" I asked, regretting the confidence I had expressed to Agathe that we would find her daughter before the police did. The street was heaving with tourists and street traders selling their wares. Men with dreadlocks and sunglasses were selling bracelets, watches, and handbags on mats at their sandalled feet. They attempted to entice their quarry by holding the goods out at arm's length and engage the passing people with compliments and mimicked accents.

Marjorie looked up and down the street, deciding which way would be the more fortuitous when she abruptly grabbed my arm and excitedly started to babble about a gallery. After a minute or two of trying to calm the woman into something bordering on coherence, I managed to decipher her words. She had apparently spoken to Marley of an art gallery she'd seen, and the girl had told her that she would check it out at some point during her holiday. It did seem a good place to start, so we set off, Marjorie practically running down the street.

The gallery stood alone in a dusty square, two sleepy pigeons sitting on a bench being the only living things in sight.

We entered and I gulped down the cool air which tingled my skin. Behind the ticket desk sat a young girl with pink hair and blue mascara. She smiled at us as we approached. "Hello, sweetheart," said Marjorie. "Sorry, I don't speak much Spanish, you must think me terribly ignorant, but I was wondering if you've seen a friend of ours. She's a lovely girl she is, with an afro and a big smile. Very friendly she is, too."

"You just missed her, she left about ten minutes ago."

We thanked the girl, Marjorie again apologising for her lack of fluency in Spanish and explained how when she was a girl you only learnt a smattering of French and not much else besides, and sure what use is that to anyone in a mining village in the north of England.

Disheartened at being so close to finding Marley, we headed back towards the town only to have our spirits lifted almost immediately. In the window of a café, I saw Marley staring intently at her phone. She looked up as we entered but didn't greet us with her customary grin.

"Marley," I said, "the police are looking for you."

"I know, I've just had a text from Penny, why on earth do they suspect me?"

"I don't know, but I think you're about to find out." Through the window, I was watching Agente Garcia take long strides towards us. He entered the café with no histrionic gesture which I would've expected from his superior and instead sat with us after first asking permission, then began speaking quietly and slowly. He explained that he had been sent to find Marley and to accompany her to the police station for questioning. His soft voice conveyed kindness, as though he were offering words of encouragement and support, instead of telling the girl that her liberty was imperilled. He assured Marley, and us, that if there was a misunderstanding, she would be back at The Orange Tree Hotel in no time. Marley listened in silence, asking no questions. She nodded and rose, following the officer to the door where she looked back at us and gave a sad smile.

53

Terry

I came on holiday to relax, to take it easy and enjoy myself, I thought that were the whole point of holidays; apparently not.

When Elle left me after remembering she had somewhere to be, I told Marge what she'd said about the police looking for Marley. Marge near snapped her neck, she turned around so fast to relay the information to Agathe. "Terry says that Elle says that the police says…" It was like a game of Chinese whispers, though I daresay you can't say that anymore, it's probably racist or sexist or something. Or is it woke? Would it be too woke or not woke enough? I don't know, I can't keep up these days.

Anyways, Elle hadn't gone two minutes before Marjorie and Agathe up and left, too.

"Are you not coming with us?" asked Marjorie, her hands on her hips, and her towel tucked under one arm.

"What for?" I asked, confused.

"To find Marley, of course!"

"Don't worry, Marge, I'm sure the police will find her and besides, she might be armed or something; you're safer here."

"Not to arrest her, Terry! We need to warn her, to help her!"

"Oh right, of course, no love, I'll stay here, keep an eye out in case she comes back to do a bit of sunbathing." They hurried off to search the hotel, leaving me to enjoy the sun. I mean, why would I want to go off searching for a wanted criminal? There's been no mention of a reward yet.

That's the problem with Marjorie, has been since I met her; she always sees the best in people. The idea that sweet, happy Marley could be a psychotic killer wouldn't enter her head. Not that I'm accusing her you understand, but the police must have a reason for banging on her door, even if they are a bit useless. And it's always the ones you don't expect, isn't it? I said to Marge that maybe the reason Marley has become so close to Penny is because she's worried that Penny will unmask the killer: her. And that she's using Penny to mislead her or give her false clues.

This whole business is so complicated it makes my head hurt. It's like one of those detective shows you see on the telly, a new body popping up every five minutes and a whole load of suspects. Maybe when it's all over I'll write a screenplay based on the case but change the names. I could get Sean Bean to play me, or maybe Liam Neeson if he's not too busy. I'd call the show Mid-summer Murders. The BBC would lap that up, getting one over on the enemy.

Anyway, as I was saying, the women went off leaving me on my lonesome, not that I minded; everyone enjoys my company, I should enjoy it myself from time to time. I reached into Marjorie's bag and pulled out my phone to check the pre-season football scores and then caught up a bit with the diary, getting it up to date.

After about five minutes I thought about having a little nap, but a bunch of the East Wingers got in the pool and decided to have a game of water volleyball. The fat fella I'd seen at breakfast was the ringleader. Him and his wife played another couple. They tossed the ball into the air and started palming it towards each other. There wasn't even a net! You could tell none of them had ever played competitive sports, not like me. Whenever one of them missed the ball they laughed, as though sport were a bit of fun which shouldn't be taken seriously. I got so angry watching them, I went down to the beach and had a swim to cool off. The water seemed cold at first but after a minute or two it were like being in a bath. I floated on my back and looked at the sky. It were sheer blue except for a few wispy clouds that looked like thin threads of cotton wool. My ears were submerged, the sound in them being like when you put a shell to your ear when you're a kid, that dull droning. After a while I closed my eyes, enjoying the peace and hypnotic sea, until a wave came and sent water up my nose and down my throat. I started spluttering and stood up, only I'd drifted out farther than I thought, and my feet didn't touch the seafloor like I expected, causing my head to go under. For a second I was worried I was drowning but my natural athleticism saved the day, my legs kicked, and my arms paddled, bringing me to the surface. I wasn't afraid of drowning anymore, now I was afraid of sharks, because I'd seen on David Attenborough that when you thrash in the water the sharks think it's a seal in distress, so I kicked my way back to shore, spluttering and spitting salty water out of my mouth the whole way.

As I staggered onto the beach, trying to fill my lungs with air, I looked up and saw Luke sitting on the sand watching me. I stopped in front of him, hands on knees, still gasping, when he said, "You shouldn't go in the water if you don't know how to swim." He had a bottle of beer in his hand, and he took a swig.

"I can swim!" I told him. "I practically played football for England! I just got a bit of water up my nose is all."

"From here it looked like you were drowning." He took another swig.

"You thought I were drowning, and you just sat there looking on with a beer in your hand, like you're sat at home on your sofa watching *Aquaman*?"

"Not *Aquaman*, more like *Moby Dick*."

I felt my fist clench and saw Luke's face break into a smile. I took a step forward, then stopped. I didn't stop because I imagined Marjorie's anger if I hit him, or Sanjay's for that matter. I didn't stop because I imagined getting arrested again, and it wasn't the thought of that tiny, dank police cell that held me back. I stopped because I realised that Luke was deliberately provoking me, that he wanted me to hit him.

I stopped and saw tears in his eyes.

Then I hit him.

54

Marley

Agente Garcia didn't put me in handcuffs or try to humiliate me in any way. He walked alongside me to the police station, knowing that his size and athleticism were all that was needed to ensure I didn't attempt to run away. The tourists we passed didn't gawk or point, Agente Garcia giving no sign that I was his prisoner. To a casual observer we could have been friends meeting on his lunch break, enjoying a walk together.

He found me in the café, talking to Marjorie and Sanjay, who had heard I was in trouble and had come looking for me. I'd been weighing up my options when the tall policeman had come and taken the scales out of my hands.

The reality was I didn't really have much choice about what I was going to do. For a few moments, romantic notions of fleeing took hold of my mind (perhaps because me and Mum recently watched *Thelma and Louise*), but they were based on the idea of adventure and intrigue, no practical reasoning had guided my thinking. Besides, I knew I was innocent of whatever it was they were intending to charge me with, so running away would only make me look guilty. And, of course, there was Mum to consider. I can't leave her, she needs me. No, I decided the best thing to do would be to wait for the police to find me and answer their questions in a straightforward and honest way and hope the trust I have in the judicial system is not misplaced, and that's exactly what I did.

The one other thought that crossed my mind was to call Penny, but I knew that when the police did find me, they would confiscate my phone and a call to Penny shortly before my arrest may look conspiratorial, especially to Inspector Moreno who is not her biggest fan.

The police station is exactly how I imagined it would be, in need of fresh paint and better coffee. Agente Garcia stood with me as I was 'booked in', my belongings put in a tray like when you go through airport security and taken away for examination, or maybe just safekeeping. Then he took me to a holding cell and said he would come to fetch me for an interview when Inspector Moreno arrived back at the station. As he turned to leave, he stopped at the door. "Would you like some paper and a pen?" he asked.

"Why would I want that?" Curious thing to say, I thought.

"Terry Smith asked for some when he was here, I thought it was maybe some sort of English custom for the police to offer in these circumstances."

I gratefully accepted the offer and wondered why Terry had asked for pen and paper. The pen, I could understand, because on the magnolia painted door were the words, *'Terry woz ere,'* but I couldn't fathom what he would want with the paper.

Garcia returned a few minutes later with ten sheets of crisp, white A4 and a black biro. My first inclination was to draw something, and maybe I will, but my first duty must be to record the day's events, so that's what I'm doing now.

Inspector Moreno arrived full of the joys of spring, as my old Sunday school teacher would say. He bounced into the cell, his mouth motoring on a piece of gum. He looked at me and rubbed his hands together as though he'd just stepped in from the cold, then issued his command: "Come."

I followed him a short distance to the interrogation room which was a dark, dreary space containing a wooden table and four chairs. Agente Garcia and Inspector Moreno sat on one side, I on the other. I presumed the chair next to me was for my lawyer, but when I mentioned this to Inspector Moreno he laughed and said I had been watching too many Beverly Hills Cop films, which I didn't deny. My mind then wandered as it sometimes does, and I had to ask the inspector to repeat himself which he wasn't too pleased about. I hadn't caught what he said, I'd been thinking how crazy it was that Mel B had Eddie Murphy's baby and was wondering what the monthly child support bill was.

"I said, your DNA was found on Russell Aspell's body. How do you explain that?"

"What do you mean DNA?" I asked. "Sweat? Saliva? Help me out here."

"I mean blood, Miss Williams."

"Blood?" A fear gripped me. Blood? That was ridiculous. Were the police so desperate they would fabricate evidence to secure a conviction? I tossed Inspector Moreno's word around in my mind. If he had said sweat or a fingerprint, I could understand, after all, I did touch Russell when I felt for a pulse. Then a thought struck me, and hope flashed again.

"Tell me, Inspector, where on Russell's body did you find the blood?"

"It was on Mr Aspell's wrist. Only a trace, but that will be enough..."

"I think I can explain."

He removed a squished-up lump of chewing gum from his mouth and stuck it on the underside of the table like an obnoxious schoolkid, before popping in another stick. I explained how I'd cut my thumb on a tape measure when helping Russell measure the gym for new equipment.

"Obviously, when I felt for a pulse, a small speck of blood must've smeared onto his skin."

"I see. Who else helped you and Mr Aspell measure this space in the gym?"

"No one, it was just the two of us."

"Oh, just the two of you? So, you expect me to believe that your DNA was transferred to the murder victim because you cut yourself when you were helping him with some menial task in the very room the murder was committed, and no one saw you do it? Do you think I'm an idiot?"

"I'm telling you the truth!" I held up my thumb, showing him the thin red line where the cut had healed.

"You disrespect me with your lies, you could have scratched yourself afterwards or done this today when you heard we were coming to find you."

"Does it look like a fresh cut? No, I don't think so!" I felt myself getting angrier than I had ever been, it was an alien and unwelcome feeling, so at odds with my natural disposition.

Agente Garcia interrupted our staring match. "Excuse me, sir, but I'm sure we can prove or disprove the witness's statement if we find the tape measure. Our forensic laboratory will surely find blood along the tape's edge. If she is telling the truth that is…" He leaned back and smiled at me out of his superior's line of sight. I felt he believed me, and that the last sentence was to stay on the right side of his boss. Moreno sat staring at me, the hamster hard at work on its wheel.

He was undoubtedly deciding the level of risk he was comfortable with. I mean, if they charged me and the tape measure was found, and then it exonerated me, he would look pretty stupid having wrongly arrested two guests of The Orange Tree Hotel. As he opened his mouth to speak, there was a knock at the door and a young policewoman entered. She approached Moreno and whispered something in his ear.

"I'll be right back," he growled, leaving me with her. It was five minutes before he returned. In that time Agente Garcia and I hadn't said a word to one another, I was too busy wondering what was so important that it meant Inspector Moreno would interrupt interrogating me.

"Very well," said the inspector when he sat down opposite me once again. "We will search for the tape measure and confirm this girl's lies before we take any official action. Now, on to other matters, I want you to tell me about Penny Haylestone's private little investigation. You know what she is up to, you'll tell me." He turned over his hands and held them out as if to say *go on*.

"I don't know what you expect me to say, she keeps her cards very close to her chest."

"What was she looking for in Dylan Forester's hotel room?"

"You'd have to ask her."

"Miss Williams, you have not yet been cautioned, no charge has been brought against you, that, however, can change in an instant…"

"No charge? I was locked up in a cell a minute ago!"

"That is customary to ensure you do not escape. As I was saying, if you cooperate you may even get out of here today, unless, of course, no tape measure is found and I lock you up for the rest of your life, but still, another day of freedom is better than none at all, agreed?"

I *did* want to get out, but I wasn't prepared to jeopardize Penny's investigation in any way, or level the playing field by bringing Moreno up to speed on *his* case, so I did the only honourable thing I could think of. I lied.

"Dammit, Inspector, you're too wily by half. Okay, I'll level with you, Penny thinks Russell was killed by a Turkish crime lord as revenge for ripping him off. You see, a long time ago, Russell stole from the Turkish gangster and as repayment was supposed to set fire to a drug rival's boat, but it didn't go to plan… there were no drugs on board."

"Tell me about this Turkish crime lord…" Moreno had taken his notepad from his pocket; his pen rapidly scratching the paper.

"He was a small-time drug runner whose family had been kidnapped by Hungarian mobsters. He butchered his own family then killed the mobsters and their families before disappearing. After that, he did business only through minions who didn't know his real identity. He thus became a fearsome urban legend, a spook story that criminals tell their kids at night."

"What is the name of this Turkish crime lord?"

"Keyser Söze."

"Kais-er So-say," said Moreno phonetically under his breath, as he carefully wrote out the name. "Aha! Penny Haylestone thinks she can bring this international criminal to justice from under my nose, she hasn't reckoned with the genius of Inspector Alberto Luis Alejandro Juan Flores Moreno. Agente Garcia, take Miss Williams back to her cell, then release her after you get me my lunch from the McDonalds across the road."

I limped out of the interrogation room; my leg had gone numb from sitting on the hard chair. Agente Garcia grinned and shook his head at me as he closed the cell door, no doubt wise to my trick.

I bet Inspector Moreno won't be happy when he finds out that I lied to him about the Turkish gangster, but at least I'll be getting out of here in a few minutes!

55

Sally

"Why did Inspector Moreno say Dylan's surname was Forester?" I asked Penny, as we made our way down the stairs from Russell's office to the pool.

"Because it was, dear. The name you knew him under, what was it, Findlay? Well, that was a bogus name."

"You mean he had two identities?" I asked, shocked.

"No. Three. Elle knew him as Dylan Freeman."

"But why? Why would he lie about that?"

"A very good question. I'm hoping Jasmine might be able to shed some light. Oh look, there's Paulo, I bet he's scrumptious in bed. You will tell me won't you, dear?"

"Penny!" She is elegant and sophisticated, with a voice like polished crystal, but she is not subtle, and certainly not quiet. We were approaching reception, Paulo only being a few yards away.

"What's the matter? It's obvious he likes you, and you're not a fool, so doubtless you'll end up in bed together. I just don't understand why you're taking your time about it, or your reticence to talk about it for that matter."

"It's not simple, Penny!"

"My dear, we're talking about sex, there's nothing simpler."

"No, you're talking about sex, I'm -"

"Talking about what? Emotions? Feelings? All of that should come later, you must take the bull by the horns."

"We'll talk about this later," I said, as we stepped onto the tiled pool area, though I hope we don't.

I spied Jasmine lying on a sunbed at the far end of the pool, close to the steps that lead onto the beach. She saw us at once and jumped up. "Hey," she said, joining us. "There you are. I wondered where you'd got to."

"Inspector Moreno wanted to speak to me. Where have you been all morning?"

"Here."

"Oh. I looked out on my way to Russell's office and didn't see you."

"Hmm, that's strange, I've been here the whole time. Although, I moved from one sun lounger to another, I must've been blocked from view. Anyway, are you hungry? Penny, would you like to join us for lunch?"

"How lovely. Shall we sit inside or out?"

We sat near to the pool bar and Paulo brought three lunch menus over. I noticed Penny smirk as he handed me one, and for a second I worried that she might say something mortifying, but she remained tight-lipped.

"What do you girls say to sharing a jug of sangria?"

"A bit early for me, Penny," I said. "I'm still a little bit delicate after last night."

"I'll join you in that, Penny."

"Wonderful, I thought you'd want something refreshing after lying in the sun all morning."

"Exactly," replied Jasmine, her face hidden behind her menu.

"I used to have a rule, you know," continued Penny. "No alcohol before five in the evening."

"Is the rule suspended while you're on holiday?" I asked.

"No, it's abolished now that I'm retired. Forced retirement, I should add. Ridiculous. Jasmine, dear, how old would you say I am if you didn't know?"

"I don't know how old you are, Penny."

"Of course, I forgot, you see I told Sally on your first night here, but you hadn't yet joined us. Well, since you don't know, look at me and take a guess."

"I'd say, maybe…fifty-five."

"Darling, you're a terrible liar, a *terrible* liar. But I thank you for it." I saw colour rise in Jasmine's cheeks and felt I was missing something, like maybe there was a joke that I wasn't part of. Penny continued. "What are you girls going to eat? The herring in tomato sauce is divine, I think I'll have that."

"Hmm, I don't want anything too carby, I want to take a few pics on the beach at sunset and don't want to be bloated. You don't mind taking them, do you, Sal?"

"Of course not," I assured her, though the thought didn't thrill me. I had to remind myself that now I felt close to Jasmine again, I should be more supportive of her and help in her new career, even if I didn't quite understand it.

Paulo appeared at our side, taking my order first. I opted for the bacon and avocado salad. When he left us, Penny got down to business.

"Jasmine, dear, I'm afraid I need your help. I need to know more about Dylan." Penny then explained how Dylan had used different surnames, three that we knew about and possibly more.

"I can't believe it! The lying rat!"

"You had no idea?"

"No, none."

"What about his family, did he ever mention them? Surely you wanted to meet them when you were together?"

"He was an orphan, or at least he said he was. I don't know what to believe now. He said he was an only child and that his parents were killed in a car accident when he was fifteen. Dylan was in the back seat, that's how he got the scar on his leg."

"I see. He told Elle he got the scar in Afghanistan, that his vehicle hit a mine."

"Afghanistan? Rubbish! Dylan was never in the Armed Forces; did he seem to you to be the type of person who could handle discipline?" Jasmine picked up her glass of sangria and I could hear the ice rattle in her shaking hand.

"Hmm. Interesting…"

"What is?" I asked, watching Penny's eyes narrow in thought.

"Only that quite often there is a grain of truth found in a lie. A competent liar must have a good memory, it is easier not to trip yourself up in your deceptions if a common thread runs through them. What did he say his occupation was when you met?"

"He said he was a photographer."

"And how did you meet?"

"Through Instagram. He messaged me saying he was looking for some models to photograph to expand his portfolio. He said up to that point he'd mainly been a nature photographer and that he wanted to diversify into other areas and that he'd come across me by chance and that I was just what he was looking for. How stupid I've been." I saw tears well in Jasmine's eyes. Penny handed her a napkin and put her hand on her forearm.

"Not at all, you mustn't say that. Men like Dylan can be very charming, and… persuasive."

"He showed me his photographs, the rainforests in Belize he'd been to, the Great Barrier Reef when he went to Australia, all of them looked so professional."

"They probably were, dear; I'd bet he took them from a real photographer's website and was passing them off as his own. Did you ever see his passport?"

"No. Why?"

"I thought not. I'd say he was very protective of it in case you noticed the different surname, and the fact that it would be missing stamps from the countries he told you he'd visited."

Paulo brought us our food. The consummate professional, he showed no curiosity or interest in the cause of Jasmine's tears, he placed our plates in front of us and signed off with, "Enjoy," before flitting away.

"How long were you and Dylan together for?"

"About eighteen months. We met shortly after Sally went off to uni. I guess I was a bit lonely, Sal and I had been spending so much time together and then just like that she wasn't around. I suppose when Dylan came along, I jumped in headfirst where I should've been more cautious; I was too ready to believe anything he told me. We broke up two years ago when I found out about him and Elle."

"How did you find out?"

Jasmine looked at me and drew in a breath. I quickly swallowed a mouthful of salad and took over the story, telling Penny about the phone call I'd overheard at the pub and that I'd told Jasmine. I neglected to mention that I had sent a cowardly text and hadn't told Jasmine face to face, as I didn't see how that particular detail could be of interest to Penny who simply wanted to know more about Dylan.

Penny twirled her glass of sangria in her hand, the orange and lemon slices swirling like they were caught in a tornado.

"Did Dylan mention if he'd ever been to Spain before?" she asked Jasmine.

"Not that I remember, why?"

"We know he used different names; I'm just wondering if maybe he had some sort of connection to Russell. Maybe they'd met before, maybe here."

"Would Uncle Russell not have told you if that was the case?"

"Not necessarily. Russell had his secrets like everyone else. I'm not conceited enough to think that he wouldn't keep them from me, his oldest friend. If he thought his life was in danger, yes, he would tell me, but I think Russell died feeling safe."

"Do you think Dylan killed Russell?" I asked.

"It's a possibility."

"But if that's the case, who killed Dylan?"

"If Dylan murdered your uncle, then whoever killed Dylan could have done so for revenge, someone who cared deeply for Russell, or…"

"Or someone hated Dylan and murdered him because they thought they would get away with it, because it would be assumed that the two murders were linked, when actually, they may be completely separate!"

"I rule nothing out until I know for sure, but you've certainly given me one clue which I need to think over…"

56

Sanjay

After Agente Garcia took Marley away, Marjorie and I took a slow, dejected walk back to The Orange Tree Hotel. We had found Marley as we'd set out to do but watching her being led away made me feel a failure. The truth is I don't know who murdered Russell and Dylan, but I cannot accept that Marley is the culprit. In fact, I'd say that out of everyone she seems the least likely to me. A girl with such a happy and kind nature surely couldn't possess the anger needed to bash a man's head in, and then poison another, calmly watching as he dies in such a horrific manner.

Jasmine is my main suspect, but even this seems too fantastic an idea. I'm not saying she had a motive to kill Russell (though I did see her slap him in the face the night before he was killed), but she certainly had the strongest motive to kill Dylan. It was plain to see how much she hated him. On the flip side, Terry seems to have hated Russell enough to kill him but no reason as far as I can tell to harm Dylan, unless it was to keep Dylan quiet if he really did know who killed Russell.

When we arrived back at the hotel, Marjorie went off to look for Terry. I told her I'd find Agathe and tell her about Marley's detainment. When I did, I was careful not to use the word 'arrest', as I didn't want to overly worry the old woman, but also, I didn't know for sure that Marley had been charged with anything, so I suppose my kindness was coupled with veracity. Agente Garcia had merely said she was needed for 'questioning'.

I was a tad disappointed in Agathe's attitude when I found her in the lounge bar eating her lunch. She seemed to blame Marley for the predicament the poor girl found herself in, but to her credit she had little doubt that her daughter would soon be back, her innocence proven, and reputation restored. She was almost blasé about the whole affair, my fears of upsetting the woman with news of Marley's detainment being unfounded.

I left Agathe with something nearing reluctance. Not because I felt she needed me but because I knew that by getting up and walking away from Agathe, I was walking towards reality. My reality. My quest to find Marley and to be useful was a distraction from my fight with Luke, and the truth that he had been seeing someone else. I wasn't sure if I could face that truth, or if I could face seeing Luke. I didn't know where he was, and I hadn't had a call or text from him all morning.

Sometimes in life you have to face your fears, and sometimes your fears face you, which is exactly what happened when I ran into Luke by accident. I had peeked out onto the pool area and could see that he wasn't there. I assumed he was in the room or out in town, as I know he hates sand and wouldn't be at the beach. I was wrong. The beach was deserted apart from him, which may explain why he was there. I reached the bottom of the steps and there he was, looking straight at me. I couldn't even pretend not to see him and run away; he was sitting only a few feet away and must have heard my flip-flops clapping on the wooden steps as I descended.

"What happened to you?" I asked, my trepidation of an awkward encounter abating as I saw to my surprise a swollen, purple lip on his face.

"Nothing, I... I fell over this morning getting out of bed."

"Luke, there's one thing I've learnt in the past twenty-four hours, it's that you're a good liar, but even *you* aren't fooling me saying that."

"Why do you care what happened to my lip?"

"I don't. If someone hit you, they didn't hit you hard enough as far as I'm concerned."

"If that's how you feel, why did you come looking for me?"

I wanted to scream. Even now, after everything he'd done, he was still making it all about him.

"I didn't come looking for you. In fact, you were the last person I wanted to see when I came down those steps."

"Well, what are you waiting for? Go away if you don't want to see me." He turned and faced the sea, white foam fizzed and disappeared as baby waves rushed and then receded on the shore.

"I still need answers. You didn't explain what I found in your suitcase, and you never told me…who."

"Why does it matter, any of it?"

"I have a right to know."

"You had no right to go rifling through my case -"

"Argh!" I screamed. "Stop making yourself out to be the victim and take some responsibility. I told you a million times last night, I was looking for a shirt, we're on holiday, I didn't think looking in your suitcase was the heinous crime of the century. But I have a right to know who you were seeing behind my back. Was it someone I know? One of our friends?"

"Our friends? You mean my friends. You are the plus-one, the tag along. If it wasn't for me, would you ever see any of them again? *Will* you ever see any of them again?"

I looked at his fat lip and wanted to make it obese. I could feel my fist clenching. I've never punched anyone before, not in the playground, not when I've been drunk, not ever. But I really wanted to hit Luke in that moment. As always, he was right. They were his friends, and I wouldn't see them again, and… I was glad. I opened my palm and smiled. I realised that as scary as a new start might be, it was better to face life alone than with someone like Luke, someone who knows they have control over you, someone who uses that control to make themselves feel important, a person who can love only themselves. Now, as I looked at his arrogant smile, I didn't care about his suitcase or his secrets anymore. The burning question in my mind wasn't who Luke had been seeing, it was this: did he think I wouldn't be able to cope without him because he is so great or because I am so weak? He'd said it last night, he'd said it over and over, that I needed him, and fool that I am, I agreed. Now, my anger and fear had, in that instant, turned into determination. I was determined to walk away and never shed another tear for Luke, though I know I'll cry floods; there's a difference between crying for him and crying for me. Only one of them is okay.

I turned and walked and didn't look back as I climbed the steps. I walked into the shadow cast by the gym above me and shivered. Seeing the pool before me, I looked around aimlessly, unsure where to go. I wanted to go home, to get on a flight and feel London's cold rain on my face, so far removed from this Spanish anguish. I cursed Inspector Moreno for taking my passport and trapping me here. I figured I couldn't even book myself into another hotel without it, and I was sure this place was fully booked given the weekly booking system between the two wings, but I figured there was no harm in asking. I found Paulo at reception talking to a young waitress. He broke off his conversation to engage with me as I approached.

"Senor, how are you?"

"Fine," I lied, before realising that my next request would make that lie obvious. "I was just wondering if there was a vacant room in the hotel."

"Another room?"

"Yes, I know your system but thought I'd ask anyway."

"Actually, senor, we do have a room. A couple in the East Wing had to leave suddenly to go back to Germany, a family emergency I believe. Housekeeping is cleaning it now. I'm afraid, though, it is only available for a few more days, then the East Wing empties and new guests arrive."

"That's fine, I'll take it."

Now I must hope that Inspector Moreno either solves the case or is satisfied enough that I am not the murderer and he releases my passport before I must vacate this new room. I'm in it now, writing on the balcony. Ironically, the room faces directly onto Luke's, the pool separating us. *Luke's*, not ours. *Luke's*. I must now get used to *mine* and not *ours*.

57

Terry

I won't lie, I felt bad after hitting Luke. I tried to console myself that it was what he wanted, I mean, it must've been for him to provoke me like that, but still… Sometimes you've got to be the bigger man.

Anyway, I were worked up after that and needed to calm myself down, so I came back to the pool and had a beer. I kept one eye on the steps leading to the beach in case Luke wanted round two, but there were no sign of him. There were none of my lot about, just the East Wingers lounging around, the same old faces. You wonder why people come abroad if they're just going to sit by the pool all day and then fly home after two weeks. People aren't active these days, that's their problem. The fat one; East Winger number one, had finished playing water volleyball and was now fast asleep on his sun lounger, no doubt he'd wake up in time for dinner. Speaking of which, I began to feel a bit peckish, after all, swimming is very tiring isn't it, because you use all your muscle groups apparently. Well, I do anyway.

I'm not in the habit of wearing a watch, never have been, so I opened Marjorie's bag to get my phone out to check the time and what did I find? Nothing. No phone. I looked again because you can never be too sure, especially with women's handbags. Ernest Shackleton had less provisions with him when he went to the South Pole than Marjorie keeps in that bag. There're handkerchiefs, painkillers, cotton buds, polo mints, lipstick, cold and flu tablets (in Spain?), Rennie's (they're for me), magazines, Imodium (also for me), lemon sherbets, hand cream, pens, you name it.

I was pondering what to do, and sucking on a lemon sherbet, when Paulo came along to collect my empty glass. "Ey'up, Paulo lad, I don't mean to be a bother, but I think we've got a bit of an issue."

"Something wrong with your beer, Senor Smith?"

"Bloody hell no, lovely it is, no, the thing is I went down to the sea and swam a couple of miles, and as I've come back I've noticed my phone's missing. Here, look..." I held up Marge's bag and the fella peered in.

"Oh, I see. I'm very sorry, Senor Smith, I will write a report and notify the policia. As you may know, this is not the first phone to go missing this week." He scarpered off presumably to make his report and left me wondering. I'd forgotten that young Marley's phone had disappeared too, did this mean there was a thief as well as a murderer running about the place?

When Paulo came back out to tell me the paperwork had been completed, I'd moved to the bar where I was reading a menu. "The usual please, Paulo!"

I was eating my gourmet burger and chips when Marge arrived back with a face like a smacked arse. "What's the matter with you?" I said, leaning forward, being careful about where the juices were dripping.

"The police took young Marley away."

"That's the last we've seen of her, then."

"It wasn't the last we saw of you!" she said, and sounded bitter about it, too.

"I'm innocent!"

"So is she! You can be so insensitive at times, Terry. And I see you didn't wait for me so we could have lunch together." She folded her arms the way women do.

"I didn't know how long you were going to be, did I."

"You could've phoned or sent a text message."

"Ah! That's where you're wrong. I went to call you to ask if you'd be back for lunch, but guess what? My phone's been nicked!"

"No! How?"

"Well, it was like this... I went down the beach for a swim. I practically went all the way to the stork's island. Then I came back and had a quick chat with Luke who was down on the beach, and then I thought to myself, I wonder how poor Marge is getting on finding Marley, she must be getting hungry, I'll just give her a quick ring and make sure she's alright. And as I looked in your bag, there it was. Or there it wasn't, rather."

"That wasn't very clever of you, was it?"

"How'd you mean?"

"It's only been a day or two since Marley's phone went missing, and young Sally's, and you decide to leave my bag wide open by the pool for all and sundry to go through while you're off having a float about? Well, that's just brilliant, isn't it."

"It's not my fault there's dishonest folk about. I'm too trusting, that's my problem. I'm too kind."

"Are you sure it's been stolen? You haven't just lost it?"

"Of course, I'm sure, I had it before I left the sun lounger. I'll have to get another one. There's bound to be somewhere in town I can get one. Probably cheaper than back home, too."

"That shop I went to the other day sells them. We can go tomorrow."

"Why not this afternoon?"

"Because I'm tired and hungry. You can go on your own if you like."

It's not often you see Marjorie in a foul mood, seeing Marley taken away by the police had obviously upset her. Maybe it brought back memories of the other day when I was in that police station and her world fell apart.

"Here you go, old girl," I said, handing her a menu. "Let's get you some grub. Cheer you up a bit." She half-smiled. "Don't worry," I continued to soothe, "I'm sure Marley will be back in no time, all charges dropped just like me."

"I do hope so, Terry. I can't face the thought of seeing Agathe. Sanjay went to find her, to tell her the news."

Marge had a club sandwich and a handful of chips. She perked up a bit, no doubt I played a part in that. I was very attentive and caring, even more so than usual. When her glass was nearly empty, I flagged down a waitress to get her topped up, got myself another each time too, it's only considerate, after all; you don't want the staff doing two trips to the bar when they could be doing one, they're busy enough as it is. I also got her some ketchup, made sure she had enough napkins. Then I helped her finish her chips, otherwise she would've eaten them all and been angry at herself for doing so. *'Oh Terry, I shouldn't have eaten all of them, now I'm going to be fat etc, etc,'* saved her the turmoil, I did. Yes, I turned her mood around with a bit of TLC, Terry Loving Care.

Almost as soon as we'd finished Marge's lunch, Penny joined us briefly. She came from the lobby and sat with us when Marjorie called her over to tell her about Marley's run in with the law.

"I'm sure she'll be out in no time," she said, fingering the pearls around her neck. "The police can't have anything they can make stick, no evidence whatsoever. Even that idiot Moreno will realise that when he speaks to the girl… or when someone speaks to him."

"And now there's another crime he needs to investigate…" I said, hoping to see the woman's eyebrows rise in surprise.

"Oh yes, your phone. I heard about that."

"How?"

"I have my sources. Are you sure you haven't just lost it?"

"Not you as well. That's what Marjorie said, though I don't know why anyone would think I'd be so careless. The only time I lose anything is in the bookies." Penny handed me a napkin; a bit of ketchup had somehow got onto my shirt. "Besides, it's obvious it's been stolen, first Marley's, then Sally's, and now mine."

"And Dylan's."

"Poor dead Dylan's, too?" asked Marge, with a gasp. "Whoever next?"

58

Marley

Agente Garcia offered me a lift back to the hotel. It was my first time in a police car. He told me I could ride up front beside him as I hadn't been arrested, but I wanted the full experience, so I sat in the back and looked out through the blacked-out windows.

When we pulled up outside the hotel Sanjay was standing next to a large plant pot, smoking a cigarette. Agente Garcia wished me a good day and then strode over to talk to him while I went inside.

My first instinct was to seek out Penny to find out if she'd made any progress on the case, but I was dutybound to first see Mum and to let her know I was back safe and sound without being charged. I found her in her room reading her Bible.

"There you are," she said, when I walked in. "So, they let you out?"

"Yes, and without charge, too."

"I should think so, although you might think twice in future about getting yourself arrested."

"I wasn't arr-"

"Interfering in a murder inquiry, such a silly thing to do. If your father was here to see this, he'd die of shame."

"Yes, Mum." When she gets annoyed, whether it's about the subject of conversation or not, she's impossible to placate. The best thing to do is agree with whatever she's saying and make a quick escape, which is what I did.

I found Penny sitting alone by the pool bar beneath the orange tree, her face tilted to the sun, her eyes hidden behind dark sunglasses. She registered no surprise at my resurrection, at least none that I could tell, she merely stood up as I approached and kissed both my cheeks before sitting down. "You've just missed Marjorie and Terry," she said. "They left a couple of minutes ago. Terry's up in arms because his phone has been stolen."

"Another one?" I asked rhetorically. "Another mystery for us to tackle."

"Was Inspector Moreno terribly upset that he was made to let you go?"

"Yes, he – hold on, what do you mean, made to let me go?"

"Well, I couldn't have you languishing in that cell, could I, dear? I need you here helping me to solve the case… and we're getting close."

"We are? Wait, first thing's first. Are you saying you got me out of the police station?"

"The British ambassador in Madrid is an old friend, and he has owed me a favour for twenty years. A quick call to Moreno's boss would've sufficed, British tourism is what keeps these towns afloat, a few words from a displeased ambassador would be quite enough to get you out. Although really, I can't see how Moreno could've held you for more than twenty-four hours, I imagine the evidence against you was flimsy as hell. What was it? Blood on Russell's body?"

"Yes, how did you -"

"I saw the nick on your finger, and you told me you checked for Russell's pulse when you found him, it seemed the most probable conclusion to draw. Forensics these days is akin to wizardry, the boffins in the white coats can pick up the tiniest trace of DNA, then they give it to the idiots with the handcuffs and they wave it around like it's a smoking gun and use it to drive whatever narrative that suits them. Hence how Inspector Moron used your cut finger to convince himself that you killed Russell."

Penny filled me in on Terry's testament about his stolen phone, laughing at the man's indignation when Marjorie suggested that he had probably lost it. "There is another theft I need to tell you about," she said. "Sally and I went to Russell's office this morning. Do you remember we looked in the safe after Russell was killed?"

"Yes…" I could guess what Penny was going to say, but I still found myself shocked when the words came.

"The money from the safe is gone."

"How? Who knew the code?"

"You, me, and Russell that I know of. Of course, someone else might have, a member of staff perhaps."

"You don't think I stole it do you?"

"No, I don't, dear. But it is very curious… Whoever knew the code might not have been looking for the money."

"What do you mean?"

"I'm just thinking out loud. It would be natural to assume that whoever stole the cash opened the safe in order to steal it, meaning they knew the money was there, but… that might not be the case. Imagine if someone opened the safe thinking it contained an important document they wanted, a will or deeds or whatever. They don't find what they're looking for, but their disappointment is softened by finding twenty thousand euros. Or maybe they found what they were looking for and took the money too. As I say, I'm just hypothesizing."

"Actually, now that I think about it, there is another way that someone could have known the code to open the safe…" Penny lowered her head and looked at me over the top of her sunglasses.

"Please enlighten me, dear."

"I've been writing a journal, a sort of diary, on my phone. I started it before the murders, on the plane in fact, just for fun to keep my creative juices flowing. Whoever stole my phone could've read the code. Stupidly, I recorded it when I was recounting that day's events. After Russell was killed, I thought I'd better write all the important bits of the case accurately, after all, it might come in handy as evidence in court one day, or even help solve the murders."

"Marley, darling, why didn't you mention this journal before? It could prove extremely useful, and it may explain why your phone was stolen in the first place. Are you sure you wrote the code in the blog?"

"Yes, look, I had it saved to my iCloud, I retrieved it when I got a new phone. Here it is." I showed Penny the journal, she removed her sunglasses and squinted at the screen. "I wasn't going to put it online or share it with anyone, it was just for me, otherwise I wouldn't have typed in the code. Pretty stupid of me I guess."

"Stupid? Nonsense. This could be a valuable clue. Did you tell anyone you were keeping a diary?"

"Not a soul. Not even Mum. Though someone could've seen me type it over my shoulder, I wasn't super secretive about it."

"Do you mind if I read it?"

"If you think it might help, by all means." I emailed it to her to enjoy at her leisure.

The afternoon was beginning to slow, it was those hours that stretch between lunch and cocktails. I ordered a bottle of sparkling water with a sprig of mint in it and Penny chose a coffee. "Mental stimulation will be needed this evening. I'm expecting my friend in London to send the internet records of the guests at any minute."

"Do you think we'll find anything that will nail the killer?"

"I hope so; time will tell. Are you alright, Marley? Here's me blabbing on about the case and you're probably still reeling from the day you've had. They didn't treat you too poorly in the police station, did they?"

"No, it was fine. Agente Garcia is not like Inspector Moreno. In fact, I don't think he respects his boss too much. When I was being interrogated he would subtlety steer the inspector, who was oblivious, of course. It was Agente Garcia who found me. I was with Marjorie and Sanjay in a café when he… Oh, Penny! I forgot to say! I haven't told you what I saw." I quickly looked around, aware that in my excitement my voice had risen and that I was probably being stared at by curious sunbathers. I lowered my volume, leaned closer to Penny and continued. "As I was saying, I was in a café when Agente Garcia found me, but I wasn't there enjoying a nice spot of lunch, although I did have quite a delicious smoothie… no, I ducked in there so that I wouldn't be seen."

"Seen by who?" asked Penny, raising an eyebrow.

"Elle or Jasmine. I saw them together in the art gallery, they were talking, confiding rather, then Jasmine took something from her bag and handed it to Elle."

"Could you make out what it was?"

"No, the exchange happened so quick, Elle took whatever it was and stuffed it in her handbag in the blink of an eye."

"Hmm, now that *is* interesting. So that's where Jasmine was this morning. She told Sally she'd spent all day by the pool, but I knew she was lying."

"Are you going to confront her about it?"

"Yes, but timing is everything. Don't forget, we need these people to give us answers willingly, not to clam up. The suspects must want to talk to us. Ideally, they would think themselves smarter than us, be a little cocky, even."

"But what if they lie to us?"

"They're all lying to us, dear, about something or other. And if the killer isn't lying to us, then I'm afraid we aren't asking the right questions. It's all about catching them out in their lies, in trapping them with proof. In truth, I'm beginning to have an inkling who the killer is, I just need more proof."

She spoke mechanically, almost to herself, her fingers toying with the pearls around her throat.

"You do? Who?" My shock was so acute I wasn't sure if my breathless words were audible.

"I can't tell you yet, dear, I may be wrong, and I don't want to influence your thoughts. Hopefully, my contact in London will send us the information we need and that will put matters to bed. In the meantime, we won't let the grass grow under our feet, we shall carry on striving for the truth. Tell me, dear, you're young, what do you know about social media?"

"Quite a lot. Why?"

59

Sally

Jasmine and I went back to the room for an afternoon nap before going to the beach at sunset as I'd promised. On the way past the pool, she stopped at the outdoor shower. She stood under the gushing nozzle for a minute, wetting her hair but being careful not to ruin her newly applied makeup. When we got down to the beach, she looked like she had just emerged from the sea, a nereid come from the deep to tempt and tease foolish, mortal men. She was wearing an apricot-coloured bikini, darkened by the water, and she bent forward then threw her hair back, the slapping of the wet strands hitting her back being the only sound other than the fizzing of the receding waves.

"How does it look? It should be wild but not straggly, like natural but not clumpy."

"Your hair looks great," I said, unsure whether I was lying or telling the truth.

Jasmine walked into the surf until her ankles were submerged, then dropped to her knees and began twisting her body with her hands behind her head. I took this as my cue to start snapping, using her phone, the camera on it being much better than my cheap replacement. The sun was dipping into the sea and her skin was aflame in the crimson-orange light, her dripping hair shimmering, the droplets falling like beads of mercury into the briny blue.

The sun sank faster than we'd anticipated, so that in a few short minutes the light had faded almost to dusk, ending the photoshoot and the day. We sat huddled next to each other, a towel wrapped around our shoulders, silently listening to the lazy waves. I wondered how many other people around the world were listening to the same sound, to the continuous currents washing the sands.

We both shivered and decided to go to our room and get ready for the evening, discussing dinner plans and what we would wear as we ascended the rickety old steps. We were still chatting when we came out of the lift, walked the short distance to the room and found Penny sitting in the armchair next to my bed, a cup of coffee in her hand.

"Penny," I said, shocked, "what are you doing here? How did you get in?"

"Quite easily, my dear. Take a seat, both of you." Her voice was cool, but with an edge to it, as though she were pointing an invisible gun at the pair of us. We obeyed, waiting for her next move or command.

"It's you I want to speak with, Jasmine. If you don't want Sally to be present to hear my questions then I suggest you ask her to leave."

"I'm not going anywhere!" I said, dumbfounded by Penny's formal manner and the underlying menace it seemed to carry. Penny looked at Jasmine and raised her eyebrows.

"Sally can stay," Jasmine said, in a shaken voice. "Whatever we talk about, she's bound to ask me later. There's been enough lies on this holiday."

"Indeed, there have." Penny looked at Jasmine as though determining the best approach to take with her. "Jasmine, why did you come here?"

"You know why, for a holiday with Sally."

"Ah, another lie. You see, dear, if it were me, and I wanted to go on holiday with my friend, I wouldn't choose to stay in the same hotel that my ex-boyfriend is staying in. Especially an ex-boyfriend who I hate as much as you hated Dylan."

"This is nonsense," I said. "Jasmine didn't even know that Dylan was -" my voice froze when I saw the look on Jasmine's face. "You knew!"

"Yes, she knew. It was Jasmine's idea to come here, remember? When she found out that Dylan was going to be here, she saw an opportunity, what for I'm not exactly sure. Did you come here to kill him?"

"No! I swear."

"Why, then?"

"How did you know I followed him here?"

"Probability. I know that Elle tagged Dylan in an Instagram post saying how excited she was to be going on holiday with him. She even put the dates and the name of this hotel. Dylan, for his part, had never put anything on his Instagram account that was personal, or that even hinted at his whereabouts. I also noticed that Dylan's Instagram account was created *after* you and he had split up. You knew his tricks, the fake photographer ruse, the fake names, it would be difficult but by no means impossible for you to find him online. So, I asked myself, if you knew he was going to be here, why would you come too?"

"I didn't kill him!"

"If you want me to believe you, you had better explain what you're doing here."

"Okay." Jasmine looked at me through watery eyes and reached her hand out to me. I hesitated before taking it. We'd been growing apart before we came here, and after a rocky few days we had grown closer than ever, and the reason for that was honesty. Jasmine being honest about her horrid relationship with Dylan and what he put her through, and me being honest about my part in their break up, and now here we were, embroiled in lies again.

"You know some of this, Sal, but not all. Dylan stole from me when we broke up. He wiped out my bank accounts, took out a loan in my name, credit cards, everything you can think of. Then he vanished, moving on to his next victim."

"Why didn't you tell me?"

"I was embarrassed. As if I didn't feel a big enough fool with him seeing someone else, I wasn't keen on anyone knowing he had completely ripped me off, leaving me thousands of pounds in debt. I felt like such a fool. I searched for him online exactly like you said,

Penny, and I found him, but there was nothing to indicate where he was. I knew he was using another fake name so I couldn't trace him. Then, one day, Elle posts about this holiday and tags him: it was perfect. Even if Russell didn't own the place, I still would've got us here so that I could confront him, so I could get my money back."

"So, you told him that if he didn't pay you back, you'd call the police," Penny guessed.

"Yeah. I spoke to him in the airport before we picked up our luggage, he was on his own, I don't know where Elle was."

"And what did he say?"

"He said the Spanish police wouldn't be interested, that only the British police could arrest him. I knew he was right, so I played my trump card; I told him that if he didn't pay me back the money, I'd expose him to Elle, tell her what he was really like."

"What was his response?"

"He took out his phone…"

"That's when you found out?" I screeched. "In the airport?"

"Hold on, you've lost me," Penny said. "Found out what? What was on his phone?" Tears began rolling down Jasmine's cheeks and I knew she wouldn't be unable to answer, so I did my best for her, knowing what she told me the other day.

"Dylan had pictures and videos of Jasmine from when they were together. Explicit stuff."

"I see. And he threatened to put these images online if you told Elle or the police about him?"

Jasmine nodded, still overcome by emotion.

"How much money did he steal from you?"

"Nearly twenty thousand pounds."

"Not a small sum, especially for someone your age. You have my sympathy, dear, about everything. Dylan's phone, you stole that, didn't you?"

"Yes, I waited for the perfect moment, right before you all set off for the island. I knew that if he noticed it was missing there would be nothing he could do about it. I watched you motor off knowing I had plenty of time to go through his phone and delete the pictures and videos and not be disturbed or rushed."

"Why did you give the phone to Elle this morning in the art gallery?"

"How do you know about that?"

"Eyes and ears, my dears, eyes and ears."

"When I was looking through it, I came across photos of Elle, too. I thought she should be the one to delete them, maybe it would give her closure, or… I don't know. It just seemed like the right thing to do."

"It was. As was being honest with me."

60

Sanjay

I thought cigarettes would taste better now that I don't have the guilt about smoking them, but they don't. Each stinking puff reminds me why I don't have the guilt, that there's no one to disapprove of my addiction.

I was slowly expelling wreaths of smoke from my tingling nostrils outside the hotel when a police car pulled up. Marley got out and dashed into the lobby, giving me a wave and a smile as she went. Agente Garcia had been behind the wheel, but instead of driving off, he came over to me, his long, slow strides almost matching Marley's excited pace.

"Good evening," I said, blowing my smoke sideways away from him.

"Hello again." He took out a packet of cigarettes from his pocket, I scrambled to offer him a light.

"I see you brought Marley back…"

"Si. The girl is no murderer, though my boss is not satisfied, so I must come here to look for proof of her innocence. I will be searching all the rooms again."

"What are you looking for?"

"I'm afraid I cannot say. Do not worry, I shall be quick and leave everything tidy."

"I had better tell you that I've moved rooms. I'm now in the East Wing, room 207." Agente Garcia raised his eyebrows and took a long drag on his cigarette.

"You have had a quarrel with your partner?"

"Something like that. Tell me, when do you think Inspector Moreno will allow our passports to be released? I don't fancy staying here for another week."

"Once he has made an arrest, your passports will be returned."

"And if he doesn't make an arrest? Let's face it, it's not looking too promising, is it? He's had two people in custody and released both without charge."

"We are getting closer. The forensic analysis report came back; Penny Haylestone was right, Dylan was killed with a combination of nicotine and digitalis poisoning which was contained within the EpiPen."

"And Russell's murder?"

He shrugged and held out his arms.

We went to my room. I hadn't yet unpacked my suitcase, its contents jumbled together, thrown in hurriedly, such was my desire to be away from Luke. Agente Garcia watched as I took out my clothes and hung them up, this apparently counting as part of his search. We chatted about Spain and London, about my life and his. I didn't mention Luke at all, as if when describing my life I was talking about how it will be and not how it was. I don't know if he was being deceptively nice in the hope that I would slip up and reveal myself to be the murderer or give him some lead, but I don't think so. I think (and hope) that his genial curiosity was genuine. It was like he wasn't wearing his uniform, and there was no barrier between us. He made a cursory search, opening the bedside drawers and checking the bathroom, and was satisfied that whatever it was he was looking for wasn't hidden in my room.

When he left, I sat on the edge of the bed. The sun was going down, its rays turning to a pinkish orange, the last blast of beauty for the day. I wondered what I would do with my evening, could I face the stares and murmurs if I sat alone in the restaurant for dinner? Penny does it with ease. She'll sit nibbling on a piece of bread, or an olive, looking around her, observing everything. She has no embarrassment and is completely at ease with herself and content in her own company. I've seen her politely turn down invitations to join others for dinner, those well-meaning guests wrongly assuming that she would like company. Of course, she came here to see Russell, and if he hadn't been killed she would spend less time alone, but still, how I envy her confidence. Maybe it's age. Maybe as you get older you give less of a toss about what people think. I guess I've always been conscious of others, hiding my sexuality for so many years, the diligence required to do so. I decided to try to be more like Penny; I could get through dinner on my own. And if the restaurant was full and I panicked, I could always walk into town and get a kebab.

I stepped onto the balcony and looked down at the pool. Penny and Marley were sitting at the bar having a drink, their heads close together. I then looked across to the West Wing, wondering how far Agente Garcia had got in his search. I wondered what he was looking for, then fear gripped me. What if he was searching for what I had found in Luke's bag? Surely not, how could it be? But then again…

Even if Agente Garcia *was* looking for something else, he would find what I had found, Luke hadn't exactly hidden it well. And if he did find it, he might think I had something to do with it. After all, I was staying in that room until only an hour or so ago. I had to think quickly and make a decision. I sat on the edge of the bed for a few minutes then pulled out my phone. Luke answered after the fourth ring. "Are you in your room?" I asked, forgoing with pleasantries.

"Yeah, why? Decided to come crawling back?"

"No chance."

"Well, I hope you're going to move out of *my* house as fast as you moved out of this room."

"Don't worry, as soon as the police hand my passport over, I'll be on the first flight out of here and out of your life."

"Is that why you phoned me? To tell me you don't need me, that you'll be alright on your own? You're only trying to convince yourself, Sanjay, we both know it's a lie."

"I don't care what you think, not anymore. But that's not why I'm phoning you. I called to tell you the police have just searched my room, and they're coming to search yours, too."

"What for?" he asked, the smallest hint of strain audible in his voice.

"I don't know, they wouldn't tell me. But if I was you, I'd get rid of that twenty grand that's hidden so well in your suitcase."

61

Terry

I have to say, I'm very pleased with how my tan is coming on. I was worried that the two murders might have affected it, what with spending practically a whole day locked in my room when Russell was murdered and another in a police cell, but overall, I think I'm browning well, much better than that East Winger. He's been here a week longer than me and he's still using factor 30 suncream. You'd think he'd know oil is the way to go, and if not, just one look at me and my tan would give him a clue. I was just admiring it in the mirror when Marjorie said she was going to have a bath. "A bath?" I said. "It's still thirty-odd degrees outside and you're having a bath?"

"I'm not going to make it too hot, Terry, I just want to relax for a bit."

"You might as well just go for a dip in the pool."

"Nonsense, it's got chlorine and bacteria in it."

"Is that why you haven't been in it yet? Bloody bacteria? Honestly, Marge, I don't know why you suggested this holiday, all you've done is sit in the shade."

"And what's wrong with that? I like sitting in the shade, it's very pleasant, and it's still nice and warm, just not too hot."

"Well, what the bleeding heck am I going to do while you're soaking in the bath?"

"Why don't you go down to the bar and have a drink?"

She didn't need to tell me twice. Paulo saw me instantly and sent one of the young waitresses over with a nice frothy beer. I was just thinking how wonderful it was to be breathing in the warm air with a cold drink, enjoying the peace and quiet, when Penny bloody Haylestone came over and plonked herself down next to me. I'd only just got rid of her an hour before. It's not that I don't like her, it's that you've got to be careful what you say. You don't know where her questions are going to lead or what motive lies behind them. One minute, you'll be talking about storks, or paella, or whatever, and then she'll blurt out something about me killing Dylan or Russell or whoever. I wouldn't be surprised if she has me in mind as being Jack the Ripper.

"Ey'up, Penny girl, can I get you a drink? What would you like?"

"Gin, thank you, Terry." A young waitress ran back and forth to the bar.

"You've not come to question me about murders and whatnot, have you?" I asked, half-joking.

"Heavens no. You've already told me everything you know, haven't you. And you withstood police interrogation, very impressive. I know the tricks and tactics they use. Underhand, quite often."

"Too bloody right. Still, if you're innocent, you've nought to worry about, do you."

"If only that were true. I wouldn't trust Inspector Moreno not to pull a stitch up job, would you?"

I scratched my chin; she was right on that one. The inspector was a slippery customer. "Agente Garcia seems a fair enough bloke," I said. "He was very hospitable when I was locked up inside."

"I wonder if he's having any luck now…"

"How do you mean?"

"He's searching all the rooms again. He knocked on my door before I came down here."

"Searching for what?"

"I didn't stay to find out, I've got nothing to hide. But I would imagine he's looking for the tape measure that Marley cut her finger on to corroborate her story. I just told him to close the door behind him and that if he wanted to speak to me, he could find me here. He did mention one thing though, as I was leaving. I was right; Dylan *was* poisoned, the substance in his EpiPen was a concoction of digitalis and nicotine, the laboratory confirmed it."

"Digi-what?"

"Digitalis, it's a poison found in certain flowers, foxglove being the common one. Not hard to get hold of around here. It's a beautiful summer flower, purple and tubular in shape, and very toxic. It's used in medicine to treat certain heart conditions, in small, measured quantities you understand. Too much, or a strong dose, and the opposite effect occurs; it stops the heart."

"How do you know all this?"

"I have some in my garden at home. Horticulture is a hobby of mine."

"You said there was nicotine in the syringe, too? Why?"

"Nicotine is an alkaloid from the nightshade plant. You may have heard of deadly nightshade? In fact, nicotine on its own probably would've caused death but the killer was making sure with the digitalis."

"But people smoke nicotine, and it doesn't kill them, does it?"

"No, but breathing in cigarette smoke and having nicotine injected into your body are two very different things. Even if you ingest nicotine, you'll be violently sick."

"Blimey, the killer was really covering all bases weren't he."

"It seems so, though I can't help but feel there was another reason for the choice of poison: pain. The effect of the combination of the digitalis on the heart and the nicotine in the blood and tissue would cause severe agony, which is what we saw Dylan suffer. I wonder..."

"People don't like blackmailers, Penny."

"How did you know Dylan was a blackmailer?" I spluttered my beer down my shirt, then coughed to give myself time to think, not that it did me much good. Penny's razor-sharp eyes observed me, then took hold of me and shook me, until finally, I was shifting and squirming in my chair.

"Do not lie to me," she said quietly yet forcefully, before I had uttered a word.

"First off, I want to make clear, I didn't kill him."

"Understood. Go on."

"It's not important you see, and it's nothing you don't already know, not really. But Dylan saw me throw the rock at Russell and was trying to squeeze twenty grand out of me to keep schtum."

"Did you give it to him?"

"Joking, aren't you. Where do you think I would get twenty thousand big ones from? I haven't worked in six months, I'm not exactly flush with cash, am I? But it didn't matter in the end, did it, because I went to the police, was cleared, and then someone killed the little rat anyway."

"Did Marjorie know you were being blackmailed?"

"You think Marge killed Dylan to protect me? The thought had crossed my mind too, but she didn't know I was being blackmailed. At least, I never mentioned it, and neither has she."

"There must be some way she could know. Maybe Dylan mentioned it to her. Maybe he was trying to blackmail her too, 'give me twenty grand or your hubby goes to jail.'"

That was a point I hadn't thought of, but I didn't consider it likely. More probable was Marjorie reading my diary and finding out about the blackmail that way. But would she really kill Dylan? Marge would be much more likely to go to the police and trust them to deal with it.

"What exactly did Dylan say to you?" Penny asked, taking the wedge of lime from her glass before biting into it.

"He told me he knew who killed Russell, and I said it weren't me. He said the police wouldn't believe that, and I'd better fork out to keep him quiet. I was about to tell him where to stick it, when he said, '*I could tell the police it was you I saw talking to Russell this morning before he died.*' So you see, he must've seen me on the beach when I threw the rock. Later on, I figured he got the same idea as me, that Russell died of a delayed reaction, after all, it were Elle who told me the story about her cousin, maybe she told him, too."

"Oh, Terry, I think you've been had."

"Had? How do you mean?"

"I don't think Dylan saw you at all on the morning Russell died, I think he was trying his luck."

"But he said -"

"I know what he said, but if you've recounted his words accurately, even you can see that he was lying. Or at least half-lying."

"What? How?" I asked, taking a gulp of beer.

"If Dylan saw you talking to Russell he would've said, 'I'll tell the police I saw you talking to Russell this morning,' but according to you, he said, 'I'll tell the police it was *you* I saw talking to Russell this morning.' Do you not see the difference? He did see someone talking to Russell, but it wasn't you. And Dylan told me he saw someone having a heated discussion with Russell in the stairwell of the West Wing on the morning of the murder. At the time I wasn't sure if he was telling the truth or fishing for attention, or if he was a blackmailer for that matter, but now I think he did see someone violently argue with Russell, the only question is who?"

62

Marley

I had dinner in the restaurant with Mum. As we passed through the lobby, I could see Penny torturing Terry at the pool bar. The poor man looked as though there was a heat lamp hovering above his head, beads of sweat were hanging precipitously on his hairline, illuminated by the hundreds of fairy lights which provided a canopy to the bar area.

The restaurant was full of East Wingers. They're a smug lot. They walk around like they own the place because they've been here for a week longer than us. Either that or they think themselves superior because none of them can be accused of murder. They've all got clad-iron alibis.

Mum and I both passed on a starter, Mum's appetite not up to it and me eager to see Penny. I assumed her contact had sent the information we were waiting for, and I was keen for us to resume the investigation, aided by fresh clues.

My haste to be done with dinner was, however, forgotten when a waitress brought my main course. Pork in whisky sauce, with a side of tenderstem broccoli doused in a chilli infused oil. The meat was deliciously tender, the perfect amount of seasoning balanced by the tang of the sauce. I savoured every morsel and was left satisfied by the rich meal. When offered the dessert menu I declined, content and happy.

"Would you like some coffee, Mum?"

"No, I need an early night, all this murder business is exhausting. Coffee will keep me awake; you know my bones need their rest. What are you planning to do this evening? Not getting yourself arrested again, I hope."

I felt a tinge of sadness and guilt. Mum had obviously (and correctly) thought that I had no intention of spending the evening with her, that I would be off crimefighting or sticking my nose in where it wasn't needed. I tried to console myself by thinking that if I helped catch Russell's killer it would bring comfort to her, but I knew this was a lie; I was helping Penny because it was exciting, not because I wanted to give Mum solace through justice.

"Are you enjoying your holiday, Mum?" I asked, fearful of the answer.

"I always enjoy myself at The Orange Tree Hotel, you know that. Though it's not quite the same without Russell."

"Russell? I thought you were about to say Dad."

"Honey, I'm used to your father not being around anymore, and I wasn't expecting to see him here, was I? But Russell I was. Your father and Russell got on like a house on fire, sitting drinking rum, fishing, laughing over nothing, and now he's gone…"

And now he's gone, so is another link to your father. That's what she was thinking and stopped herself from saying.

"I'm sorry I've left you on your own and been running around so much, Mum."

"That's alright, you've always had boundless energy ever since you were a little girl, I just can't keep up with you anymore." She kicked the wheelchair next to her, before continuing. "But just because I can't keep up, doesn't mean it's right for me to clip your wings and hold you back. You go and help Penny find whoever killed Russell, you've got a better chance than that oaf of a policeman."

"You really think so?"

"I do. You're a bright girl, you just get a little distracted at times, and Penny is as sharp as a razor. You go solve the murders, then we can enjoy some time together."

"Yes, Mum." I left her with a new resolution in my heart. Just because I hadn't been seeking the killer for my mum's sake up to that point, doesn't mean I couldn't from now on.

When I stepped out of the lobby and onto the tiles of the pool bar, I saw Penny sitting alone and joined her.

"Hi. No Terry?"

"He left me ten minutes ago; I've been reading this since. Here, take a look." Penny handed me an electronic tablet. On the screen I saw a report with names and email addresses along with websites listed and search engine results. The report was split into sections, each one allocated to a different hotel guest. I saw my name on there and winced, unsure what embarrassing searches I'd find.

"How far back do the searches go?" I asked.

"Two months."

"But whoever killed Dylan will only have searched for poisons and EpiPens in the last week."

"True, but we may find something related to Russell. That would be a real scoop."

"Have you found anything interesting?"

"Not yet, but I've only got as far as you and your mother. You appear to mostly look at art supplies, and your mum appears to spend more time on IMDB.com than she could actually watching films."

I placed the tablet between us so we could read together. Marjorie was next on the list, there was nothing to indicate she had searched for Russell or the hotel other than a visit to TripAdvisor, which also included restaurants and shops in the local area.

When we reached Terry, Penny told me of her recent conversation with him and how Dylan had been blackmailing him. If he hadn't mentioned it, we would've been enlightened by his internet search history, anyway.

'What is blackmail?' – *Blackmail is the demand of money....*

'What is the going rate for blackmail?' - *Blackmail and extortion are serious crimes...*

'What's the difference between blackmail and entrapment?' – *The biggest difference between blackmail and entrapment...*

'Entrapment' – *Entrapment is a 1999 film starring Sean Connery and Catherine Zeta-Jones*

'Catherine Zeta-Jones pictures' – *Images results*

'How old was Sean Connery when he died?' – *Sean Connery was 90 years old when he died on 31st October 2020*

'Who will be the next James Bond? - ….

"Nothing much to help us there, I'm afraid," said Penny.

Sally was next. Her searches mainly centred on various publishers and the 'career' pages on their websites. There were also searches for flat shares and estate agents.

"Jasmine is next," I said, swiping my finger on the screen to scroll down the page. "Oh, hello…" My eyes immediately latched onto a name on the screen, and not the one I was expecting. Jasmine had already told us of her quest to find Dylan, so I wasn't surprised to see his name at the bottom of the screen, but the name that made me gasp when I saw it was *Russell Aspell*. There were several variations of the same generic search. *Russell Aspell, Russell Aspell – Spain, Russell Aspell – The Orange Tree Hotel.*

"Interesting…" said Penny.

"Maybe she was looking for a motive as to why someone would kill him," I suggested fairly.

"I don't think so; look at the dates. Jasmine searched Russell's name after she arrived at the hotel but *before* he was murdered. Will this girl ever stop lying to us?"

The rest of Jasmine's search results showed clothes and fashion websites, a few model agencies and hair style articles.

"Who's next?" Penny asked.

"Dylan." The results for the second murder victim were underwhelming. I had hoped to find a clue about the many lives the man seemed to lead, but he was as guarded on his internet search history as he was on his social media. Pornography, BBC news, and Sky Sports appeared to make up the entire range of his interests.

Elle's results confused me, until Penny enlightened me with what she had discovered. It seemed Elle had a growing unease about the man she was in a relationship with. She had searched for information about hard drives, storage clouds, and the dark web. It seemed she too was worried about Dylan having pictures of her in his possession, out of her reach and control.

This left Sanjay and Luke. "It looks like Sanjay makes a lot of work-related searches. There are lots of links to his local area and articles he's written," I said. "Other than that, it's which podcasts are hot right now, a bit of celeb gossip, and a lot of eBay browsing."

"What about Luke?"

"The same, really; shopping, cooking recipes, nothing to get excited about. The only person who warrants further investigation is Jasmine I'd say."

"She's certainly keeping secrets from us."

"And no one has searched for EpiPens, or how to replace the adrenaline in them with another substance. How is the search carried out? Is it by device?"

"No, it's through email, phone number, everything linked to that particular person."

"So, if someone got a new phone and made a search, the results would still appear on this?" I asked, tapping the tablet in front of me.

"Yes, because the phone is linked to you. The same goes for email addresses, if you use multiple, a work one for example, the results will still be here." I was disappointed, I thought I'd found a way that someone could evade the search by using a different phone or laptop, but of course, these days, all devices need registering before use.

"We know Jasmine's motive for killing Dylan, but why would she want to kill Russell? She now seems the most likely killer, don't you think?"

"No…" Penny said, staring at the tablet. "There's someone at the heart of this case, who's not on that report."

63

Sally

Although I was disappointed Jasmine had kept another secret from me, I could understand it. To have someone you trust steal from you is bad enough, on top of Dylan's affair it must've been a real body blow, and that's before you take that revenge porn is taken into consideration.

As soon as Penny left us, Jasmine went into the bathroom to change out of her damp bikini. She emerged a few minutes later wearing a pair of denim shorts and a tight top. She was still dabbing her hair with a towel when there was a knock at the door. We both sat in silence, expecting another knock and then whoever it was to go away defeated, but we heard the electronic beep of the access card reader and the door opened. Agente Garcia stood in the doorway. "I'm sorry, senora," he said, seeing me stare at him. "I thought the room was empty. I am authorised to carry out another search, with or without you present."

"In that case, it'll be without," I said, more rudely than I intended. Jasmine followed me, not speaking until we stepped into the lift.

"Are you angry at me? I don't blame you if you are, I was just so embarrassed."

"I'm not angry at you. I just wish you had told me; I could've helped."

"How?"

"I don't know, a problem shared and all that…" Jasmine opened her mouth to respond, then shut it tight. I wondered if she was going to say it was cash that she needed, not support. Twenty thousand pounds is a lot of money, especially when some of it is debt. The pair of us have never been flush, our mums being single parents, but at least my dad sent a few quid home now and again when he got shore leave from the oil rig (if Aberdeen's pubs hadn't taken it all). But Jasmine's father had never been on the scene and doesn't get mentioned. Jasmine's mum has a personality that fills the whole house and has always earned enough that money worries are on the horizon and not around the corner. I've never heard her mum make a bitter comment about her father, or lament him not being there, she's not the type of woman to look back or dwell on anything; she rushes forward, usually leaving chaos and laughter in her wake.

The pinging lift broke our uneasy silence as the doors opened onto the lobby. Paulo came from behind the reception to greet us. "Good evening, ladies, would you like a table for dinner?"

"Yes, thank you, Paulo, a private table if there is one, away from the other guests." I wasn't sure if Jasmine intended to continue our conversation regarding her stolen money but if she did, I didn't want anyone else hearing it.

As he escorted us, Paulo dropped his voice and spoke just loud enough for us to hear him. He bowed close to me, and I caught a whiff of his strong, masculine aftershave from his dark, stubbled throat.

"I'm afraid the police are back in the hotel, senora. Agente Garcia is searching for something and has the correct documentation with him. I could not stop him."

"That's okay, Paulo. If it helps catch Russell's killer, the police can look wherever they please."

The restaurant was bustling. I was glad of the noise and clamour, hoping it would drown out our discussion. Paulo took us to one of the few vacant tables and pulled it close to the wall so that we were as isolated as could be. The candleflame in the middle of the table flickered, then settled, vanquishing a shadow on the wall.

I looked around the room as Jasmine inspected the menu; I'd decided on the swordfish with mango salsa as soon as I saw it. I noticed Luke sitting alone by the window which separated the restaurant from the pool. He was pouring red wine into his glass. When he set the bottle on the table it was empty. He looked up, met my gaze, and held it. I noticed a dark yellow bruise on his jawline, as if he'd fallen into something. At his foot lay a leather satchel, more fashionable than practical.

"The ratatouille sounds good," said Jasmine, bringing my attention back to our table. "I think I'll have that." She snapped shut her menu, and as though that were his cue, Paulo appeared and took our order.

"What do you think Agente Garcia is searching for?" she said. "It must be something specific, they've already searched the hotel."

"I'm not sure," I answered. "Probably the stolen phones."

"You'd think they'd be focusing on the murders, not a couple of nicked phones."

"Unless they think the phones are somehow linked to the murders," I said.

"How? It's not like Russell's phone was stolen, and we know I took Dylan's, and that was nothing to do with his murder."

"The police don't know that."

"True. I hadn't considered that. You don't think Penny will tell them I stole Dylan's phone, do you?"

"No, I think your secret's safe with her. And don't forget, we don't know who stole Marley's phone, or why, or, if it was in fact stolen and not lost."

"I still don't see how it could be connected to the murders."

I considered the possibility that the police were, in fact, looking for the cash that had been stolen from Russell's safe, but as far as I knew, Inspector Moreno wasn't aware of the money's existence never mind its theft. Of course, I have wondered if I should tell the police of the stolen money, but I worry it would put a spotlight on me. My uncle is murdered, I'm revealed as his heir, and I'm concerned about money? It would look like I'm making a fraudulent claim to get extra cash at best, and a suspect for his murder at worst. No, best to say nothing, you can't miss what you've never had, and that money has never been mine as far as I'm concerned.

The swordfish was exquisite, perfectly complimented by the sweet and spicy salsa. The restaurant began to empty as we ate, the noise level dropping as a result, and our voices, too. When I looked up, I could see that Luke had finished his wine and was now showing his affections to whisky instead. To my surprise, he was still looking at me, his drunken stare more disconcerting than before. If he wasn't gay, I would've felt more uncomfortable; it was like he was leering, or unsure about something, trying to figure something out. His eyebrows were knitted, and he was leaning forward on his elbows, his whisky tumbler suspended from his limp hand like a worthless car in the mechanical claws of a scrap yard grabber.

We charged the meal to our room and I ordered a coffee. Jasmine's phone rang, its vibrations edging it towards the end of the table and making her wine ripple faintly in its glass. She glanced at the screen and said, "It's my mum, I'll be right back." She left the restaurant and I looked again at Luke. As soon as our eyes locked, he got up, picked up the satchel and came over to me.

"Can we talk?"

"Erm, sure," I said, hesitatingly.

"I mean somewhere more private." If I hadn't seen him finish a whole bottle of wine and more besides, I wouldn't have known he'd been drinking. His voice was clear, and he stood straight, without the slightest wobble. I still felt uneasy but decided to go with him.

"Paulo," I said to the man as we passed him, making sure Luke heard me, "when Jasmine comes back can you tell her I'm with Luke at the beach and I won't be long, thanks."

We passed the pool bar unnoticed and uninterrupted by any of the other guests, and descended the wooden steps until the hard boards beneath our feet were replaced by sinking sands. We half-sat, half-leant on the huge rocks which sit at the base of the cliff face.

"What do you want to see me about?" I asked, the darkness and solitude heightening my unease.

"I want to give you something, two things, actually. First, advice."

"Go on," I said, intrigued.

"You know I am here because I was Russell's solicitor?"

"Yes…"

"Your uncle has, in the past few months, had issues which he has made disappear through, shall we say, inappropriate methods."

"You mean illegal?"

"Yes."

"What sort of issues?"

"It's to do with the legal ownership of the hotel grounds, the boundaries to be precise. The deeds show that the adjacent property own the land that a section of the restaurant sits on, where you were sitting at dinner, in fact. The rightful owner is an amicable old guy and was happy to accept payment from Russell for the land and had no wish for any hassle."

"So, what was illegal?"

"The payment, and certain tax implications."

"I'm sorry, I'm confused, you said you wanted to give me advice?"

Luke bit his lip before continuing. "I discovered the discrepancy when looking through Russell's files. I was looking into a different, now resolved issue. I can tell you that my firm will have nothing to do with this matter, it could put its reputation at stake. I, however, will make the problem disappear. I can shift funds around to ensure the correct tax is paid and there will be no fallout onto you."

"Why would you help me if your company would wash their hands of the situation?"

"To make amends."

"For what?" For a second, I thought Luke was about to confess to Russell's murder.

He had explained the financial peril of the hotel in clear layman's terms, but I could smell the whisky on his breath and wondered if the alcohol was loosening his tongue. Instead, he opened the satchel and held out a lumpy plastic bag. "It's twenty thousand euros I took from Russell's safe."

"You? How did you get in? How did you know the code?"

"I watched Russell enter it one day. To answer your first question, Russell gave me a spare key so I could work in his office without him being there."

"Why did you take it? Are you that strapped for cash that you would steal from your murdered client?"

"He didn't take it for himself," said a voice in the darkness. I turned my head and watched Penny emerge from the murky dusk. "Isn't that right, Luke?"

He nodded, his lips quivering.

"You see, dear, Luke took the money to give to Dylan. Another victim of blackmail stands before you."

"What dirt did he have on you, or do I not want to know?"

"You do know, or at least you would if you put the pieces together," Penny said. I was at a loss for words, so Penny continued to supply them. "You yourself provided me with the clue needed to solve this particular mystery. Remember the phone call you overheard in the pub all those years ago? Dylan didn't start seeing Elle until eighteen months ago, so it wasn't her you overheard him talking to on the phone. It was Luke, or 'L' as Dylan called him. Then Marley heard Luke talking to someone on the phone when she and I went for cocktails, she heard, *'You bastard! How am I supposed to do that? It's too much money. I'm warning you; I'll kill you!'*"

"I didn't kill him, I swear." Luke had found his voice, but it was weak and faint.

"I know you didn't, I saw your reaction when he died, you were... grief-stricken. I could see that Dylan was someone you cared for, or at least had cared for at one time. That was when I knew you had been lovers, and then learning about Dylan's history of blackmail it took no great leap of imagination to conclude that he wanted money to keep his mouth shut and not tell your sordid secret to Sanjay."

"I stole the money and Sanjay found it. He wanted to know where it came from, so I told him."

"Did you tell him who it was that you were having an affair with?"

"No, I didn't see that it mattered, and besides, I didn't want Sanjay to be suspected of Dylan's murder, he found out about the affair *after* Dylan died."

"Can you be sure of that?"

"What do you mean?"

"Never mind. So, there you are, dear," said Penny, turning to me again. "It appears the offer on the table is take back the twenty grand which is rightfully yours, accept Luke's help in the hotel's financial matters, and all he asks for in return is that you don't tell the police about the theft or the affair. Personally, I think it's a pretty good deal."

64

Sanjay

I scoffed my dinner down like a starving dog. The restaurant was almost deserted, I'd waited until what I judged to be the last possible moment when I would be seated without being told the kitchen was closed. By the time my prawn linguine arrived the only other occupants were a couple who were finishing two glasses of tawny port.

Exhausted by the day's events I went straight to bed after dinner, the bed feeling huge because it was empty. I feared I wouldn't sleep, unused to being alone, but I drifted off and woke this morning to the sound of birdsong.

I had no appetite having eaten late, so I decided to spend the morning by the pool, thinking the murders over in my mind. If I could solve them, I could get out of here sooner and also make definite plans for my true crime book.

I was the first guest to the pool, well, except for Terry whose towel was draped over a sun lounger, although the man himself was absent. I chose a sunny spot as far from Terry's lounger as possible and plugged in my earphones and closed my eyes. For a few hours I thought, listened, surmised, calculated, and ultimately failed to unmask the killer.

When I opened my eyes, I saw most of the other guests working on their tans. Luke was not amongst them. I went to the bar to get a fruit juice and on my way back to the lounger was persuaded to sit with Marley, Agathe and Penny beneath the orange tree. Marley's radiant smile pulled me in like a tractor beam, and I was still grateful to Agathe for her kindness, but the truth is I didn't need my arm twisting to join them; I hadn't enjoyed conversation or human company since Agente Garcia searched my room yesterday afternoon.

"How are you this morning, Sanjay?" asked Agathe, patting my hand.

"Never better," I lied. "I've had a perfectly relaxing morning by the pool."

"I saw. You looked like you were fast asleep."

"Or dead," said Marley.

"Marley, please. There's been enough death around here, we don't need to joke about more."

I looked at Penny who hadn't uttered a word. She was wearing a long-sleeved black and white polka dot dress and was staring towards the sea.

"How is your investigation going?" I asked, looking at my smoothie. Marley waited for Penny to answer, but the lady sat stock-still as if she hadn't heard me speak. After an uncomfortable few seconds of silence, Marley took the reins.

"Erm…we're closer than when we started," she said, vaguely.

"Any solid suspects?"

"Just about everyone."

"Even me?"

"Of course," Marley replied, laughing.

"Not me too, I hope?" asked Agathe.

"You can't have special treatment, Mum; everyone must be investigated equally and fairly."

"Me? Your own mother who brought you into this world and raised you? You're supposed to be finding Russell's killer, why would you waste time on me?"

"Don't worry, Mum, you've been ruled out as a suspect now."

"I should think so too, thinking your God-fearing mother could -" Agathe rambled on in this way for a few minutes longer. I stopped listening and watched Penny, who seemed absorbed in whatever thoughts were occupying her mind. She was leaning back in her seat, though her body seemed rigid, tense even.

"Oh, Sanjay, where did you spring from, I didn't see you there," she said when Agathe had exhausted herself.

"I've been sitting here for five minutes, Penny; you've been in your own little world."

"I'm sorry, I must appear very rude. It's just this murder business, it's testing my intelligence as well as my patience."

"It is baffling, I admit. I mean, how did the killer get in and out of the gym to kill Russell?"

"Hmm. A good question, but not what I'm thinking about right now."

"Yeah, I suppose figuring out who the killer is must take priority."

"Not quite. Unmasking the killer isn't the problem, it's proving who the killer is that's the sticking point."

"You mean -"

"Yes, I mean I'm almost sure I know who the killer is, but the problem is…" Her voice trailed off, and she was again lost in her own thoughts. I looked at Marley who shrugged and raised her eyebrows, clearly desperate to know what Penny had figured out but frustrated at being kept in the dark.

"And your room, Sanjay, is it alright?" Agathe addressed me, concern in her voice.

"Yes, thanks. It's just the same as the old one."

"That's nice. I've never been in the East Wing, always the West. Russell made sure especially, ever since my first visit when I told him I liked the sun reaching the balcony in the mornings. Has Luke tried to win you back yet?"

"Er, no."

"He will."

"I wouldn't be so sure. The only person Luke thinks is worthy of his love and attention is himself. He has too much pride to ask me back, even if he wanted to, which I doubt. It appears he wants something else in life. Maybe someone funny, and kind, and good-looking."

"Then he's a fool. Sometimes you already have what you are looking for, you just don't know it."

I watched Penny's eyebrows rise above her sunglasses and her head slowly turn. Then she stood, the suddenness of her ascent knocking over her chair. She stared down at Agathe and asked, "What did you just say?"

65

Terry

Blimey! What a day. I'd better start at the beginning.

I got up nice and early and bagged my favourite sun lounger before tucking into a hearty breakfast. It were the perfect start to the day; the sun was shining, the air was warm, my belly was full, I could have a snooze and top up my tan. Little did I know what lay in store.

When we came out of the restaurant to the pool, Sanjay was there, and looked to be asleep. Marjorie pulled an umbrella over to her side taking good care its shadow didn't come anywhere near me. She sat in the shade and did one of her sudokus or whatever they're called until young Elle came down with a towel slung over her shoulder and a book in her hand. Marge cajoled her into sitting next to her.

"The poor girl," Marge had said to me over breakfast, seeing Elle alone. "It must be terribly lonesome for her, what with her boyfriend being dead. I must have a chat with her and see she's alright."

I could hear Marge nattering at the girl, "Are you alright, love? I saw you at breakfast, you looked tired. I suppose you haven't been sleeping well what with… you know. I remember when my budgie Percy died, oh it was a shock. Just there at the bottom of the cage one morning. I barely slept for a week, but this is much worse, isn't it. I mean, Dylan was your boyfriend." I sat up on my elbows to see if the girl was crying, but she was perfectly composed.

"I slept okay," she said. "I'm just tired waiting for the police to arrest the killer so I can go home. As soon as they give me my passport back, I'll be on the first plane out."

"That's the spirit. A fresh start for you, love. If you need anything, or just someone to talk to, we're here anytime, isn't that right, Terry?"

"Absolutely. Terrible thing to happen to a young girl like yourself, but at least you're young enough to find another fella, try to pick a better one next time. What's that you're reading, anyway?" I asked.

"It's a book about minimalism?"

"Minimalism? What's that when it's at home?"

"It's about living with the bare essentials. About decluttering your life, being efficient, and not wasting space."

"Oh, I see," I said. "I would've thought that would only be available on Kindle." Marge and Elle then started talking about clothes or something and I lost interest.

The pool area filled up with guests. Marley, Agathe and Penny were sitting in the sunny part of the bar and I watched them for a while. Penny likes to sit under that orange tree, her face in the sun, but I've never seen her go for a dip. In fact, I've never seen her wear anything that isn't long-sleeved. She's not going to get the best possible tan like that. She wasn't talking to Marley or Agathe, she was sitting like a statue, almost frowning, like she was deep in thought. Probably, I figured, trying to crack the case. Up to that point she hadn't had much luck; her friend had been killed in a locked room and as far as I could tell she had no clue how the killer had got into the gym, or who had committed the crime. I was convinced the card reader on the door was faulty and the murderer got in and out the normal way and there wasn't any great mystery. Of course, I found out this afternoon that I was wrong, and it's not often you'll hear Terence Smith saying that.

For two hours Penny sat still, the only evidence that she wasn't dead was when she occasionally played with the pearls around her neck. Marley and her mum didn't disturb her, they drank their drinks and chatted, or sat in silence enjoying the sun. Then, Sanjay got up and joined the three of them. They talked for a few minutes, but Penny still didn't seem interested in what anyone else had to say, until bang! Out of the blue she jumped up and practically ran into the lobby. The other three were left sitting in wonder, I don't think they knew what were going on. They turned and looked at each other and I could see them babbling away but they were shaking their heads, obviously ignorant as to what Penny was up to.

It were about ten minutes later that Paulo did the rounds. He came over to us and whispered, "Senor Smith, ladies, excuse me, but Senora Haylestone wishes for all the West Wing guests to gather in the restaurant if you please be so kind." "Bloody hell," I said. "This is the hottest time of the day, and she wants us to go in the shade. Alright, Paulo son, if it keeps her happy, the last thing I want is her on my back again. Do us a favour though, and bring us in a beer, will you."

We gathered our things and made our way inside. I held the lobby door while Marley pushed her mum through. In the restaurant we found half a dozen tables had been pulled away from the rest, their chairs arranged so they were all on one side facing the window which looks out on the pool. Luke, Jasmine and Sally were already seated. Elle sat next to Marge and me. Paulo brought me my beer and then came back with one of those big silver coffee pots and a stack of cups.

"This is exciting," said Marge. "It's like we're at one of those Ted lectures and some important person is going to speak to us. I'll pour the coffee while we wait. Who takes sugar?"

"What's this all about?" asked Agathe.

"Paulo told us Penny wanted everyone in here," said Sally. "Do you know what's happening, Marley?"

"I've no idea. Penny was sitting with us and then hurried off. I haven't seen her since."

"Well, somebody had better explain what's going on soon. I don't want to sit here all day," said Luke, his arms folded over his stomach.

"It could be anything knowing Penny bloody Haylestone," I said. "She's probably going to point at a gun at all of us until someone confesses."

"You already have confessed, remember?" I looked around to see Penny sweeping into the room. She strode past us, her handbag slung over her shoulder, and stopped at the window. "But I don't need a gun, or a confession. I know who the murderer is, and now, I can prove it."

66

Marley

It came to her in a flash, the answer she had been looking for. Mum had uttered a few seemingly innocuous words and Penny had jolted like she'd been hit by lightning. Then she'd called Paulo and had all the suspects gather in the deserted restaurant where we wouldn't be disturbed. I figured that Penny must've cracked the case, but I couldn't be sure. I mean, her behaviour had been unusual, erratic even, but I didn't want to get my hopes up, or tell the others what I suspected in case I was wrong. We waited a few minutes and then Penny came in and stood in front of us. She looked elegant and composed, as though content to have solved the mystery, but also acutely aware of the gravity of the situation; this investigation having been steeped in the murder of her friend. She placed her handbag on the table in front of her and looked at each of us in turn. When she looked at me, our eyes locked, and she gave a solemn nod. I trembled, knowing for sure that the killer was in the room. I looked around; Luke, Sally, Jasmine, Mum next to me, Sanjay on my left, Terry, Marjorie, Elle, all seated. Standing to our left, near to the door was Paulo, who I guessed was waiting to show the police in when they arrived.

"I think you can all guess why I've asked you here. Amongst you sits the killer of Russell and Dylan. Amongst you sits a cunning, ruthless criminal who planned with meticulous skill, not one, but two murders. That's right; both murders were planned, the only difference was that one of the murders was forced upon our killer. An unforeseen happening meant that two people had to die, not one. But even that murder was thought-out and engineered in a cold, calculated manner, before being adeptly executed. Of course, the murderer had luck of their own along the way, old grievances, false confessions, and improbable love triangles all helped to obscure their identity by making me turn my head the wrong way time and again. And the task of unravelling the mystery would've been even harder, had the group staying in the East Wing not been on a trip to Seville when Russell was murdered. Had they been here, the pool of viable suspects would've been twice as large. As it was, we were left with a very definite cast of suspects, the question which needed to be answered was not only who killed Russell, but how?"

I felt the room bristle as sweaty palms rubbed thighs and everyone squirmed and fidgeted. Penny had said that one person was the culprit, so I guessed that the innocents in the group were fearful of being wrongly accused.

"The most obvious suspect, at least in the beginning, was Terry."

"Ey'up! I-"

"Quiet! As I was saying…Terry was an old rival of Russell's from their school days, and we had all seen Russell accidentally knock Terry into the pool the night before the murder and Terry swear revenge. The fact that Terry later confessed to killing Russell would ordinarily make this a cut and dry case, however, facts are often at odds with stupidity. Terry also had a motive for killing Dylan, who was blackmailing him. What Terry didn't know (or couldn't figure out) was that Dylan was shooting in the dark. He told Terry he had seen him talking to Russell before he was killed, Terry had in fact spoken with Russell that morning, but Dylan didn't know that. Dylan *had* seen someone talking with Russell on the stairs leading to the first floor…" I looked around to see if anyone gave themselves away as I still didn't know who this person was, but everyone sat frozen, watching Penny.

"…but it wasn't Terry. The next person to consider was Marjorie."

"Me?" shrieked the little woman.

"Everyone must be considered a suspect, and you are Terry's wife, it's not inconceivable that you would kill Russell to defend his honour. Perhaps you knew Dylan was blackmailing your husband. Maybe you thought you could kill him and not be suspected as there would be no obvious link to Russell's murder.

"Then, of course, we have Sally, who stands to inherit this hotel as well as any money Russell may have had. Inheritance has always been strong motive for murder, and the bond between you can't have been that strong considering how infrequently you saw each other. Next, we have Jasmine, who has lied at every turn.

"Agathe, on the other hand, is sadly without her husband Reggie. Did she blame Russell for his death and seek her revenge? Or Marley for the love of her father?

"As Russell's solicitor, Luke was sent here to help deal with certain financial matters. Did he see an opportunity to steal some money, to divert funds into his own account and then kill Russell to prevent being caught? And as for Sanjay, well, I can think why he might like to kill Dylan, but Russell? Perhaps Sanjay is one of those psychopaths who make their own sport. A journalist who yearns for greater acclaim and prestige, who would commit murder to document the investigation and influence the events to make a more intriguing and mysterious case. He could even keep a false diary in order to mislead any investigator who might come upon it and throw suspicion away from himself…

"But, as I said, the murderer's identity is not the only mystery here; how Russell was killed inside a locked room is also key to the case, for without knowing the *how*, the *who* can't be proved, at least not in this case.

"And then, a few minutes ago, Agathe uttered a few careless words, and my mind went racing. She said, 'Sometimes, you already have what you are looking for,' and I realised that the key to the whole thing, the locked-room murder, and the killer's identity was already in my possession. And this is it…" Penny reached into her handbag and held up a mobile phone.

67

Sally

We gathered in the restaurant where Penny promised to unmask the murderer. She hinted, nudged, and poked at us before reaching into her bag for something tangible. The room took a deep breath and then let out a confused sigh as she held up a mobile phone like Moses did with the Ten Commandments. It took a minute before the silence was broken by "Hey'up! That's my phone!"

"Yes, it is, Terry. I stole it from you," said Penny, her tone firm and unapologetic.

"You? You're the one who's been going around nicking people's phones?"

"No, I only stole *your* phone."

"What? Why?"

"To protect it. Ironically, to stop it from getting stolen. You see, when murders happen, a missing phone can be a coincidence, two vanishing phones tells me something fishy is going on. Marley's phone went missing first, then Sally's. I tried to connect the two, I tried thinking of what the two had in common. After all, Marley and Sally were strangers until they met here, what could be on their phones that linked them. I thought I'd sussed it, but then Dylan's phone was stolen. That threw me off course, until I found out that Jasmine had taken it, and the reason why. I was satisfied by what she told me, and that Dylan's phone was not in any way linked to the theft of Marley's or Sally's, and I reverted again to my previous line of reasoning. I figured that the two phones must contain something that the killer wanted."

"My journal!" said Marley.

"No, dear... your camera. Both phones were used to take pictures on the first night by the pool. Terry also took photographs at dinner before taking an unplanned dip, though his phone was safe and dry on a nearby table. I didn't know what I was looking for, and I'll admit, when I took Terry's phone and looked through the pictures from that night, I didn't find anything unusual, at least not at first glance."

"But, Penny, I don't understand," said Marley. "You say you took Terry's phone yesterday, but you only worked out who the killer was today?"

"That's because it wasn't the photographs that made me realise who the killer is. I took Terry's phone hoping the photos on it would reveal the killer, but remember what your mum said, 'Sometimes, you already have what you are looking for,' well, that's when I realised the evidence I needed could be on the phone, but *not* be a photograph.

"So, I looked through the phone again, and that's when I knew that it was *you* who killed Russell Aspell... Marjorie Smith."

There was a clatter and crash of cups and saucers as the shock of the revelation caused a few of us to lose control of ourselves. I dropped my coffee cup, the splintering fragments flying like shrapnel from a grenade, the smashing porcelain echoing through gasps of shock and denial.

When the initial surprise subsided and the room quietened, I looked at Marjorie and was surprised to see her sitting calmly. She was returning Penny's stare, poised and ready to continue listening, to hear the condemnation about to be thrown at her. Terry, after nearly falling off his chair, recovered and bellowed, "You what? Marge? I don't bloody think so!"

It wasn't Penny who replied but Marjorie, who, without breaking eye contact with her accuser, raised her hand in front of her husband's face and held up one finger. 'Hush' it said, 'let this woman speak.' Terry, either through shock or disbelief, obeyed and repositioned himself on his chair, ready to hear the evidence Penny had to provide.

It was at this moment that I noticed Agente Garcia enter the restaurant. He stood next to Paulo by the window, the handcuffs dangling from his belt glinting in the afternoon sun.

"The problem of the locked room," Penny continued, "told me that Russell's murder was either planned long in advance or was thought up quickly by someone with fine intelligence. I can tell you all, it was the latter.

"To most here, her husband included, I would say, Marjorie would not be thought of possessing an exceptional mind, but that is because people see what she wants them to see, and people lean towards their own prejudices all too easily and don't observe those around them in their true forms. In my line of work, I have come across some brilliant minds, some truly extraordinary people, and countless times have I seen such people dismissed, ignored, or overlooked because of how they look, or dress, or how their accent sounds, or what school they went to. Marjorie thought of how to murder a man inside a locked room and nearly got away with it."

"But why a locked room?" asked Sanjay. "Why make it so mysterious?"

"Because Russell's death was not meant to look like murder, it was supposed to look like an accident. Allow me to explain...

"Russell was found by Marley and Marjorie inside the gym. The door was locked, and access recorded through the hotel security system. The windows were also locked, and Russell was found with three wounds to his skull in an empty room. It was assumed that he was struck three times with the bar found leaning against the stanchion next to his body. However, no blood was on the bar, and we later discovered that one of the wounds had been caused by Terry who threw a rock at Russell earlier that morning. So now, reimagine the scene. Russell is found with *two* wounds on his head, not three. But that still means that someone must've struck Russell twice over the head with some heavy object, right? Wrong. Russell was alone in the room when he died."

"How? That's impossible," Luke said.

"No, it isn't, bear with me. I've just shown how three wounds should actually have been two, now, let's go a step further. Imagine a body with one fatal wound found in a locked room, what would you assume?"

It was Marley who answered, her voice wavering and unsure. "I'd think something fell on his head, something heavy."

"Exactly. And you'd think it was an accident."

"But we know he was struck twice on the head, the two indentations -"

"Caused by one object: a dumbbell, which fell from the I-beam above Russell's head, and then rolled along the floor to the foot of the weights rack. The dumbbell was placed on the beam and when it fell, the two weighted ends struck Russell's head simultaneously. I imagine, Marjorie, you thought the dumbbell would be found beside the body and it would be assumed Russell accidentally dropped it on his head when exercising?"

"Yes. I didn't even notice the bar leaning against the stanchion. When I entered the gym, I saw the dumbbell lying by the weights rack. While young Marley was frozen in shock, I quickly looked for blood on it, but there was none. The impact must've happened so quickly the dumbbell had rolled away before the bleeding began. Then I dashed over and removed the other thing and stuck it in my pocket."

"Ah yes, the other thing. Because, of course, you had to make sure Russell would be standing exactly where you needed him to be, so you stuck a note to the stanchion. What did you write on it that was so shocking he stopped to stare at it?"

"*Russell Aspell, today you will die.* I only needed him there for a few seconds. You see, I knew his routine, he told me at dinner; thirty minutes on the treadmill then fifteen minutes weight training. The same every day, like clockwork."

"But how did you make the dumbbell fall when you wanted?" asked Sanjay.

"Ah," said Penny. "That is where this comes into the story." Moses held up the mobile phone again, and this time we all looked at it with the awe and respect it deserved.

68

Sanjay

I had sat stunned and silent as Penny had revealed Marjorie to be the killer, I only found my voice again when my curiosity overcame my shock. Penny had explained that Marjorie had placed a dumbbell on the I-beam and that this makeshift murder weapon had fallen onto Russell's head exactly when she wanted to. What I now wanted to know, was how had seemingly sweet, simple Marge done this.

"Sometimes, you have to go backwards to go forwards, they say," said Penny. "It is the same in this case, Marjorie rigged up her trick backwards. She took Russell's access card the night before the murder when he was drunk and started to set up her trick by placing the dumbbell on the beam. She placed a pen behind the dumbbell and tied a fishing line around the pen. Marjorie then walked across the gym to a window where she dropped the fishing reel into the flowers and bushes below. The window is hinged horizontally at the top and opens six or so inches at the bottom, it snaps shut under its own weight. What did you use to wedge it open, Marjorie, out of curiosity?"

"I put another pen in the right angle of the window frame and rested the window against that. I did it the night before when everyone was having drinks by the pool. I said I was going to phone my Sarah. Everyone was chatting and having a good time and I knew no one would miss me. Russell had left his access card on the table where he was sitting, I didn't think he'd miss it if I took it for a short while. I went up to the gym and began setting up."

"And you put a doorbell camera on the window ledge pointing at your chosen spot where the dumbbell would fall. You made sure the fishing line was close to the doorbell camera and the pen that was holding open the window so that when your trick worked, the pen that was tied to the fishing line would pull the camera and other pen clear of the window leaving no trace of what you'd done inside the gym. Then, you went down to the flowerbed to finish off the trick. You pulled the fishing line until it was nearly taut and applied the catch on the electronic fishing reel. All it needed was for the catch to be pressed and the line would automatically retract, pulling the dumbbell down, the reel spinning, bringing the line, the doorbell camera, and the pen down to the flowerbed for you to pick up later. The window fell under its own weight and snapped shut when the pen was flung out by the retracting fishing line."

"But Penny," said Marley, "how did Marjorie cause the fishing line to retract when she was nowhere near the flowerbed?"

"That, dear, is where this phone comes in. You remember you said Marjorie was using her phone to bid online for a piece of jewellery for her daughter's birthday? You said she tried to phone Terry, to keep an eye on the auction, but it wasn't Terry's number she called. The call log on this phone has no record of an incoming call from Marjorie on the morning of Russell's death. The phone Marjorie was actually calling was a burner phone. I'm guessing-"

"There's no need to guess, I'll tell you how I did it, although it seems you've figured it out. The pen was just long enough so that both ends touched the weighted parts of the dumbbell. It was perfect. I was sure the trick would work. When I was satisfied with the setup of the gym, I gave myself plenty of slack and tossed the electric fishing reel into a plant pot from the window. The next morning, before Russell went into the gym, I got up early to finish off the trick. I stuck a fishing rod handle into the soil of the plant pot, just the handle mind, I obviously didn't want a huge rod sticking up for everyone to see, and I attached the reel to the handle as you do. As you said, the catch on the fishing reel needs pressed once, this causes the reel to retract the line automatically, it saves a fisherman the exertions of manually winding the reel in over and over again when spin fishing. I reeled the line so it was nearly taut then set the catch. I then balanced the burner phone, as you call it, half on the reel, half over the catch.

"You see, I knew Russell's routine, but on that morning, as luck would have it, he deviated from it. I had arranged to meet Marley at a quarter-to-eight. Russell should've been off the treadmill by seven-thirty and been standing staring at the notice telling him he was going to die by seven-thirty-five, but he decided to spend ten minutes doing stretches first. I could see it all. I had the doorbell camera synced to my phone. I sat in the lobby watching him, urging him to get to the spot I had in mind to kill him. Then young Marley showed up in the lobby and I was between a rock and a hard place. I considered abandoning my plan. I could've triggered the trick then and Russell walked away unscathed and no one any the wiser, but I was committed. As Marley and me walked up to the gym I told her about a necklace on eBay I was bidding on for my Sarah, which was true. I even showed her it on my phone, but I was toggling between apps – eBay and the doorbell camera. As we got near the gym, I got the luck I needed, I saw Russell move around the stanchion and read my note. I told Marley I was going to phone Terry but really, I called the burner phone which was balanced on the fishing reel. The vibration of the ringing upset the precarious balance of the phone, and the upright phone fell, knocking the release catch. The fishing line retracted, pulling the teetering dumbbell, and Russell fell, dead."

"You killed him as I stood next to you?" cried Marley. "That's horrible."

"I'm sorry, love, it was nothing personal. I'm sorry you had to see him lying there and the blood and everything, but it had to be done. Russell had to die."

"Why? What did he ever do to you to deserve that?"

"Ah. Now we come to the crux of the matter: the motive," said Penny, taking over the situation once again. "The most baffling aspect of the entire affair, made all the more difficult to unravel by false assumptions. All of us, I think it's fair to say, assumed that Dylan was killed because he knew something about Russell's murder. Whether he saw the murderer, or because he implied he did, he got killed as a result. But we were wrong.

"I figured out the locked-room murder by thinking backwards, and that is also how to figure out the motive for these crimes.

"Dylan wasn't murdered because he knew who killed Russell: Russell was murdered because he *would* know who killed Dylan. You see, Russell's was the improvised murder, and Dylan's was the planned one. It was Dylan who Marjorie came here to kill.

69

Marley

It all began to make sense. We had been looking at the whole thing the wrong way round. I sat enthralled as Penny explained how she had broken the blurry puzzle into tiny pieces and put them together again until a coherent, clean picture emerged.

"We come back to the photographs that first set me on the right track," Penny said. "I couldn't know what Sally or Marley had photographed, what detail or incident captured was important to Marjorie, and likely they didn't know themselves. The one thing about Dylan's death that bothered me more than anything else, was the hatred of his murder. Someone had gone to great lengths to not only kill him, but to ensure he suffered the most agonising death possible. Someone possessed the knowledge needed to replace the adrenaline in his EpiPen with poison, but when I reviewed everyone's internet search history, nothing suspicious came up. How could this be? I asked myself. There are no doctors or nurses amongst us, no one who would know how to disassemble an EpiPen, yet that is exactly what someone here had done. In truth, all the important clues welded together in my mind at once. If Marjorie had used a burner phone for her little trick with the fishing reel, could she have used one to search poisons and EpiPens? She could, but she didn't. Not quite. Because when I realised that Dylan was the intended victim all along, I realised that his murder had been planned for many months, and there was someone else at the heart of this mystery whose phone search history I hadn't checked, the person who this whole sad affair is all about: Sarah. Marjorie's daughter."

"I can speak for my daughter, if you don't mind, Penny."

"As you wish."

"I did it for her, for the life that he robbed from her. No, she's not dead, though she's not much alive. Paralysed from the neck down, confined to a wheelchair, and all because of him. She eats through a tube and can't speak. I phone her so that she can hear my voice, though I'll never hear hers. Do you know what they call her? A vegetable. Not a statue, or a rose, or anything else that's still and beautiful – a vegetable."

"Was it a car accident? The same where Dylan got the scar on his leg?"

"Yes. He'd been drinking and was going too fast. He walked away with that scratch, but my Sarah will never walk again. I wanted to paralyse him like he did her. That's why I chose the toxins I did. You all saw him, didn't you? He suffered, yes?" Marjorie had a strange, eager smile on her face as she asked us this, as though she wished to be reassured that she'd inflicted the agony she had craved to.

"I knew when I killed him the police would check our phones, so I got one registered in Sarah's name. I control her email account and bank and everything. It's not an easy thing to take apart an EpiPen, they're spring-loaded, you have to be careful. I bought one online and brought it with me. On the boat journey to Stork Island, I swapped it when no one was looking. As everyone was taking care getting off the boat I swapped the gin bottles and dropped the bottle and the EpiPen in the sea. It all went perfectly."

"Except for the photographs."

"Yes. I knew that Dylan had a severe allergy, Sarah had told me years ago. They were a couple at university, so I never met him. I saw him in court, of course, when he was sentenced for the accident. Four years for ruining my Sarah's life and out in two for good behaviour. Is that justice? He sat in the dock and didn't look at me. Why would he? The conceited, arrogant rat. He showed no remorse for what he'd done. But you have to understand, killing him wasn't enough, he *had* to suffer."

"He had to have an allergic reaction and use the EpiPen?"

"Yes. I'm sorry for Russell, I didn't want that to happen, but he'd seen me with shellfish on my plate at the first-night dinner. He'd even commented on them, asking me was I enjoying them. Then Terry told everyone that I didn't like shellfish, which is true, but I didn't know Terry had said this until later when he told me about how he got knocked in the pool. I'd been phoning my Sarah at the time, you see. Wishing her a goodnight, not that she can say it back.

"I knew when I killed Dylan, that Russell would know it was me, and then there was the photographs to prove it. Me standing with the plate in my hand, prawns in full view. I couldn't wait to kill Dylan; I was going to do it the next day but then Terry spoiled everything by announcing to the whole world that I don't like shellfish."

"The cheek of it!" Terry exploded. "You kill two people and somehow it's my fault? Bloody typical."

"Oh, shut up, Terry! Not everything is about you."

Elle, who had been sitting silently, now interrupted with her own question. "There was no competition, was there? You invented it so Dylan would be here."

"Yes, love, but I hope you've had a nice time anyway. You poor thing going out with him."

"But you gave me two options to choose from, here or Turkey. How did you know I'd choose here?"

"Giving you two options would look less suspicious when he died and the police investigated, but I knew you'd choose here because you had food poisoning when you went to Turkey. You wouldn't want that again, love. I've been following you on social media, it's how I kept tabs on Dylan. He disappeared and went off the radar a few times over the years, but I always managed to find him again. You can do anything if you're determined enough."

70

Terry

I said it were Marge! Didn't I? I said it were her!

Still, it did come as a shock hearing it. I didn't know she were so cold and calculating. Imagine. Killing an innocent man just so you could kill another one in the way you wanted. At least it were Russell bloody Aspell and not some decent bloke.

I shouldn't be so shocked, really. I know how much she loves Sarah. It's heart-breaking seeing her in that wheelchair and seeing Marjorie doting on her. That's why I was surprised Marjorie wanted to come here; I couldn't imagine her leaving Sarah with her carer for two *hours*, never mind two *weeks*. Now I understand.

The revelation knocked me for six, truth be told. I haven't even written in this here diary since it all happened two days ago, and I've grown very fond of my new hobby, so that just goes to show the effect it's had. Penny was kind to be fair to her. As soon as Agente Garcia led Marge away, Penny took me to the bar and got me a large beer with a whisky chaser and asked me if I were alright. I didn't know what to say I don't think. It's all such a blur. I've had plenty of women walk out on me before, but never in handcuffs. Still, at least I'll be doing the divorcing this time, that'll be something new.

Everyone's been kind really, not just Penny. Not one of them have judged me or avoided me for being married to a psycho killer. Even Luke came and sat with me and had a beer, and he still had a bit of a bruise on his cheek from when I thumped him. I don't think him and Sanjay will be making up anytime soon, though.

As soon as Marge was safely behind bars, Inspector Moreno came to the hotel and handed back everyone's passports. Sanjay took his and booked himself onto a flight for this morning. He leaves in an hour or so.

Speaking of Inspector Moreno, I don't think he were too pleased that it were Penny Haylestone who cracked the case and not him. He stormed in, dished out the passports and stormed off, barely saying a word to anyone. He left Agente Garcia to finish off the paperwork and get the final statements off people. He were nice and all. "Senor Smith," he said. "I'm sorry to have arrested your wife. I hope you understand."

"No worries, mucker," I said. "You were only doing your job. Say, will I have to come back for the trial?"

"You will be called as a witness I imagine, si."

"And who pays for that then, your government or mine? Flights aren't cheap you know. And I need extra leg room, what with my dodgy knee." He said he'll get back to me.

I don't know if I'll be able to face staying here when I do come back though. Too many memories. There's a nice new five-star resort getting built just up the road, you can see the water slide they're putting in from the car park. Maybe I'll stop there if the Spanish government are footing the bill. If not, I could always stay here, I'm sure Sally would be glad to put me up. Anyway, that's all in the future, I don't need to worry about any of that now, I've still got a few days left to perfect my tan, and Paulo hasn't run out of beer yet.

71

Sanjay

I've given up on the true crime book idea. Being detached, reading a few pages about a murder that's happened far away and long ago while tucked under your comfy duvet at night is very different than seeing and feeling the raw reverberations of violent crime up close. To write the book now would mean having to relive it all, and not just the murders, but the breakup with Luke, too. It's best just to forget it.

To be honest, I think part of the reason why I've lost my appetite for the project is the killer's identity. If Terry had've been the killer, or even Elle, a beautiful, aggrieved girl whose passions resulted in murder, I think I could write it. But Marjorie? It just seems wrong. She committed horrible deeds and I doubt whether psychologically she is of sound mind, but her actions were born out of love. I had imagined the killer would turn out to be pure evil, and that their capture would be a bright finale at the end of the book, the final revelation an exploding star. But what I imagined was wrong. I wonder if that is how Penny saw what no one else could, she saw darkness where we saw light? She had the worldly wisdom and experience to know that life is not full of happy endings, and that you must seek for truth in the darkest of places, where you don't want to find it, but must have the courage to look anyway.

I never suspected Marjorie because she was too nice, too timid, but that's exactly it, isn't it – too. She was *too* timid. What was it Penny had said? *People see what she wants them to see, and people lean towards their own prejudices all too easily, and don't observe those around them in their true forms.* Could this not apply to how I saw Luke, or how Elle saw Dylan?

After Marjorie was taken away, an exhausted silence fell over the hotel. We sat around the pool, staring and thinking, still absorbing what we'd heard and trying to make sense of it all. I saw Penny sitting beneath the orange tree, a well-earned gin in front of her. Her head was tilted to the sun, her long sleeve-covered arms resting on her lap. She turned to me as I took the liberty of sitting next to her. "Hello, Sanjay, dear. Are you alright? I haven't had much chance to check on you since you moved rooms. I imagine you'll be off as soon as you can."

"Yes, I need to get away from here, and I need to move out of the house before Luke flies back. It's his house, and-"

"Listen. You can mope, cry, and spit in anger all you like, but never doubt your self-worth. Don't look back, keep going forward. That's my advice. You're a handsome young man and have a lot to offer."

"Thank you, Penny, that's very kind."

I realised then, that what I need, that what's been missing in my life, isn't a good relationship, but a good friendship, and now, having come here and met some wonderful people, I think I can say that's a problem no longer.

72

Sally

The end of the affair had come like an avalanche, a rush of information crashing down as Penny unleashed her torrent of revelations until it was finally over, and we were left in a daze by the event.

Once Marjorie had been led away, we stumbled outside, blinking rapidly in the afternoon sun. Jasmine and I went for a walk along the beach to clear our heads. We walked barefoot in the surf and watched the waves wash away our footprints, the shifting sands erasing the memory of the imprints, the sea being the master and us the intruders. We held hands as we walked, until, exhausted by the day's proceedings we dragged our feet back to the bar where we ordered the punchiest cocktails on the menu. Penny soon joined us, and I ordered a third.

"There's still one thing we don't know," I said, more to Penny than Jasmine.

"What's that, dear?"

"Who was it that Dylan saw Russell talking to on the stairs before the murder."

Penny took a long suck on her straw, but I didn't miss the short, sideways glance she gave to Jasmine. "It's not important now. It can't have been anything to do with the murder because it wasn't Marjorie," Penny said.

"It was me," Jasmine said, looking straight at me.

"You? Why were you arguing with Russell?"

"I wasn't arguing with him. Not exactly. I was telling him I needed space, that I needed time to think, but he was pushy, desperate even."

"What are you talking about?" I asked, beginning to imagine the worst.

"Not what you're thinking, dear," said Penny, assuaging my fears somewhat.

"You know?" Jasmine asked Penny.

"Yes, I know. Russell didn't tell me, though. He didn't need to. I saw him act differently, I could tell that something was eating at his brain and that it wasn't necessarily a bad thing. He was thoughtful, yet happy, I'd say. And, of course, we later found out that he'd instructed Luke to draw up a blank will…"

"Would one of you mind telling me what it is you're talking about?"

"It was your eyes that made me sure, so dazzling and blue," said Penny, ignoring my request. "The only person I've met with eyes like that was Russell."

"You mean…"

"Yes, Sally. You and Jasmine are cousins."

I couldn't believe it. I thought the day couldn't have any more surprises in it and then Penny dropped that into my lap. Jasmine and I are cousins? How did I never work it out? I sat thinking, not caring if Penny and Jasmine were waiting for me to say something. "When did you find out?" I asked Jasmine, still gasping in shock.

"The night we arrived. He came to our room, and I just knew. It was like looking at a mirror. In that moment I could tell that he was thinking the same thing. Remember you and him went for a drink while I phoned my mum? Well, I confronted her. She took it in her stride as a matter of fact. She told me she fell pregnant when she came here all those years ago with your mum. Remember you told me in the airport? I couldn't believe it; she never even told him. Then, at dinner that night, he kept trying to talk to me, but I kept away from him. Not only did I not know how I felt, but I also didn't know how I should feel. I mean, what is the normal reaction a person should have when you unexpectedly meet your dad for the first time. Later that night I went to the car park. I just wanted to be alone for a few minutes to try and get my head around things. He followed me out, he was excited, and I found it too full on, too overbearing. I slapped him. I know I shouldn't have done, and that he didn't deserve it. I felt so guilty when he died, I hadn't even apologised. I felt sick. I'd only just discovered my father and then he was murdered."

I stood up and hugged her head tight into my chest. I had no words to offer, no advice to give. I looked at Penny and she smiled before turning her face to the setting sun.

73

Marley

Elle was the first to leave. She booked a flight the minute the police released her passport and took a taxi straight to the airport.

Sanjay left yesterday morning. He didn't want to linger any longer. I tried to convince him to stay, to enjoy himself, but he was determined to start afresh and do it as soon as possible, though he did say he'll miss us, especially Mum. They've already arranged to go to the theatre next month. I know Mum is looking forward to continuing their friendship back in London.

Luke left an hour after Sanjay. He flew to France to visit his sister who's holidaying there. He said he would've gone earlier but he'd promised to help Sally with something and wouldn't leave until it was done. I don't know what the task was, and I don't want to know, I've had my fill of mysteries for a while. I promised Mum when the killer was caught we'd enjoy ourselves, and that's what we've been doing.

Yesterday, Paulo drove us into town, and we sat at the harbour where Dad would go fishing. We ate ice cream and watched the sun set. "You should go back to the university," Mum said as we watched a fishing boat return with the day's catch.

"But who would look after you?" I asked.

"Don't worry about me. Besides, I have four children. It's about time your brothers started doing more around the place, they've had it too easy for too long."

We enjoyed dinner together in the hotel, then Mum had an early night. I found Penny sitting in her favourite spot beneath the orange tree, reading a book, a glass of wine for company. "Did you enjoy your day, dear?" she asked when I sat next to her.

"Yes, I did. It was great spending time with Mum. I neglected her when we were hunting the killer, but now I can enjoy the last few days here with her."

"I'm glad."

"I know she misses Dad, but I think she's enjoying herself now. Is this the first holiday you've been on since your husband died?"

"Heavens, no dear. I've been abroad dozens of times since Anthony died."

"Dozens?" I asked, wondering if I had befriended a millionaire.

"My dear, Anthony was murdered nearly forty years ago. I've been a widow for quite some time."

"He was murdered…"

"Yes, he was, though his killer was trying to get both of us. A car bomb, you see. It was a North African arms dealer who found out we worked for the security services. He had been supplying his merchandise to some Irish terror groups and we were closing in.

Anthony and I got in the car one morning and were about to set off when I realised I'd forgotten my briefcase. I don't think I'd ever forgotten anything before…" As she spoke, her eyes searched the sky for stars, but they were diluted by the hundreds of fairy lights all around us. "I went back into the house. Anthony started the engine. That's when it happened. Of course, I don't clearly remember what happened after that, the shock, you see. I'm told a neighbour had to use all their strength to pull me from the car. The windows were completely blown out from the explosion and the driver's door was on fire. I'd put my arms through and was trying to get Anthony out but of course it was too late, and I didn't really know what I was doing. That's how my arms came to look like this." She rolled up her sleeves to reveal shiny, wrinkleless skin. Skin cleansed and discoloured by flames.

"Oh, Penny, I had no idea."

"Of course you didn't, I never told you."

"What happened to the person who planted the bomb?"

"Russell Aspell happened to him."

"What do you mean?"

"Do you remember when we were in Russell's office, I told you I owed him?"

"Yes…"

"Well, Russell was here at the time; the hotel was under construction. We got word that the bomber would be passing through on his way back to North Africa. Russell intercepted him and killed him. I asked him to do it, and he did. A good friend.

"The security services were, and are, unaware of the fact. I was still in hospital being treated for my burns. We had a code, or watchword if you like, that he was to send me when the bomber was dead. I still remember sitting in the hospital bed when a nurse handed me an envelope. I opened it to see six words typed: THE WAGES OF SIN IS DEATH. I knew it was done."

"That's what was on the note we found in Russell's desk!"

"It's the same note, dear. I returned it when I sent my own watchword when I helped Russell out recently. He was in a spot of bother."

"What kind of bother?"

"Financial. Russell was always bad with money, but recently he had overstretched himself and I bailed him out. It was the least I could do."

"And you sent him the other note I found: REMEMBER THIS: WHOEVER SOWS SPARINGLY WILL ALSO REAP SPARINGLY, AND WHOEVER SOWS GENEROUSLY WILL ALSO REAP GENEROUSLY. That's why one note was yellowed and fragile, because it was forty years old, and the other was crisp and new."

"Yes, dear."

"And no one ever found out what happened to the bomber?"

"No. I think a few colleagues suspected what happened, but it was never mentioned in my presence, and his body won't be found, at least not while I'm alive."

"You know where Russell hid it?" I asked, incredulous.

"Can't you guess? I just told you the hotel was a construction site at the time…"

"You mean the bomber is buried here?"

"My dear, he's lying six feet beneath the seat you're sitting on."

74

Sally

I went to the airport with the others, but I didn't get on the plane. I still have too many things to sort out here; the inheritance (Jasmine must benefit too, it's what Russell wanted), the food and drinks' deliveries, the bookings; running a hotel is going to be hard work and will take some getting used to. Luckily for me, I have Paulo by my side. Quite close by my side...

I said my goodbyes in the departure terminal. So much has happened in the two weeks since I was in this airport, I still haven't fully processed it all. Agathe was so sweet and promised me she would still come back to The Orange Tree Hotel every year, even though Reggie and now Russell are no longer here.

Terry gave me a kiss on the cheek and said he'd had a lovely time, it was just a shame about Marjorie being a murderer and all that had put a bit of a dampener on things, but overall, he was still happy to give the hotel a five-star review on TripAdvisor. I told him that if he needed to come back for the trial, he would be welcome to stay here free of charge. He was so happy I feared he was about to get down on one knee and offer to make me wife number five.

Penny was rather coy about her plans; she wasn't getting the same flight as the others, and I got the impression she wasn't flying to England. What I do know, is that wherever she goes won't be prepared for what's in store; she's a marvellous lady, but there's never a dull moment, and I'll miss her.

I squeezed Jasmine tight, happy that we had grown so close again, and that although our friendship might peak and trough and we may have silly fallings out now and again, we would always be bound together by blood. She was my family.

"Promise me you'll come back," I said to Marley as we hugged.

"Of course I will, who do you think will be bringing Mum…"

"And because you want to?"

"That, too. I miss the place already and can't wait to return, even though I hate flying. I mean, I really hate it."

Thank you for reading Sun, Sea, and Murder, it really was a pleasure to write. If you enjoyed the book I'd kindly ask you to please leave a review on Amazon or Goodreads. Ultimately, it's reviews which determine an author's success and which help bring the book to a wider audience, so thank you.

Acknowledgements

Firstly, I'd like to thank my fiancée Corinne for your support and encouragement throughout the writing process. I'd also like to thank Steve Cardwell, Ed Oakley, and Rosie Gleeson for your feedback on early drafts of the book, your input and suggestions really were invaluable. I'd also like to thank my editor, Kathryn Hall for your hard work and continued support.

Lastly, I'd like to thank everyone who has enjoyed *The Mystery of Treefall Manor*, and who have supported me in my writing career so far, let's hope there's plenty more murders yet to come!

The Mystery of Treefall Manor:
The Mystery of Treefall Manor: An Inspector Graves locked-room mystery eBook : SAVAGE, J.S.: Amazon.co.uk: Kindle Store